THE HERETIC HEIR

G. Lawrence

ISBN: 153504439X
ISBN 13: 9781535044394

For my parents… for their love, their humour and compassion.
For bringing me into this world and always impressing on me that it can be changed for the better.

TABLE OF CONTENTS

PROLOGUE

Richmond Palace, London
February 1603

Death sighs softly at my ear.

I almost smile, pulled from my thoughts of the past by that slight noise which no other mortal can hear. He waits still for me to follow him, but I have other affairs to attend to.

Death has had to wait for me for a long time. He has had to be patient. He must have thought that he had my soul surely within the grasp of his hands many times, only to be thwarted at the last moment.

I can almost hear skeletal fingers rapping against the wood of the table before me. Poor Death. I sense his exasperation with me; that even now, when the end is surely here, I delay him once again.

He is not the only one to have felt thus. Many others have found me confusing, perplexing, bewildering… Perhaps it was my greatest strength; to have never been as I was expected to be. The unexpected is enticing, alluring… dangerous. That is why I was feared, that is why I was loved. That is why I will be remembered where others fall to the wayside of history. Oh yes, I will be remembered. They will speak of me long after I have left this life. The minds of the people will remember their Elizabeth.

Death can wait for me a while longer. I am a fine prize for his collection. I am worth the wait. Soon enough, I will step into the dark maw which marks the passage of the living to the realms of the dead.

But not yet.

Not yet… Poor Death, my old friend.

You must tarry at my side a while longer.

Listen to my tale a while. Remember with me when I was young, when I sparkled like the sun in a sultry sky. Remember with me when you almost took me once before.

For to live close to the throne, is to live close to Death.

And to be the unwanted heir of an unhinged queen is to dance with Death.

Take my hand once more, poor Death, old friend. I shall lead you on a merry dance.

CHAPTER ONE

Forty-Nine Years earlier...
Whitehall Palace, London
Palm Sunday, March 1554

It was early in the morning.

Blue and grey, silver and white slipped the first hints of dawn over the gardens of Whitehall Palace.

I had not slept. She had not answered my letter. There would be no reprieve, not now, not for me. Sat by my window, my glassy eyes staring at nothing and everything, I listened to the first jumbled calls of the birds in the trees... watched as the light returned to the world.

They came for me early. They did not want any crowd to gather, any resistance to grow. So, quietly they came... to take me from palace, to prison.

As the door opened, I looked to my side; the pupils of my ladies were wide with fear as they stood by me. The whites of their eyes glistened in the muted light as we looked to the dour faced men, and they beckoned to us, their low voices telling me what I knew already.

That I was arrested under suspicion of high treason against the Queen, my sister; that I was to be taken to the Tower of London. And what they did not say was possibly worse; that if I was found guilty, then Mary, my sister, my queen, would take my head in payment for betrayal.

Out of the room they guided us. We scurried fast and quiet at their urging on hushed feet behind their guards, down the stone corridors of the palace, past the staring portraits of my ancestors, the Kings and Queens of England. I sought to hold my chin up, for pride, for dignity, even as we scuttled like mice down those paths. My pale face was pinched, ghostly, but I held it high; so should be the face of the daughter of a king.

The first cold rush of the morning hit my skin as we left the palace and even beneath my fur-covered shawl, I shivered. Breathing in gulps of the frosty spring air, I sought courage from the very air and earth of my family estates.

I was afraid. I knew well enough that my survival did not rest on whether or not I was guilty. It rested on my sister and her suspicions of me. Therefore, I had good reason to feel fear.

I breathed in again, forced my shoulders back and my head up. My father once walked here and he would have never shown fear to any enemy. I am the daughter of a king, I thought. I cannot quail now like a mewing child; not when I need my courage the most.

The gardens were damp; cobalt and navy blues of the dissipating dawn lit our way through the paths. Small pockets of silver mist still clung to the horizon, drifting gently in the breeze. The grass and water of the river were black in the dim light, tiny drops of moisture shone from leaves and trees.

I looked up and back at the darkened windows of the palace. Little lights, as red as bright fire against the dark shone from the palace windows as the servants started their morning's work to warm the rooms of the Queen, to light the candles and the fires. I looked to see if I could see *her* eyes; perhaps to make one final plea to her, my own blood, the daughter of my father. But there was nothing. My sister did not show herself that morning.

But I knew she was there.

Something deep in my soul told me that somewhere beyond that stone and glass façade were the dark, watchful eyes of my sister, catching one last glimpse of me as her guards led me to imprisonment and possible death at her command. I could feel the bright heat of her hatred and suspicion for me. Jealousy and resentment, distrust and doubt, guilt and fear… all those emotions she sought never to acknowledge in herself…. I felt them burning into my back as I marched behind her guards.

I knew she was watching me.

Down through the gardens we hurried at the ushering of the guards, soft step on well-tended path. They were taking us by water; quicker, quieter than mounting horses and riding through London to the dreaded fortress. They did not want to give any a chance to halt our progress. They feared my popularity with the people of England.

The boat bobbed on the dark water calmly, merrily; it was too happy in its task. I stopped before the boat; my courage seemed to drain from me. I looked about me and my heart skipped within my chest with a heartbeat of fear… Could I run now? Could I flee my captors, call for help? I would not get far.

Lord Sussex held out a pale hand to me, startling me from my thoughts of escape. His face was eerie in the strange light, strained and pale from the task he now performed. He had little love for it, I knew well. A small smile for him, not lit in my eyes or believed in by my heart, touched my lips. I took his outstretched hand and stepped into the vessel. My ladies, Kat and Blanche, following my lead as always, stepped in after me. Rain fell on our heads and an ill wind chilled our bones.

I heard the shallow, scared breathing of my ladies as they sat beside me. Felt flesh tremble with dread against my own. I slipped my hands into theirs, and gave one brief squeeze before folding my hands before me and sitting straight.

I was the daughter of a king. That one phrase echoed in my mind. I was the daughter of a king. I must have courage, like a king.

I was the daughter of a king.

The daughter of a king… I thrust those words out to mask the coward within me, trying to cover her, silence her with my refrain.

The daughter of a king… The daughter of a king.

I knew I must stay calm, as much for my ladies as for me. I fought to retain control over myself as I sat on the rude seat. I sat straight and tall on the uncomfortable plank. No cushions were provided on this journey for a princess of the Tudor line, but more than enough guards. Comforts were for treasured royalty, not for prisoners.

Winchester and Sussex talked in hushed tones at the head of the boat. The quicker this was over the better for both of them; the worse for me. Down the River Thames we moved. Soft waves caused by other boats bobbed the boat up and down, and on the horizon, the red dawn approached. People were already up and moving in the city; carts rumbled through the rough streets, horses snorted white clouds of breath in the chill dawn light. Boats started to ferry people back and forth to the city. There were shouts from the waterside and the sound of inn doors opening, for today was Palm Sunday and under the rule of my sister, the old celebrations had been brought back. The common people were gathering to take part in the revived ceremony of the old Catholic ways, to carry crosses made of palm leaves to mark the day that Christ entered Jerusalem, starting the journey to his own death.

Was my journey, nodding along in the black water, lit by the gathering lights of the sunrise, to end in the same way?

They were taking me to the Tower of London. Into that fortress where so many kings and queens and princes and lords had been taken into the arms of God. It was a royal place to die indeed. I almost laughed at the thought. At least, in the place of my incarceration and execution, my sister was finally admitting I *was* of royal birth. Had I been the daughter of a lowly musician, as Mary had professed at times to believe, then she would have just had me tried and then hanged like any commoner.

Would I be fated instead to stand on a scaffold, to knee before a baying crowd as my mother had done? Would my head be cleaved from my body by clumsy blows of the axe, or a sharp sword? Or would my end come with a quiet pillow forced down on my face in the dark of night? Would I stand shaking before crowds of common and noble peoples as I faced death, or simply see the small shining lights of one man's eyes in a dim, gloomy chamber, as his dagger plunged into my flesh?

Those thoughts were too awful to linger on. My lips seemed to move by themselves in prayer. Although I could not hear the words in my own ears, I hoped God could hear me.

In the gathering light of the day, the great Tower loomed close as we approached, its towers, dotted about its battlements reached into the skies. The Tower had all the freedom that its inhabitants did not. I looked up, my neck bent, at the White Tower.

I am Elizabeth, prisoner.

Traitor to the Queen. Enemy of the Crown.

I am Elizabeth, prisoner.

And on this day, I fear to die.

CHAPTER TWO

Seven Month Earlier...
Wanstead, outside of London
August 1553

Kat's deft fingers made good the clasp at the back of my neck; she straightened the necklace from behind, and then walked in front of me to better view her work. My long fingers rested on the little coral beads, glistening like diamonds and trimmed in bright yellow gold, which hung around my white neck. They winked at the ruby and diamond brooch fastened to the front of my white gown. It winked back, as though the trappings of royalty shared a secret that morning.

Kat's warm brown eyes studied me carefully, and then a nod of approval was given. Her work on me was done.

I turned to inspect myself in the mirror. My long white gown was edged with gold cloth and green silks. My sleeves hung long and wide, accentuating the slim bend of my waist. The beautiful necklace and brooch, both presents from my royal sister, the new Queen of England, set the picture off perfectly.

Long red hair, flowing down my back in thick folds to proclaim my maidenhood, flashed and gleamed in the sunlight from the window. Pale skin and dark, deep eyes; a tall and lithe figure completed the picture of the nineteen year old maid who looked back at me gravely in the mirror. I would never be a beauty like some of those at court, but I was certainly more unusual, more memorable than many of those blonde-haired, blue-eyed does. And I was a princess; that they would remember me for if nothing else; the second richest noble in the kingdom, after my sister Queen Mary, the second daughter of the great *Bluff King Hal...* Elizabeth Tudor, heir to the English throne.

Kat's face appeared behind me at my side. She was smiling at me.

"You look beautiful, my lady," she said. Her voice was hushed in awed appreciation of the pretty picture before her. Her charge, the child she had sung to, the girl she had raised, was now a woman grown and bled, a premier noble of the land, one of the most appealing prizes for marriage in the country, and in the world.

I smiled at her. I was always vulnerable to flattery; being never as sure of my own beauty as those with conventional good looks, I was more prone to falling against the warmth of obsequiousness and praise than others.

We all have our flaws. We cannot help them, but it is certainly in our interests to recognise them so that they do not become our weaknesses.

I touched the necklace again. These gifts from my sister glowed with the warmth of her present happiness. Raised like a phoenix from the flames of rebellion and deceit to take the throne on a wave of popularity, Mary felt as though all her trials in life had finally brought her to her birthright as queen. She was the eldest child of Henry VIII, the discarded, humiliated daughter of his first marriage. The woman that Warwick and the Grey family had tried to bypass by placing our little cousin Lady Jane Grey on the throne. My sister, Mary Tudor; the first Queen of England to rule unchallenged in her own name.

Her army had flocked to her across land and sea, eager to put wrong to rights and place the daughter of *Bluff Hal* on the English throne. Mary's rise to the throne had seen off her enemies, and now those foes languished in the Tower of London, their fake Queen, little Jane Grey, amongst them. Mary was ready to ride triumphant into London, with me, her loyal Tudor sister at her side.

None of this present glory, however, solved the problems that waited for us just ahead on the road. Once the dust of the festivities was settled and the last merry shout receded in the darkness, there would still be concerns to resolve. Mary was the first Queen of England, the first woman to inherit the throne of England in her own right. Not since Matilda, the granddaughter of William I, the Conqueror, had a woman sought to rule in her own right. Matilda had brought the country to civil war in her pursuit of the crown against her cousin Stephen, who also claimed the throne of England, and only much later, when Matilda's son took the throne, was peace restored to England in truth. Later Queens, consorts who tried to weild power through their husbands, were vilified, their names and reputations blackened. To most people, a woman should ever be in the background of power, not at its head. Few people believed women should hold power, and certainly not on their own, without a male to guide them. The country of England and the courts of the world were asking that day; could a woman truly rule alone and rule well?

Opinions were not divided. The country thought not, the Royal Council thought not, the Church thought not and above all, my sister the Queen thought not. It was not accepted that any woman could or should have the power to rule alone... Not without a husband to aid her.

Mary would have to marry to rectify this *unnatural* situation, and her husband would then hold the reins of power... natural order would be restored and all would be well. But who should her husband be? Only time could tell us who would take such power... and that made us all nervous. If he was a foreign king, from another land, then England could be annexed under the power of another country, or empire. If he was an Englishman born and bred, then he might not have the might England needed to survive in the arena of international affairs. Oh yes, the question of whom should become the King of England was a heated one.

Then there was the other problem, that of religion. The past two reigns of English kings had seen much division in the paths of faith. Our father, Henry VIII had broken with the See of Rome in his quest to marry my own mother. Setting himself up as Head of the Church of England, *Bluff Hal* had installed his own spiritual laws in the faith of England. Our brother Edward had made England a wholly Protestant country, forging past our father's approach to religion, which in essence had always been a Catholic Church, but with the King as the spiritual leader of his people, rather than the Pope. Following the rules and laws laid in foundation by our father, and set in stone by his son, Mary should continue to uphold the Protestant religion as the faith of England.

But we all knew she would not.

The fire of the Catholic faith was as much a part of her as the blood that flowed in her veins and the rhythmic beat of her heart. It was her mother's faith, her only childhood comfort, and the one truth she clung to in her soul through every hardship, degradation and sorrow she had encountered in life.

There was no path that Mary would take us down that was not lit by the flames of the Catholic faith.

I was raised under the teachings of our father, tutored by the greatest reformers and Protestants this country had to offer. All I knew of the Catholic faith was the darkness and dimness of its superstitious trappings. All I felt when I gazed into its Mass was its obscurity. I had been raised to have a personal connection with my faith, a close understanding of the Holy Scriptures and an aversion to the fakery and corruption that so riddled the Church of Rome. There were many in England who viewed the Catholic faith as I did, with suspicion, and many more who abhorred it with a fervour akin to hatred.

Whatever my upbringing, I did not, however, grudge another man to worship God as he saw fit to. I was well with my faith and my manner of communicating with God, and I wished others only the same. But my sister did not think as I did. She did not hold that God could be worshipped in more ways than one. In her vision of the world, there was but one God, one faith and one right.

And all else must bend or be broken.

I breathed in as I gazed at my own young face in the mirror. I had seen and learned so much in my short time of living. So much had I had and lost, been given and had broken, so much had been taken from me. But I had grown under the tuition of the rough master of life, for although much had been stolen from me, so too had I learned much in return. I had known much danger, and I had yet found ways to survive. I had known much loss, and I had learned still to find joy. I had been thrown into sorrow, and clambered out of that pit with the hands of true friends. Much had I lost and much had I gained in my short life. Fortune's Wheel continued to turn about me, within me, and still I remained; tested, challenged, thwarted… until my character became resolute. Such is life, to know and to face the challenges of a winding path and to emerge ready to walk on once more.

My grave little face stared back at me. Although both I and my reflection knew this was a day for celebration, we both also knew that there were times coming that would test us.

I turned to Kat, and she nodded to me.

"I am ready," I said, and together we walked to the door, to join the triumphant procession of the new Queen into London.

The reign of my sister, Queen Mary I of England, was begun.

CHAPTER THREE

Richmond Palace
February 1603

Envy is a canker which consumes the soul.

It can start with so small a thing, so slight a gesture or word, and grows to take hold and possession of all that was once good and gracious in a person and their soul.

The simple jealousy as one woman longs for the long hair, or shining eyes of another. The envy which comes riding on the back of desires which have been thwarted. The jealously which grows within the heart when one longs to be released from the body and mind we are encased in and be another person. All these, are dangerous enough.

But the jealousy that grows between one person and another, where one comes to see the other as embodiment of all that they could have had and did not receive, that, is the essence of all the worst of sins.

Those people who come to swim in the dark waters of such jealousy never seek to question why *they* are not capable of being all they want to be. They simply squirm in the impotent knowledge that they are not as they would wish to be, and they blame others for the ills of their life.

The heart hankers for its own selfish wants; it does not heed the mind that speaks of caution, patience or restraint. If the heart is refused its pleasures, it will rebel. Turn traitor against the whole, even to its own destruction. In the seeds of the jealous mind are sown the end of the world.

Even angels fall prey to the darkness of envy…

Lucifer, that angel once beloved of God, whom God called the *Morning Star*, fell to the blackness of envy. And as he knelt bowed and cowed, broken and defeated before God, and was sent to the bowels of hell, Lucifer's heart resounded with the pestilence of jealousy, the unfulfilled and tainted blackened husk that envy had made of his soul. The same flaw rests in all of us that God created; we are all touched… anointed, painted with the same brush which caused angels to fall, kingdoms to crumble and men and women to turn on their own kind and kin.

It is the greatest test that God has given us, whether we can make the best of all He gave to us, without destroying others for possession of that which we can never truly have. Envy is never sated; it never grows less, only more. The tiny prickles of its horrid flame lay spark to more and more… until the mind is consumed by its fire. The only easement is to remove the source, to kill the host, to destroy the reason for the fire of jealousy.

The heart is jealous, the heart is treacherous, and it is always with you, shaping your decisions, whispering to you in the dead of night.

Above all others, the heart is the most dangerous enemy.

CHAPTER FOUR

London
3rd August 1553

London was a riot of colour, activity and people on that summer's day as we two Tudor sisters rode into the capital. The *coup* of Warwick and the Grey family was over; their armies now surrendered or absorbed into my sister's own forces, and the traitorous leaders locked away in the great fortress of the Tower of London, awaiting the judgement of my sister.

Bonfires had blazed through the nights previous, their heavy, sweet scent still hung over the streets; men had sung songs of valour and of adventure, of sorrow and loss and love... all fuelled by the ale and wine freely distributed in the streets by Mary's men. It is always good to reward those who have stood at your side after all. The people of London, and of all England, had cried out in adoration and support for the daughters of Henry VIII, now rightly restored to their place in the succession. It had been a merry time in England since my sister won her throne.

Mary and I, together with a huge retinue of servants and guards rode up to London in the bright morning's sunlight on that lovely day. It was to be the Queen's official entrance into London before her coronation.... the first in a long line of celebrations which would mark this first sole Queen of England taking the throne.

England is at her finest on the rare days where her gentle sunshine warms the skins of her people; when the soft breezes ruffle the leaves of the oak and the petals of wildflowers, promising a balmy evening to come, to toast a cup of wine in the company of friends. I breathed in the air like an elixir; soft and sweet to my palate and stirring to my blood.

The clatter of the hooves of our retinue should have been enough to deafen the pagan storm-gods of old, but it was drowned out by the massive din of the people of London shouting and cheering to welcome home its Tudor daughters. The streets were cleared and the crowds held back by lines of guards as we rode forth through the cluttered streets. Banners, tapestry, painted cloth and pennants were hung from all the windows and balconies, Tudor colours of green and white smothered the stalls and the streets, and from every crevice and every window I could see the happy, shouting and excited faces of our people welcoming Mary, and me, into London and into their hearts.

On occasions like this, I shone. The excitement of the people awoke a tempest of thrilling exhilaration in my blood. As they waved and cheered to me, I waved and smiled happily back. Each time I caught the eye of a man or a woman shouting, I raised my hand to them. It is often the little things in life that people remember, and my little waves and nods, my smiles and laughs, brought wild cheering and support from the crowds. They loved to know that I had seen them.

And I loved to be seen by them.

It is so easy to forget as a prince, when one is often locked away from the people, that it is not the trappings of power which make one royal, it is the people. If you are loved by your people you will always be a better ruler, a secure ruler. But love, when it is true love, must work both ways; I loved them and they loved me.

We were fools for one another from the start, England and I.

Mary however, was awkward in front of the masses. I believe her early life had made her both bold and scared in times of strain, and these elements do not mix happily when confronted with crowds of people. She understood little about how to make the crowds react to her as they did to me. She waved but little, she said less, and most of the time she looked as though she was either haughty or indifferent. It was the greatest time of triumph in her life, and the people were ready and eager to love her. If she had but smiled a little and spoken to them, as I did, they would have been hers for good; but her stilted reaction to the outpouring of their love confused them and it was noted with disapproval that she was gruff and uncomfortable with them.

Strange, is it not, that it is not our abilities that make us princes, but our blood? Mary had almost the same blood in her veins as me; our father's blood, Great *Harry's* blood ran through us both and he had the ability to charm a woman at a hundred paces just with a smile, to win a man as a life-long friend, simply by placing an arm about his shoulders. But in Mary that ability of our father's charm had not bred true, as it had with me. Strange that two sisters can be so different.

As we rode along, a man waved violently at me from a first floor balcony overhanging the street. London was riddled with such overhanging shops and inns; little buildings built on top of more buildings, clambering for the skies over one another. I waved at him gaily and smiled warmly. He was so overcome with excitement at catching my eye that he waved more and more enthusiastically, leaning so far from the balcony that he toppled and fell headfirst from it!

I gasped in horror and then laughed as I saw that his friends behind him had caught his legs; dangling from his ankles the man hung out from the building like a pig in the farmer's barn. Then, still dangling, he turned himself towards my approach once more and continued to wave to me as his friends laughed, grappled and fought to pull him back onto the rickety platform. I laughed so well and so heartily that I thought I should have done myself an injury! Others in the crowd saw the spectacle too and there was a lot of merry shouting and teasing. As I laughed and the crowd laughed with me it felt as though we were friends indeed, sharing in such a jest with each other.

Every sight along our triumphant procession only served to enliven my spirits. I felt as though I should never grow tired or weary again. I waved, I shouted, I nodded and I smiled, and not a one of those gestures was feigned. I was enjoying myself a great deal. This was a great day for the Tudors, and I was happy in the company of the people of England. London was welcoming and as she opened her arms to me, I hurried to her embrace.

We stopped along the way to watch little entertainments that the people had put on. Mary and I sat on our horses next to each other as a group of children came out to sing us a pretty song. As I watched their tiny faces lifted in song to us I was smiling, but not so my sister. Her face was grave and lost in thought as she listened to those tiny angels. I wondered what on earth she could be thinking of on this day that should make her face so grim and staid, but I did not ask. As they drew to a close, their small faces ruddy with the effort of their song, I leaned down and asked my man Parry to give them a little coin each, and then spoke thanks to them for their performance. My sister said little, and faces of the crowd around us dropped from eager vibrancy, to grumbling disapproval at Mary's lack of enthusiasm for their pains.

It was becoming a common theme of the day. I wish I could have thought of a way to say something to Mary; but it is often not safe nor sensible to query the actions of a monarch.

My poor sister. Perhaps her childhood taught her never to make the best of anything. She could never see beyond the sorrow that life had caused her, never rejoice where rejoicing was due. Mary always carried with her the air of a martyr, long-suffering and full of sorrow. But a martyr is supposed to die, not to live. Those who continue on living whilst wearing the clothes of a martyr become tiresome and draining to be around.

Even her clothes, although of the finest materials, did not suit her. She would always mix the *most* regal of colours, the crimson, the royal purple and the Tudor greens, but she would crush them together in such a way that was most unbecoming, and often quarrelled with her hair colour. In the simplest of green or white, lined with silver or gold, I stood out like a fresh flash of lightening in the sunset. Mary tried hard to flaunt her royalty, but for all her pains ended up looking like one of our garishly garbed court fools.

But I was determined not to let my sister's wooden, impassive appearance spoil my enjoyment of the day. This was a day of triumph where the rightful heirs to the Tudor throne had prevailed; even if she, the Queen, did not take pleasure in that, I, the heir, would do.

We rode through the streets of London to the Tower of London. It was traditional that the monarch should stay at the Tower in the days before their coronation. In that great fortress the traitorous Warwick, John Dudley, and the Greys were now kept, as prisoners of the Crown. Did they watch our triumphant approach from their prison windows? Did they watch as the rightful heirs to the throne were restored, and did they quake as they thought on their fates?

As we clattered up to the gates I looked around. The Tower of London was like a miniature city encased in its own walls. Great walls marked by many towers enclosed streets and roads, guard rooms, chambers and royal apartments. The great White Tower stood at its centre, a castle unto itself in the centre of the citadel, stretched up to the skies, surrounded by the clear blue of the heavens. It was beautiful. And yet, for all its beauty and magnificence, I felt a chill as I looked on its walls. Here was the place my grandmother and namesake, Elizabeth of York, died of childbed fever. Here was the prison in which my servants had been kept after the scandal of the Seymour affair. Here was the last resting place of my mother, Queen Anne Boleyn, the abandoned and disgraced Queen of Henry VIII. She had faced her last moments on earth here before her head was taken by the sword, and my life had changed forever with the loss of my mother.

There had been others too... Queen Catherine Howard... the murdered King Henry VI... other nobles of the realm, other servants, other souls, all who had found their way to Death in this place.

As we passed through the gates and into the streets inside the Tower walls, I saw Kat shiver slightly beside me. She remembered this place well enough. She had been a prisoner here too.

They had brought forth prisoners from the cells and the towers that my sister, in her fairness and majesty, was to set free. It was a tradition of the coming of a new monarch to show mercy to the prisoners of the last. Not those of the recent *coup* against Mary, of course, but prisoners who had been placed here by our father and brother in their reigns; prisoners who had long been a part of these stone walls.

They stood on the grass before the chapel, awaiting the mercy of their new queen. Squinting slightly in the sunlight were three figures. Edward Courtenay, imprisoned by our father after Courtenay's father had shown support for Queen Katherine of Aragon when our father had sought annulment of his first marriage. Courtenay's father had lost his head for that betrayal, and his son, Edward Courtenay, had spent most of his life in the Tower of London. Then there was Stephen Gardiner, once one of our father's most trusted men, imprisoned during the early reign of our brother for his too-Catholic views. Gardiner was a man I had no love for, for not only had he allegedly worked against my own mother during the last days of her life, but he had been instrumental in the attempted plot to disgrace and destroy my beloved stepmother, Queen Katherine Parr; a failed conspiracy to have her arrested on charges of heresy. Katherine only escaped arrest and questioning by taking to her bed feigning illness, and then gaining the mercy of our father, Henry VIII, which saved her life. I remembered the day all too well when I saw pale fear ride on the face of by beloved stepmother… and I remembered too when Gardiner turned up in the palace gardens to arrest the poor Queen, and was sent angrily away by the unpredictable temper of my father, who had, by that time changed his mind on the proposed imprisonment and removal of his last wife.

The last prisoner was my own aged great-uncle, the Duke of Norfolk, that slippery eel of our father's court. He had been imprisoned for treason along with his son, Henry Howard, Earl of Surry, who had dared to quarter the royal arms of Edward the Confessor with his own heraldic titles. Our father had been determined to execute Norfolk for his son's treachery, but, fortunately for Norfolk, King Henry had died before signing Norfolk's death warrant. Norfolk's son, Henry Howard, Earl of Surrey, had not been so fortunate and had gone to the block a few days before our father's death. Norfolk was left to rot in his prison through the reign of my brother. Although Norfolk was my great-uncle, the brother of my Howard grandmother, Lady Elizabeth Boleyn, I had no great love for the man. Through my childhood I had heard stories of how he threw his nieces, my own mother and her cousin Catherine Howard, at the marriage bed of the King, and then abandoned them when they had need of his support. Norfolk had presided over the trial of my mother Anne Boleyn, and her brother George, and had helped condemn them for treason and adultery, sending them to their deaths. Although Norfolk's Howard blood linked him to women my sister had no cause to love, he was a Catholic, an able and ruthless politician, and an experienced general, and so Mary was willing to forgive him.

These three men were to be restored to their old positions in the reign of my sister. She intended to show her mercy to England.

She greeted them each in turn; first Courtenay, his tall figure and pale but handsome face lit up with all the adoration of a puppy for its master when Mary restored to him the title of Earl of Devonshire. Courtenay was, like Mary and me, a great-grandchild of Edward IV, a prince of the blood royal. It was almost from the first moment of Mary touching his shoulder, bidding him to rise, that whispers of their marriage started. Who better for an English Queen to marry than a man of similar lineage and royal blood? I am sure that to rise from the bonds of a prisoner to the trappings of a king would have suited Courtenay. Such a match also seemed to suit the wants of the people of England. Whether or not Courtenay was to the taste of my sister, however, was another matter.

Gardiner was given back the title of Bishop of Winchester, and more, as my sister made him her Lord Chancellor. As they stood talking together I saw his little eyes light on me with disapproval. A Protestant princess was not what he wished to see standing beside his Catholic Queen. Gardiner was my enemy long before we even met. The faith I held was enough for him to despise me, but then they also said he had hated my mother in her short years as Queen, so to him, I believe, it felt as though he had ample reason to work against me.

Then Mary came to my own great-uncle Norfolk, general of my father's armies. As Norfolk tried to bend his gouty, aged knee to her it looked as though he might topple over, but Mary reached out and bade him stand rather than kneel before her.

This gesture of compassion roused the crowd to cheer for her and my uncle looked at her with both gratitude and respect. He was her loyal servant, Norfolk said, and he meant every word.

Mary addressed the crowd. She was a good Catholic, she said in her deep voice, and she hoped that her country and its people would also embrace her own faith, but there would be no *compulsion* to turn to her faith. She wished us to love our neighbours, to refrain from the use of such terms as "*papist*" or "*heretic*" and to but love each other, as she loved us.

Her words were an echo of our father's statements on faith to his people, and the crowds gathered around us heard that ghost of *Harry* in the mouth of his daughter, and approved of it. They did not care now, to remember all that our father had done which they disapproved of, or aught that was done in his name which brought fear to their lives. In death, our father King Henry VIII had become a paragon of kingship to them. In death, he had become sanctified as their greatest master. To echo his words was clever of Mary. She sought to remind them of the great man who had stood in the place she did now; to call her people to her, to give their loyalty for her Tudor blood. I, who was to become so adept at this trick, recognised it and approved it immediately. It was well for the people to remember the greatness the Tudors had brought to these lands. It was well for them to remember who the true sovereigns of England were.

As Mary spoke those words of inclusion and acceptance in terms of religion, she looked over at me. Her Protestant half-sister, standing before the crowds at her side should have been a clear sign of the truth of her words. But even as she spoke of tolerance and peace between the faiths of Christianity, I saw her eyes narrow slightly at me. This pretty speech may bring comfort to the people of England today, I thought, but on the morrow we should see what *acceptance* of religion really meant under the rule of my zealous Catholic sister.

CHAPTER FIVE

The Court of Queen Mary I
Greenwich Palace, London
1553

"It would seem my sister sets great store by ladies who are as high of virtue as they are dull of beauty and wit," I whispered to Kat as we stood in the audience chambers of the Queen.

My lips barely moved as I spoke, a trick I had worked on for some time and was quite expert in. Kat stifled a giggle and covered the outburst by coughing slightly, gaining a look of disapproval from Lady Jane Dormer, one of my sister's new ladies in waiting and the only attractive or lively one of the whole flock.

We were at court, in waiting for Mary's coronation and watching as she chose her household. My sister had chosen many noble ladies of utterly unimpeachable character to be her chamber women. Every one of them was chosen for their temperament, their likeness to her, their morals and their religion. Every one of the dour birds flocking to my sister's side was a Catholic. There was not a Protestant amongst them. It was clear that under Mary's reign, Catholics would be favoured, and Protestants would not. In that at least, we were starting to see the light of truth. Mary had spoken of tolerance when she rode into London, but it was clear where her personal preference lay.

If only everything had been so easy to read...

In those first few weeks of Mary coming to the throne, there had been some general confusion. We waited for the coronation of the Queen, and in that space of waiting, there was much to be done. Confusion always reigns when people have no precedent for the events unfolding before them. This was the first time that a queen had ruled in her own right, and as of yet, without a king. Mary was not a consort; she was the sole ruler of our country. Usually those officers awarded places in the sovereign's household were as important as the Council, and often too, held posts in both the household of the monarch and in the affairs of state. But here, with a female ruler, it was not the same. Would we have given weighty importance to the counsel of Jane Dormer or Susan Clarencieux on matters of war or trade? No... and for good reason.

Women surrounded Mary who were educated enough to know how to hold conversation, dip salt delicately at dinner, do household accounts, play music, dance, embroider and perhaps sign their name. These are goodly skills to have for a life at court, but were not the skills one wanted in a person in charge of, say, the Royal Fleet. These women had no understanding of international affairs; some of them had limited understanding of their *own* affairs. It was doubtful that these horribly good women chatting to my sister so deferentially understood much beyond the borders of their own household, so, no. A king's household might mean one thing for the country, but a queen's must mean something else, at least until she married. The Queen had a household that did not hold sway with the affairs of the state, and a Council that did not play a part in the everyday life of the sovereign. It was unusual for everyone, to say the least, to take on this new construction of the court.

Perhaps I am harsh on my own sex. It is not every woman in England that had the benefits of the education our great father insisted on for his daughters. Most women were tutored only in the most basic and rudimentary of skills for life. At the present time, here and now, most women have no place in politics because they are *allowed* no place in politics. They understand nothing of international affairs because they are not expected, or often endorsed, to engage with them. It is a cycle which keeps women in the home, away from the seat of power, which is I suppose, the ultimate aim in a world ruled by men. They like not us interfering in their games. In these matters I must admit myself relieved that as a princess I was allowed a lot more engagement with affairs usually reserved for the male sphere, although even I could never abandon with ease the eagerly assumed prejudices against my sex. It was a hard path to wander for a young woman, to sit between the two sexes and carry both their ideals within her. But I believe I was gifted with the courage to walk it.

Looking around at my sister's ladies, I could see that the Queen's court was likely to be a very good, very devout and terribly boring place to be. I wanted to sigh a little, but I restrained myself. My brother's court had also been rather lacking in lightness, entertainments and sparkle. Edward had enjoyed plays and interludes, but preferred ones with a moral end and little mirth. His court had been filled with older men going about affairs of state in a most serious manner. I remembered the snap and the sparkle of our father's courtly entertainments. I longed for a court such as his. But the nature of the court reflects the soul of the ruler, and Mary was amply surrounded by her felicitous frumpish females, just as she wanted it to be. Enjoyment may have to wait, I thought, until they can convince her to marry.

Perhaps then, we might have a king who loves to dance, laugh and make merry, as our father had.

My sister seemed to have grown a degree of constancy in her actions that I had little seen before she came to the throne. She kept her house as she did her Council; just as Mary's women were unwieldy and lacking in grace, so too was her Council. When Mary came to the throne there were hard choices to be made; available to fill the spaces in her Council there were either those men who had been loyal to her cause, or there were those who had, at first at least, backed the traitorous *coup* of Warwick.

Although I am sure she would have wanted to choose only from the first group, the second were too many and too strong to ignore. Every man of them came to her on bended knee, apologising most profusely for their support for Warwick and the Grey family, and insisting on their loyalty and deference to her.

Of course they did... what else were they going to say to her? They wanted to keep their heads on their shoulders and power in their hands.

I doubt Mary believed them. Some of the protestations made it sound as though Warwick had resorted to the powers of witchcraft in order to control their every thought, deed and word; the length of their speeches and the sheer talent in mummery that some of them had shown had been astounding. I saw tears creep from eyes, hands raised to the heavens and protestations of innocence which would have made the angels blush. Such fakery! Such deceit! It is amazing how quickly men can forget loyalty to one master for fear of the next. Mary knew it well enough too I am sure. Yet she could not send all of them away, or to the block as she may have wanted to; to do so would have decimated England's nobility, and she needed them on her side. Many of them held considerable power in their own lands; they had men and standing armies at their command. It would have been madness to have only taken those who she trusted to her Council.

Trust them, she did not. Need them, she did.

Perhaps in not knowing quite who to believe and who to not, Mary's Council was amassed... and I do use the term *amassed* here with good reason for it was a huge and cumbersome group, made up of Catholics and those loyal to Mary, and of reformers, Protestants mainly, who had toiled and worked for the changes in England and in her Church that my brother and father had started. Perhaps Mary had wanted to show her professed acceptance of the faiths by including both Protestants and Catholics in her Council, but I believe she could have done that with but half the number she chose to guide her.

A few men make for good counsel, a large number of men, makes but an argument.

We were all waiting in the wings until her coronation, watching every move the new Queen made as we tried to fathom the course our new ruler should take us on.

Fair weather or foul ahead? I knew not. But I had reasons already to be wary of our new queen.

My sister had already brought me to her privately on several occasions to ask that I embrace, as she did, the Catholic faith. The "*faith of our father*" she said to me, which baffled me completely. It was our father who broke from Rome, made himself Head of the English Church, annulled his marriage to Mary's own mother to marry mine without the blessing of any but the English Bishops, resulting in excommunication from the Catholic Church... and yet here was my sister telling me that our father had been an obedient Catholic? Conservative he may have been in his beliefs at heart, but a good, loyal and steady Catholic, subject to Rome and the Pope, our father had not been. Our father had been determined to have his own way in his life, and no man or priest, no matter how high, would stand in his path.

It is strange, the things that our mind allows us to remember; it is as though sometimes the more painful aspects of the past are sieved out by our own selves and so the past we remember is *always* sunny, the people more *refined* than those we know now, the winters short and full of glistening snow, the summers long and full of laughter.

I wondered if my sister could remember the truth. But she smiled at the blank look on my face;

"The *original* faith of our father," she insisted, "which is the only true light in the world. I would wish, sister, you could discover in the Catholic faith the peace and the strength that I have found these long years. Sometimes, in the darkest of times, my faith was all I had, and it fed my body and my spirit and I am here now, come into my glory as the Lord wished it to be, because of that faith. "

She paused and looked at me, her dark eyes narrowed slightly as they were often prone to do. Mary had poor eyesight, and often had to squeeze her eyes in their lids in order to see clearly. The expression this created was actually quite unnerving. Her dark eyes were large and beautiful, they were one of her best features, but when she gazed thus, she looked as though she could pierce through to the centre of the soul. They were like the eyes of a bear when it has seen the hounds released into the pit; the beast that sees where and how it needs to attack, in order to win.

I smiled a little at her. "My Queen, Your Majesty," I bobbed into a curtsey. "I was raised in the faith that *our* father thought was most *suited* for me and I have known no other. I would not wish to disobey the wishes of our great father, in changing the faith he gave to me. Nor would I wish to act against my own conscience. I have known only the reformed faith and no other. I would beg you not to ask me to alter it."

Mary stared at me a little. I could almost see her mind churning over the words I had spoken. She wanted me to be Catholic; I was her heir and she wanted England to return to being Catholic, to be Catholic and continue Catholic. No matter what she said in front of the people, that was the truth. If she could convert me to her faith then she and I would be working for the same aims. If she could convert me to Catholicism, there would be no danger from religious dissenters who might want to supplant her with a Protestant. If she did not have children and I came to the throne, then she would know that her country would remain in her faith. It was her ideal situation. If I was to become Catholic then all her fears for the present and the future of her reign and the country would be removed.

But I have never liked being told what to do. I have never changed an opinion or belief simply by having someone tell me that I should, without any other reasoning or argument. No one responds well to being forced to do something. My faith was my own, I understood it, I drew strength from it, and I was not going to change it.

But for now, there was little question of another uprising, there was little thought of plotting against her; she allowed the subject to drop, whilst still asking me to consider her requests which I duly promised to do. She and I walked in the afternoon sunshine in the gardens at Greenwich together, talking of other things and leaving religion to one side. Greenwich was always a favourite of royal palaces for me, since it was the place of my birth and christening.

There was a sense of mounting excitement in the air, Mary's coronation was fast approaching and it would be a great celebration for the people, noble and common alike. I was feeling quite happy; my men Parry and Cecil were keeping a watchful eye as ever on the mood and affairs of the people and the court. Kat was spending her time finding out every wisp of gossip that could be reeled in from any source and I was making friends about court. I felt as though between us, my servants and I had a good grasp on the comings and goings of the court. I liked to be well informed. I will admit that a certain amount of that interest comes from the excitement that gossip may rouse in the heart, perhaps something that Kat taught me when I was small, but there is another use for such information.

It is good for a prince to have eyes on all things and in all places. Although I was never as well informed then as I am now, it was the very start of some of the most valuable lessons I learnt as the heir to Mary's throne.

Be watchful; be aware; forget nothing; remember all.

These are the things that a prince should learn to practise and perfect, if they wish to hear the coming of a storm before the first raindrop has hit the ground.

CHAPTER SIX

The Court of Mary I, London
1553

Those in the eye of the public are players. The face that one must wear in front of the crowds is hardly the same as the one lain on the pillow at night.

In the days before my sister's coronation, it looked to all the world as though we were the best of friends. Side by side we rode and feasted, watched plays and saw entertainments. Side by side we walked in the gardens and appeared before her people.

Yet in private, we were rent apart by Mary's constant and unending pressure on me to convert my faith, and become a Catholic. My own faith, which was nurtured in me by my tutors and my upbringing, is something that to me is intensely important. But I have never had that need that others have, to impose my own faith on their hearts and souls. Later in my life, I would say to my people that as long as they obeyed my laws and went not against them in public, then I cared not for what was truly within their hearts. My relationship with God is one which I understand perfectly, for God is the only one who I know can see into the secrets of my heart. It was He who made me, and He who caused me to survive to the station I now hold. The choices of faith I made later in my own reign were for the unity of my country, not the satisfaction of my own soul. But in others… the quaking uncertainty of their own faith makes them seek to overcompensate by stamping their religion on others around them.

Those who shout the loudest, are often the most insecure.

So it was with my sister. Her childhood and all the suffering she had endured under our father had made her see her faith as a *cause*, and she was determined not only to follow it, but to brand all others with it as well. For her, the love for her mother and the love for her faith were bonded together and perhaps as she sought to restore England to the faith of her mother, she felt she could ease the guilt of having succumbed to the will of our father, in renouncing her mother all those years ago.

Every audience we had together only served as another opportunity for Mary to pressure me into converting to her faith. She spoke to me of the inadequacies of my upbringing, the lack of understanding on my part of the grace of the Catholic faith, the arrogance of thinking that a personal relationship with God was possible without the intervention of the priests and the See of Rome. She reviled our brother's reign, sorrowed that he had been lost to the true religion, advised by men who were wicked and driven by the devil to the wrong faith, she said. She pressed on me my *ignorance*, my foolishness and my lack of sight. Every time we met she pressed me more and more. Every time we met the strain and the atmosphere between us became more forced. At first, it simply annoyed me; no one likes to be told they are a fool by another, after all. But in time, my irritation was replaced by other emotions.

I was nervous.

My sister sought to change the very fabric of my soul, and under her reign it was not hard to see that the Protestant faith would not be allowed to continue either publicly or privately in the hearts of any of her subjects. Mary did not see that she was pushing me into the exact same position that she had endured under the reign of our brother; just as Edward had scolded Mary and publicly upbraided her for her defiance of *his* religion, so she was trying to do to *me*. Edward's pressure on Mary to convert to Protestantism had almost caused her to flee the country, and had certainly left her in fear of her life. She talked of it as one of the worst times of her life, and yet could not seem to see that she impressed the same torments upon me. Perhaps it was because she was the elder, and elder siblings always consider themselves right where the younger are wrong; or perhaps because she was the Queen; or because she was simply Mary, my sister with a goodly share of the stubborn Tudor will. Mary wanted me to convert, and it was becoming an obsession to her.

Under the guidance of Parry and Kat, *I* parried, I danced around her speculation on my religion. It was the religion my father had chosen for me, I said. I had known no other, I repeated… I smiled and I bowed to her even as I evaded and protested… But I knew we could not last long before matters should come to a head.

God did not want me to end my life as a martyr. If he had wanted me thus, he would have given me less imagination and less instinct to survive.

When Mary had stood in defiance of our brother and his religious changes, she had an Imperial cousin across the water in Spain on whom to call if her situation became desperate. I had no such arsenal. Alone stood this Princess of England, and when one has nothing to call on but the wits that God gave, the actions taken have to be different. I could not threaten invasion from a foreign power, but I *did* have an army, or at least, the possibility to call many thousands of men from my estates to protect me if it came to outright rebellion. I was the second largest landowner in England after my sister; the option of force and rebellion was open to me… which was why she viewed me as so dangerous. A powerful Protestant heir to her throne was not what she wanted.

But I did not want to rise up against my sister. Rebellion has a dangerous habit of going awry, and I wanted not to find myself in the position of an imprisoned traitor. And more even than this, such an action would go against my personal beliefs. I was Mary's heir; she was in line to the throne before me. I understood, as many do not, the importance of respecting the line of kings. When people rise against the natural order, chaos sets in. God's hand comes to batter down on countries that do not respect his own plan for their fates. No… other methods had to be used in order to find a peace between us in matters religious. I did not want to fight my sister, not with sword and the flesh of men. I would have to find another way to ease her demands on me.

We had reached a fraught point in our relationship, so early on in her reign. Mary had not even been crowned yet, and we were arguing like we had when I was a little girl. But this time there was much more at stake. Mary was the Queen, and however high I stood in the land, I was her subject. She wanted my obedience, and I was willing to give her my loyalty, but not my soul.

I went to Mary and before her I burst into tears. "My Queen and royal sister," I pleaded. "I have heard it whispered about the court that you are displeased with me on the matter of my faith, and that you have spoken many hard words about my person."

Mary's face clouded with anger at my words, she liked not that her words had found their way to me. Perhaps she had not thought her private and not so private musings on me would reach my ears with such ease, but as the Queen, her words were never private. I held out my hands to her, unfeigned tears of fear stood out in my eyes as I looked up at my sister. I knew well enough the danger which disapproval could bring to bear on the shoulders of a subject to the sovereign.

"But I have never sought to be a source of displeasure to you. My youth was such that I was raised in the reformed faith of our father, and knowing no other, this faith I have clung to all my life. If the religious upbringing I was given was unfit, then it was the fault of those who raised me, for I was never taught the doctrine of the Catholic faith. And even though I might know a different path to faith than you, Majesty, the Christian creed to which I adhere, is still as a follower of the word of Christ."

"There is but one path, one God and one faith, sister," Mary intoned coldly as she looked down on me. I do not think she believed in my tears, although the fears which brought them forth were real enough.

"If Your Majesty would be willing," I said, reaching out my hands to her, "then I would take instruction from a learned man with your approval, so that I might see if I could turn my heart and my faith to the same as your own."

Mary looked somewhat pleased by this and I continued. "If you would perhaps agree to send me books, and a priest to learn from, then I could see if I could temper the flames of the faith I was raised in, to see indeed the light of your faith, my Queen."

I am sorry to tell you that it was all lies. But I did not want to lose my head or my freedom to the ill-will of my sister. Nor did I want to convert. I was not going to change faith.

Mary looked at me and pursed her lips. "You will attend Mass with me this Sunday," she commanded, looking at me thoughtfully.

"I would not wish to attend Mass until I had been properly instructed…" I started, but my sister cut me off.

She held up her hand. "You will attend Mass with me this Sunday," she repeated. "To show in good faith, sister, that you are indeed willing to allow the light of God into your heart."

I nodded slowly. I did not see there was a great deal I could do to remove myself from the situation. But I little wanted to be surrounded by the popish idolatry which I saw the Roman Catholic faith to be; the thought made me quite cold. Mary had spoken of tolerance in faith, so should that tolerance not also stand for me as it should for others? Obviously not. I did not want those of my own faith to think I had abandoned it so easily, nor for others to think that the heir to the throne was so weak that she would cast off her faith so quickly in the face of disapproval of her sister. But the situation was fraught, and I was afraid that the Queen, my sister, might come to see me as her enemy. I would have to attend Mass, but I would have to manage it in such a way to please Mary, *and* to appease my Protestant supporters.

Life often hands us riddles with which to play.

Mary insisted that I attend Catholic Mass, and I did so. But all the way to the royal chapel I complained of a great pain in my stomach and my head, and through the Mass I groaned loudly. It was noted and reported about England. The Lady Elizabeth had been made to attend Catholic Mass, the people whispered, and she suffered for it in her body and her spirits.

I was pleased to hear this rumour, brought back to my ears by Kat, of course, for I wanted those who were of the same faith as I to know that I followed instruction and ritual in the Mass, not by choice, but by the demands of my sister.

Mary seemed satisfied enough, for now, that I had attended her Catholic Mass. Even if I had gone protesting, I had attended. I had obeyed her. To her mind it was a step in the direction of having me obey her completely and convert. She gave me presents for my submission; more strings of coral beads to match the ones she offered to me in joy at her ascension. My little plan had worked, it seemed. I was becoming as slippery as any creature of the seas in my dealings with my queen.

I had gone to the Mass, yes, but not without letting the Protestants of England to know that their Princess had gone under pressure, and not from choice. Their Princess was still of their faith.

But my path was to lead me down a more dangerous road than I imagined when I started walking it.

CHAPTER SEVEN

London
1553

We rose early on the day of Mary's coronation; the warmth of the summer was dissipating under the coming turn of the seasons, and autumn was starting to show his golden face. The white breath that smoked from men's mouths and the russet colour of the leaves on the trees heralded the end of the glorious summer.

I dressed with care. My gown, chosen for me by my sister, was of crimson velvet and cloth of silver. On my neck I wore the necklace long ago bequeathed to me by my stepmother Katherine Parr; that same necklace which once my own mother Anne Boleyn had owned and worn. The golden initials *AB* were hidden down the front of my gown, for my sister would hardly approve of seeing the initials of the woman who replaced her mother on the throne on the day of her coronation, but the pearls could be seen, glistening in the morning light, catching the reflection of the silver in my gown, winking in the mirror.

It was a risk to wear the necklace, but I felt that on the day when I stood as heir to the throne of England that a part of my mother should stand with me. I wanted her strength to fuel mine in the days yet to come. In some ways, I thought that if I wore her necklace, then she might be able to see me, to see how close I was to the throne.

The past few days had seen the leaders of the traitorous rebellion against Mary come to their unhappy ends on the executioner's block. Warwick and his lead rebels had been tried and executed as we had expected, but they had also made their ends in this world as converted Catholics. A new twist on an old tale of treason; that prisoners arrested for treason, not heresy, should be made to convert their faith before death. I held some suspicions that Mary had bargained with them; to save some of their children from a sentence of death, the rebel leaders could convert to be Catholic. Amongst those spared for now was Warwick's fifth son, that bold, dark boy who had once promised to make me a pirate queen when we were but children. Did Robert Dudley wish now that he had in truth run away to sea as we had spoken of all those years ago?

Had Robert watched his father shiver on the scaffold of his execution, renouncing the faith which had apparently caused him to rise against my sister? Did that handsome boy now fear that he might spend all his life rotting in the Tower of London as so many had done before him? What a waste to the world that would be, if such came to pass.

John Dudley, Earl of Warwick and Duke of Northumberland died having recanted the faith for which he had risked all, and protesting the infinite majesty and mercy of my sister the Queen.

Mary, in great mercy, however, *had* spared the Lady Jane and her gaudy husband Guildford Dudley from the block. Tried and condemned for treason, they were as yet saved from death by the goodness of the Queen's clemency. Mary, much like the rest of us, knew that our little pale cousin Jane was not to blame for the unrest that had occurred in this country. Jane had been a flag, a figurehead. She was no true traitor. Jane had been used, because of the connections of her blood, for a task made by ambitious men. Mary wanted to be merciful where it was due, and the survival of our pallid Protestant cousin in the Tower gave me relief, and a little hope for my own self; that Mary might extend her mercy to me in her obsession regarding my faith. Perhaps, some day Jane would be allowed to walk free, even though she was a fierce Protestant which Mary liked not. For now at least, Jane would most likely be happy enough; as long as she had her books and a light by which to read, Jane had what she wanted most in life.

It was almost time to set off. I walked to my position in the cavalcade, flanked by my ladies Kat and Blanche, and smiled at the woman chosen to stand beside me in the fanciful chariot Mary had ordered for the occasion. My aunt, Anne of Cleves, dressed in the same silver and crimson cloth as I, looked pleased and honoured to be chosen as one of the premier royal ladies of the procession. Her short time as our father's wife had been a blessing really, for when their marriage was annulled our father had made her into his *beloved sister.* Perhaps through gratitude at her having obeyed his wishes so quickly, Anne had been made a very rich woman and an independent one. She was growing aged now, little lines appearing beside her eyes, but she always seemed so content… and she had never sought to marry again, perhaps preferring to retain her own power after almost falling victim to a dip of Fortune's Wheel in marriage to a king who loved her not. She pressed my hand as it rested beside hers on the chariot and I smiled at her, pleased to be beside a woman who so represented all I understood of the nature of survival and temperance.

The crowds were wild as we traversed across London to Westminster. Cheering and waving, ignoring all of the solemnity of the occasion, they were anxious to show their support and joy. My sister was some way ahead of us, and throngs of nobility surrounded us in a sea of gold, silver and green.

Mary was anointed with all the care and rights that would have been given to a male king. To do otherwise should have sent the country into a state of pure confusion. But there was doubt as to whether a female ruler could hold the same powers as a man. That doubt was not only carried by her people or her Council, but it was held also by Mary herself. A woman had never ruled in England, not alone; all the authority of the Crown was based on there being a male king, not a female. Mary clearly doubted her own authority in some respects, as on the eve of coronation, she issued the Earl of Arundel with her own powers to ennoble the new Knights of the Order of the Bath. This ancient Order of knights was so named for the rituals of cleansing and purifying both their bodies and souls for their induction into the sacred Order. Knights of the Bath were created at coronations and it was a great honour to be so chosen. There were, however, some problems with the ceremony itself which my good sister clearly had reservations about. The tradition of this ceremony maintained that after searching their souls in the company of God through the night, the new knights should then be stripped of their clothing, bathed and be given their new status by the King… whilst the knights stood bare naked in their baths.

My pious sister would have had trouble even *seeing* her new knights past the hazy fog of her blushes had she had to perform such a task, so we all understood her reluctance to knight the new members of the Order of the Bath. But Arundel also dubbed the Knights of the Carpet later before the nobility… and that ceremony was attended by all, fully clothed. There were clearly aspects of kingship that my sister felt she was unable to undertake.

Those roles that required the military, or essentially masculine, she felt were beyond her scope of power, and she made that clear in her actions at her coronation.

Mary required a husband to complete the circle of her power, and to take on the tasks of kingship she felt were beyond her. That was what everyone said, and that was both what Mary believed, and what she wanted above all other things. As we sat together at the feast after the coronation, she made no pretensions that she was not as keen as her Councillors for her to be married, and to have a child. Mary was thirty-seven years old; still a virgin, untouched by the hands of men. Although women have been known to give birth at such an advanced age, it was not a common occurrence, nor one that was not fraught with danger. But the realities of birth, and her own possible death because of it, did not seem to touch my sister's idealized image of her future; when she spoke of a husband, she blushed, but when she spoke of a child, she shone. I believe my sister had longed for a child for years. In many ways, she would have made a good mother.

But I did not relish the idea of her marrying, and even less of her tired and worn body producing an heir, even if it would make her happy. Yes, it was selfish, I know that well enough, but if Mary could breed, then she could replace me in the line of succession. This was also a thought in her head I am sure. If she could have a child then she could see her throne passed, not to her Protestant half-sister, daughter of the woman who had destroyed her life, her mother and her childhood happiness, but safely into the hands of a Catholic prince or princess of her own royal blood.

The continuation of her dream to restore Catholicism to the land for good depended on her production of an heir to replace me.

Four days after the coronation, Mary's first Parliament was called and it repealed all the religious changes that had been made by our father and our brother Edward; England was a

Catholic country once again. In that first Parliament, there was another ruling. Parliament decreed that the marriage between Henry VIII and Katherine of Aragon had been lawful, and Mary was the legitimate issue of that marriage.

Mary reversed her own bastardry. She revoked the decrees of our father.

My sister was seeking to rewrite history, to turn back time, so that she might make all the sorrows of her childhood disappear. In Mary's new history of our family, our father and her mother had never truly been separated by mine. Mary's mother was the true Queen of Henry VIII. Mary's birth was lawful, our country was Catholic.

Although it was not said outright, this proclamation meant that as Mary's birth was lawful and legitimate, mine was unlawful and I was a bastard. For if her birth was legitimate, then my birth was not. I had been born when her mother was still alive. I had been born therefore not to a lawful queen, but to a woman Mary sought to make now a mere addendum in history; my mother was cast now as just another mistress of King Henry VIII, rather than his queen.

With that proclamation, Mary's attitude towards me altered. Although her feelings for me had been souring for some time, it seemed that the proclamation of her legitimacy pulled up all the old hatred and bitterness that she had felt towards my mother, and my existence only served to remind her of all her past sorrows.

I was the bastard Princess once again… the heretic heir to Mary's Catholic country…and my sister was starting to see me as the source of all that was wrong with her country, and all that had gone wrong in her own life too.

I was in danger.

CHAPTER EIGHT

Richmond Palace, London
1553

"So," I said slowly, wondering if I had heard my old friend and lady of my bedchamber correctly. "The Queen is passing comment that I am *not* the daughter of our father Henry VIII?"

Kat looked at me with a grave expression on her face. Her warm brown eyes were sympathetic, but there were lines of anger growing at her eyes and mouth.

"Yes," she said simply, "that is indeed what I am hearing from the ladies of the royal bedchamber." Kat paused and shook her head. "As though anyone could doubt who your father was!" she exclaimed, showing her displeasure with a clucking noise like a mother hen punctuating the end of her sentence.

William Cecil, the appointed administrator of my lands and wealth, had returned to court to keep me updated on the latest accounts and surveys of my lands, and was looking at Kat with some horror. Cecil had long been a supporter of mine, and was becoming my good friend. He had recently been elected to Parliament as a knight of the shire for Lincolnshire and was about the court a great deal, as well as still managing my estates and affairs. He was a slippery and pragmatic survivor, my Cecil, and I was most fond of him.

"Doubt indeed!" Cecil looked from Kat to me with an appalled expression. "Why, you are the very image of your father, *more* so than the Queen... of a certainty!"

"What say you, Parry?" I asked of my Master of Coin as I looked out of the window to the gardens of Richmond. Parry made a soft grunt of dissatisfaction at the unwelcome news, which made me smile, although the situation was hardly amusing. In the wake of Mary's coronation and the proclamation of her legitimacy, there had been a change in the winds of court as there was in the weather of the land. Rain fell in never-ending storms, reflecting perhaps the temper of the Queen. Mary was not happy with me. She was making sure that everyone knew and understood her displeasure.

Kat had uncovered that Mary was discussing me, not only with her ladies, but it seemed with several trusted Councillors, and the Spanish Ambassador, Renard. In addition to my apparently *unconvincing* attempts at engaging with Mary's religion, my sister was also starting to question my birth, wondering aloud if I were the child, not of our great father King Henry VIII, but of the lowly musician, Mark Smeaton, who was executed along with my mother and the other men accused of crimes with her.

I did not speak of my mother in public; my relationship with her was like my own with God, a personal and private one. But yet, although I had known so little of her in life, I could not believe that she was guilty of the crimes they accused her of when she was sent to her death.

There had been many reasons for the men about my father to move against my mother; she had been a powerful influence on

King Henry, and men with fierce ambitions had not liked her interference. When she had failed to give a son to the King, despite numerous pregnancies, there had been a chance to remove her from her position, and set up another queen who more agreed with the ambitions of those men about my father. My father had grown weary of his fierce and flirtatious queen, and when she ceased to please him, she had lost her most valuable weapon, his protection.

Over the years, I had gleaned this information and made my own conclusions on why and how my mother had fallen from grace. Although I would never discover the whole truth, I believed the accusations against her had been false, and that she had gone to her death for the sin of failing to please her king, rather than for the foul charges of incest, adultery and treason which had been used to stain her name. But not all believed in her innocence as I did… my sister clearly, thought my mother capable of anything, and was now quite comfortable to use the slanders thrown at my mother, against me as well.

I certainly was not the daughter of a court musician. I was the daughter of Henry VIII.

If my father, in all his wisdom and with his greatly suspicious mind, had thought for a *moment* that I was not his daughter he would have had me removed from his court and his family in less time than it took to skin a hare. And Cecil was right. My red hair, pale skin and little mouth did not come from the dark haired mother that bore me, but from the Tudor father who passed the colours of the Welsh dragon down through my blood. Mary looked less like our father than I did. Edward too, had resembled more his mother, apart from his little stubborn mouth. My dark eyes and lithe figure, my long thin fingers and elegant hands were things I had taken of my mother, but the rest, all the rest, was Bluff King Hal.

Cecil looked worriedly at me. "You must not take these rumours to heart, my lady," he counselled. "No one can doubt that you are the true daughter of the late King. They have only to look on you to know it."

I shook myself from staring at the window and turned to them. These three were amongst the best people I had ever known. I gave them a little smile.

"I do not believe that any but the King *was* my father," I said. "But that is not the problem. Mary is making clear day by day that she likes not that I am her heir; she will find excuse for action against me. If she can convince people that her suspicions on my legitimacy or my religion are enough, then she will be able to move against me. She is not inspired by any Godly or goodly impulse in this, however much she may wish to believe it. She is encouraged in her ill-will towards me through the cankers of jealousy and the spirit of revenge. She has never had any person to hold to account for all the wrongs done to her during the annulment of her mother's marriage, and that, she seeks to do now... whether she knows it or not."

Kat looked sharply at me. "But you had nothing to do with anything that happened to the Queen as a child, my lady," she rushed on, her face drawn with concern. "You were a babe in arms, you were an infant! There was nothing done then that was your fault..."

I held up a hand and stopped her. "*That* is reason talking Kat," I smiled at her sadly, "and reason has nothing to do with either of the emotions I have just described. In the darkest places of her heart, Mary sees me as the cause for her and her mother's pain, and there is no one left that she can take revenge on... but me. All her ill will to me has nothing to do with my religion or her reason, but if she can use them as excuses to move against me, I believe she will."

I looked at the three serious faces before me.

"What should we do then?" asked Parry.

"What we always do, my dear Parry..." I said. "Watch, wait and be careful. If Mary wants to act against me then she will have to have good reason. The Council are not likely to allow her to remove me from the succession without a full-proof motive. After all, she has no easy heir to replace me with. Our Grey cousins, the Countess of Lennox and our cousin Mary of Scotland, are all more distant in the succession, and there would be divisions within the country at any of those choices. And besides…" I paused and smiled a little. "They will fear what the people of England may have to say about my removal as heir, or aggression against me; they know I am popular in the hearts of the people."

"You are, indeed," Cecil's warm smile lightened my heart a little.

"Come," I said. "We know what is occurring, and we know its reasons. Now is the time to ensure that we keep a goodly eye on the comings and goings at my sister's side. What else has been occurring at court, besides her slander of my birth, religion and parentage? Anything of more import than that?"

Parry grinned; he often found my flippancy engaging. I saw no point in always wallowing in gravity, even if the situation was quite grave.

"The Queen has been meeting most regularly with the Spanish Ambassador, Simon Renard," Parry informed us. "It seems that she is most anxious to carry on good relations with her Imperial cousin of Spain."

"Umm…" I tapped my nails on a window sill. "Mary is looking for a husband… does she look to Spain? The Emperor Charles is quite old now, although they were once promised in marriage when she was a child."

"The English will not accept a king who is foreign to rule over them," Cecil warned. "It would be unthinkable that England should become annexed as a property of Spain."

"I do not think my sister would allow that," I said. "But it is troubling. She has always felt more Spanish than English, I believe, and her devotion to her saintly mother is such that a match with her cousin would feel right to her, I know. My father, too, married outside of England at times in his reign."

"But the Queen's husband will have powers that no incoming female consort would ever have!" argued Cecil. "It is agreed that the Queen must marry, but to marry into the Empire of Spain and take our country away from all its independence and glory? That cannot be borne."

"Indeed not," agreed Kat. "What about the royal cousin she so lately removed from the Tower? Edward Courtenay would be a fine match, and he is English at least. Marriage to him would not bring the risk of a foreign power becoming master over England."

"Whatever happens, my friends," I said. "I think we can be sure that the Ambassador of Spain will be pouring notions of marriage to her Catholic cousin into Mary's ear with ease and happiness. Mary may be old to be a maiden bride, but she rules one of the principal countries of Europe now, and in that respect she is a fine match. But you are right; the English will never accept being mastered by a foreign power. It is strange, is it not, that an island already so made up of different peoples should be so intolerant of those who come from across the water?"

"It's not just those across the water my lady," said Parry with a laugh. "I was born a Welshman in blood and bone. For most of my life I have lived with the suspicion of the English. It's something to do with all the mist in England; it makes Englishmen naturally a fearful race since they can't see beyond their own front gate."

I laughed. Cecil and Kat joined in, but of course my clever Cecil could not help but retaliate. "It is misty in Wales much of the time too, when it's not raining that is..." Cecil quipped back to Parry, "how come you to explain that the Welsh are not fearful?"

Parry looked affronted. "The Welsh are never fearful, my lord," he said. "We know what lies beyond our gates... the English.

And if the English are all we have to fear then good Welshmen shall *all* sleep easy in our beds."

I held up a hand as Cecil looked as though he might jump at Parry. They were good friends, but joking has a way amongst men of becoming a fight with little provocation.

"My lords, since I am made of both fine English *and* Welsh blood then I shall fear neither of you. I would rather be surrounded by honest Englishmen and Welshmen alike. But my sister is not made of all the same blood as I; I believe her Spanish blood is calling her home. Let us keep an eye on this matter, for I believe that she will lean to Spain in her choice of husband."

I looked out into the gardens again. A mist was starting to appear, grey and foggy its silver fingers stretched out across the gardens obscuring the horizon.

Parry looked out over my shoulder and grinned. "See?" he nodded at Cecil, "mist."

We laughed again. But this was just a brief alleviation of the fear I felt settling about us, much like the mist. Creeping over me was my sister's displeasure as her ill-will toward me was becoming obvious. I had to be careful in my public observation of religion, and in my speech around court. Eyes were watching me, other than hers, which would not be displeased to see this Protestant heir to the throne removed. As long as I lived and was the heir, the radical Catholics would see me as a threat.

Not long after this discussion, my sister started to give precedence to our Catholic cousin, Lady Margaret Douglas, Countess of Lennox, over me, at court. I was at times, instructed to enter a ceremony behind Margaret, or that she should take my place at a feast beside Mary. Margaret Douglas was the daughter of our father's eldest sister, Margaret Tudor, from her second marriage to Archibald Douglas, Earl of Angus. Tudor blood ran therefore in Margaret Douglas' veins, but not as thickly as it did in mine. She came of a match made between a princess of England and a noble house of Scotland, whereas I came directly of the line of the kings of England.

By giving my place to our Lennox cousin Mary was making clear her disapproval of me as her heir and showing that I might well be replaced. Mary stopped seeing me in private and started to avoid me about court. I was followed and observed by her spies. She sent daily instruction on my religious conversion and demanded constant updates on my attendance at the chapel royal. Mary was threatening my place in the succession, advancing those of lesser birth above me, and haranguing my person. I knew that I could not continue long at court under the pressures I was now facing. But I also did not want to leave the hub of power.

Mary was coming closer each day to making her choice of husband. I wanted to be close at hand to see what should come from this, most royal, of marriages. Would she follow her head and marry where the English people would want her to? Or would she follow her heart and find a husband of Spanish blood?

The heart is the most dangerous enemy, and all too often it becomes the master of the mind.

CHAPTER NINE

The Court of Mary I, London
1553

Life is full of liaisons lost to time, distance, or the changing nature of the heart.

Sometimes a love was never meant to be; sometimes it is not as strong as those involved wished it were, and sometimes, life simply gets in the way of two hearts once intended for each other. Once an impression is made on the heart however, it does not leave.

If love is thrown aside, then that love will turn to hatred. The bitter cuts made by the knife of abandonment may forever fester, and will not be forgotten. If love is betrayed, the heart will be overwhelmed by fantasies of recrimination and revenge. If love is made and then separated by outside forces, it will become longing, and even when we realize that we may be better off where we end up, in such longing there is still attachment to a love that never was.

And sometimes, even when love is nothing more than a fiction, it can endure. Sometimes love is false fiction, for only one heart reaches out in adoration of another, but that love is not real, not tangible. It slips through the fingers like the air we breathe. Love, when it comes from one heart alone, is not true love, but that does not mean it is not still powerful.

When Mary was a small girl, her mother and our father betrothed her to her grand cousin Charles V of Spain, a man much older than she and already in possession of a huge empire. Katherine of Aragon's love for her homeland was such that although royal betrothals are made and unmade faster than the turning of the seasons, Katherine convinced Mary that this betrothal was sealed by love. When Mary and Charles married, her mother promised, they would have such as the love that Katherine and her husband, Henry, had, a true love, an equal love, and Mary would return to help to rule the country that her mother adored and dreamed of, the hot and sultry shores of Spain. There were many fictions in such tales, as we were to see later.

Telling tales to a small girl about her future marriage may seem innocent enough, but perhaps not... It does depend on how seriously the girl takes those stories. Mary fell for her mother's promises with all enthusiasm, and when she was eventually told that Charles, who was around twenty years older than she, had married another, it broke her tiny heart.

Mary had a jewel the Spanish Ambassador gave to her from Charles when they were betrothed. Mary carried it in a pouch, kept close to her heart, since she was a little girl, and still wore the little gem even now she was grown. As the Queen, Mary had many more fabulous jewels to adorn herself with than this little thing, but yet still she wore it.

There was a deep sentimental streak in Mary, as there had been in our father, as there was too in me. That little jewel meant a great deal to my sister.

So, when the question of her marriage came to the fore, I knew that Mary would hark back to those echoes of love still sounding in her heart. Echoes of a fabled, mythical love which existed before all of her sorrow and pain; the fulfilment of the marriage her mother had so wished for, the marriage that would see Mary restored to happiness… marriage to the man she had loved and idolised as a child.

There was but one small problem with this fantasy; Charles was an old man now, a wasted and weary emperor whose exploits had been as great as his chin was long. He had been married much, and was not taken with the idea of marrying again.

But he had a son.

Charles' son was a young man, a handsome prince, who was the heir and would one day be the ruler of the Hapsburg Empire. So, if the father was too old then why not the son? The Spanish were keen for it; Mary might be an old woman by the standards of marriage, but she was also the Queen of a strategically important isle, and this match would mean another advantage over the French, which the Spanish were most keen on. They had no love for their neighbours the Valois kings of France, with whom they were presently at war.

Mary was horribly keen, and terrible at disguising it. How often had she longed for a family that loved her? A husband of her own, and children to grace her days? And here was the handsome, young son of Spain being offered to her… I am surprised she was able to keep still on her throne in her excitement.

But the English were not keen. A king married to our queen would have power in this land which was unknown, uncharted. With this first ascension of a queen to the throne, it was hardly known what position her king should take… Would he have overall power of the land, just as a man should have by law when he married a woman and took on mastery of her house? If Mary retained her own power, and had power over her husband, would this be out of the bounds of the laws of God and man? If Mary's husband was king of another land, would England become annexed as part of the property of that country?

No one really knew, and it made Englishmen uneasy in their beds to think they may have fought to put their Tudor queen on the throne, only to have her hand her power over to a foreign potentate. The English wanted to be ruled by the English. I understood my countrymen well enough; they feared a foreign power squashing out their individuality and power. If Mary took this route, she would have opposition on her hands.

There was another option; Mary could marry an Englishman, a noble. Our father had, after all, married often into the noble lines of England, so there was prescience for such a match. Our cousin Edward Courtenay had been put forward as a possible suitor and he may have proved a good solution to the problems which worried the men of England so. But I believe Mary's mind was made even before she had seen the portrait of the striking Prince Phillip of Spain.

The French Ambassador, Noialles, who had started to visit me on a regular basis, told me that Phillip had a salient collection of salacious portraits in his private collection; female nudes whose forms seemed less to represent appreciation of art, than appreciation of the naked. He whispered it to me with a delighted yet horrified expression which caused me to smile and laugh a little. I'm not sure if he intended me to relay this to my dour sister, looking for ways to discredit the Spanish Prince in the eyes of the Queen, but I had little opportunity to do so these days. I think really the Ambassador just wanted the rumour of Phillip's dalliances to be cast about court to increase the fears of the populace, which in truth, needed little encouragement.

My sister eventually received rather helpful and timely *divine* intervention in her choice of a husband. One morning, Mary and her lady in waiting, Susan Clarencieux, had just bowed before the communion bread when the Spanish Ambassador walked into the Queen's audience chamber. Suddenly, Mary was taken…. possessed…. with the Holy Spirit, to reveal that she was destined to marry Phillip of Spain by the will of God.

It is odd, is it not, that a piece of bread may be capable of transmitting God's thoughts to a person? In the Bible when He spoke to the prophets or fore-fathers, He generally did not do so through a pastry or a loaf. To the Protestant within me, that bit of bread was just a symbol of the bread broken at the Last Supper. To Mary, that bread was the incarnation of the spirit of God. So I suppose there was always going to be a difference in the way we viewed the Host. All the same, it seemed God had a remarkably political sense of timing about Him that day, as He sent His spirit to inform Mary she was destined to marry Phillip, just as the Spanish Ambassador arrived in her chambers…. But there is a saying that God works in mysterious ways, and here so it seemed He did, with Mary and His wishes for her country. God wanted Mary to marry Phillip, apparently.

I believe we would all have found the little scene more convincing, had the bread told Mary to marry Courtenay, rather than confirming the desires of her own heart.

The refuge of the uncertain is often in the pretence of power; I wondered myself over the years if Mary had really fooled herself by her own play-acting in this matter. Sometimes when we want something enough, it becomes easy, too easy, to convince ourselves that it is not only right that we want it, but that it is *meant* to be.

The heart is a dangerous enemy. Mary's heart was leading her down a path she might come to regret. But it now seemed the Queen had the direct approval of God on her side, to achieve what she desired.

CHAPTER TEN

The Court of Mary I, London
1553

Mary wanted to marry Phillip of Spain.

Assured by no less than the Holy Spirit that her choice was the right one, she made her will plain to those around her. She wanted to marry, she needed to marry; not only as it was the right condition for a queen to have a king, to complete her ring of royalty, but also to bear an heir for her country.

And God *wanted* her to marry into the arms of Spain, or so we heard from Mary.

Mary's Council were divided on her choice; yes, they wanted her to marry and as soon as possible; but many were uneasy with the idea of a foreign prince coming to marry their queen. With all the rights a husband should have of his wife's property, essentially and in all terms traditional under the eyes of God, this would mean that England would belong to Spain. The English were afraid to lose their country, to become but a part of another power; but more than that, they were afraid to relinquish their identity, their independence, something they had become proud of, justifiably.

If the sexes were reversed and our queen had been a king, there would have been no problem with marriage to a foreign princess. That lady would have travelled the wide seas to England, bringing with her riches and no personal power other than those diplomatic persuasions princesses are often trained in to advance the interests of their homelands. A foreign *princess* would have brought no confusion to the ritual of royal marriage. But with a queen bringing a king to her… that was different.

Most men fear change; for in the unknown lurks every deep shadow of possibility. Those of limited imagination will simply refuse change for as long as possible, and blame change for anything untoward that occurs, retreating into memories brim full of past and history to tell us how good things *used* to be. Those of more imagination, more realisation, will learn how change can be cultured and altered to suit themselves.

Some men benefit from change as they would do from stagnation, and some will benefit from neither. Some are active in this life, and some are passive. We must all of us seek to find the best of any situation life hands to us, using all the wit God gifted to us, to carve our own space in the ever-changing world.

Mary knew that her people were averse to the idea of her marrying a foreign prince. Our father, although he had done many controversial acts in his reign, had still granted his people an impression of their own power in the world. England had grown, broken from Rome and still stood tall. We traded with other nations, fought enemies and we were still here, still standing; this little isle in the middle of the seas, a nation of sailors, adventurers and bold risk-takers. Mary was in the process of threatening that very special sense of her people's identity. There were many rumbles against this marriage; from her Council, her nobles and, more importantly, from the common man.

Kings only hold their power through the will of the common man. Although in the simplest terms, it seems as though the King is all-powerful, it is not so. A king is a fragile thing, made of flash and appearance, of sparkling gold and recognition of family blood. Throughout history, thrones have been given, stolen and taken, and it is not only having a claim to a throne which means a king may hold it. It is only through either love or fear that a king may hold his crown. Mary ascended to the throne on a wave of love from her people, and now it seemed that her personal desire for love was the emotion most likely to make her risk everything she had achieved thus far.

Mary succeeded in manipulating her Council into agreeing with her marriage to Phillip of Spain by flatly refusing to consider any other suitor. They realized that if they were to have a king and an heir to secure the Catholic future, then they would have to agree with the Queen. Then, on the 16th November 1553, Mary faced the House of Commons to do the same. The Speaker started by presenting a petition, on behalf of the realm, asking the Queen to marry into an English bloodline, to choose a man from her own realm to be her king. We all knew they were thinking of Courtenay, although no name was mentioned.

Mary's Lord Chancellor, Gardiner went to speak for Mary, but she stopped him, and stepped forward herself. She thanked the House for its wish that she should marry, but went on:

"The English Parliament has not been wont to use such languages to their sovereigns. And where private persons in such cases follow their own private tastes, sovereigns may reasonably challenge an equal liberty. We have heard much from you of the incommodities which may attend our marriage... we have not heard from you of the commodities thereof; one of which is of some weight with us, the commodity namely, of our *private inclination*. We have not forgotten our coronation oath. We shall marry as God shall direct our choice, to his honour, and our country's good."

Mary was magnificent; even I will admit that to you. Her speech was clear, strong, bold... insisting that her will and her *private inclination* in marriage was the only right one, and it was approved by God. Mary was in essence claiming that her choice was divinely inspired, that her will was God's will; if it was God's will then that she marry with Spain, no one should stand against it.

It is a sure, yet, interestingly unimaginative way for a person to put to an end an argument... Stating they have *divine* approval of their choices, rather than relying on the certainty of their own will, or on argument of logic and reason, seems rather... unfair. For my own part, I have little believed that God would intervene so in the everyday tasks of man; He gave us our qualities and the wit to make our choices, and therein His work is done, and ours begins. It is we, His people, who make the choices for good or ill that shape our world, and our responsibility is to try to make the best choices we can, to show to Him we acknowledge and honour His gifts to us.

Mary was *using* God to ensure her own wishes were carried out; something no mortal man or woman should ever take lightly.

But no one was going to argue against her since she was sure she had God on her side. To counter the argument, her Councillors or Members of Parliament would need a holy intervention of their own, and there are only so many interventions that can be ascribed to God before things start to appear faintly ridiculous.

In December, a marriage treaty was drafted. It must have been the oddest marriage proposal that was ever made. Phillip was to be the *King Consort*, a king, but one in *name* only. He would hold no governing power in England and neither would his nobles. He would not take any part of England as part of Mary's dowry, and Spain would not be able to draw England legally into any of her wars or conquests. Mary would not leave England; her prince would have to come to her.

An odd proposal and a novel one for this age… in which a woman brings nothing but her body to the bed of her husband!

The Spanish were so keen on having a foot in England that they agreed to all the terms. I am sure they thought that once their handsome prince stepped into England, he could charm Mary so thoroughly that she would acquiesce to their needs later. In the country, however, the muttering grew to openly spoken discontent, the whispers started to turn to growls of anger that our queen was to give herself, and England, to a Spanish prince. The common man did not understand, or care to try to understand, the marriage proposal being laid down. They understood that their queen would be subject to her king as any woman was to her husband, and that was all. Their queen was opening her legs and her country, to consensual conquest by the Spanish.

At court, Mary was still making my life a misery; giving Margaret Douglas precedence ahead of me in court activities, giving our Lennox cousin rich gifts and allowing her to live at court without paying for room or food. My household and I were not given any such honour. Mary muttered to her Ambassadors, particularly Renard of Spain, of the trouble I gave her and was obviously not above degrading my lineage and birth to them. She did not move publicly to remove me as her heir, but I think she wanted to, more than anything. Such an action would be a balm to the hurt and sorrow of her childhood humiliation.

Her pressure on me to alter my religion was such that I now had to attend Catholic Mass at the chapel royal frequently. I never went without at least a little protest, but I could not refuse entirely. The iron will of my sister was stuck around my waist, pulling me and thrusting me, trying to force me into her idea of what I should be. But I did not think her will was right… I was seeing enough of her mistakes in this, the youth of her reign, to know that trouble was coming.

It was becoming intolerable for me to stay at court, both personally and politically. I decided that it was time I retreated into my estates. If the common opinion was so against this marriage, then it was best for me to be apart from the spectacle of it. I did not want the people associating me with the ills that they believed Mary was bringing to their country. In a personal sense, my every step was being watched, my sister was becoming overtly hostile to me and her constant pressure on me to change my religion was starting to make an impact on my health. Worries of the mind so easily come to plague the blood and bone of the body. I had found this in times past when I had faced situations of anxiety; sometimes I had feigned illness to escape danger, but now, with Mary's pressures and disapproval on me like a weight about my neck, I found I was affected with a constant tiredness of soul and body. I needed to leave the court for a while.

I went to Mary a little before Christmas, and asked to remove to my country estates at Ashridge.

"The court and the airs of London are making me feel weary in my body and my mind, Your Majesty," I said as I knelt before her. "Since your glorious ascension to the throne, there have been so many entertainments and diversions that I believe I have exerted myself and depleted my strength. I was so happy to see my good sister take her rightful place as queen, that I failed to notice the weakening state of my health." I looked up at her and smiled pathetically, "I hope, Majesty, you will forgive my absence at your side for your first Christmas as queen, but I am in truth feeling most feeble, and I fear that further exertion might have a lasting effect on my health."

She looked at me, narrowing those dark eyes with her strange way of seeming to see through a person's skin and into their soul. If she could indeed have seen the truth there within me, it would have said quite different things to her than the words which came from my lips.

My soul spoke thus: … *my strength fails me under the constant barrage of your stubborn will. I am not sick in body, but in mind, through your constant criticism and complaint. I have done all that I can to appease you, to publicly show my loyalty to you, but I cannot change the nature of my own soul, nor the blood that flows in my veins.*

I cannot change that my mother supplanted yours in the affections of the father we shared. I cannot change the past, but I am your sister and true subject; I believe in the dynastic right of your rule, but I cannot and will not alter my soul in order to satisfy the cravings of your heart. I can never be a Catholic. If I were your queen, I would be satisfied if you but showed obeisance to my wishes… if you but showed in public that you were loyal to me and my will. I would not seek to change your private nature nor your personal faith. If I were your queen, I would treat you with more fairness than you are presently showing to me.

An accident of destiny gave you to me as sister, and you are the only other person in the world to share the true blood of our father. As such, I am bound by duty to love you, but I would like with all my heart, to love you as a sister and to have that love returned. For you to accept that I cannot be other than what I am. I cannot convert the way I believe and am instructed by God. We are both made by Him, but He has made us different. Surely, though I worship in a different way, we still both worship the same God? Surely, though I hold a faith of different practise to yours, this does not affect my loyalty to you?

At that last meeting, I turned to her and spoke with a wish that seemed to me later to have come from some shadow of the future which fell on my present.

"I would, Your Majesty, that should you hear aught which might give you to suspect ill of me, that I might be allowed to talk with you in person. To show that although others may accuse me of many things, that I am, in truth, your sister by blood, and your servant in honour."

Mary nodded to me, assuring me that I was always welcome in her presence, as her kin and as her subject. Perhaps she knew what was in my heart as I knelt before her, perhaps not. But either way, I think she was relieved to see me go. We parted before the court as the most affectionate sisters you ever saw, with many embraces and good wishes. She gave me parting gifts and smiles.

It was all pretence. She was as suspicious of me as I was wary of her.

I rode out from London before the first light on the next morning. As we mounted horses in the courtyard, and the first creaks of the many heavy carts carrying our household supplies, beds, clothes, plate and furniture, were heard, I breathed in the icy cold air and let it out of my body with a shuddering sense of relief.

I had started to dread each morning as the coming of another day of courtly humiliation and religious bombardment. Not many more days could I have taken being forced through the doors of the chapel to listen to the priests muttering in Latin. Not many more days could I have kept that false smile on my face as I went about my day, knowing my own sister was spreading filthy rumours against my mother's already blackened name and thereby, my own. Not many more times could I accept the humiliation of having my repulsive Lennox cousin, Margaret Douglas, placed before me in court.

I breathed in again and felt the cold air revive my spirits. It was better to fall back, to watch and wait, to see the lie of the land at a distance to decide on the next step. The persistent bombardment of my sister's *private inclinations* had to be taken in small doses.

In the dark blue-grey of the winter's morning light, I spurred my horse on and with my personal guards, rode ahead of our main party and out into the world. The further we rode out from London and the overbearing atmosphere of the Queen, the further my spirits were lifted.

As we rode through the countryside, whenever we were slow enough for them to approach, the people of England would stop in their work and come to look on us. Here and there people were brave enough to come forward, and when they did, I tried to stop and talk to them. A woman brought us icy-cold ale fresh from her store and it was so delicious after a long, hard ride on the frosty ground that my thanks were perhaps overdone. She looked at me with such gratitude for my enthused acceptance of her small present and blushed as she muttered her thanks. I was truly grateful to every person who came forth to give us presents. The people who came to me that day were offering me bread and ale which would have made up their own suppers, and yet they offered it to me freely.

When one has more than enough, it is never hard to be generous. When one has little, generosity means so much more.

We visited with nobles along the journey, stopping to feast and use their homes as our beds, and it was a merry journey for me. As we drew near the estate and the familiar sights of Ashridge House started to show themselves in the distance, I started to feel at ease. I was coming home. Even if I had not a conventional home where a family of kin may meet my homecoming with warmth and smiles, I had my own manner of family; Kat, Blanche, Parry, Cecil, John Astley and my servants; they were my family.

I pulled up my horse to stop on a hillock as the house came into view and my guards did the same. I looked around at them and smiled, my face flushed with the ride and the cold air. They smiled back at me with genuine grins of affection. My men were as loyal to me as they were to my standard. I was *theirs*, their own princess; a youthful and comely maid who commanded swathes of men with the surety of a man. They told me often that I reminded them of my father, and I loved them for that. My household was a merry place to be in service. I rewarded loyalty and good service amply and made provision for the families of my servants. Many lords are mean with their money and their favours. They think that a servant should be honoured simply to serve. I was of a different set of mind; I was honoured to be served *by* them, honoured to be surrounded by those loyal to me.

"I fancy I smell a roasting deer on the wind," I said to them with a wide grin. "Who here thinks he can beat me to it?"

My men laughed as I kicked my horse into action and sped across the rough ground towards the house. Then there was a roar on the wind, and they were after me. I heard their horses' hooves racing behind me and their shouts of encouragement and challenge to each other. I urged my horse on faster; my mount was fine, and he carried a smaller weight than theirs. Behind me, I could hear their shouts as they came closer to me, and I laughed, feeling their determination even as I heard their voices. No man alive likes to be beaten by a girl at anything, even if she is his master and commander.

I reached the house first, but I sent the best cut of meat at the table to the guard who came in second after me.

CHAPTER ELEVEN

Ashridge House, Hertfordshire
Christmas 1553 – January 1554

Christmas was merry at my house at Ashridge, although a much smaller affair than celebrations at court. Once a Priory, Ashridge was taken by my father from the Church during his reformation of the houses of religion in England. Although I might more usually have chosen to go to my estates at Hatfield House, I felt as though further distance was required from my sister, to calm my nerves. Released from the domineering presence of my sister, I was cheered and enjoyed a fine Christmas with my servants with much dancing and entertainments. But we kept a careful eye on the court; Parry gathered news on the forthcoming marriage and on the whispers from the country on what people thought of it, and we brought dispatches together to talk on in the long cold evenings by the fire.

When we had ridden out from London, I sent a letter back to my sister asking her to send me such things for my newly converted Catholic chapel at Ashridge; copes, chasubles, chalices and other Catholic adornments and ornaments. I hoped she might take this as further public evidence of my 'conversion'. Mary had showed enough times, after all, that she often believed what she *wanted* to believe.

The problem was that in my case, she did not want to believe anything good of me. She sent the items I requested, and continued to ask for proof in letters of my attendance at Catholic Mass. It seemed I was not going to get away with just these public shows of obedience to her will. Mary wanted my soul to bend to her wishes, not just my knee.

It was bitterly cold that winter. I wondered if God was taking offence at His name being so easily bandied about by the mouth of England's Queen, and took steps to show His disapproval through the bitter weather. We heard that the Thames froze over, that a temporary market was erected there and that people even made a great fire on it to roast beef and mutton. The ice did not melt as the fires blazed on it, dripping the cooking fat of the roasting animals, sizzling against the solid surface of the river.

At Ashridge we were surrounded by great falls of snow that covered the countryside in a glittering, thick blanket. Although it was beautiful to be sure, such times also spelled danger and times of hardship for those who were not well-cared for in a great house, such as I was. I instructed that the outer-lying villages and farms of the estate should be given succour from our kitchens of meat, bread and wood to burn whilst the snows persisted. Then, after thinking on it, I sent word to Cecil at court that the same should be true on all my estates. If I could help my people in hard times, they would remember that kindness, and reward it, I hoped, with loyalty.

In January of 1554, the Spanish Imperial embassy arrived at the shores of England, and rode through the snowy land to

London to meet the Queen. Prince Phillip of Spain was not amongst them yet, but this was the first wave of the coming wedding party who were making everyone in England nervous. When the Spanish nobles rode into London, they were pelted with snowballs by young boys of the city. The welcome the Spanish received from the people of England was as frosty as the snowballs that exploded against their backs, as they rode into their new land.

The English nobles tried to make up for their chilly welcome with courtly courtesy and many entertainments, but it was clear as the ice on the Thames that the Spanish were not a welcome sight to the people of England.

In late January, my men in the country heard whispers of an uprising planned against Mary and her crown; a series of co-ordinated rebellions from key areas of England. The West Country, Kent and Leicestershire were all mentioned, as well as the names of several lords; Sir Peter Carew, Sir James Crofts, Sir Christopher Aston, Sir Thomas Stafford and Earl Edward Courtenay… whom Mary had only just released from his prison in the Tower, were all implicated as leaders, as well as Henry Grey, Duke of Suffolk, father to the still-imprisoned Lady Jane Grey. The leader of the rebellion was Sir Thomas Wyatt of Kent, a man whose family estates neighboured those traditional lands of the Boleyns, my mother's family. *This* Wyatt's father had been arrested at the same time as my mother, but had been the only man to escape those accusations with his head still on his shoulders.

The main grievance of the plotters was the proposed marriage with Spain and the possible annexation of England that many feared this would lead to. Many of the rebels were also Protestants, like myself, and feared that Mary's wish to marry into Spain would outlaw Protestantism entirely, but also might bring the dreaded Spanish Inquisition to our shores.

The plot was, of course, quite simple. Mary would be deposed, her marriage to Phillip and union with Spain ended, and

I should be made Queen and married to Edward Courtenay, uniting the last blood of the Angevin kings with the Tudor line. It was even said that the King of France was to offer his help to the plotters, providing a force to invade England on the back of the first waves of rebellion. The King of France, Henri, little wanted to see a match made between his neighbours in England and present enemies of war, Spain. He much preferred to cause disquiet and unrest. The mention of help from a foreign country made the plot seem more serious.

The rumour that Henry Grey, Duke of Suffolk, father to our still-imprisoned cousin, Lady Jane Grey, was implicated in the plots brought a chill to my heart. Mary had released the Duke, in her benevolence, from the Tower in the late summer of 1553. His possible involvement in yet another plot against the Queen was dangerous. His daughter, Jane, was still a prisoner held in the Tower. Mary had been lenient thus far with our cousin, but would she continue to be so, if Jane's father was once again found to be a traitor to the crown? Henry Grey was gambling with his daughter's life; if he was unsuccessful in this rebellion, then I feared what might become of Jane.

But then how often do men such as Grey stop and consider that they may fail at something? It seems to me that men willing to risk the lives of their families for a chance at power have very little in the way of forethought for what might happen if they fail.

Over-confidence can be a disease which destroys all in its wake.

The plot was madness... of course, most plots are so. And it was not only Jane who was in peril from the wild plans of these desperate men. *I* was being thrust into its very centre like a pawn in a game of chess, put forward as a Protestant puppet-replacement for Mary on the throne. At this stage, we knew not if the plot was truth or mere rumour, but we were soon to find out.

It was coming to the end of the first month of the year when one of the rumoured rebel leaders, Sir James Crofts, rode past Ashridge on his way to the Welsh Marches. It seemed from his messages that the rebel plot was indeed likely to go ahead, for he was riding to bring men to his banner. I would not meet with him, not wanting to be pulled into outright treason… but I did not report his passing to Mary either. For one thing, if the plotting came to naught, then I did not want my sister further convinced that I was a danger to her and her throne. Seeing as I was marked by the rebels to replace Mary, then to alert her to such a plot, before we knew if it was likely, would only count against me in the end and add to her suspicions of me. Crofts sent word to me to move to a castle I held in Donnington, north of Newbury, for my own safety. Similar messages were sent to me by the leader of the rebellion, Sir Thomas Wyatt.

I did not answer either in person, nor in writing, for I knew what would happen should such be discovered. But I sent word, verbally, by a messenger, William St Loe, expressing total non-commitment to their plans and pretending that I understood not the truth of their messages. I was comfortable at Ashridge, I said in my messages, and had no desire to move houses.

I started to gather my men to me, quietly; if there was an uprising and if it was successful, then I might need to fight for my own life and royal rights. I was the second-largest landowner in the country and I had a great many men I could call on if I needed an army. I am sure that was one reason why the plotters wanted me on their side; I could amass a force akin to Mary's guard if I had the will.

But the men I gathered to my houses, at Ashridge, Hatfield and Donnington amongst other estates I owned were not gathering there to rise against my sister; they were gathered to protect me if the need came.

I was not going to become a *tool* for the rebels to use to justify their cause. I was not going to be used as a puppet-queen to mouth their wishes and words. And I was certainly not going to go willingly to the altar at their urging to marry anyone, least of all that pretty dullard, Edward Courtenay, who had spent most of his life staring at the walls of a prison. I wanted not a husband who was fine to look on but useless for counsel, company or conversation. What would I do with such a flower? Put him in my button hole and wear him as an ornament? I would not be forced into marriage with anyone, nor made to share my power with another just because an accident of birth had made a man royal. If I ever came to the throne then I would be *I* who ruled, and no other. I would show the rebels I was not simply another piece to be moved around a chess board at their bidding. I had seen enough of that from the example of my cousin Jane Grey to know that such a fate was not for me.

Through Parry and Cecil, I knew soon enough that I was not the only one who was aware of the planned uprising in England. Mary and her Council were alerted to danger, and the Spanish Ambassador Renard rushed to tell Mary of a French fleet apparently massing in Normandy, readying for invasion. Courtenay, still at court when he was supposed to be rousing Devonshire for the rebel cause, was interrogated by Gardiner's men and broke down under questioning. He betrayed the other plotters.

At first, I am not sure how seriously Mary took the plot; the easy capture and confession of Courtenay must have given her reason to think perhaps that all the plotters were as dull of wits as he, and therefore may have posed little threat to her.

The plotters were uneasy, their planned uprising depended on speed and surprise, but surprise was being fast lost to them.

My sister sent word that I was to join her at court *for my safety*, but I pleaded illness and took to my bed. Once more under the covers of pretended sickness, I watched and waited to see what this uprising should bring. I had done the same, not so long ago; pretending to be ill when my sister had ridden to take the throne from Warwick and Jane Grey. Now, just as then, I wanted to see what course should give me the best advantage before choosing my side… and I was hardly assured that my sister's intentions to me were entirely benign. I wanted to be a captive of neither side.

History has a way of repeating itself, perhaps because we never learn from its lessons.

Mary did not want me at her side for my safety; she wanted possession of my person in case the rebels looked likely to succeed. She may also have suspected that I was involved in the plot, in which case my head would not be secure on my little shoulders if I was in her keeping. I wanted to give my person neither to the rebels by moving to Donnington, nor to my sister by moving to London.

In the South West, the Midlands and the Welsh Marches, the planned rebellions rose and then fell. Carew and Crofts both failed to raise any men willing to march with them on London, and although Henry Grey did a little better, raising one hundred and forty souls to his banner, but they were largely his own men. His numbers spoke little for his leadership.

Grey and Crofts ran when they heard that the French ships at Normandy were disbanded by the King of France, who feared that the insubstantial rebel forces raised would simply prove an embarrassment to become involved with.

All seemed to have gone awry for the rebels. But, in Kent, Sir Thomas Wyatt *had* amassed a large force in support of his plan. He had some three thousand men. He marched on Rochester, took the town with fair ease and from there, he planned to march on London.

The Queen saw early victory as her forces routed a detachment of the rebels in Hartley Wood, but when Wyatt issued a proclamation from Rochester against the marriage with Spain, more and more men marched to join him. Anti-Spanish feeling, resentment, fear and anger at the Queen and her Council drove men to Wyatt's banners and swelled their numbers. Soon a large force was marching upon London, set on removing Mary from the English throne. It was only a few months since her forces had taken London and deposed Queen Jane Grey, now another army sought to depose Mary, to make either me or Jane Grey the Queen. I wondered truly if they cared which; as long as they had a figurehead.

Within days the South of England descended into chaos... And the rebels were marching on London.

CHAPTER TWELVE

Ashridge House, Hertfordshire
January 1554

"They say his father loved your mother..." Kat's familiar voice came cutting through my thoughts as I stared at the warm fire burning in the hearth of my chambers.

"*They* do say a lot of things to you Kat," I said, perhaps a little harshly. "Whoever *they* are, they do seem to be in constant conversation with you."

She looked at me with a little amusement, her gaze rich with the warmth of love. No matter how much I grew, nor how many estates, titles or power I held in my hands, I would always be the little girl she raised.

"My mistress is not in the mood for conversation?" she idly started to pluck a golden stitch in her embroidery that had gone awry with all the irritating pretended nonchalance of one who *knows* they have something interesting to share. "Then I shall not bother her again."

I sighed. I was restless, anxious, waiting for word on the rebellion that was tearing a swathe through the southern countryside. Although the men fighting in Wyatt's rebellion were fighting under a banner of righteousness as they saw it, this was not stopping the sackings, burnings and abuses which are always suffered by the common people whenever an uprising occurs. War brings no good to common people.

It was also not helpful to my mood that at any time I could become a captive of either these rebels, or of my sister. The rebels wanted me as a figurehead to use against my sister; precisely what my sister really wanted of me, I had yet to discover. So yes, I was uneasy. As England suffered from unrest, so did I.

But my Kat had a way of tickling and tempting me with her gleaned snippets of gossip and finally I had to give in, my curiosity raised. I turned my head to her and stared at her as she plucked her golden thread on the bed covering she was making. A smile at first just touched the side of her lips as she saw my head turn from the corner of her eye, and then spread to cover her face, lighting her countenance. Some people only smile with their mouths, but with Kat, her smile became an extension of her whole body, an enjoyment so palpable that you could taste it in the air, like baking cakes or sweetmeats. She raised eyes to me that danced with glee at having gained my attention. Her soft brown eyes reflected the prancing flames and sparkled with her desire to tell me all.

"Go on," I muttered, with much ill temper. "You have won, have you not? Tell me what *they* say."

She laughed; "you were always the same, even as a girl," she exclaimed. "I know you too well! You were never able to resist so much as a snippet of information, most likely why you took to your books with such ease. Never was there a mind I saw so ready to learn as yours."

I smiled at her. Kat and I had been through a great deal together and it looked as though we were coming to another story to add to our chronicle. Perhaps a little conversation that was not of war and blood and power would help to ease my mind. I nodded to her. She turned to me, and as she thought on how to start her tale she started to re-stitch her covering, her fingers occupied as her mind thought on her story.

"When your mother was young and first came from France where she had been a lady in the service of Queen Claude, she made an immediate impression at the English court." Kat looked up to ascertain if I was listening, which I was, intently. I did love to hear tales of my mother, ones which were not tainted with the hatred some still seemed to hold for her.

"They say that when Anne Boleyn walked into the court, all eyes turned to her; for she had something the other women did not; a spirit and a spark all her own. She was never a true beauty, not like her sister, your aunt Mary Boleyn, not like the Bessie Blounts of this world, but in that too was part of the interest... because she had something that was *more* than beauty. All the Howard women have that appeal, that charm, something that is handed to them through their blood, and she had it from her mother just as you have it from yours." Kat paused and pulled her golden thread through the cover.

"*This* Wyatt's father was a young lord at court then, a poet of a little renown, and when he saw your mother he was struck hard and true with love at the mere sight of her. But Tom Wyatt was already married, and his love for her could never come to anything. He offered her the place of his mistress, they say, but Anne Boleyn was not a woman to be so easily bought! Later, she even refused the same position when your father offered it; she was to be a *wife*, honest in the sight of God, and nothing less. Your father, the great King, moved heaven and earth to have her, but Wyatt, being but a lowly lord, could not do so. So... poor Tom Wyatt, he could only watch as Anne was pursued by the King and eventually as the King won her heart, Wyatt had to step away from his love for her. They say he left the country for a while, worked for your father in foreign lands and tried to bury the love he had for your mother in the arms of other women. But…" she paused and her eyes lit up, "he wrote his poetry to her... about her. She was his *muse* and even now with both of them gone and in the arms of God, those words of his love, and loss, writ in verse still live on."

"Why was he not executed by my father with the others?" I asked bluntly. "If my father knew of his love for my mother, why was he not suspected with the others?"

Kat looked sorrowful at my mention of my mother's fall and execution, and that of the men accused with her. Kat's story had been one of love and romance; she did not want an unhappy ending to her tale.

"He was arrested, but your father did not believe he had done anything," she replied and shrugged. "But I wondered always how the King had believed in the guilt of the others. All through the country they say people whispered against the execution of your mother and the men accused with her. They said that the charges seemed too incredible to be believed."

"But none stepped forward to help them, of course," I spat bitterly, frowning. "Wyatt was lucky more than anything to escape with his head. Perhaps he had more powerful friends than the others accused with my mother."

"Perhaps," Kat frowned a little, "perhaps by that time it was such an old liaison that none could stand witness to any truth in it."

"It is a lesson to learn, Kat," I said. "That those who survive are often just luckier than those who do not. We'll never know truly why they killed my mother, or why they chose those men to accuse with her, but once they had her trapped, her friends taken with her, there was nothing she could do. Perhaps if she'd been more popular with the people, they could have saved her. Look at this situation now; the country rises up for one queen or another or another. There are *three* of us now that men have sought to place on the throne. Which of us will live and which will die? Which will be luckier than the other? If the rebels win, then Jane Grey or I could find ourselves on the throne, but we will be prisoners to the will of others. If Mary wins once more, then what will become of Jane and me? We live our lives on Fortune's Wheel, and where it may turn, none ever know for certain."

Kat looked at me sadly. I think she had hoped to wrest me from my melancholic mood with a tale of love and romance, but I had brought us back to death and betrayal.

I smiled at her a little, feeling guilt for having spoiled her storytelling. "So you think this Wyatt knows of his father's long lost love for my mother?" I asked frivolously. "You think this is why he raises banner to fight my sister and place me on the throne? For the remembrance of love lost?"

Kat grinned at me, pleased by my flippancy. "It would make a good story wouldn't it?" she let out a merry little laugh. "The truth is that life is unfortunately more complicated, and less pretty than it is in books or tales. Who can say what stirs a man's heart to war? Perhaps only the longing all men have to rush off and fight would be enough. But if we had the choice, I would like to believe there was an *ideal* behind it all, there was a good reason to fight, if fight we must… and to my mind, love would be a better reason than most to fight and die for."

I pulled the rich woollen blanket around me as I felt a little draught creep towards me through the tapestries covering the walls. Outside the wind howled and shrieked about my house and estates. It was a cold winter in which our Englishmen had chosen to raise banner and revolt against their queen. Perhaps the fire of rebellion was keeping them warm, but I doubted it. I would have thought there were many thousands of frozen and unhappy men camping out there in the dark night.

"Do you remember his poetry... Wyatt's?" Kat asked and I shook my head. I am sure I had read some of his poetry, but my tutors were more given to make me read the works of Cicero and other masters of rhetoric and history. Poetry and romances were seen as dangerous diversions from true knowledge that my tutors believed would dissolve all the good sense and intelligence they had instructed into me if I was allowed to read them, making me into a simpering, silly woman rather than a wise and learned princess.

People often are suspicious of books, or perhaps rather of the words inside books. The changing ideals of the world are often shaped by words that spark ideas, by stories that move our emotions. We are inspired by books and words; inspired to act, to change, and consider things anew... which is why people consider them dangerous. Words are not empty marks on paper, but arrows which may thrust deep into the soul of men. If words and ideals contained in books are different from one's own, therein is the threat. That is why so many books come to be banned and outlawed... they are seen as dangerous influences on us...

But I believe that the *reader* is the one who shapes words to their own meaning. A thousand people could read the same text and see a thousand different ideas. Writers and their books are but platforms for the imagination of a million minds. We can take nothing from books but that which is already possible in our own imaginations. The threat or the possibility created by words is already in us, and it is our divination of the meaning of words which brings either good or evil.

Books by themselves are just books... bound and collected papers with marks on them. It is the reader that gives life and meaning to them, by lifting them from the shelf, by reading them and entering another world.

Kat thought for a moment, calling from her memory the words of the poem, and then she spoke; her voice was soft with reverence for words of love and sorrow declared by a voice long lost to Death's kingdom, for a woman I wished I had been granted more time to know.

"Whoso list to hunt, I know where there is a hind,
But for me, alas, I may no more;
The vain travail hath wearied me so sore.
I am of them that farthest cometh behind;
Yet may I by no means my wearied mind
Drawn from the deer: but as she fleeth afore,
Fainting I follow. I leave off therefore,
Since in a net I seek to hold the wind.
Who list her hunt, I put him out of doubt,
As well as I may spend his time in vain;
And, graven with diamonds, in letters plain
There is written about her fair neck round about;
Noli me tangere, for Caesar's I am,
And wild for to hold, though I seem tame."

"Beautiful," I murmured thoughtfully. "And think you that was written for my mother? She is the hind Wyatt cannot catch? Her love is as impossible to gain as it is to catch the wind in a net?"

Kat nodded; a little look of peaceful happiness on her face. Such is the power of poetry.

"The words are lovely," I sniffed, frowning a little. "Although my father would not have given up as Wyatt did. I doubt my mother would have thought a man *fainting* after her was very impressive."

Kat looked a little annoyed, pulled from her happy revelry of love by my words. "No," she said, "and that was why Wyatt failed, of course. Only the greatest man can match the greatest woman, and your mother was destined to match your father." She looked at me with a strange look on her face.

"What is it?" I asked, still thinking of the poem she had recited.

"Nothing, my lady, it's just..."

"Just what?"

Kat sighed a little. "Perhaps it is your upbringing and the responsibility that was given to you as a princess of the realm; perhaps it was that your first experience of love was not without danger." She paused, and I felt a little shard of an old pain thrust into my heart as her words brought Thomas Seymour to my mind. Like an ache in the bone from an old wound, it had been years, and yet his face was still clear to me when I closed my eyes. Gone was the sharp pain of first loss, but in its place was a longer lasting throb. A dull pain that reminded me of the depths that dangerous love had carved into my silly young heart and of the effect he had had, not only on my heart, but on my life. Yes, my first experience of love had been at best confusing, often fearful and painful, and at the worst, threatening to the safety of my life.

Kat went on, oblivious to my thoughts, "... but I would wish that someday you could be able to love without questioning it... without having to *examine* it with that logical and practical mind you have. I would that someday there could be a man that was worthy of you, in station and in wit, and that such a man might show you there was a softer side to love and to life. That way..." she paused and looked ruefully at me, "you might one day be able to enjoy a romantic poem... without picking it to bits like a roasted capon."

Her rueful expression deepened. "I *liked* that poem," she said with a touch of resentment.

I laughed. "Kat, you mistake me. The poem is good and full of great sentiment of love; you do well to like it for it is clever and rich in feeling. And I would wish the same as you.... that when these dangerous days are done, that there might be softer times for me. But..." I stopped and rose to pinch her sides, tickling her playfully until she started to laugh and squirm away from me.

"But! Any such man as you speak of shall have to learn to keep up with me and *not* fall behind!" I laughed, my merciless ticking fingers finding their mark on her sides. "For there is nothing in this world that is impossible, not if one tries hard enough to attain it; find me the man who *will* hold the wind in a net… the man who knows not how to give in, and I will make *him* my husband!"

Kat rose and danced away from my poking and prodding. I chased her around the room, tickling her into submission. We stopped as my good guards knocked at the door, hearing the din within, to check we were not being murdered. I fell on my chair weakened by laughter as Kat waved my guards from the chamber and turned to me flushed with mirth, shaking her head at my naughtiness. Perhaps it seems frivolous to you, that we should take time to find merriment in amongst the horror of revolt and uprising. Perhaps my young mind should have been set only upon the movements of troops and the messages of the court. Perhaps a princess should only have room in her mind for the serious nature of the world. But a little light relief can do wonders for a mind encased in worry and clothed in concern.

As I retired to my bed that evening, I thought on Kat's words. Would there ever be such a man for me? One who could match my temper and my position… one who was interested not only in the titles I could bring him, but in the person I was? Would there be a man who wanted *Elizabeth,* for herself, for love of her? I believed that rare and precious element was what my parents had once found together, no matter how ill it had gone between them at the end. My father had spent most of his life chasing the ideal of marriage, the ideal woman, the ideal of love itself. Had he ever truly found it? I knew not, but I reasoned that if he had, then it must have been only fleetingly, for he seemed to have lost or abandoned those he loved with alarming regularity. My sister too was risking the affection and loyalty of her people for the ideal of love. Whilst I could see all the danger inherent in the pursuit of love, I could also understand the wanting of a heart... the yearning to be loved by another, truly, honestly, and completely. To be loved for the person who sat on the throne and under the crown, and not just for the crown and throne alone.

If the rebels succeeded in their plans and I fell captive to them, then shortly I might be married off to Edward Courtenay. Even with all the noble blood which ran in his veins and, yes, a handsome face, I could not see a man with no experience in life becoming everything I should look for in a husband. In all the men at court, in all the nobles of the land, was there such a man that should satisfy me in mind and spirit enough that I would wish to stand beside him all my days? Would there be a man, such as I had once thought Thomas Seymour might have been to me, who could make my blood dash, my pulse ricochet and who could master so my heart and body?

But... would I want to relinquish the power of my position to another person... even if I loved them? Could I ever retain my power *and* marry, as my sister was trying to do?

It seemed a thing impossible.

"In a net I seek to hold the wind," I muttered, as I looked out through my bed hangings into the frosty and frozen land.

CHAPTER THIRTEEN

Ashridge House, Hertfordshire
January- February 1554

News of the rebellion reached us in fits and starts at Ashridge, but the worst of news always travels faster than the best. My nerves were most ill; I was worried and anxious and it made my temper short. I often snapped and slapped out at Kat who received every harsh word and every mark of my long-fingered hands with a silent look of reproach. She dared not say anything to me then of my rough treatment of her, but I was sure she was storing up comment for later.

In London, Mary and her Council had become increasingly worried about the rebel forces. They could not be dispersed it seemed, by the local sheriffs or law keepers. This was going to require a true military intervention. Mary dispatched my uncle of Norfolk, a seasoned general to be sure, but also an old, bent man of eighty years, to see off the rebel forces that marched on the city of London. As he rode out to meet them, the Whitecoats, a central part of the Queen's Guard, deserted Norfolk and went to join the rebels. The rebel's rousing cries of "*A Wyatt! A Wyatt!*", as five hundred more men joined their forces, from the Queen's Guard, must have resonated in Norfolk's ears like the sound of shovels digging a grave. His remaining men lost nerve and heart with their task. Overnight, many hundreds more deserted.

Norfolk and his leaders ran back to London, cringing and whimpering from the rebels like submissive dogs. The ordinary soldiers of Mary's guards were left behind by their leaders, so they turned their coats inside out, so that none could see the insignia of my sister on their chests. What once had been symbols of pride to these soldiers they now feared to display on their bodies. Some of them joined with the rebels, throwing aside their loyalty to their queen, some of them fled back to the protection of the city walls. Mary's own armies and men were turning against her. Chaos had come to pay court to England.

I cannot imagine that my sister was best pleased with the pitiful response of her supposed military giants. Norfolk grovelled at her feet for his part in the failure to stop the rebels. I am sure the old man grovelled well; it was an undertaking he had practised often during my father's reign... along with betraying his family, and abandoning them to save his own skin. Uncle of mine Norfolk might have been by blood, but that man I would never call my friend or my kin. He had used my mother, her brother and their cousin the merry Catherine Howard when they had been of use to him, and abandoned them when it served his best advantage. The man did not understand the notion of loyalty to any but himself; I liked not such people. I was almost pleased to hear that this time there was no other Norfolk could blame for his failure. It is satisfying to see one who has squirmed out of responsibility for so long feel the full weight of it on their shoulders at last.

For Mary, dealing with the failure of the Duke of Norfolk would have to come later, for my sister had other, more pressing problems on her mind at that moment.

The rebels, their numbers swollen not only by common men from village and town, but now too with Mary's deserted armies, were becoming an almighty force, one that might be capable of actually taking London. They sent demands that Mary was to be handed over to them, and the Tower of London was given to them. Not surprisingly, Mary and her Council refused. The people of London, who previously had murmured with sympathy for the rebel cause, were outraged by the bold demands of the rebels, but were also scared by their march towards London. London started to panic; preachers in the streets spoke out against the wedding with Spain and called to the Queen to give in to the demands of the rebels. Looting began in poorer areas, shops and houses were boarded up, and common people started to try to flee the city. Mary was losing numbers as well as ground to the rebels.

My sister was in trouble. If London stood not with her when the rebels arrived, then she was truly in danger of losing this battle.

The rebels, bolstered in numbers and enthused in spirits, slowed as they reached London. Their success so far gave them time, so they thought, to make sure they came at London by the right path. They had reached Southwark, but they faltered as Mary's man, Sir John Brydges sent word he was prepared to unleash the great guns of the Tower of London on them if they tried to enter by that path. The rebels had nothing like the power of the cannons of the Tower of London at their disposal. Their weapons were those of farmers and carpenters. They turned about, and went to find a better door by which to enter London.

It was then, as the rebels paused to decide their next move that Mary decided to act. She rode out from Whitehall Palace and into the city, her remaining guards at her side. She went to the Guildhall to rally her people. If the people of London would not stand with her and defend their homes with her Royal Guard, then Mary may well lose all and become a captive of the rebellion. But the love that the people of London had for her only a few months ago as she rose to the throne was not as sure now as it had been then. On such a wave of love and popularity had Mary risen to the throne, I am sure she found this sudden reversal of her people's affection for her almost inconceivable. Although the Queen could be assured that many thousands about the country *had not* risen against her, there was still a substantial force on its way seeking to depose her. Their reasons were clear to all now: Mary's proposed marriage to Spain; her refusal to consider a contender for her hand that would suit her people; and the old Tudor stubbornness. All these had left her with fewer friends and many enemies in a short space of time. Even those who had not risen against her seemed to be sympathetic to the cause of the rebels. Up and down the country, whilst men did not rise to fight against Mary, they did not flock to aid her either. I am sure there were plenty of lords in the countryside waiting as I did, to see how the rebels would fare, before committing to either side.

But Mary was always at her best under the worst of strain. And if her youth had taught her anything, it was the value of a well-placed lie. Her submission to our father's demands when she had agreed that his marriage to her mother was no true marriage was a good example. Mary had ever believed that her mother Katherine of Aragon was the true wife of King Henry VIII; Mary had gone against her own feeling, had lied to appease our father, to save her position and her life. Mary had lied then, and she would lie now to do the same.

Mary stood in the Guildhall, its expanse filled wall to wall with people all anxiously waiting to hear what their queen would say about the approaching hordes. Mary walked forward. She spoke of her grandfather and father, the great kings Henry VII and VIII. She spoke of her lineage descending from the houses of Lancaster and York, both combined in the blood of the Tudors. And then, she held out her coronation ring to them; holding her thin hand up in the pale winter's sun so that all might see the flash and sparkle of her coronation ring.

"I have it on my finger," she proclaimed, her deep voice gruff with attachment and with fear. "It never hitherto was, nor hereafter shall be, left off my hand."

She shook her head and spread her hands before them. She had the strength to rule them, she maintained; it flowed deep in her blood. She had the right to rule them. That, too, was granted to her through her lineage. But more than those qualities, she *should* rule them... she had been called to rule them by God Himself, because she loved them. Tears sprang to her eyes as she told her people that she loved them as a mother loves her children.

"On the word of a prince, I cannot tell how naturally the mother loves the child, for I was never a mother of any. But certainly if a prince and governor may as naturally and earnestly love her subjects, as a mother loves the child, then assure yourselves that I being your lady and mistress, do as earnestly and tenderly love and favour you."

Mary was showing that her coronation ring was a *wedding* ring that married her to her country; as she was married to England, so the people of England were her children. She had the right to rule them, as all kings had done before, but she *should* rule them because of her love for them. Those who were coming to take her throne from her were acting against all the laws of man and God, she said, and she asked the people of London to stand with her, to fight, not only for their homes and their families, but to see right prevail in England.

Yet still there was muttering about her. The people asked each other about the marriage to Spain, and Mary, hearing this, responded. She told them that she had agreed to marry a foreign prince, yes, but this would not impede on the lives of the English, nor do anything to damage its lands. She would never do anything that *was not done to benefit her country*, and her people must believe this of her. All these things she spoke of to them, in a voice which throbbed with passion and pain.

She won their hearts again. Seeing her standing before them, invoking all the powers of a king, with the persuasions of a woman, with the compassion of a mother, was a heady combination of emotions for the people of London. They came to remember why they had opened the gates of London to her forces when the previous *coup* had happened; they remembered our great father, they remembered the gentle kindness and generosity of her mother Katherine of Aragon. And then Mary gave them her best argument; she swore to them that she would not marry at all, unless her people were content. She would not marry into Spain unless asked to by her Council. She told her people that as much as she was the lord of these lands, she was also its servant… bidden only by the will of her people.

There it was. The well-placed lie.

I almost choked when I read the dispatches on her speech from Cecil. It was clear that whilst the common men of London knew much, they in truth knew little of their queen. Mary was known to be a pious and religious woman, and I am sure they would have taken her word, both as a queen and as a woman of well-known faith. But they did not know her as I did. Mary was quite happy to use truth or fiction to her own advantage when she needed to, and if she chose to lie to her people now, I am sure she would have excused her untruth easily. She so often used God to excuse her will and wishes. Perhaps it was He who intervened here? Once again speaking through her mouth and uttering untruths which would call the people of London to her side at her time of need? I am sure she excused her lies thusly to herself; God, it seemed, was ever on hand to support Mary in her own mind.

Mary could not rely on her position as queen to call them to her side, so she resorted to lying to them instead. I do not blame her in truth; for I would have done the same... but I would not have lied to *myself* on the matter. Therein was one of the many differences between we two Tudor sisters.

Mary needed the people of London. She would lose the city without them. She had already decided on the marriage with Spain for her own personal gratification, but she was not going to say that to her people, not now... not at the crucial moment. She won them. They believed her. They accepted her promises and were ready to stand with her against the rebel army. London after all was their home. Their families lived there. Their livelihoods were in its streets. The people of London little wanted to watch their home and hearth burn to the ground.

Wyatt's men marched on to Kingston Bridge, but found the people of London were breaking it down, chopping it up, burning and throwing as much of it as they could into the river, to stop the rebels getting in.

Mary's people were working for her once again.

But the rebels were not defeated, for Wyatt's army had an advantage. When fist comes to sword, a soldier is a good man to have at your side. When it comes to mending bridges, it is always good to be surrounded by labourers and carpenters. The bridge was made passable, and the rebels flooded into the city of London. There were thousands of them and they marched with the rage of righteous anger at their backs. Like a mighty wave they washed through the outer streets and thronged into the streets and squares. They tore down the shutters that merchants had placed over their shops to protect them, they burned and they stole. The sounds of screaming spread through the streets, the sounds of men struggling against one another for life and for honour… the sound of women trying to defend themselves and their daughters against men bent on rape.

Even men with the best of intentions become as animals when they are encased in the mentality of a horde.

Inside London, the rebels broke off into smaller groups; some passing into Charing Cross… but some marched to Whitehall, to the very heart of the court. I don't think they could have known that Mary was in Whitehall Palace, but the fact that the rebels seemed to be marching straight for her must have caused concern for her and the court.

The rebels were rioting through the streets, smashing and burning as they went. The Queen's Guard seemed to have been caught unawares by the sudden invasion from Kingston Bridge and by the ferocity of the invading rebels. They fell back, allowing the rebels to take more ground.

Panic broke out in the streets as the people of London tried to either flee or turn their shops and homes into makeshift forts. The rebels became beasts, leaving their sense and reason behind; looting, stealing… crowing their defiance against the Queen with their rousing call of *"A Wyatt! A Wyatt!"* As the rebels progressed through the city, it seemed there was little resistance to oppose them. The fear of the streets became a disease which infected all those within the city. London was faltering, and falling to their power.

Mary was now standing in the very centre of the rebellion invasion; her seat in Holbein's Gate, that massive gateway which bridges sections of Whitehall Palace across the east and west of the main thoroughfare, gave her ample opportunity to watch as the rebels swarmed like wasps over the city. She watched as the remains of her guard lost courage and, led by the Captain of the Guard Sir John Gage, ran *away* from the rebels shouting "Treason! Treason!"

Not the most helpful or bravest action they could have taken for their Queen or their people.

Mary's guards were craven, and they were allowing the rebels to gain ground in the city of London. The panic had now reached the court at Whitehall. Noble women and men alike brought their personal guards to them, seeking ways to escape the palace by water, or to hide within rich apartments. Some ran screaming, so we heard, through the halls of the palace, entirely losing their wits in the excitement and fear of the bedraggled army marching on them. Later, people would tell you those who ran screaming through the halls of Whitehall Palace were all women… but for my part, I heard of a few noble lords who lost their courage that day too.

Mary's cowardly guards, who should have been holding order on the streets, ran for the palace, scrambling through the gates to hide inside the court itself. They were turned back out by palace guards who thought that the other guards should be doing their jobs outside in the smoke-ridden streets, rather than guarding the safe inside where *they* were. The guards were fighting each other now, rather than the rebels. None had the verve to fight for their Queen, all seemed lost and all about Mary was falling into ruination.

Chaos had taken London. And in the midst of this, in her palace, stood my sister, watching London erupt into flame, watching rebels run through her streets screaming insults against her name and sacking the homes of her people. They were very close to the palace now, and her guards were failing her. Would the rebels take the palace? Would they take her? The thought must have come to her mind, for her Council urged her to prepare to flee by water.

But yet Mary refused to run. She stayed, standing at that window, watching.

What must she have thought as she stood there? Watching the people who had so recently fought at her side to win her the throne rise up and set her city to flames, seeking to rid themselves of her as queen? It must have been a harrowing time, for in amongst her fears for her people, her person and her power there must have also come the thought that she was being attacked and rejected by her people. She had come to them with love, and now they hated her. They wanted her gone.

We Tudors, we have never been very good at accepting rejection. Our father was well-versed at rejecting others, but the thought of not being loved as he wanted to be was unimaginable to him. I believe the same was true of Mary. And in the darkest parts of my heart, I will admit that it was true of me also. The Tudor heart seems to live very much on the surface of the body; in many ways the kings and queens of our line have been masters of the tricks of words, speech and show. We know how to put on a pretty play and dance to our people. We know how to stand tall and regal before them. We know how to write history to our advantage. But underneath all that pomp, the Tudor heart is thin, fragile, delicate. The hatred which poured into London on that day must have been a bitter potion for Mary as she watched from her high window.

Amidst all the confusion, the palace guards finally got the outer gates to Whitehall Palace closed and allowed most of the city guard within as well. The rebel forces were not strong enough, or well-armed enough to bring the gates down. This army did not march with cannon; they barely marched with sword. They fought with scythe and pitchfork, with lighted taper and with dagger. They were not trained in the art of war, but had won their way through the city on the back of sheer numbers, force, anger and vigour. They could not bring down the great gates, and they had no munitions to enable them to do so.

But that did not mean their enjoyment was to be done for the day. They were overjoyed with their success, and, they wanted more.

They marched on through the streets to Ludgate, but found the bridge closed to them there. Rather than seek to discover how or why the bridge was closed, they pressed on. The rebels were starting to thin as pockets of them went about the streets, spreading apart from one another, transforming the great ocean waves of their invasion, into small rivers and streams. They were wandering into great danger by dispersing so, but they hardly knew it, so excited were they by their triumphs thus far. They were becoming scattered and ill-deployed. They lacked the discipline of a guard, the knowledge of generals. The rebels were too thinly spread about London now. Their numbers looked less and less impressive the more they dispersed. It gave the people of London heart to see that the rebels were not as numerous as they had thought, and the Queen's Guard started to comprehend the same.

The rebels did not realise that most exits from the city were now being blocked or destroyed. Even as they milled about London, crowing for their victory, they did not understand that London was closing slowly about them like a trap.

Finally, Mary's troops were bolstered… Encouraged by the reckless, random meanderings of the rebels, the Queen's Guard came together. They finally understood that they had more men than the rebels had, better weapons, and if they had the courage to stand, they could beat them.

The rebels could not get out. The Queen's Guard moved against them at Ludgate. The rebels realized only too late that they were outmanned and outmatched, and they had nowhere to run. The fight was brutal, and ruthless. Mary's guard fell on the rebels like wolves on a carcass. The rebels were without direction, without escape, and man by man they fell under the sword of the Queens' Guard, or submitted to arrest.

Wyatt surrendered, hoping to buy the lives of his men with his own. Others around him followed suit. London saw the dusk approach her with cheering and shouting as the voices of the victorious sounded over the groans of the dying and the captured.

Mary had seen her capital invaded, and she had crushed those who dared to move against her. Her generals and her own guards had let her down, her people had lost much; but shops and walls could be re-built and new generals could be found with more courage than the last. She had survived, and she had won, that, was what mattered on that day in London.

By five o'clock Wyatt was being taken to the Tower of London by water, a prisoner whose fate was not hard to follow in the stars appearing in the night's sky above him.

CHAPTER FOURTEEN

Ashridge House, Hertfordshire
February 1554

The rebellion was crushed. The Crown was victorious… and now my sister was determined she would not be challenged for her throne again.

I stayed in my bed at Ashridge, pretending illness still, worried and wondering as to whether my sister would seek to incriminate me in any of these dealings. The rebels had contacted me, after all, and even if I had made no move to plot with them, Mary had made it more than plain that she already resented and distrusted me. Would this rebellion prove a perfect opportunity to rid her of me?

The Duke of Suffolk, father of the still imprisoned Lady Jane Grey, gave himself up and was brought to the Tower of London under armed guard. Perhaps he was hoping for clemency, since he had surrendered, or perhaps he just thought he might not get far as a wanted man on the road. He was a well-recognised figure by now, having dealt so deeply in seemingly every rebellion of the past few years. His part in the last failed *coup* had brought the lives of his daughter and the rest of his family into grave danger. Now, for the second time, in little more than a year, Henry Grey had proved himself once more a traitor, proved that his daughter was a constant danger to Mary's crown… and this time Mary was not going to be lenient.

If there had been any doubt in this matter at all, it was dispelled as Gardiner, Bishop of Winchester, and Chancellor of England, preached before the court on the Sunday following Grey's arrest. The rebels who were not already in the arms of God were in chains, and the Queen and her Council had won back the city. But this was clearly not enough for Mary, or her guard-dog Gardiner. Gardiner preached that the Queen had previously shown herself to be too merciful to those who would threaten the peace and prosperity of her rule. Obviously entirely missing the irony of such a statement, since Gardiner himself had been recently released from imprisonment by Mary's mercy, Gardiner went on to both plead and demand that Mary give no quarter to the rebels. Her clemency was a *womanly weakness,* Gardiner said, which, although was born from Christian charity, was not beneficial for her people. Now, Gardiner said, the Queen must show mercy *to the country,* by ridding her lands of such traitors for good.

Gardiner spoke, but I am sure it was Mary who had written those words. Her Chancellor would not have spoken in such a manner unless his words had been previously approved by the Queen. All those standing there on that Sunday knew that blood would soon follow word.

Jane Grey, my little, serious, studious cousin, was tried for treason, and condemned to death. She had been a figurehead for the rebels of both this rebellion and the last, and her father had shown repeatedly that his family could not be trusted to be loyal to the throne, unless Jane sat upon it. Jane's husband, Guildford Dudley, was condemned with her; as was Wyatt, leader of the rebellion; as were his men; as was Henry Grey, Duke of Suffolk.

The Queen was tending to her garden, removing all the weeds.

Mary sent me a letter of all that had happened since the rebels were defeated. Her words were cold, hard and short. She wrote of the sentencing of Jane and the others. Then, in the last lines, Mary wrote to call me to London. Her Council wished to question me about the troubles in the country of late. She knew that I was ill, she wrote, so she was sending doctors to me to ensure I was fit to travel, along with a battalion of her guards to ensure my personal safety through our troubled land.

It was not hard to read the true message beneath the one which was written on this parchment.

Mary had Jane and the rebels in her power, and now she wanted me. She suspected me, she feared my personal power, the armies I could raise, the religion I believed in, and the love the people had for me. Doctors to care for me and a guard to ensure my safety? I thought not. Those doctors were being sent to assess if I really was sick or not, whether or not I was lying to the Queen… and her guards were sent in truth to arrest me, capture me.

I was in danger. Great, great danger.

I took the letter and put it against my heart as I suddenly felt all the air leave my lungs. The room was suddenly so bright that I could not see; the air too thin to breathe. I struggled to rise from my bed as I felt the weight of fear and panic rushing over me, as though I stood under a waterfall, trying to hold my head up against the might of the water's flow. Kat rushed to me as she saw me try and stand from my bed and waver like a drunken man in the ale house. I was deathly pale and she grabbed me as I started to fall.

"What news, my lady?" Kat cried, shaking me. "*What?*"

She held my body to hers. I felt the warmth of her skin on mine burn me, as though I were made of ice and water rather than skin and bone.

"She will kill my cousin," I whispered, feeling sick, turning my ashen face to Kat's and seeing my own panic mirrored in her eyes. "Jane Grey… Mary is going to kill her."

Kat gasped. "But the girl is… but a girl," she said. "Mary could not execute one so young, and we all know that Jane had little true place in the uprising. She did not want to be involved."

I shook my head. "It does not matter," I gasped, rising waves of panic pulsing through me. My breathing had become fast, shallow and strange. "It doesn't matter Kat…. Mary has been scared by this rebellion… she will not tolerate any who oppose her now. Jane is a focus for opposition to her rule; the Queen will not allow her to live."

I was breathing fast and thin; I could see stars dancing before my eyes in blackness. I felt dazed. "Jane was such a small creature when last I saw her," I said, my voice sounding high and eerie, unlike myself. "She only wanted to have her books and be done with the world…. And now the world is done with her, and she will die."

I burst into tears. There had been enough times I had looked down somewhat on my cousin Jane for her seriousness, her constant reading and her innocence of the world. For a moment, when I heard that my sister had ordered Jane to be put to death, I could feel nothing but the horror of that reality… the horror of what Fate had in store for poor Jane. But then came the knowledge of my own fate… I could not breathe, I could not think. Never had I been so paralysed with fear. Jane had not been involved personally in this rebellion, how could she have been… locked away in the Tower of London? She was being removed for being a focus for rebellion. As long as Jane lived there was a Protestant alternative to Mary.

But my cousin was not the only, nor the nearest alternative to Mary as queen.

I was.

Jane Grey was to be executed when only her father had taken part in the rebellion, not her. But whilst Jane's name had been linked to the rebellion, the rebels had made clear that *I* was the true focus of this newest uprising, the centre of the plans they had to restore stability to the lands of England. True enough, Jane's name had too been used by them, but my name had been spoken more.

"She will kill Jane," I gulped at the air, barely able to catch my breath. The dancing stars were whirling before my sight like so many fireflies in the marsh lights. I was about to lose consciousness. "And then she is coming...for me."

CHAPTER FIFTEEN

Ashridge House, Hertfordshire
12th February 1554

There are some days in life which fall like the leaves of the trees in autumn; so numerous, so alike in shade and shape, that they seem to barely make an individual impression in the memory. Many people would count such days as wasted; littered with small things of trivial importance that do not bend the mind, nor tug the heart to form any remembrance of that day. Yet I, who have seen so many days that, for good or bad, have been stored in my memory branded and bound as individuals, like books in a library; I, would say that the more trivial and unremembered days a person may have, the more peaceful and temperate their lives must have been.

Although it may well be said that with greater knowledge of sorrow, so comes greater understanding of joy, there is also much to be said for the life of a person who has seen little of either true comfort or intense pain. It must be an uncomplicated existence, to maintain a life of quiet nonentity; passing through life with gentle nothingness... living, dying, and never making impression on the world. Or so it seems to me, but then, we always envy that which we do not have ourselves.

I was clearly never fated for a life of gentle quietness.

February 12th, 1554, is one of the days that have burned themselves into my memory. It should have its own shelf in the library of my memories. In the glaring light of fear, so many things become lucid ... In the grip of misery, so few things are missed by the mind. I remember that day well.

At ten o clock that morning, Guildford Dudley, son of the *queenmaker* Warwick, met his maker, at the command of my sister, publicly on Tower Hill. Tower Hill was a place of execution for traitorous nobles. Not given the privilege granted to those of royal status or blood, to die in relative seclusion within the walls of the Tower of London, Tower Hill was a most public place to die. Thousands of people would gather to watch executions for entertainment. The spectacle of death became a day out for the people of London.

In that same place of execution had my own uncle George Boleyn once stood before the multitudes that turned out to watch him die. My uncle George, so Kat told me, faced his end as a gentleman and a noble, showing great courage in the face of death. My mother too, had been a lioness at her end within the confines of the walls of the Tower of London, upon its sheltered green.

Guildford, I was told, was dragged to the scaffold blabbing and wailing, screaming his innocence and attempting to blame anyone but himself for his treachery; no one was listening to him. He spent his last moments on this earth much as he had lived, as an undignified, spoilt and foolish young man. He did not die cleanly for he flinched from the fall of the axe. It took several attempts to chop through his neck.

My cousin Jane watched her young husband's body brought back in a cart, his bloodied body covered with a sheet. She watched in silence, they said, her fingertips touching the glass of the window lightly. She shed no tears.

I wondered whether Jane had cared for her gaudy little husband at all. It had not been her idea to marry Guildford Dudley, she had been forced to wed and bed him, and from what I had seen of him about court there was little to recommend him either as a husband or as a man. In life he has struck me as boastful, conceited and thoroughly absorbed with himself. Although all the Dudleys were blessed with charm and good looks, it is easy enough to spoil a fine dish when one overseasons it with too much salt. Like such a dish, Guildford left an unpleasant taste in the mouth. Guildford had been a pretty, petulant, petty little fool. His mother had doted upon him, making him her favourite and giving in to his every wish. His brothers had been fine soldiers and gentlemen, and every one of them had more to recommend them than Guildford... but Guildford had been chosen as the one their mother wanted to be a king. Jane had been given no choice in marrying him, and I could think of no one less suited to her than him. Jane was of a serious and studious bent of mind; she loved thought and books and words above the trappings of material show. Their marriage had been like matching a strutting peacock with a studious owl.

But for all my dislike for Guildford, the boy hardly deserved death for the crimes of being a spoiled child. Traitor he may have been, but he was used as a tool for the plots of his father just as Jane was. Guildford had not the wit to be a true danger to the throne of England. I could not tell you if Jane had any true regard or affection for her husband, but I am sure she felt pity for him on that day, no matter what indignities she had had to suffer as his wife and bedfellow.

They buried Guildford in the Chapel of St Peter ad Vincula in the Tower of London; his short, garish life was spent.

Later that morning, the Lady Jane Grey came out from her rooms. Her gown was black and trimmed with black velvet. Her pale skin must have seemed even whiter than usual against that dark material. As she walked towards the scaffold her lips moved in silent prayer and she held on to her prayer book with a tight grip and white fingers. It was the volume which Katherine Parr had granted to Jane upon her death, and Jane had kept it with her all the time since.

Jane spoke only a few spare words to the crowd, and then knelt to pray. "Have mercy on me O God," she whispered. "Wash me thoroughly of my iniquity and cleanse me from my sin. The sacrifices of God are a broken spirit, a contrite heart, O God, thou wilt not despise...."

Her ladies helped her to untie her dress at the back. Jane removed her gloves with shaking hands. As the executioner asked for her forgiveness for the task he was about to perform, he stepped sideways, and Jane saw the block. Her courage faltered.

"I pray you," Jane pleaded, her voice catching in her throat, "dispatch me quickly." Then as she knelt, she looked up at him with fear. "Will you take off my head before I lay me down?"

The executioner assured Jane he would not strike until she was prepared, until she indicated she was ready by holding out her hands. Jane nodded to him, but looked nervously at him as she said her prayers. She might have been a lady of royal blood, but she was also just a frightened little girl facing death. She was pale as a ghost and shaking, praying for God to give her strength to die well, to die clean, and to receive her soul into his arms. Tears crept from her eyes, but she dashed them away and continued to pray. Determined Jane had been in life, and determined she was in death... to ensure God knew she was coming to Him, and to ensure that He had a place for her soul in His arms.

She must have looked so small, huddled there in prayer.

The crowds muttered angrily; they saw her fear, her youth, her smallness, and they did not revel in her death. Jane looked fragile; like a little child. Her seventeen years seemed less than they were on the little and slight form of her body and face. In fear, we all seem smaller than we do in courage.

Her women did not want her to see any more. Jane was growing terrified, her prayers faltering on her lips as she glanced over and over at the block. Her words were becoming slurred with terror. Jane's women feared that she might run or flinch from the axe. To do such would mean more strikes of the blade, strokes which would fall on her shoulders or head. If Jane moved then the executioner might miss his target, prolonging her suffering and pain. If they could blindfold her, the executioner might have a chance to take her head off in one strike. Her women put a cloth on her eyes as a blindfold, but as they stepped back from her, Jane lost her sense of where the block was. She stumbled, groped for it, afraid the headsman would not keep his promise if she took too long to lay her head on it, her hands flailed out, desperately trying to reach it.

"*Where is it?*" Jane cried out in a shaking voice, tears darkening the blindfold on her little face. "I cannot find it... *What shall I do?*"

Her voice was almost hysterical; high pitched... a child in distress. Her ladies and her servants were beside themselves with grief, rushing to grasp at her flailing hands. They guided Jane to the block, placing a hand on each side of the gully in which she was to place her head. As Jane found her position, she grew calmer, her panic subsiding, her sobs falling in volume... The guards took her ladies back and away from her. The crowds about her on Tower Green were weeping with her now, for her... they did not cheer and shout insults as was traditional at such a time; they pressed cloths to their streaming eyes and prayed sincerely for the soul of this young woman.

Jane laid her head down and spoke. Her voice was calm, blank yet steady. She had found the block. She had found her way to death.

"Lord, into Thy hands I commend my spirit," Jane gasped, and she stretched her arms out, trembling at her sides, as a sign she was ready for the strike of death.

The axe fell.

The executioner kept his promise. He struck true and clean, and Jane died quickly, without suffering. She too was taken to the Chapel of St Peter ad Vincula. Somewhere in that Chapel were laid the remains of my mother; her last resting place on this earth unmarked, and her coffin an old arrow chest they had hurriedly stuffed her body into for burial.

It was as though the Tower of London was being slowly filled with the bodies and blood of my family.

Death is always sudden, and it is always a shock. But when death comes to those who have barely tasted life, to the young, it is all the more bitter. Jane was but seventeen when she died. My poor little cousin; she had no temper for politics and courtly intrigue, she would have been happiest in a life that contained nothing but a room full of books and enough bread to live by. If she had been allowed those simple pleasures then she would have lived a life of quiet scholarship and retreated from a world that she was little suited to live in. Jane did not glory in court life, in power or in showmanship. She was not vainglorious and she had not wanted to rule this land.

Lady Jane Grey had been made a queen by men who used her blood and body to fulfil their wishes and dreams, and as they fell, so did their tool in the operation.

In this world it seems that women are often nothing more than vessels. Used to carry power, persuasion, or a child to further a line; women are often nothing more than an implement used and then discarded by the ambition of men. Jane had been used as such an implement. She was used and then thrown away. What she wanted of life had never been held to be important.

Mary was aware that Jane had been used as a tool by the ambitious Warwick. She was aware that Jane would have been happiest pottering around her tower rooms with her books for the rest of her life. Mary was aware that Jane was used by those whose station, sex and blood commanded her obedience to them as a woman, a daughter and a wife. And yet, she still sent Jane to her death. Mary had not been given a lot of choice. To leave Jane alive was to leave alive a threat to Mary's throne. But it was Jane's father, in truth, who signed his name to his daughter's death warrant. Had he not risen up once more against Mary in his daughter's name, Jane might still be alive.

Might… but I have cause to doubt that Jane would have survived for long, even without her reckless father. The wheels of politics were against her, just as her own kin were. The Ambassador of Spain, Renard, had insisted that before his master Phillip could be allowed to come to England, that the threat that Jane posed must be removed. Mary had enabled her marriage by shedding the blood of our cousin; to most of us, that spoke of a cursed beginning to any marriage.

The blood that flows in the veins of the royal houses is as much a danger as it is an asset and a privilege. That blood may make one a king, or it may make one a corpse. Mary had taken a step that I not thought her capable of; killing an innocent, or as near as one could get to an innocent in this world, to preserve her own power, to bring about her marriage. Mary had proven, perhaps, that she had the strength to take the hardest of choices for her survival upon the throne, but at what cost?

She had killed a cousin on this day… Would she one day, kill a sister too?

The devil dances in many forms; I think he found his way into the masque of England on the day my sister sent that girl to her death.

On the day that Jane walked out to die on the scaffold in the Tower of London, a party of armed guards and Privy Councillors arrived at Ashridge. They were taking me to London. I tried to parry them with my poor health; most of my household could swear honestly that I had not left my bed or my rooms in my recent sickness. But they had brought doctors with them at my sister's command. Mary was becoming wise to my wiles; she knew that I was lying. She knew that there may be other reasons I had not wanted to join her at the time of the rebellion. What those reasons were, I doubt she knew in truth. She simply suspected the worst of me.

Mary's doctors diagnosed me with 'watery humours', they felt my forehead and tasted my urine and agreed when looking at me that I looked and seemed ill. As well I might, for the thought of what might happen to me under the power of my sister had caused me to shake and shiver in truth. Despite this, Mary's doctors proclaimed that I was well enough to travel... unsurprisingly. They had orders from their mistress... I was not to escape the Queen this time.

I had no choice but to go with them.

I continued to protest my sickness; I was too ill to ride a horse. They bundled me in a litter and we started to wend our way to London.

Every step took me closer to Mary, and, I believed, closer to my own death.

CHAPTER SIXTEEN

The Road to London
February 1554

The litter rocked from side to side as it carried me towards London. Though my sister's guard carried my person with care, every rock and bump we passed, every slip on icy ground we endured, caused pain to my body, and to my troubled soul.

The fear and the anxiety caused by my sister's impetuous summons to London had caused me to become unwell in truth. I was sick in heart and sick in mind, and my body was now sick also. Fear had become a disease which brought forth real and great physical suffering. My joints were swollen and puffy, filled with liquid of some unknown source which gathered painfully within me. My stomach ached and my face, too, swelled up, causing me discomfort as my skin stretched and burned under its pressure. My head throbbed and my belly moved uneasily, like a man unaccustomed to the waves of the seas may feel as he stands upon a boat. I could not keep down food and only could barely drink liquids. My skin and eyes were bright with fever. I was sick in truth.

Much as the troubles of my mind had come to wreak havoc on my body during the time of the death of my stepmother, Katherine Parr, now it seemed my fears were being played out in the fabric of my own form. Kat fluttered at my side; uneasy and worried for my faltering health, she tried to press me to eat or drink, but I could do neither. Food did not pass my mouth, ale and wine served only to taunt my dried tongue and broken lips with their sharpness.

Every step we took towards London was, for me, a step closer to the fate I feared awaited me. Mary was now rid of Jane Grey, one figure for the machinations of those opposed to Mary's rule, and now I was sure she was going to rid herself of me.

I tried to think of all I had done or had not done as the rebellion unfolded. I tried to think of what I would say when I was questioned. I needed to have everything clear within my own head. I would not explain further than was necessary why I had not joined my sister when the rebellion had broken, and I needed to have my wits about me if there was any chance I was going to survive this.

I had not gone to London, as Mary had requested, but all could see, now at least, that I was truly unwell. Even if I had not actually been ill at the time of the rebellion, there was no evidence of that now. Mary could not prove that I had not been ill. That was in my favour.

I had replied to the messages of the rebels, but only in word, never in person and not in writing. So it was but my word against theirs if they talked of it under torment of pain or suffering, or to save their own skins in the Tower. I had not undertaken the suggestions they put to me to move house. I had remained at Ashridge and had not taken any active part in any uprising against my sister's crown. That too, was in my favour.

What had I really done that they could prove made me a traitor to my sister? If inaction is a sin as much as action, then perhaps they could prove me guilty.

But I knew well that the suspicions fixed upon me now were much more to do with the content of my character and most importantly, my religion and the focus my being gave to those who opposed Mary. As long as I lived, there would be an alternative queen to Mary for the throne of England, and a Protestant one; a focus for rebellion and religious dissent; a vessel, as much as Jane Grey had been. As long as I lived, I could be used as a tool for the rejuvenation of the Protestant faith in England. I was sure that Gardiner and Ambassador Renard would not simply sit back, and allow such a focus to remain alive if they could. I was a threat to the world they wanted, a threat to the religion they held most dear in their hearts.

I looked out of the litter and into the lines of men that had been brought to accompany me to the city. Although surrounding me were the Queen's Guard, and Mary's Privy Councillors, there were also around two hundred of my own men. My faithful Parry had organised my men to accompany us, and with little time to complete such a large task, Parry had done well to gather so many. The presence of my own men was making the Queen's Guard nervous, twitchy; Mary's guard cast sideways glances at my men to make sure that they were not planning to attack them, to take me and ride away with their princess to raise fresh rebellion against the crown.

But that kind of desperate action was not behind Parry's reasoning in ordering my guards to accompany their mistress to London. Parry was too clever to allow such moments of madness to enter his head. If I rode into London with my own guards, it reminded the people of my own station. I was not some rebel brought to heel by Mary and the Council; I was a princess of the royal Tudor house. I was the heir to the throne. I was *Harry's* daughter.

I would ride before the people with all the trappings of power, even if I was a prisoner. In reminding them of my station, Parry reminded the people of my position, my father, my lineage… and my own self. I had been popular with the English common man from the very start. Sympathy for the loss of my mother, even though they had hated her, had developed into affection and love for the young princess who was gracious enough to stop and talk with them, to offer them a smile and give a coin to those who pleased her. My houses showed munificence to those who needed succour in times of hardship and my name was spoken of well and with love. My guards were proud to serve my name and house. With my red hair and pale skin, I was the image of my father but with the grace and charm of a young comely woman. I showed the people the continuation of the old ways, a steady and unchanging link to the past that they now remembered in hindsight as being ever peaceful and bounteous. But in my youth, there was promise for the future, and set against the staid and stiff presence of my aging sister, who was taking England down paths unknown and feared, I was their hope for a better future.

Those who walk with the blood of kings in their bodies are emblems for their people. We are not wholly human, for in many ways we become the embodiment of the identity of a whole race, a whole people. I was loved by the people for my blood and myself, but in their growing dissatisfaction with Mary, I was also becoming looked to as a light, an emblem for their future.

Before we entered the city, I had Kat and Blanche change my gown into one of white. Perhaps it would remind the people of the times they had seen me in glory, at Mary's entrance to London… Perhaps it would show them my youth, for the white cloth accentuated my skin and hair. But I also wanted to make sure that I was seen by the people for other reasons. The Ambassador Renard, I had been told, had spread salacious gossip regarding my illness around the court, and this in turn had leaked out to the people.

He was telling anyone that would listen that my swollen body was due to pregnancy, from some "*vile intrigue*". Exactly who I was meant to have engaged in "*intrigue*" with was left unsaid; perhaps some spirit had been ushered into my chambers and then floated out through a crack in the plaster after coupling with me? It seemed nothing was beyond the imagination of some people. When I was told this by Kat, ever the mistress at gathering gossip, I could not help but remember the days when I was in disgrace during my brother's reign, and rumours had flown up and down the country that I was carrying Thomas Seymour's child. Then too my enemies had sought to discredit me by making me appear a wanton or whore in the eyes of the people.

It is the refuge of all simpletons to try to slander a woman with her sexual reputation, real or imagined; such people have not the imagination to devise anything new or interesting to attack her with. The easiest way to disparage a woman's name is to accuse her of whorish behaviour, even though the same is never true for men who engage in loose practises. Look throughout the annuals of history and tell me of any woman raised to power, who men had cause to be nervous of, and tell me if she was not slandered in such a way. If you can find one, then I will be much impressed. And now, that fool of an Ambassador was trying to start rumour against me in such a manner, and it was wholly unfounded.

Now was the time to show this lie up to the people. *They* would decide who spoke truth.

Much to the chagrin of the Queen's Guard that surrounded me, I ordered the sides of the litter pulled up as we entered London. I am sure they would have wanted to keep me concealed, as though I were hiding away, brought to London in shame… but I would have none of this.

What little courage one has should always be shown to enemies; I was not going to crawl to the palace of my sister in ignominy.

With the sides of my litter drawn up, I looked out at London with all the valour I had left. My body was drawn up straight against my pillows to show that my swollen limbs and flat belly were nothing like the body of a woman carrying a child. My pale face was drawn with fear and with tiredness, but my eyes sparkled like dark fire as I faced down the last few miles of this terrible journey. The people could see that I was truthfully unwell.... and that I was assuredly not pregnant.

As my litter passed, there were no roaring crowds as there had once been. No people rushed forth to give my men presents for me; there were no tiny children brought scuttling forward to sing sweet songs to my ears. There was only the hushed and scared silence of a world watching and waiting, wondering what might happen next. The execution of young Jane Grey had shocked even the most hardened hearts of London, and they feared now also for me.

As I stared out at the rows of shops and inns, men took their caps from their heads, women bobbed indelicate curtseys towards my litter. Some of them had tears in their eyes as they looked on me; a young woman, obviously sick and carted around under armed guard. I heard mutterings that this was *no way to treat their princess.* I wanted to smile, that was just what I wanted to hear; but I knew that I had to maintain my wasted appearance, in order to gain the sympathy of the people. I needed them now. I needed their sympathy, their pity.

I needed all the weapons I had against Mary.

One man shouted out, "God save Your Highness!" but the guards pushed him rudely away. No one else dared to utter words of support aloud for me, but in each eye that held sympathy, in each doffed cap, every teary eye and graceless bob of curtsey, they were giving me their support.

I was taken through Smithfield and then to Whitehall. Mary was in the palace in her apartments, and I asked to be taken to her, but she refused. They took me to a secluded and remote corner of the palace near to Mary's privy garden. There, the Queen's Guard took over all roles from my servants and turned them out, and my guards were sent away; I was allowed to keep my own ladies, Kat and Blanche among them, but that was all.

I was in Mary's house; I was in Mary's power. My sister, who refused to speak to me or see me, was gathering the evidence that could be used to remove the menace of the heretic heir from her reign, for good.

CHAPTER SEVENTEEN

Whitehall Palace
February- March 1554

There are some people in this world for which the pleasures of trivial pettiness are a constant delight. Those people revel in the small and the stupid, the little gleanings of happiness that come not from attacking a person in the open light of the day, but who take vengeance by inflicting many, small torments on one who is unable to respond.

Such a petty creature was my cousin, Lady Margaret Douglas, Countess of Lennox.

Margaret never really liked me. She was one of those who maintained that my birth had been illegitimate, and therefore she thought *she* should outrank *me.* As the daughter of my father's eldest sister, Margaret Tudor, and her second husband, Archibald Douglas, the Countess thought she had more Tudor blood than I, and although she never spoke those words before me, little, craven, dullard that she was, she spoke it often enough behind my back at court that I knew her mind. She had always been furious when I was honoured above her, and yet she could say nothing… until now. Her elevation of status under my sister had gone to her head. Unable to attack me personally, both due to my own guarded position and the cowardly nature of her heart, Margaret Douglas took instead to inflicting discomfort upon me in other ways.

She had ordered that the chambers below where I was guarded should be turned into temporary kitchens for her use. As I sat above, wresting with the fears of my heart and the ills of my body, thinking any day that I, like poor Jane, should be carted off to lose my head, I was kept awake by the sounds and smells of a kitchen ordered to make any delicacy the Countess desired, at any time of the day or night. Most often, it seemed, she wanted fish, ensuring that she picked the very smelliest of those creatures to consume. She kept her servants busy… but then, she had to feed that giant mouth of hers constantly, I imagine. Hateful harridan.

But such is the refuge of those who are as small in mind as they are in character. I am sure, during those days, she could imagine with great satisfaction the swaying of my stomach under the assault of the stink of cooking fish and fat and the pounding of my head exasperated by every bang and clash of kitchen pots. The guards complained too of this to Kat, as the smells of the food were annoying to them as much as they were to me and the constant noise of the kitchens, too, caused pains to their heads as well as ours.

To the ravages of a mind already beset by worry, the everyday noises caused by those merely going about their business can become maddening. The mind needs peace and quiet in times of trouble, and I was ever the advocate of having space and time to think of my next move. But with the crashing of the kitchens below me, I was constantly disturbed, and unable to gather my thoughts, which, I am sure, was just what my spiteful cousin of Lennox wanted. Margaret had no reason to be a friend to me; after all, if I were removed from the succession, perhaps she could step into my place.

I vowed not to forget the actions of my cousin at this time of my troubles. If I was ever in a position to, I would make sure she regretted her petty pleasures at my expense… at length.

On the 23rd of February, Jane's father, the foolish Duke of Suffolk, met his end on Tower Hill. Not spared the roars of the crowd as his daughter was, he went to his maker surrounded by many who were happy to watch his fall. The crowds cheered with enjoyment as his head fell to the wooden platform. They had stayed quiet for his daughter, they had wept for his daughter, but I do not think anyone mourned the loss of Henry Grey.

I little knew Henry Grey, nor wanted to. Blinded by ambition, his part in Wyatt's rebellion gave Mary every excuse to execute Jane Grey. If Suffolk deserved his death, Jane had done little to deserve hers. He would always be guilty of having murdered his daughter, not by his own hands, but by his own actions. Such men who know nothing but their own ambition at the cost of all natural loyalty and fatherly protection are not worth their weight in horse droppings.

In late February, Sir William St Loe, the messenger I had used to relay my non-committal communications to the rebels, was implicated in the plots and taken to the Tower of London for questioning. When I heard this, I glanced suddenly at Kat, remembering the days when she and Parry had been taken to the Tower during the Seymour scandal when I stood accused of possible treason to the Crown. Under the pressures which are known only too well to those men who toil within the Tower, Kat and Parry had eventually given evidence that did not entirely damn me, but certainly did not clear my name either. I am sure Kat remembered the same, for she cast her glance away from mine and looked at the floor in shame. Kat may have felt as though I suspected the same would happen again. I was not foolish in my love for my servants, but I did not believe that she or Parry would ever betray me now. Much more than just my reputation rested on this present affair.

St Loe was strong, and he resisted the questioning and whatever else they did to him in the Tower with bravery. Torture was a common enough method used to loosen the tongues of men for the preferred outcome of the monarch, even if its use was not admitted to. But St Loe resisted whatever methods were used upon him. The message I had given to the rebels was told to his interrogators, but it was so obscure that the Council could do little with it. My careful reply could not be altered and changed to suit their deadly purpose.

In mid-March, Wyatt was brought to trial. I had feared that he might seek to lessen his own sufferings by implicating me, but he did not. He admitted he had written me a letter, but that my answer had not come back to him in writing. He spoke of the contact between us as being small, incidental to his own plans. His contact with me therefore seemed innocent enough, even if his further actions had not been.

I wondered then if Kat was right. Had his father ever spoken to his son of his love for my mother? Was the saving grace here not what I had spoken in reply to Wyatt, but the remembered and honoured love that his father had once held for my graceful mother? Love comes in many forms, and those who would respect it and honour it may do much to save what tattered remains are left of goodness in this world.

It did not seem, however, to matter much what Wyatt said about his interactions with me. Wyatt's trial served as a platform for Mary's Council to mount their attack on me. The day after Wyatt's trial, the whole Council, in one body, came before me and accused me outright of having had involvement in Wyatt's rebellion.

They stood before me, headed by Lord Chancellor Gardiner, who looked like a fat snake that had just swallowed a whole rabbit, so pleased was he. Some of the Council appeared nervous, hiding away at the back like cowardly dogs. Some faced me; the pleasure in their faces was undeniable. They thought, here, that finally they could be rid of this girl, this known Protestant, this daughter of a woman condemned to death for treason and adultery. Oh yes, there were plenty of men there who wanted me not as heir to the throne. They liked not my descent from such a mother, and they feared my religion.

I was a weed they wanted to pull. But I was not going to let them.

I held my chin up and pulled myself to my full height. I was taller than most women, a quality taken from my father's blood. My red hair fell around my shoulders, teasing at the velvet fabric of my white and green gown, proclaiming my youth, my virginity and my descent from Henry VIII. I was the daughter of my father, I was the child of my fierce mother; I was a princess of England, and I was not going to give in to these men without a fight.

I looked at them calmly, and then I spoke.

"It is strange to me, my lords, to find myself here, under such guard at all, for the world and its peoples know that I have ever been a loyal and righteous subject of the Queen, my beloved sister. How is it that I could have taken part in this rebellion that so tore our country asunder? When these traitors rose up against my sister's grace, I was laid low with the self-same illness which beset my body and mind as when I was brought to this place. Ask my doctors, my lords, ask my servants.., they will all tell you the same truth. I have been a loyal subject to my sister, the Queen. Those who would tell evil lies of me, those who would implicate me in such matters, know themselves that I have done nothing against my sister, nor ever would do."

I paused and looked scornfully at them. "For I, unlike *some* in this realm, understand and honour the process by which a king is made king, not only by the blood of the great father that Her Majesty, the Queen, and I share, but also by the hand of God, who moves us in our earthly tasks for His glory. My sister is the Queen, chosen by birth, and by God, and I am her humble servant. I have never, nor would ever, take arms against her, for she is the rightful sovereign of this land, and I am her sister, her servant, and her kin. I have done nothing to deserve such treatment of my person."

Gardiner shifted and narrowed his eyes at me. "The Queen has ordered that you are to be taken to the Tower of London on the next available tide," he sneered, "pending further investigation into the crimes against her country and her crown."

The words struck me like a knife to the chest. I had to try not to gasp. I am sure that my face must have become more pallid, as Gardiner looked pleased, but I would try hard not give the Lord Chancellor further satisfaction than that.

"Whatever further investigation is required to clear my name of any wrong against the Queen will be met with my full cooperation," I said stiffly. "But all any further investigation will prove is my innocence, and loyalty, to Her Majesty."

As they left, they did not bow; they did not take their caps from their heads as they should do for respect of a member of the royal line. Kat noted it and looked grimly at me. I nodded. I knew, too, what that mark of such disrespect implied.

In their minds, no matter how brave or resolute my words, I was condemned.

CHAPTER EIGHTEEN

Whitehall Palace
March 1554

Power is a curious possession in this life.

True power comes from the certainty of the soul, from the hand and will of God, from the actions of a person in their everyday life who knows where they want to be in the world.

The power granted to people by possession of title, or through the acquisition of money, is something that people will state they know surely about a person, and yet it is as fragile and insubstantial as the glittering of sunlight on a pond's water; as fleeting as the glint of gold on the body of a fish as it turns in the watery depths; as transitory and ephemeral as the touch of a person who loves us.

Power is but an illusion, but we all would swear we could see it; the gold that shines on a finger, diamonds that shimmer in the sun, rich cloth and great houses, titles, wealth and guards. These are the things that make up our perception of power, but as they are removed one by one, we must then find out in our own selves if our power is indeed an illusion, or if there is anything truly worthwhile inside us.

When we face danger, when we stand alone… that is when we find out whether there is anything truly powerful inside us, or if it was all nothing but a screen of smoke, a puff of gunpowder, a wink of gold.

On the evening of the Council's visits to my chambers, the last of my maids and household servants were taken from me, leaving only Kat and Blanche to attend on me. Mary's guards marched around and around the corner of Whitehall Palace where I was held captive; on the morrow, when the tide was right, they would take me to the Tower of London.

When they first came for me, I met them at the door. Winchester and Sussex, men not eager to do this duty, but afraid not to carry it out, told me they were to take me to the Tower that day, as soon as the turn of the tide gave them the right conditions.

"I wish to see my sister the Queen," I pleaded, but the grave men shook their heads in unison.

"Her Majesty will not see you, my lady," replied Sussex.

"Then I must be allowed to write to Her Majesty," I insisted. Again they shook their heads.

"Her Majesty will not allow that either, my lady," Sussex again maintained. He gave me a small smile, a sad smile. He did not like this task which had been placed on his broad shoulders.

I waited until it was nearer to the time when we should catch the boat to the Tower of London. Then I begged once more for the right to write to my sister.

"I am a princess of England, a daughter of Henry VIII," I implored. "Such small mercies as I ask for, even a man of no substance would be granted. Will there be no such justice for a daughter of the Tudor house? Will the daughter of King Henry VIII see no clemency in this state?"

They relented. I sat down to write perhaps the most important letter of my life... I was in truth writing *for* my life. Words had never been as important as they were now to me. Mary would not see me in person, I was sure, because her Council feared I might get her to relent if she saw me in flesh and blood. They were the ones holding me back from her. If I could reach her in words, if not in person, I might still have a chance to save my own life. I tried to impress on Mary her own promise to me when last we parted; that I was not to be condemned on the words of others, without having the chance to see her in person. Such, she had promised me then, but it seemed my sister would not hold to her promises now.

"If ever I did try this old saying, that a king's word was more than another man's oath, I beseech Your Majesty to verify it in me, and to remember your last promise and my last demand that I be not condemned without answer and proof; which now, it seems I am. For without caused proved, I am by your Council, from you, commanded to go to the Tower. I know I deserved it not, yet it appears proved.

I protest before God, I never practised, counselled, or consented to anything prejudicial to you or dangerous to the state."

I paused. My hands were shaking a little as I wrote on. I was writing for my survival. I could not fail now. Surely, all those years of study and translation, of gleaning the wisdom and the feeling in the words of others as I studied could not fail me now. I begged for an audience with her.

"Pardon my boldness, but I have heard of many cast away for want of coming to their prince.

I pray to God, that evil persuasions persuade not one sister against the other."

I finished. I read over the letter, and upon doing so, a little chill crept over my heart. The suspicion of an idea seemed to enter my heart even before it arrived, formed in my head. As I wrote, I had not noticed that I had come to the end of my persuasions and petitions to my sister after one, and one quarter, pages of parchment. If I sent this letter to my sister in its present state, what would stop someone along the way intercepting the letter and adding words that were not my own to the blank space on this second page? Words that might be used against me, words that might incriminate and condemn me, even though they were not my own?

The cold fluttering of my heart spoke to me and I took up my quill and drew long, diagonal lines across the blank space of the page, carefully scoured lines which showed where my quill had ended its words. When, and if, my sister saw this letter, she would know that I believed the *evil persuasions* I spoke of in the letter were real, and that I believed her men intended to do me wrong. At the bottom of the letter under my signature I wrote *"Your Majesty's most faithful subject, that hath been from the beginning and will be to my end. Elizabeth."*

As I wrote, the tide had turned. The chance had been missed for them to take me to the Tower this day. Sussex and Winchester told me we would have to go at first light in the morning.

My letter had won me a reprieve, but only for one night.

CHAPTER NINETEEN

Whitehall Palace
Palm Sunday, March 1554

It was early in the morning.

Blue and grey, silver and white slipped the first hints of dawn over the gardens of Whitehall Palace.

I had not slept. She had not answered my letter. There would be no reprieve, not now, not for me. Sat by my window, my glassy eyes staring at nothing and everything, I listened to the first jumbled calls of the birds in the trees… watched as the light returned to the world.

They came for me early. They did not want any crowd to gather, any resistance to grow. So, quietly they came… to take me from palace, to prison.

As the door opened, I looked to my side; the pupils of my ladies were wide with fear as they stood by me. The whites of their eyes glistened in the muted light as we looked to the dour faced men, and they beckoned to us, their low voices telling me what I knew already.

That I was arrested under suspicion of high treason against the Queen, my sister; that I was to be taken to the Tower of London. And what they did not say was possibly worse; that if I was found guilty, then Mary, my sister, my queen, would take my head in payment for betrayal.

Out of the room they guided us. We scurried fast and quiet at their urging on hushed feet behind their guards, down the stone corridors of the palace, past the staring portraits of my ancestors, the Kings and Queens of England. I sought to hold my chin up, for pride, for dignity, even as we scuttled like mice down those paths. My pale face was pinched, ghostly, but I held it high; so should be the face of the daughter of a king.

The first cold rush of the morning hit my skin as we left the palace and even beneath my fur-covered shawl, I shivered. Breathing in gulps of the frosty spring air, I sought courage from the very air and earth of my family estates.

I was afraid. I knew well enough that my survival did not rest on whether or not I was guilty. It rested on my sister and her suspicions of me. Therefore, I had good reason to feel fear.

I breathed in again, forced my shoulders back and my head up. My father once walked here and he would have never shown fear to any enemy. I am the daughter of a king, I thought. I cannot quail now like a mewing child; not when I need my courage the most.

The gardens were damp; cobalt and navy blues of the dissipating dawn lit our way through the paths. Small pockets of silver mist still clung to the horizon, drifting gently in the breeze. The grass and water of the river were black in the dim light, tiny drops of moisture shone from leaves and trees.

I looked up and back at the darkened windows of the palace. Little lights, as red as bright fire against the dark shone from the palace windows as the servants started their morning's work to warm the rooms of the Queen, to light the candles and the fires. I looked to see if I could see *her* eyes; perhaps to make one final plea to her, my own blood, the daughter of my father. But there was nothing. My sister did not show herself that morning.

But I knew she was there.

Something deep in my soul told me that somewhere beyond that stone and glass façade were the dark, watchful eyes of my sister, catching one last glimpse of me as her guards led me to imprisonment and possible death at her command. I could feel the bright heat of her hatred and suspicion for me. Jealousy and resentment, distrust and doubt, guilt and fear… all those emotions she sought never to acknowledge in herself…. I felt them burning into my back as I marched behind her guards.

I knew she was watching me.

Down through the gardens we hurried at the ushering of the guards, soft step on well-tended path. They were taking us by water; quicker, quieter than mounting horses and riding through London to the dreaded fortress. They did not want to give any a chance to halt our progress. They feared my popularity with the people of England.

The boat bobbed on the dark water calmly, merrily; it was too happy in its task. I stopped before the boat; my courage seemed to drain from me. I looked about me and my heart skipped within my chest with a heartbeat of fear… Could I run now? Could I flee my captors, call for help? I would not get far.

Lord Sussex held out a pale hand to me, startling me from my thoughts of escape. His face was eerie in the strange light, strained and pale from the task he now performed. He had little love for it, I knew well. A small smile for him, not lit in my eyes or believed in by my heart, touched my lips. I took his outstretched hand and stepped into the vessel. My ladies, Kat and Blanche, following my lead as always, stepped in after me. Rain fell on our heads and an ill wind chilled our bones.

I heard the shallow, scared breathing of my ladies as they sat beside me. Felt flesh tremble with dread against my own. I slipped my hands into theirs, and gave one brief squeeze before folding my hands before me and sitting straight.

I was the daughter of a king. That one phrase echoed in my mind. I was the daughter of a king. I must have courage, like a king.

I was the daughter of a king.

The daughter of a king… I thrust those words out to mask the coward within me, trying to cover her, silence her with my refrain.

The daughter of a king… The daughter of a king.

I knew I must stay calm, as much for my ladies as for me. I fought to retain control over myself as I sat on the rude seat. I sat straight and tall on the uncomfortable plank. No cushions were provided on this journey for a princess of the Tudor line, but more than enough guards. Comforts were for treasured royalty, not for prisoners.

Winchester and Sussex talked in hushed tones at the head of the boat. The quicker this was over the better for both of them; the worse for me. Down the River Thames we moved. Soft waves caused by other boats bobbed the boat up and down, and on the horizon, the red dawn approached. People were already up and moving in the city; carts rumbled through the rough streets, horses snorted white clouds of breath in the chill dawn light. Boats started to ferry people back and forth to the city. There were shouts from the waterside and the sound of inn doors opening, for today was Palm Sunday and under the rule of my sister, the old celebrations had been brought back. The common people were gathering to take part in the revived ceremony of the old Catholic ways, to carry crosses made of palm leaves to mark the day that Christ entered Jerusalem, starting the journey to his own death.

Was my journey, nodding along in the black water, lit by the gathering lights of the sunrise, to end in the same way?

They were taking me to the Tower of London. Into that fortress where so many kings and queens and princes and lords had been taken into the arms of God. It was a royal place to die indeed. I almost laughed at the thought. At least, in the place of my incarceration and execution, my sister was finally admitting I *was* of royal birth. Had I been the daughter of a lowly musician, as Mary had professed at times to believe, then she would have just had me tried and then hanged like any commoner.

Would I be fated instead to stand on a scaffold, to knee before a baying crowd as my mother had done? Would my head be cleaved from my body by clumsy blows of the axe, or a sharp sword? Or would my end come with a quiet pillow forced down on my face in the dark of night? Would I stand shaking before crowds of common and noble peoples as I faced death, or simply see the small shining lights of one man's eyes in a dim, gloomy chamber, as his dagger plunged into my flesh?

Those thoughts were too awful to linger on. My lips seemed to move by themselves in prayer. Although I could not hear the words in my own ears, I hoped God could hear me.

In the gathering light of the day, the great Tower loomed close as we approached, its towers, dotted about its battlements reached into the skies. The Tower had all the freedom that its inhabitants did not. I looked up, my neck bent, at the White Tower.

We landed at the Tower's wharf, heavy rain fell upon our heads, and wind billowed sudden and cold down the passages and streets of the Tower complex. We passed quietly on foot across the wet drawbridge and into the narrow, dark passageways of the fortress itself. Armed men guarded the route, their grim faces lit by flickering torchlight. All along the route I was to take, man after man after man was stationed in a line, each bearing arms.

"Are all these men here for me?" I asked of Sir John Gage, Mary's Captain of the Guard, who had arrived to see us into the stronghold.

"No, my lady," he replied, and I heard his voice shake with the lie it held.

"Yes," I said, almost calmly. "I know it is so. It is needed not for me, being but a weak woman."

As I passed, some of the guards broke from their structured order, doffing their caps to me and muttering, "God save Your Grace."

I nodded in thanks to those who spoke as I passed, but I could say little. The fear bubbling inside my body was so strong now that I felt weak; my feet scuffed and stumbled at the stones of the paths as we walked. My hands grasped at the folds of my clothing. I was losing my courage and my spirit in the maw of the great prison.

We passed the Tower menagerie, where brutal beasts roared in the darkness at the sound of our heels. Kat jumped high in the air at the sound of a lion who bellowed in the dim light. I reached behind me, grasped for her hand and squeezed it; her skin was clammy and cold, her hand was shaking with fear.

We came to pass near to the open expanse in the centre of the Tower complex and then I saw it, there, on the Tower Green. The platform on which my poor cousin had so lately met her end still stood. There, my cousin Jane had spoken her last, had groped for the block, and they had taken her head. The boards of the platform had been scrubbed, but Jane's blood still marked the wood. I could see it… that dark stain glistening in the falling rain, in the early morning's grey light. I felt the chill finger of Death pass down my spine and I shivered.

Had my enemies left the scaffold there so that the sight would quail my spirits further? Or, was it left there for stark and practical reasons? Was it to be used also for me, to walk my final steps on? Was that where Mary intended my life to end?

I stood stock still for a moment, staring at it, the rain fell on my face and my hair, and yet I hardly noted it. The wind blew about me, stealing around my ankles with its icy fingers, and yet I did not flinch. There was another type of coldness which had overtaken me, much more powerful than the ills of the weather. That platform... that dark stain of Jane's blood... If my enemies had wanted to scare me, it had worked. Sudden and cold was the feeling that swamped my heart as I saw the last construction of my kinswoman's death. Gage, Winchester and Sussex roused me from my frozen terror. I must continue on, they said. My steps faltered as I tried to turn from the sight of the platform. Was I to be taken to a dungeon, or to one of the towers? I knew not. Rich prisoners were usually kept in the towers which punctuated the walls of the great fortress, perhaps I was to be taken to one of those. But as we resumed our march and I saw to where they were taking me, I felt a surge of hysterical laughter swell inside me.

No dungeon, no tower. They were taking me to the royal chambers of the Tower complex. The inner ward of the Tower... the south-east block.

The royal chambers... traditionally used by the Queen consorts of England in our father's reign.

I stood before the building and stared at the painted bricks. I felt as though I was almost outside of my own body, a floating ghost already, looking at the thin figure of a young maid staring blankly at a building. Sussex looked a little confused as to the pallor of my face.

"My lady?" he gently tried to rouse me.

"These chambers were built by my own father," I said in a quiet voice. It was a strange voice, it did not sound like my own, though it came from my mouth. Sussex nodded in assent, still confused.

"He built them for the coronation of my mother," I murmured. "This is where she also stayed... before they took her to her death."

I saw a small look of horror pass over his features. Perhaps Sussex had not remembered what significance these chambers would have for me, perhaps he knew not what special cruelty my enemies had planned. To place me in the same rooms that had seen the last days of my mother's life... that was sweet torture, was it not? I could almost imagine the glee on Gardiner's face when the idea came to him; a delightful piece of spite... a fitting reminder for the bastard daughter of a condemned traitor... to put her in the same prison where her mother had been held before her death.

Our world is one where most people are unable to read and instead interpret the world through sign and symbol. The crest of heraldry on a tunic shows where a man's loyalty lies, the banner over a butcher's shop shows what he sells, the show of a woman's hair may tell whether she is married or a maid.

All the signs and messages my enemies had given to me spoke of one fate and one fate only.

The glistening scaffold of Jane's death, the dark faces of the armed men, the passageway past the great, imprisoned beasts, and now, to be put in the same rooms that my own mother had been imprisoned in before they killed her.

All these symbols whispered one word to me.... Death.

I breathed in, a last deep lungful of cold morning air. The rain was weeping down my face, bedraggling my hair and gown. My hands were frozen stiff with fear, my body shaken and terrified. But I was still a princess, I was still alive, and I was not going to give in to my fear before these men.

"Come," I said to Kat and Blanche, whose faces, like mine, were drawn with the haggard look of fear.

I pulled into me all the strength that I had left, and walked in. Into the gracious prison, into the padded, richly furnished gaol they offered me; into the rooms, the walls that my mother had stared at in the last days of her life.

I walked in, and with every step I took I felt the cold metal of the executioner's sword racing towards me.

I am Elizabeth, prisoner.

Traitor to the Queen. Enemy of the crown.

I am Elizabeth, prisoner.

And on this day, I fear to die.

CHAPTER TWENTY

The Tower of London
March 1554

I had to swallow hard to force any moisture down my parched throat. I could not breathe. My hands shook at my sides. I was wet through. The walls seemed to close around me. Every step I took into the rooms which witnessed my mother's last days and now, perhaps my own, made it more difficult to draw breath.

I felt as though I was being suffocated; a firm and steady pressure, like a pillow pushed over my face. As I walked in and looked at the room, I felt as though I was ready to faint dead away. I put out a hand to steady myself and found two pairs of hands gently take hold of me. Kat and Blanche, their pale faces almost green in the light from the candles and the fire were at my side. As their hands touched me, as the door closed behind us, I was suddenly no longer the strong-willed daughter of *Bluff King Hal,* I was no longer the stoic princess who held her chin high as she walked into this prison past armies of guards.

Looking at the faces of the two women who had guarded my person since I was a child, I burst into tears.

The others did not follow us in. There are many emotions that men are uneasy with witnessing of women, and a young woman of but twenty years facing not only her own death, but being immersed in the memory of her mother's, is perhaps one best left to women to attend to. There are many types of strength; if men face battle without reserve, you could place a strong bet that they would flee from the sight of a woman weeping.

A key turned in the giant lock on the door. Grating metal against metal, it did its work and we were locked into this opulent prison. Men were posted at the door, and I was left as a bird in a cage waiting to be plucked for the kitchen.

From outside the door I heard their voices; Sussex and Winchester and Sir John Gage, Constable of the Tower and Mary's Captain of the Guard. Although Gage had spoken kind words to me upon entering the Tower, I knew he was no friend to me in truth. His love for the Catholic faith and the Pope would not allow him to become easily endeared to a Protestant. Gage had also been the man chosen to oversee the execution of my young step mother, Catherine Howard. He was used to seeing the high fall low. But Sussex and Winchester were another matter. They were uneasy in this task.

"What will you do, my lords?" I heard Sussex say. His voice quailed as he whispered to them. "She is a king's daughter, and she is the Queen's sister… and you have no sufficient commission to do this. Therefore go *no further* in this commission. Let us use only such dealings that we may answer for hereafter."

In the centre of my panic, I felt as though a drop of water had fallen into a pool of ink and cleared a space in the darkness with clarity. Sussex is warning them not to abuse the position I am in, I thought. He worries there may come a time when any such action against me will be revenged.

Sussex does not believe I go to my death here.

Sussex believes I may live.

The thought came to me as though it were spoken in another language for all the sense it made to me at first. But then it inspired within me clear thought once more. There may yet be a chance that I am not to be murdered here and now, I thought. Not to be combed from Mary's hair like some burr picked up as the fleet-footed horse flies through the forest.

Then there was another thought, chasing on the last one's tail... There may yet be a chance, that if Sussex is as uneasy with my imprisonment, that others were too.

I had thought that if I was not murdered this night in the Tower, then I might die by legal means, facing the axe or the sword on the Tower Green. But perhaps, perhaps there was yet still a chance for life.

The sun was starting to rise outside and still the rain fell, lashing the outside of the walls of my prison in earnest; soon the morning would be with us in truth. I looked around the room and suddenly I had never felt more tired than I did then. It was as though all the troubles and trials of my entire life had come to rest upon my shoulders and my head just at that moment. I felt old, as old as Cain who wanders the world alone, as old as the angels who fought for God against Lucifer. I had lived but twenty years, but I felt as though I had seen a hundred lifetimes.

"I would lie down," I murmured weakly to Kat and Blanche. They helped me into the bed in the next room, moving the covers and stripping me of my soaking gown and sleeves as though I was still an infant. Their familiar hands soothed the fear and trouble within my mind, and I think I fainted into the arms of sleep before I had even lain down.

At first, I could see nothing. Darkness surrounded me and all I heard was the sound of my own breathing as I lifted my head. I was prostrate, lying on some soft, warm and moist ground. I raised my fingers to my mouth and on them I tasted the sweet coolness of the morning's dew, the tears of night, shed as she gives way to the coming of a new day where she must hide herself away.

There was in my head a nagging notion that I should be somewhere else, that there was something most important that I needed to care for, to see to, but I could not remember it. All I knew was a sense of relief, for in this soft and darkened place there was not fear, and there was not worry. My head felt as light and loose as the clouds that roam across a summer sky. Boundless and obliged to none, I lay in peace on the pliant ground.

Far away, a light was rising; a gentle orange glow murmuring on the distant horizon. But for now, I was disguised still in the darkness. I watched it idly, my fingers entwining in malleable and yielding velvet mosses, my eyes flickering slightly with the flush of colour growing ahead of me.

As the light rose, gently, so gently, I started to see more around me and beside me. There was a presence. Not something that startled or scared me, but a gentle and watchful presence. I could never tell you how I knew, but I knew it was a friend.

I moved my head slowly towards the feeling of the something beside me, and as I did, my eyes widened as I looked into the dark, bright eyes of a hare sat politely beside me. Its black eyes reflected a mirror image of my own face in the dim light, and I saw my own dark eyes staring back at me. As I looked into the eyes of the hare, as I saw my own eyes there reflected, I reasoned that here and now I could see into infinity; the mirror images of our eyes reflected each others' again and again and again, stretching back and back, smaller and smaller into the space where no mortal man may see or know.

Disappearing into that portal of infinity, I blinked, and the hare looked away. The moment and the vision were lost, but in that brief moment of infinity I saw, I understood that no fear or terror was contained therein; only wonder and possibility.

I pulled my body up to sit. Unlike any hare in the world of man, the hare beside me was little startled by my sudden motion. It watched me right my body with a calm interest and a twitch of its nose.

This hare too, was unlike any I had seen or known. Those I had hunted, those my dogs brought to me, were creatures of the undergrowth, brown and worn hard by the rigours of the life they lived. But this one was white, as white as the coat of a lamb, the silver frost of a winter morning, the thick ice of a pond in January. Its huge, dark eyes pondered on me as I stared at it, but still it did not move from my side.

The glow on the horizon was spreading now, and the landscape before me was emerging from its blanket of darkness. Light spread from the fingers of the orange dawn over the fields and meadows before us. Tiny lights shone where the dawn glistened from a dew drop, or shone off a grass blade. As the sun rose, the hare stretched its long-limbed body and sniffed the cool, clean air.

The white hare looked sideways at me. For a moment I thought I recognised something in those dark, brilliant eyes. But in the dream-state I was in, my mind was too slow to see whose eyes looked back at me from behind the hare's. For a moment we sat still, transfixed on each other, and then in one bounding leap, it sprung across the fields, towards the coming of the dawn.

I rose, as though to follow it. But the beauty of its graceful dance across the field and into the light caught me. I did not move my feet for fear of losing sight of the wonder before me. So free and so joyful was every one of the movements it made as it danced into the light, I was captivated by its every step.

The white hare reached the crest of the hill, the very source of the light, and there, silhouetted against the brightness of the sun, it stopped.

Its dark shape against the yellow daybreak stood, as proud and as free and as wild as any being I had ever privilege to see or meet. I breathed in through my nose, feeling the still-cool air bite at the inner flesh of my nostrils. If I owned anything, I should have given it up in that moment to be as glorious as the being that stood in that sunrise.

I watched as slowly the hare's shadow on the sun seemed to stretch, growing longer and longer until it was little more than a line stretching across the middle of the sun itself. And then it was gone.

Before I could taste fear or panic in my heart or mind, another shape rose from the place where the hare had stood. Not the white hare, but a bird of prey. It seemed to rise from the shadow of the hare itself, as it flapped strong wings and flew into the skies.

As it swooped over my head, the warm winds carrying its body, I saw crystal white feathers beat the winds to its will.

A white falcon soared through the skies.

The light of the sun rose in full and I was bathed in the comforting warmth of a summer's day. Not too heavy was the heat that basked on my face and my body, but the sun seemed to touch the bones of my body and remove the stiffness of tired muscle and sinew.

My ears heard the cry of the falcon as it flung itself through the air. The wild, free call of a beast of freedom and fortitude.

I lifted my face into the sun and smiled, feeling warmth and peace envelop me.

I opened my eyes into the darkness of the room in which I lay. For a moment I thought I lay on that cool, sweet floor of moss and grass, but I did not. Beside me were the sleeping figures of Kat and Blanche. Before the burning fire, our gowns dried, steaming gently in the dim light of the fire. Outside the locked door were the guards of the Tower, their step still patrolling along the corridor.

I reasoned I must have slept all day, and woken in the night.

I felt the chill of fear and despair start to rush into my blood once more as I remembered what had passed that day before, and how I had come to be here. I rose from the bed, careful not to wake either of my women, and I walked to the window. Rain was lashing down outside, pelting the window with uneven strikes. From here I could just see the scaffold on which my cousin Jane's life had been ended. It was perhaps, the self-same spot on which the last construction of my mother's life had been erected. This place, this Tower, this small corner of the world was where so many had come to breathe their last... In this fortress many of my kin had shed their blood and died on the orders of my father, my brother… my sister.

Kin slaying kin. Family murdering family.

We were all stained with the blood of those who had passed before us, those who fell to the whims of politics or passion. I thought of Thomas Seymour, put to death by his own brother the Protector. I thought of old Lady Margaret Pole, one of the last of the old line of kings, executed by my father. When she had died she had run from the executioner, and he had hacked at her old, frail body before she spluttered her last on that block… an ungainly, ungraceful, terrifying end to life.

There were many ways to die here, for those of royal blood, for those who threatened the safety of the sovereign.

I thought of them then, of the women most close to me who had died here… of Jane Grey, of the little, merry Catherine Howard… of my mother. I thought of the words people had spoken of those women; of their bravery in the face of death. I thought of them standing before the great maw of mortality; prayers on their lips for mercy and pleading for peace everlasting with God. My kin had faced death with courage; they had not run from it like poor Lady Pole. The women of my family had stood proud and strong for the last time on this earthly plane, and if they could, then so could I. If I was to die now, then I would make such an end as to be able to stand shoulder to shoulder with these ghosts of my past in Heaven. But I would not give up all hope for life as yet. The strange dream still echoed within my heart. I remembered the dark, glittering eyes of the hare, and I remembered another pair of dark, beautiful eyes that once looked on me with love and adoration. I remembered the soft stroke of her hands on my face, the feel of her kiss on my forehead. I remembered those eyes…

There was no creature in this world or the next, who had eyes such as my mother's. Not even me.

For reasons that I cannot explain with clarity, nor ascribe to any rational sense, I knew that my mother had been that spirit of freedom and liberty who had entered my dreams that night. I knew that her soul was as free as the flight of the falcon who had screeched over my head, as wise as the eyes of the white hare that had come to my side and brought me peace. The thought of her, free and flying in the winds of the heavens, brought me peace in that dreadful first night in the Tower of London. And I knew, with all the certainty of one who has had such a vision, that she died innocent of those crimes they had accused her of; for how else could her soul be so free, so light and so beautiful, if God himself did not understand her innocence? It was perhaps the first time in my life that I truly and completely believed that she had done naught of wrong to bring about her death. Others had spoken to me of her innocence, and I had wanted so much to believe them, but that dream, that night, gave me more certainty than I had ever known in the goodness of my mother.

I sat for a while that night, at that cold window. I thought on the manner in which my kinswomen had met their ends in this place. They had faced death with the courage of lionesses, and if they could do this, then if it came to it, so could I. I would not cower before mine enemies and disgrace the nobility of my family. I would stand as they had, I would not fall under the cloak of fear. I would make a good end to the little life I had lived… if I had to.

But another thought came to rest with me that night. I would make a brave last end if I had to; but if I could face death with courage, then I could too, face life with that same courage.

The threat of death and danger was still before me. The menace of my sister's hardened heart was still a force that could end my life. But when I needed it the most, something had come forth to warm my soul, to take me away from my troubled worries. Something had come to give me back that spirit of strength that I had lost as I entered these chambers.

I climbed carefully back into the bed and as I closed my eyes I thought on those dark, sparkling eyes that had looked out at me from the distance of infinity inside the white hare, the same eyes that glinted in the face of the wild falcon soaring above me. My mother's spirit was free in death; the thought brought me comfort. Perhaps if I did come to die in this place, then I would see her once more; we would be joined, flying in liberty together, on the wings of Heaven.

But until that time, I would fight to live.

CHAPTER TWENTY-ONE

The Tower of London
March 1554

For days, they simply held us without word from my sister or her Council. I understood they were trying to gather evidence against me, so, for the moment at least they would not attempt to simply murder me in the dark of the night. They wanted to try me, to question me, and to have proof of my guilt to display to the people of England.

My mind was troubled; the peace of the first dream on my first day in this place had helped me when I was at the very verge of collapse, but I could not escape the dread of what was to come. Kat and Blanche tried their hardest to keep my spirits raised, but the rooms in which we were housed, as comfortable and opulent as they were, did not allow my ladies to rest easily either.

Quite apart from the general dread of our fates to come, Blanche and Kat were nervous in those royal rooms. They shivered often, though the fire roared full and warm in our rooms.

They did not like to be left alone; almost unconsciously they became as one person, moving and walking, sitting and sewing always near each other. They especially avoided the window seats; there seemed to be something that repelled them from that area of the chambers. I asked Kat if there was something more than just our present fate that made her ill at ease and she looked at me with a slightly guilty, fearful expression.

"Never would I wish to speak ill of the dead," she said in a low whisper. "But I feel as though we are *watched* in here."

"We are," I nodded, indicating with my pale hand at the guards outside the doors and the ones patrolling outside around the Green.

Kat shivered. "No," she murmured. "It is not them… there is another *presence* inside this room, and I wonder…" she broke off and looked at me, warily, worriedly. As my servant and companion Kat was honour-bound to tell me the truth, but she did not want to. She did not want to admit to me that she feared the spirit of my mother still walked these rooms.

To do so, she feared, would firstly upset me, but also might mean that the soul of my mother was not at rest. A soul who is not at rest may be not taken into Heaven. I reached out to her and took her in my arms. My good Kat, always working to try and protect me, and here and now this was the least she felt she could do for me.

"If my mother's spirit is not at rest, Kat," I said and felt her jolt a little as it must have seemed I read her mind, "then it is because I am in danger."

We separated and I saw her brown eyes flood with tears. "How is it that you always know what I am thinking?" she asked.

"You, Kat Astley, are as an open book written in the plainest, boldest English," I grinned at her and she managed a little smile in return.

"If your mother is still here," Kat whispered looking around her, her pupils widened with fear that speaking of it may in fact bring a phantom into sight, "if your mother is still here, then it is because of the wrongs done to her, and to you, my lady… not because of any mortal sin she may have committed. There was never any sin that she made that could have been wicked enough for God to not take that good lady in his arms."

I nodded. I did not know if the feelings of coldness and watchfulness that Kat and Blanche said they felt in these chambers were the effects of the spirit of my dead mother occupying this space with us, as they seemed to believe, or just the imposing and terrible dread of our own fates. Kat and Blanche, however, seemed convinced there was a presence within these rooms.

I was not allowed to go to the Chapel, but I was allowed of course to hear Mass in my own rooms; the *Catholic* Mass that my sister prescribed in her effort to save my soul. As the priest that she sent to me droned on in Latin, I would recite the Lord's Prayer, in my own native English, inside my head. It was not as though I did not understand every word that the priest pronounced, badly, before me in Latin; it was just that when I spoke with God, I felt as though He understood me better when I spoke to Him in the tongue of my own country. Why would God have given us different languages if He did not understand them all and wish us to use them to our betterment? So, pushing the sound of the priest into the background of my mind, I closed my eyes and sought to talk to the One who made me.

In my darkest hours, I have often talked to God. It is sad, perhaps, that I have not given as much thanks during the happiest times of my life for His goodness. But it is when we are most close to death and danger that we ask for His help; I am no different to every other mortal in this respect.

Help me, I prayed.

Help me to know that I have found the right path to you. You were the one who made me; as individual and as strange and thoughtful as you made me, I am here as you intended.

You have shown me death and despair; you have shown me joy and love. I was given the path I walked to you in childhood, but if it were not the right one, let me know. Does it matter to you which signs and symbols I observe, what language I use when I talk to you? My sister believes it matters more than anything else, but I do not agree with her.

Does it not matter more that I feel you within me, that I believe you to be present in every day and every action I take? I would wish to make you proud to have brought me into this world. In everything I do, I hope to accomplish that duty to you.

All that you have given me has made me who I am. All the wealth and glory, all my friends, and enemies too. All the joy of knowing love and the horror of having those you love removed from your side by the hand of Death.

If you made me, then it was you who made me to survive.

If I survive this challenge, here, where I am the closest to death I have ever known, living in the shadow of my mother's fate, surrounded by the ghosts of the Tower, then I will know that you meant me to survive for a greater purpose.

But if I should not survive this, I would ask you to take my soul to the same place as my mother, my father, to my good stepmother Katherine Parr and to Jane. Entering death and knowing that I might see those faces so sweet to mine eyes once more, would never be so terrible a fate.

As the Mass finished, Kat and I rose to leave. Walking into the other room, I must have looked more peaceful as she squeezed my hand and gave me a smile.

I smiled back. "I forget sometimes, Kat, this must be more awful for you even than for me, since this return to a prison in the Tower must remind you of the first time you were taken from me and kept within these walls."

She shook her head. "At least the rooms are more comfortable now," she said with a little smile. "If you ever have to be a prisoner, be one in company with a prince."

I laughed a little. Then Kat's face took on a more serious expression. "I worried the most *then,* my lady," she said, "because I was not with you. I did not know what they were putting you through and for all your wisdom, you were still but a girl when they took me from you. All the discomforts of this place, of the cell they kept me in then... they were little to the discomforts of my own mind. And after Parry talked and I failed you as well, I would think over and over what I thought your different reactions might have been, if you still loved me or hated me, despised me, or wanted no more to do with me. It was torture of a more lingering kind that took my sleep and pained my body."

She paused. "And here, even though I am not at ease within these walls," she shivered a little and looked around as she had become accustomed to do, fearing the ghost of my mother, "even though I am not at ease, I am with *you.* You have been my sole care and thought in this world for so many years and I would follow you into *Hell,* my lady, if that was where your footsteps took you. As long as I am by your side, then I know I am where I am supposed to be."

My eyes filled with tears as I took my friend into my arms. "Kat... " I whispered as I choked into her shoulder.

"I love you, my lady," she cried into my shoulder. "You are the daughter that I would have always wished to have had."

All I could do was nod into her soft shoulder as I wept into it. "I love you too, Kat."

CHAPTER TWENTY-TWO

Richmond Palace
February 1603

Death is a strange and enticing character. He is the last companion on a journey all must take, and whilst his visage shows an aspect of fear and trepidation, there is also something about him that can become inviting, calming, and alluring. Death is not attractive to those who have never known pain and suffering; but to those of us who understand how hard the battle of life may be, the ultimate enemy can sometimes come to look like a friend.

I cannot tell you of my trials in those days and weeks in the Tower of London, not in truth. I can show you passages and conversations, I can tell you of my pale white face haggard and drawn with fear, and the pounding of my chilled blood in my veins, but the truth of my heart was such that no mortal can explain.

Resting so close to the arm of Death, though I feared his every step at my side, I began to see that therein was also an escape and a release from the torment I was presently under.

Death began to look to me as an old and trusted ally, one I had long known. Death began to look like a cool and calm place, away from wrestling with the life I had so little known then, and yet was already beginning to be so very tired of living. His call in my ear started to sound most warm and pleasing. His step at my side started to sound inviting. To those who have known much of suffering and pain, Death can start to appear as a much easier option than staying for another round in the fight of life.

At that time, I even chose the method by which I would meet my end if I was given the choice. I decided within myself that if I was to be executed, I wanted my end to be by the sword rather than the axe. It was not simply that those learned in the sword are cleaner at the ruthless task of taking life than those untutored, and often drunken, beings who are often chosen wield the clumsy axe; it was not just that the sword was the method of my own mother's death and I felt therein another connection with her. I felt in some ways as though my life had been a battle, and if I was to meet my maker, it should be at the end of a sword, in the manner that a king may die on a battlefield. If I was to end this life now, the manner of my death should reflect the life I had lived.

In those chambers, built for my mother at the height of my father's love for her, we sat and waited to see if Mary would send me to the block for the threat she believed I represented to her country and her faith. In those chambers I passed dually between calmness at considering the peace of death, and the most awful, desperate hope that I might survive.

I am an old woman now and I know how little I had seen of life then; had I died there in the Tower, there were many ills I might have avoided by passing from this life early. But I should also have had to give up the greatest glories and loves I found later in life.

I knew that not, then.

Life is not the easy option; it never has been. But we were granted it, and all that we are granted, we must rejoice in. There is so much sweetness in life that we cannot taste unless we also sample the bitter, so much more joy we can contain if we are hollowed out by loss and sadness first. Life is a double-edged sword itself. Two sides to every life… and in order to nibble at the happiness of love, we must also sip from the cup of sorrow.

The heart is the greatest enemy, for we never know how it may serve us in times of trial. It may quail in the face of pain, or it may cry strong and true as a lion. We only know if it is friend and ally, or enemy and rival, when we come closest to our destruction… when the heart is put to the test.

Death comes to look like an old friend to those in the grip of suffering and pain. And it is only in the primal will to survive that we find the might to refuse the beckoning hand of the companion of our last and greatest journey.

CHAPTER TWENTY-THREE

The Tower of London
March 1554

It was Good Friday when they came to take me before the Council. Neither Kat nor Blanche was allowed to accompany me as I walked in before those sombre men whose faces were hidden in shadow at the back of the great chamber. Did they wish to frighten me, sitting in a row behind that dark wood table? Or were they seeking to hide their faces for shame, knowing that nothing wrong of me could be proved?

As I entered the room, a full half of my inquisitors rose, and were then chided by the half who still sat; I almost smiled. The divisions of opinion about my guilt and position were as clear to me then as could be. It gave me heart, to see their split opinion laid bare.

I drew myself up to my full height, and walked through towards them. I had chosen my dress with care that morning. Tudor green and silken white silk and velvet shone on my body and my long red hair was loose about my shoulders. The daughter of Henry VIII was before them, and I was not going to let them forget that truth.

A chair had been provided for me before them, and I sat, sitting near to the edge and pulling myself up to look as regal as I could in front of these men. My blood was royal and they were but the servants of the Crown. I was a princess and they were mere men. I was not going to be convicted by mortals bent on corruption or vanity. If I could face Death with courage, I would face life with the same. This chant resonated within my heart as I turned my eyes on the men sent to question me.

"We are here today to ascertain the guilt or innocence of the Princess of England, Lady Elizabeth Tudor in the recent rebellion against the grace of Her Majesty, Queen Mary I," said a voice. I raised my eyebrows at them and said nothing.

"What were your intentions, Lady Elizabeth, in refusing the invitation of Her Majesty, the Queen, to come to court when news of the vile rebellion against her reign, started in this country?" The voice of Lord Arundel was bold and strong, but it was not accusatory. I looked into his face and I fancied I saw a flush of chagrin at his task. It gave me hope, and that gave me strength.

"I had no *intentions,* my lords," I said in the strongest and surest voice I could. It rang out, steady and true, through the hall, echoing and bouncing from the walls and I was pleased to hear it. It did not betray the quaking in my heart.

"I had no intentions of anything, when I was *unable* to come to the side of my most beloved sister during the recent horrors we have seen. Much as when my sister was forced to fight usurpers and traitors for the throne which was lawfully her own, I was taken with great illness. I have had these attacks of illness during times of conflict before. Were it not for the ills of my body I should have flown to the side of my royal sister. I should have certainly felt safer and more at ease by the side of Her Majesty than I did in my house, alone, with but my personal guard to protect me."

"But what of the plans we hear that were made to remove your household to your estate at Donnington?" asked my enemy Gardiner, his snake eyes flickering with the enjoyment of seeing me finally within his power. He was relishing the notion of being rid of this heretic who hovered too close to the throne for his Catholic liking. "A house, that we hear, was being fortified even as you amassed your personal guards… perhaps in preparation for joining the rebellion against your own sister?"

I looked at him and creased my brow. "Do I have such a house, my lord?" I asked, and my puzzled aspect deepened as though I was mystified by the question. I spread my hands before me and shrugged. "I have so many houses, being a princess of the line and blood of the royal house of Tudor, and greatly honoured by my sister's benevolence, but I admit, I cannot recall the estate of which you speak."

I looked around the Council and smiled at them. "Women are often wont to forget already gained riches when there are so many they hope to acquire yet, is it not so, my lords? The dress or the necklace that *may be* is always more enticing and memorable than that which a woman *already* possesses."

There was a little guffaw from some of the men at the table, and then there was also a great nudging and glaring, as those who had *not* laughed sought to express their disapproval to those who had. I smiled magnanimously at those who had sniggered, and I could feel their warmth growing towards me. Men, I have learnt, do so love to find companionship through jokes about their wives. I was already winning the affection of some of them, for my little quips humouring their sensibilities.

Gardiner looked furious; he was here to terrify me into submission, not to have the Council giggle at my jests. If he lost here, before all these men and lords of the land, the shame would be much greater.

"This is not so, my lady," he said, his face starting to redden at the cheeks and temples. "For you instructed Sir James Crofts, one of the rebel leaders, to help you repair to Donnington and to amass your forces there, for the purpose of rising against Her Majesty, the Queen."

"There was much talk, my lord, when word of the foul rebellion reached us, and I was in danger of my life, sick in my bed. There was much talk that we should take my household to this place or the other to ensure my greater safety." I smiled at the Council. "My servants are true and loyal to me, as servants should be to every good master; they take most diligent care of my person. If there was any such talk of repairing to another estate, then it was spoken of to protect my person. But in the event, I was too ill to be moved."

I looked back at Gardiner. "But I do not remember one house more favoured than another... unless it was because it was situated further from the seat of the abominable uprising. And at no time did I order my standing guard to amass for any reason, other than to protect my person against the rebels. After all, my lord, they were rising against my own royal sister, I feared what they might also do to me. I could have been murdered by the rebels, or held as captive to ransom against my beloved sister the Queen. I am but one small maid, my lord; what good would I have been against the might of so many men bent on treason and unrest? In times of danger, I may call on my personal guard to protect my person, as is the right of any noble lord of England."

"You instructed Crofts and others to move your household to Donnington," Gardiner repeated, sticky sweat was starting to break out across his ruddy forehead and yellowed cheeks. I liked the look on him. My calmness was infuriating him. He wanted me lost and floundering like a lamb caught in the marshlands. He wanted me to implicate myself. But I was no lamb to trot willingly to his slaughter.

"You know as well as I, my lord that I never met with this man, Crofts, nor ever would meet with such a traitorous cur as he. Whosoever has informed you of such is lying and I can call on many witnesses to prove so. I was taken ill, and kept to my bed at Ashridge. A princess of the house of Tudor does not receive men to her bedchamber! My servants can answer honestly for me in that regard. My servants discussed the movement of my household for the greater security of my person, my lord, many times during this season of unrest. But as you see, I did not move anywhere due to the ills of my poor body, and even if we *had* moved to another house, my lord, what of it? Can a prince not go to a house they legally own?"

I frowned at him. "Has it become treason to talk of moving from one house to another, my lord? If so, then the common man will prove better off than a prince of a royal line. I never understood my reason for being moved into this place of imprisonment, and now I see that treason is *most easily* arrived at in the minds of members of this Council. What else is there that I am here to answer for, my lords? For it seems that I am held to answer on the most trivial of matters under suspicion of great crimes but with no evidence other than talk amidst my household of moving from one house to another house... which I legally own."

I looked around at them and saw many of them blush with embarrassment. My heart was lifted and I almost wanted to laugh; *they had no proof of guilt.* The ones who wanted me dead were simply hoping I could be drawn into tripping myself up through fear, and admitting something they could twist against me. But my cool reserve was ending this hope, and if I stuck to my story, they could not make my own self an enemy against me. I had been careful in my dealings with the rebels, and that was paying dividends to me now. This Council had nothing solid they could argue against my innocence.

Whether or not I could still be executed for nothing was yet to be seen, but here and now, they held no power over me.

I lifted my chin, and moved my eyes along the darkened row of faces before me. "I believe that there are many in this realm who would seek to persecute this daughter of England for the purposes of evil; those who would spread treachery and discord between two sisters who came of the same beloved father and great king of this land. I stand accused of great malevolence against my sister, the Queen, and I say to you as I would say to her, that I am her most loyal servant, more loyal than *some* of those who seek to remove me, not for the good of England or the Queen, but for the secret satisfaction of their own sinful hearts. I have done no wrong against my sister, my Queen, or this realm and I remain Her Majesty's servant until death take me from this world."

I narrowed my eyes at them. "But until that time, it should be remembered that the word of a prince is more sacred a bond than that of any other man or woman; for in the heart of a prince is the will of God, and much as my sister the Queen, much as my father the late King, my word and my promise are *sacred.* I have never, nor will ever, do anything other than respect and honour my sister and the majesty of her position. Our great father taught us of the sacrosanct nature of kingship. My sister was placed here by *God* to be our Queen, and I honour her with all reverence, respect and love. I only wish that such were true of *all* her subjects."

I rose. "If that is all we have to discuss here, my lords, then I believe we are at an end to this audience."

Embarrassed, chagrined and shamed by a young maid only half their age, they let me walk out from the hall and back to my quarters. Gardiner sat staring at me as though I were a creature of another world, and possibly that was exactly what he believed.

He had expected me to come crawling before the Council, terrified and cowed; but it had not been so. I could see his serpent eyes narrow on me as I rose to leave, and I knew he was thinking on new ways to achieve his purpose. It was not over; they would go back and re-group for another battle. Gardiner, especially, would not allow me to simply slip from his clutches now that he could almost taste my blood on the block.

But my heart had stood the test of its resolve and courage in the face of adversity.

The first battle in this war was mine.

CHAPTER TWENTY-FOUR

The Tower of London
April 1554

The stench of burnt blood and roasted flesh hung sickeningly around us like a cloying cloak. Everywhere one moved, the scent hastened to follow. It festered in the air, wavering and dancing around us until it filled our noses and lined our lungs. It seemed as if there would never be another breath of clean air in the world.

They had taken Wyatt, once the proud leader of the rebellion, now a man broken in body from their torments in the Tower, and walked him to Tower Green to his place of public execution. Kat whispered to me that the guards had told her Wyatt's interrogators had tried over and over to offer him freedom or quicker forms of death if he implicated me directly in the rebellion, but he had refused.

Although he and I had never met, Wyatt had refused to make his death easier by causing mine.

There are some people in this world who never act but for the satisfaction of their own wants, and there are some who sacrifice their own comfort and wellbeing for that of a stranger. The latter kinds of people are to be honoured; they walk hand in hand with the angels.

On the scaffold Wyatt turned and spoke to the people; he spoke of me and of Edward Courtenay who was also now held a prisoner of my sister in the Tower. Since Courtenay's confession to Gardiner on the rebel uprising, Courtenay had been returned to the place he had already wasted so much of his life in as a prisoner. I wondered if he felt as though the Tower of London was in truth his home, for it seemed that he was fated to always return to its walls. Poor, foolish Courtenay; how little he had ever really seen of life outside of prison walls.

"Whereas it may be said and whistled abroad," Wyatt said as he stood on the scaffold, "that I accuse my Lady Elizabeth's grace and my Lord Courtenay; it is not so, good people. For I assure you they, nor any other now in yonder hold, was privy of my rising or commotion before it begun. I have declared no less to the Queen's Council. And this is most true."

The guards tried to hush him, pulling him back from his final speech. One of the men there, one of Gardiner's men no doubt, tried to say to the crowd that Wyatt was a liar who had "passed papers" to me, but the crowds were not listening to the others who spoke; their attention was held by the figure of the man about to meet death, and his words of my innocence had already sunk into them and taken root. When a man faces death, his words are taken with more gravity than when he lived. That Wyatt had chosen to exalt my innocence with the last words he would speak upon this earth carried great weight with the people.

"God save the Lady Elizabeth!" someone cried out from within the crowds; guards jumped from the platforms and swarmed from the sides of the throng to capture the man who had shouted support for me. But the crowds jostled, holding back the Queen's Guards so they could not find the man who cheered my name. The crowds were grumbling; they had not liked Wyatt's invasion of their homes, but there were many who agreed with his grievances against my sister and her marriage. The people of London were also not pleased that they were not allowed to call my name. They liked not my imprisonment in the Tower in the first instance, and now, Wyatt, a man facing death, was absolving me of treason against my sister. The people of London were on my side.

The guards hastened Wyatt to his end then, for they feared that my popularity with the crowd, and Wyatt's last vindication of my name, might put forth a riot in their midst.

We were always good friends, you see, England and I. England's people loved me, more so perhaps since I had come in ignominy to the Tower of London. Their love for me turned their hearts to know pity for me when I was brought low; an important lesson for all those who maintain that fear is the only way to rule well. If the people had feared me when I was great and at my liberty, then they would have delighted in seeing me fall. But they loved me, and so, their hearts felt sorrow for my incarceration. That pity and love, was what made me so very dangerous to Mary and her men. But it was also what was holding them back from taking my life. They feared what the people might do, should I be condemned to death.

Most people are not leaders; they seek one to follow. But those who follow are not sheep to merely bleat at their leader's command. They require a leader they can believe in. If the leader they have disappoints them, they will find another. This is why Mary feared me so, and why I was being kept locked away in this place. She feared the love the people had for me, and the anger they presently felt for her.

Wyatt's end was not easy nor was it clean. They cut his belly open, extracted and burned his bowels whilst he was still alive.

They prevented him from passing into blissful unconsciousness by shoving cloths soaked in vinegar up his nose. They cut off his manhood and threw it into a fire before the scaffold, and then, eventually, when the platform was soaked with his blood, they cut off his head.

The stench of Wyatt's burning flesh floated down to us in the Tower confines, and once it arrived, like any unwelcome houseguest, it was impossible to remove. The scent sickened me to the core and tears came to my eyes as I thought of that man, descended of noble poets and warriors, now a chopped and burned mess of blood and bones. I prayed that God should forgive Wyatt's sins, whatever they may have been, and take him into His arms in Heaven. Wyatt had, to the last, refused to make his own passing easier by accusing others. For that sacrifice, he deserved a place in Heaven.

They chopped his body into four, and took those quarters and his head to Newgate where they boiled them just enough to preserve the flesh for display, and nailed them up about London to show what happened to those who rose against the Queen. Wyatt's head was placed on the top of the gibbet at St James', but within the week, clever, courageous and quiet hands stole the gaping head away from public show, to bury at least a part of him with dignity in the cool, soft earth of England.

The next day the Council came to me again. The faint smell of burnt skin and roasted fatty marrow was still lingering on, through my chambers in the royal apartments, through the rooms of examination, through London. I had been unable to eat the day before due to the reek and the thought of what poor Wyatt had endured. But now I felt strong, resolved. With his last words Wyatt had exonerated me. The people of England now believed in my innocence; for if a man about to meet his maker would speak of my innocence, then, they reasoned, it must indeed be true.

I walked in as before, but this time more of the Council rose to their feet as my soft shoes padded across the floor.

I nodded to those who had risen, and they sat down. There was a different air in the room on this day. Wyatt's public exoneration of me had been embarrassing for Mary and her Council, and this, coupled with the lack of substantial evidence against me, was causing the common man to mutter into his beard with wonder at my continued incarceration. There were enough people willing to pass on gossip for the whole of the country to know what feeble pretences they held me here with. The Council feared these soft murmurs may turn to shouts of rebellion once more. They needed to keep control. They needed a reason to keep me here, or to execute me. They feared, now, to do either.

It is a good thing, when one's enemies are confused. And there were other events adding to the confusion and the general feeling against Mary.

There was a strange tale that one of the guards told Kat. In front of a plain wall in Aldgate there was a mysterious voice that was heard to speak in my favour from the very stones. The voice, it was whispered, was not of this earth, but was sent as a messenger of Heaven. If people shouted, "*God save Queen Mary!*" There was no reply… but if they shouted, "*God Save the Lady Elizabeth!*" Then, a divine voice replied "*Amen, so be it.*" Later, this astounding wall was also said to condemn the Catholic Mass as idolatry in the same beatific voice, and then sent all those gathered to shout at it running in hysteria from it by shouting *"The Spaniards are coming! The Spaniards are coming!"*

I am sure that, in truth, few of Mary's Council, or the common man, actually believed that God had sent an angel to speak in my favour from a wall in Aldgate. And if He had done such, then God must have been truly in an odd humour at that time. But the episode spoke volumes for my popularity in England. People thronged there to shout; "*God Save the Lady Elizabeth*" with all their might at the wall, stating innocently, if jostled afterwards by the Queen's Guards, that they only did so in order to hear the fabled voice reply to them.

It made me smile to hear that people so dared to shout my name with support and love. Such is the value of such love and loyalty, that no man can buy it and no man unmake it. The realisation that my popularity was only growing the longer I was held prisoner was causing the Council to fear, and in fearing, they were hesitating on what to do with me. If they were clever, they would have murdered me quietly on the first night they took me, but the longer I stayed alive, the louder the shouts for me became. They feared rebellion again with certainty, but they feared other considerations as well. How many of the Council feared the future, wondering whether if my aged sister should die and I came to the throne, I might look back at this time and take revenge for these slights and humiliations vested on me?

Ah yes, there was a turn in the tide on this meeting. I could feel it as surely as I could smell the awful burnt flesh of Wyatt.

There were other events, too, which spoke of Mary's growing unpopularity in the country. One night, when Mary was at prayer in her privy chamber, a dead dog was flung through her door. The poor hound had been throttled, shaved, and dressed as a Catholic monk before some twisted soul had run the halls of Mary's palace to heave their wretched message through the door. Unbelievably, the perpetrator was not caught; Mary's guards had apparently been playing at cards in an outer chamber and not seen anyone... which led everyone to believe it must have been a member of the court, for who else could know so well how to disappear within the confines and crowds of the palace? Mary herself was so sickened by the dead dog thudding to her feet in the middle of her prayers that she had vomited. I am sure the thought also crossed her mind that had this night-time visit been paid by an assassin rather than a messenger, then she would be dead.

So yes, there was a feeling of unhappiness and unrest in the country, and the Council were as aware of it as Mary was. It was coming to invade her most private moments, as well as her public ones.

I sat before them and once again drew myself up to stare them down. Gardiner was absent this time, which I thought was odd. What was the old snake up to?

"Well, my lords?" I asked after waiting a while in silence for them to start. "Shall we talk of houses once more, or have we perhaps moved from that material discussion to another? Shall we today speak of what *gown* I wore on which day and how that speaks of my loyalty to my sister the Queen, perhaps?"

There was rumbling and mutters, embarrassed faces yet again. I felt rather elated, jaunty even; for when one lives in the shadow of Death for so long finding a tiny release of humour is quite rejuvenating.

"My Lady Elizabeth," Arundel started again, the only one brave enough to face me without Gardiner here. "We are here to ask you today if you know of any action of yours, or your servants, which, however unwittingly or unconsciously done, could be admitted to being treasonous?"

I stared at them for a moment, and then let out a little laugh.

They stared at me with surprise.

"How now, my lords?" I said still laughing. "You can find no proof against me and so you come to *me* to ask that I provide proof against *myself* for you?" I laughed more heartily at the downcast eyes before me. "I am sorry, my lords," I laughed, struggling to contain myself.

"If you could answer truly, my lady," asked Arundel, flushing earnestly.

I shook my head at them in true wonder, banishing all merriment from my voice. "I am amazed that it should come to this," I said to them. "When my father was alive, there was no man, nor woman, that stood before his court that was not brought there without *some* accusation of guilt. Never has any king been known to present his own prisoner with a question as to *what* their guilt may be. If you stand in judgement over my person and my life then I would hope that you had some understanding or idea of what you accused me of. But the truth is simple, is it not, my lords? You *know not of what to accuse me because there is nothing to accuse me of.* I am the loyal and humble servant of my sister the Queen, and you have nothing to prove otherwise, because that is the simple truth. I say again to you that I have never done, nor ever will do, anything that would harm or impinge upon my sister, or her crown, or country. Not only through God-given loyalty to she who was chosen to rule this country, but also through the bonds of loyalty that one sister may have to another, for the great father we shared and for the ancient and noble house we both come from. I am innocent, my lords; there is no proof you can find against me, because this is the truth. The longer I am held here, the more it does only to dishonour you."

I stopped and saw they were staring at me. With the light from the windows shining on my head I must have looked for all the world like an angel, but with the anger in my voice, with the shimmering red hair on my head, I wondered, too, if I was reminding them of my father.

Up in the gallery I saw a curtain twitch suddenly. I looked up. There was a noise of footsteps on the rushes and the wooden floor above, and just for a moment I saw the flash of gold and pearl ornaments on a rich crimson dress.

It was then I realised that Mary herself had been in the corridor above this room, and she had listened to every word I said. She could not bring herself to meet me in person, but she *was* finally listening to what I was saying.

Perhaps there was hope of release for me still.

CHAPTER TWENTY-FIVE

The Tower of London
April 1554

It was soon after that day that I was given permission to walk in the privy gardens of the Tower, under guard and with my ladies, but only at set times in the early morning or late afternoon. Mary was granting me a little freedom, but she did not want me seen by too many people.

After weeks of being locked up in the chambers of my mother, a little walk each night and morning came as a blessed relief. Just being out in the airs of April were enough to start a colour returning to my pallid cheeks, giving me the feeling as though there was something to look forward to each day. Kat and Blanche, too, relished the feel of the breeze on their skins and the smell of herbs, crushed in their hands, as we walked and talked on our little wanders around the garden.

The guards did not impose on us; I think that Kat's ways had won over hearts already disposed to our situation. They looked on me with pity, but they also with some admiration. I talked to them little, but often, about their families and children. Since I remembered details individual to each of them, they warmed to me, and even started to bring in little gifts their wives sent to us; fresh baked bread and new needles for our stitching. We could have asked these things of the Tower Warden, Master Bridges, and had them with little problem, but it pleased the guards to give us these presents and we took them happily. Life is much easier when one has friends.

On those walks we sometimes saw the children of the Tower's servants. Most of the time they were ushered away from us, but as our walks became more regular we started to be allowed to talk to them. There was a little girl named Jane and a little boy named Martin who came to see us often. Both of them had grown up in the Tower of London itself and were no more than six or seven years old. Most of the time they worked cleaning or cooking with their mothers, but they had begged and begged, they told us, to be allowed to come and talk to the "*pretty princess*" who wandered here each day.

I realised they were talking about me and I beamed; those who see their defects in beauty all too clearly are the most susceptible to flattery.

There was another reason they wished so particularly to see me, Martin said, whispering this to me and looking around to see if anyone was watching.

"What was that?" I asked, drawn into the excitement of the game he and Jane were playing, or so I thought.

"There are two men kept in the towers," Martin whispered to me. "Who both asked that I bring messages to you..." he trailed off a little, his tiny brow frowning. "But I can't remember which one was which," he said miserably. I smiled gently at him, saying that it was alright that he did not know, and he beamed back at me, looking at me with reverence for such a little kindness.

Jane, clearly a little older and also obviously in charge, tusked at Martin. It was the dark haired man, she said, who had asked them to say that "*the princess should not fear, for many in this country love her,*" and the blonde haired man who said that "*our troubles may make us stronger.*"

I stared at them, suddenly worried and looked around quickly at the guards; they were far off and in conversation with each other. "Who were these men?" I asked. I was fearful in case this was a trap, a subtle way to ensnare me into saying something against the Queen and incriminating myself.

Jane smiled and twirled a little blond tendril on her finger. "The dark haired one is called *Robin,*" she said. "He is most handsome, and he says that one day you and he will sail the seven seas as pirates!" She laughed and bounced a little on her heels; her eyes glittering with the memory of the dark haired adventurer.

"Robin..." I muttered, thinking fast. "Robert... Dudley?" A sudden image of a bold-faced boy I knew when I was just a girl flew into my head; as dark as a Spaniard and as clever as an owl. Once friend and companion to my brother, since his father, Warwick's, execution Robert had remained locked inside the Tower. His one remaining brother Ambrose was here too, having escaped the block.

"Aye!" exclaimed Martin, a little too loudly and earning a look from the guards and from Jane to quiet him.

"And the other was... Edward Courtenay?" I asked and the children nodded delightedly.

I thought for a moment.

Was it true that these children had carried messages of support to me from two men also prisoners in this awful prison? It was not impossible. Servants cleaned rooms, made fires, brought meals... and Robert and Edward would be held in arrangements suitable to their rank, after all. The manner in which prisoners were held in the Tower of London depended on their station in life. Noble prisoners were kept in good quarters, no matter their crime, and men of no title were kept in common jails. So it was not impossible that these children could have seen and talked with them. The possibility of such messages warmed my heart a little, but I could not help but be suspicious. There was nothing of evil in these children, certainly, but that did not mean that others with hearts of malice could not use such innocents against me.

"Should we carry a message back to them?" Jane asked eagerly. I looked at the little faces and I wanted so much to trust them, so much to believe that there was nothing behind this but simple messages sent secretly from one prisoner of the crown to another. But I had been as careful as the vixen at night; however much I wanted to, I could not let my guard down now.

"Say to them that I thank them, but that I trust in the goodness and mercy of the Queen, so I have no need to fear." I said. There, in that sentence there was nothing but reverence for my sister and nothing that could be used against me should it be discovered.

They mouthed the words back a few times with looks of heartfelt concentration on their faces as they strove to remember my words exactly. Jane seemed to get the pattern of the words before Martin, but I made sure they both knew it, so that the little boy would not feel left out.

"But you must remember to keep this a secret," I cautioned. They both nodded eagerly. Who loves a secret more than a child?

That night I sat in my chamber thinking of the messages given to me by those children. Somewhere in this prison were two men, two men I had barely met, who had independently sent messages of hope and friendship to me via these little children. When had they given such messages? Perhaps a while ago when I first came to the Tower, and only now the children had had the opportunity to deliver them to me.

I admit… I lingered more on my memories of Robert Dudley than those I had of Courtenay. Courtenay seemed rather a foolish man to me, and I had little temper for fools. But dark Robin, with those glittering eyes... that sharp wit and confident manner. He had remembered how we talked of running away on ships once when we were children; how strange are the things we remember! But I was touched to think he did recall, and more touched to think that he hoped I remembered too. Those days when he served in the house of my brother Edward, when my father was still King and Edward, Mary and I were brought together as a family… How long ago all that seemed now… My father and brother were long dead, and my sister held me captive in her fortress.

I wondered if Robin Dudley was still as handsome as he had been before he had come to the Tower. I had been at his wedding at court some years ago and had found his face most pleasing to my eyes. As I stared at the fire, my mind wandering with pleasure along the remembered angles of a handsome face rather than the present fear of my situation, there came a knock at the door. Kat and Blanche glanced at me and looked worried. We were generally left to our own devices in the evening, and we had long since eaten supper. Kat went to the door and knocked back to signal it was fine to enter the chamber; the door was opened from the outside.

Master Bridges, the Tower Warden, was at the door, looking visibly pale; his clothes were splattered with mud, as though he had come straight to me from a long hard ride.

"Master Bridges," I said and gestured him to come in. Although we were, of course, prisoners, there had been lately much more of a sense that I was simply residing here with my ladies; the guards and warden all treated us with respect.

"My lady," he said fervently, his face pallid and sweating a little on his brow as he bowed shortly. "God *save* you."

It sounded as though God might well *need* to save me from the tone of his voice. I must have looked alarmed at the tone and words of his address as he swiftly brought forth a piece of paper from his bag and ushered Kat to close the door.

"My lady," his voice low and urgent, "this was brought to me this afternoon." He handed me the paper and I brought it under the candle light to read.

My heart seemed to stop dead in my chest.

It was a warrant for my own immediate execution.

All colour drained from my face, the moisture from my mouth, the air from my chest. I stumbled backwards and sat down. It was as though the hand of Death was suddenly pushing my shoulders down to make me kneel before the might of his presence. Just as I had started to hope once more for a chance at life! Just as I had come to hope that I would escape this incarceration! Just as I had started to want to live more than anything again! How cruel was my sister that she could give these things back to me only to wrest them away? I stared at the paper and then up at Master Bridges.

Kat and Blanche rushed to me and Kat made as though she were going to shout at Master Bridges, but he held up his hand.

"My lady," he said softly, and I looked up numbly into his face at the sound of a voice laced with kindness. "My lady, regard closely the signature and seal on this letter," he urged.

Dumbly I pulled the paper back before my eyes. At first I stared at it without reading the words or even seeing the page at all. And then I stopped, and looked, and stared. The seal was not that of my sister. It was a royal seal, but it was not her seal. The signature.... it was *like* her hand, but it *was not* her hand. I looked up at him, some colour must have returned to my face for I felt my cheeks flush.

"This is not my sister's hand," the words burst from me loudly. Master Bridges shook his head slowly at me.

"Then... from where did this paper come?" I demanded.

"I know not my lady," he said. "A messenger delivered it to my servant."

"What livery did he wear?"

"He wore none that my servant could recognise," Master Bridges frowned. "When it first arrived, I was much surprised. With executions in peaceful times we normally get warning with days, sometimes weeks, to prepare; so the order that you were to be taken *immediately* and executed was strange in any case, and then I noted the seal and then the signature." He regarded me with something akin to protectiveness and I felt like bursting into tears on him.

"I took the paper to the Queen herself," he said. "And when I presented her with it in private, Her Majesty swore she had never seen it, nor had ever ordered it and she promised to investigate who had sent it to me with all speed."

He smiled gently at me. "I truly believe, my lady, that Her Majesty was horrified; she did not send this letter nor issue this order. The Queen said that she would find out who had tried to do this unlawful act to "*her sister*" and thanked me for my diligence and care for your person."

I stared at him. I think I was a little in shock; partly to think that my sister was referring to me as *her sister* once more, and partly as had good Master Bridges simply carried out his orders, I should be now dead. There was someone, and I had a shrewd idea of who that person was, who was willing to act rashly and boldly to see me dead.

Gardiner was the only one who could have copied Mary's signature so well, and as Lord Chancellor, was one of the only men with sure access to a royal seal even if it was not my sister's personal seal.

I looked at the paper again and then I rose suddenly and embraced Master Bridges. He was taken by surprise and patted me roughly on the back. Good man that he was, he was embarrassed by my show of affection and blushed a ruddy red colour. As I released him, Kat pounced on him, followed then by Blanche who, as she embraced him, also muttered a blessing over him in her native Welsh. I think the poor man didn't quite know what to do or say. He spent most of his life ensuring that prisoners were secure before their execution; he was unused to them responding to him with affection.

"I am the servant of the Queen, my lady," he said, red-faced, but looking somewhat pleased at our outburst of warmth. "And Her Majesty has ordered me to hold you here with respect for your station. If you were guilty of any crimes, you would be executed by her order and I would ensure such, in accordance with my duty. But I will not have any other person issuing orders here. This palace is where the Queen's will is done and no other." He looked stern and shook his head angrily. "From now on, my lady; we will double our efforts at checking your foods and increase your guards. An enlarged watch will be put on about you, for your protection, and if anything out of the ordinary happens, then I will be informed." He nodded to us.

"Do not worry, my lady," he said gruffly. "We will see that no harm comes to you."

"Unless Her Majesty orders it," I murmured sardonically and then pursed my lips. I had not meant to say such out loud.

Master Bridges looked at me with kind and serious eyes. "I do not think the Queen will do anything to you, my lady. I cannot pretend to know the will of a queen, but the look in her eyes when she heard my news of this betrayal held all the alarm of someone who fears losing someone they love. They say that when you were a babe she looked after you, cared for you. I can't imagine that such love, deeply rooted in a heart, would wane so fast." He shook his head. "No, my lady… I do not think it's your sister that you need to fear now."

"I hope you are right, good Master Bridges. With all my heart, I hope you are right."

CHAPTER TWENTY-SIX

The Tower of London
19th May 1554

What is it in the sense of separation between two people which brings forth the best of emotions that you once felt for them?

My incarceration at the orders of my sister and my brush with death were, looking back, perhaps the best thing that could have restored feelings of compassion in her heart towards me. We were never at peace when we were adults in the same room, but when we were apart, perhaps Mary remembered me as I was when I was an infant, small and helpless; left without a mother just as she once had been too.

Separation pulls at the memories of the heart, and this time, escaping death by the slightest of margins, I felt grateful to the sentimental streak in my sister's nature that enabled her to have the grace to save my life.

Perhaps it was more than that though. For any prince or ruler to have power usurped from them as someone had striven to do in ordering my death was insupportable. Mary had shown enough fear about her ability to rule as an independent woman, but she was not a person to take outright disobedience lightly. She had shown that she was prepared to take sword to any who challenged her power, having had to do it twice now, in her ascension and in her overthrow of the rebellion. But now someone had chosen to order the death of her sister without her consent; that power belonged to the Crown, and was not for any other to wield.

Whoever's was the hand was that wrote my name, and forged Mary's, on that hateful document, made a mistake in trying to by-pass the authority of royalty. For in the moment when Mary saw that one of her Councillors, for it must have been someone with access to a royal seal, had tried to take power into their hands, she was immediately filled with distrust of all of them, and perhaps, a little more sympathy for me.

Stubbornness and pride were traits we Tudors shared aplenty. Mary was not going to allow someone else to make her choices for her, especially when it came to family.

Two months after I arrived at the Tower of London, on the very anniversary of the day my mother walked out from these chambers and to her death, I was taken forth from my prison by a massive guard of hundreds of men under the charge of one Sir Henry Bedingfield. I was not being released, but I was being moved at least from these chambers and this fortress.

Kat was not allowed to accompany me; only Blanche would remain of my original servants. Perhaps Mary remembered all too well the scandal with Thomas Seymour in which Kat had been hauled before the Council, accused being a poisonous influence on my morality. Perhaps Mary felt the same had happened again now. For whatever reason, the removal of Kat from my side was a bitter medicine to swallow. She was taken away on the morning before I left, to be placed under custody of her brother and sister in law.

Before she left, her eyes overflowing with tears, I took her in my arms. "This is not forever, Kat. It was not so the last time, as it will not be so now. One day, you and I will be together again."

She nodded, but she could say little to me through her tears.

"As soon as I am allowed," I told her, "I will send for you to return." Then I took a ring from my finger and placed it on hers, "a token… to remind you of me." Tears rolled down my cheeks as I spoke to her.

Kat looked at the ring and then smiled at me. "There was never any token that could replace the space in my heart that you occupy, my lady," she said, sniffing. "But this ring will stay on here as you have placed it, until such time as I can return both it, and myself, to your side."

And with that, for the second time in my life, my beloved Kat was taken from me. I watched her leave with a heavy heart, but at least she was going to the care of family for her house arrest, rather than the last time when she had been locked in a cell.

When it was time for us to leave the next day, I turned to take one last look at the chambers of my mother. Despite the constant shivers and fearful glances of Blanche and Kat, I had felt nothing of a foreboding phantom presence here. Blanche, however, hurried out as soon as she could, grateful to be leaving the rooms which she believed to be haunted.

Before I left, I whispered, perhaps to myself, perhaps to the mother I barely remembered who had met her end on this day so many years ago. "I go from here today, not to my death," I murmured to the empty room. "In time, I hope for freedom. Perhaps one day, I shall come back here not as a prisoner, not as a subject, but as a queen."

As I turned to leave, I stopped as I fancied I heard a little sigh, as though someone had been holding their breath anxiously and had then released it in relief.

I smiled as I shut the door to the chamber behind me.

Perhaps I had but imagined it, perhaps not.

CHAPTER TWENTY-SEVEN

The River and Richmond Palace
May 1554

We left the Tower by barge. Still a prisoner, still under guard, but at least I was leaving those grey walls. As I was walking through the narrow streets of the citadel of the Tower of London and down to the waters of the River Thames, I thought of the men still imprisoned, of the children who brought their messages to me. What would become of the handsome Robin Dudley and the foolish Edward Courtenay?

What would become of *you*, I thought to myself, is perhaps what you *should* be asking.

But still, as I walked towards the barge that would carry me hence from this prison, I could not help but look up at the towers and wonder if those men were looking down upon my leaving. The messages that little Martin and Jane had passed back and forth between us had not been discovered, but another slightly unfortunate event had taken the children from being allowed to meet with me.

The children had decided amongst themselves that since I was a prisoner within the Tower that I needed keys in order to become free. Jane and Martin could not see why such a comely and gracious princess should be kept as a prisoner, and had decided together it was a mistake to be rectified by them. From the pantry, the children stole keys for me; they were in fact the keys to cupboards in which were kept valuable spices and sugar, but the children reasoned that keys opened doors, and therefore I should have them to open the doors of my prison.

When they had given me the set of keys, hidden in a bunch of flowers they had picked for me, my heart had skipped a beat. I had looked on them with such a feeling of love, and perhaps for the first time I had wondered what it might be like to have a child of my own. Their love, like their reasoning, was so simple, so open… it was something quite beautiful. But although I had thanked them for the keys and their flowers, I told them that I must give up the keys to the guards who patrolled about my chambers still.

"Why must you so, my lady?" asked Jane, looking fearful, for she did not want to be caught doing something naughty.

"The prison in which I live now, Jane, is made much more of suspicion than it is of lock and key. My sister, the Queen, must come to believe in my goodness once more, and to do that, I must deal honestly with her in all things."

Their little faces had creased with fear when I took the keys to the guards, who visibly paled when they saw such things in my hands.

"Please," I said to the guards, "do not punish the children harshly… they only thought it a game."

But, nonetheless, that little game as I had called it, caused the children to be prevented from meeting with me, and although I had acted honestly, the guards took up a more diligent watch than ever on me in the last weeks I was within the Tower confines.

I missed the gentle goodness of those two children, and their bright and merry company.

It was only a few weeks later that I was told I was to be moved from the Tower to another residence, still under watch, but more at liberty than I had been before.

I thought then, as I gained my liberty, that it is often the way of people to turn our heads so easily from contemplating the fate of another as a light of freedom comes to us. So easy to turn from the cares of others, in happiness at our own changed fate; but that was not so for me this day. I thought much on Robin and Edward and the messages they had sent to me. Did they wonder, as I did, what this life would hold for them? Did they think of freedom and yet still fear they would never see its grace once more? Did they dream of a day when they might walk from the Tower as gentlemen? Did they wonder on the fear that one day they might die by the hand of private and quiet assassin… their lives to pass from the light of this one to the obscurity of those forgotten by history?

I too wondered on this fate… now that the threat of public execution seemed to have dissipated, would I instead face the peril of quiet assassination? Although it had not been proved, despite investigation, whether Gardiner and possibly the Spanish Ambassador, Renard, had been behind the sudden, sneaking attempt to have me executed, I still believed one or both of them was behind it. Who else would so dare? Renard had no love for me; a Protestant heretic… and Gardiner had made clear that he was my enemy. If Gardiner had failed once to have the sentence of death posted to my account with that warrant of execution, would he now attempt the hushed methods of those who practise quiet death as their profession? Would he dare? I would not have thought it was beyond the ambitions of either Gardiner or Renard. Even if Mary had made clear that she did not want me dead, I was far from convinced that she wanted me, in truth, anywhere near the court or her seat of power. Could my enemies, with time, work on her, convince her to have me quietly removed… to slip from possibility of anything I could be capable of in the future, helped on my way with a potion, or a knife?

Not easy thoughts for a woman surrounded by guards and soldiers. At liberty, and yet still a prisoner.

Four hundred guards accompanied me; men on the barge and men along the Thames where we set forth into the waters. I almost smiled to see so many. What did they think one small maid of twenty years could do? Just a few guards would be ample to overcome my small strength. But as we set off into the waters and through London, I came to see that the Council and Mary feared not my personal, bodily strength… No, they feared the love that the people of London, and of England, felt for me. As our barge sailed out from the Tower confines, word spread amongst the people of London that I was set free; rejoicing broke out in the streets as people came together to tell each other that *their* Princess Elizabeth was at liberty. They did not know I was in fact being moved to another prison. Shouts of support and happiness reached my ears from the banks on which crowds stood jostling to get a glimpse of me. It made the guards nervous when I turned to wave to them from the boat, and Sir Henry Bedingfield, my gaoler, asked me to stop.

"If I should stop *now* Sir Henry," I replied, "will not the people think something is wrong? Perhaps they will come to think, as I have suspected, that I am to be moved from the Tower of London to a place of secret execution?"

He looked rather aghast when I said that; I had spoken loudly, and plenty of the soldiers and guards around me had heard. Blanche went a strange, pale green colour when she heard those words. Much as I would want always to act in a manner that eased my servants, especially loyal women such as Blanche, the suspicion of assassination was strong with me. By calling attention to it publicly, it would make it all the more hard for someone to go ahead with any such plan and get away with it.

"If I continue to wave to the people who love me as they loved my father, as they love my sister," I said to Bedingfield, "then they think there is no harm being done to my person. You would not want them to take action to protect me on this most public journey we make, would you, Sir Bedingfield?"

Bedingfield looked at me, his dark brow creased with worry as to what to do. He was utterly loyal to my sister and her reign, this I knew well enough. When my sister had first striven to take the throne from the *coup* where Jane Grey was placed on the throne, Bedingfield had been the first man to fly to Mary's standard answering her call to arms. His own father had served Mary's mother, Katherine of Aragon, in her last sad days, and Bedingfield's grandfather had served our grandfather, Henry VII, and fought at his side at the battle of Bosworth Field. Sir Henry Bedingfield was a Catholic through and through, and a man of most traditional manners and understanding. He was loyal, trustworthy, and if his intellect lacked some of the sophistication of those brought up with better tutors and academic understanding, he understood enough of the world to get by.

Mary had chosen him, no doubt, because he was, from the top of his dark head to the ends of his stout feet, *her* man. A servant she felt she could trust; a thing that was becoming a rare commodity for my sister, surrounded by the snakes and dogs of court. He grunted at me, and I took that as an affirmation of the sense of my words. I continued to wave and to smile at the people who were by now thronging in masses on the bank.

If I had decided to, I genuinely believe I could have started a riot in London that day.

As the barge passed the Steelyard, the Thames base of the Hansa Merchants, a league of merchant traders who held ancient and vast international influence, the guards and I jumped to hear the sound of cannon fire. For one moment, I thought that we were under attack and someone was seeking to finish my life under a reign of fire… but no! The merchants were firing a salute to my barge as we passed their base. Bedingfield, ruffled and shaken, ordered the oarsmen to row faster, to speed our way along the river and through London which, it seemed, had turned out in full to celebrate my 'freedom'. It was becoming almost like a procession of glory, a royal progress if you will, rather than the movement of a prisoner from one gaol to the next. It was all rather pleasing both to my own vanity, and to my jostled spirits. I was particularly enjoying Bedingfield's many worried expressions; they were so varied and colourful. I was starting to think that I should have to write to my sister, and thank her for providing me with such an entertaining fool on this journey.

I was taken that night to Richmond Palace; the stronghold that my grandfather, King Henry VII, had rebuilt with its fantastical turrets and domes. As we stepped out from the barge and I was hurried up into the palace, I wondered again, and out loud, if anything violent would to happen to my person that night. Whenever we passed a crowd of people, held back by the guards that came with us, I tried to speak loudly about the possibility of my assassination. If I could stop this threat, just by making it clear I thought it was possible, I would not refrain from shouting it from the battlements themselves. Bedingfield became more and more anxious and disturbed the more I mentioned assassination, and he started to cast glances at me that were almost hurt, that I should address this possibility under his care and his watch of me. But I cared not. I should not go quietly into that destiny unless I had no other choice.

I was free of the Tower, if not free in actuality, and I was determined to fight for my life.

After a night of constantly disturbed sleep, both through my own dreams of assassins lurking in the bedchamber, and the pounding feet of Bedingfield's guards outside, I was taken across the Thames, where we set out on horse for the ancient palace of Woodstock, where, as Bedingfield told me, I should be kept under house arrest.

As we came to land on the bank opposite Richmond, I grinned as I spied a small gathering of faces that were most dear to me: Parry, John Astley and the Lady Elizabeth Sandes, a lady of the court who had served my bedchamber in the past. My servants, who had been taken from me, were now waiting to petition Bedingfield to let them join the travelling party, and serve me once again.

They waited politely and cautiously as Bedingfield went over and examined them, and my friends asked that a message be sent from me to them, so that they may know I was well and under no threat. When Bedingfield came back and asked that I send assurance, I said bleakly to tell them the words; "*Tanquam ovis*" which made Bedingfield blanch slightly.

I went on to modify. "Tell them this, Sir Henry," I said from the midst of the guards surrounding my horse, "*Behold, I send you forth as a sheep in the midst of wolves; be ye therefore wise as serpents, and harmless as doves.*"

He looked reassured; at least he did not have to go and tell them that I was simply *Tanquam ovis....* a *Lamb to the Slaughter.*

As Bedingfield went to go back to them I called out to him, "if you will not allow the men loyal to me to join my party, then at least allow the woman. The Lady Elizabeth Sandes served me long ago in my bedchamber and I have had all women but Mistress Blanche taken from me. It is not in keeping with the position of a princess of England, to have but one servant of the body."

Bedingfield didn't like the idea, but he had been most disturbed by the flocks of people through the city, and now this watchful party of my servants come to check my progress. My constant talk of assassination and his fears that my popularity might bring the wrath of the people on him had been enough to unnerve him. He allowed Lady Sandes to join our party, but said no others of my servants would do the same. Little did he know that the woman he had returned to my side was possibly the most *Protestant* Protestant in England. I fought back a smile to think how angry my sister would be when she heard. Mary did not approve of Lady Sandes at all.

The Lady Sandes made her way through the guards on her little blonde horse with a look of undisguised glee on her face. She and Blanche embraced whilst both still on horses, and I was touched when Sandes leapt from her saddle and prostrated herself in front of me in an elegant curtsey, professing her loyalty and love.

It was good to know that I indeed had friends in this world.

I was more amused when Bedingfield returned from having talked to Parry looking thoroughly disgruntled.

"What is the matter, Sir Henry?" We were still held in the same pattern at the side of the water, and the guards were starting to look restless.

He grimaced and turned to me. "I am now informed, my lady," he muttered, looking somewhat as though he was suffering from confined wind of the bowels, "that the cost of my soldiers and myself as your Head of Guard are to come from your own pocket, and as such, your man, Master Parry, has *insisted* that he accompany your household to see to the paying of the soldiers' wages, and to the smooth administration of our foods and other requirements." Bedingfield grunted, chewing distractedly on one of his finger nails.

I stared at him. "So," I asked slowly. "The cost of my imprisonment is to fall on my own shoulders?"

"Indeed, my lady. Such is the decree of the Queen. She insists that I am to take care of the financial arrangements since she does not want Master Parry to have any involvement with your person. However..." He trailed off. I knew what Bedingfield was thinking.

Bedingfield was not equipped to act as an accountant or administrator to something as vast as my lands, titles and tithes, my incomes, payments and privileges. He was a guard, a soldier, chosen for his loyalty to my sister, but not for having the brain of a clerk. He was not capable of doing the office that Parry presently did for my household, and he knew it. I was trying hard to suppress a smile. This must be an intolerable condition for Bedingfield to be in. Even though I would have to pay for my own incarceration, the enjoyment of seeing Bedingfield beholden to me for wages to pay his men and foods to feed them, and everything else in the prison I was going to, would almost be worth it. Better yet, it gave me an excuse to keep Parry nearby and to meet with him often. I smiled at my friends, my heart lifting by the moment.

It never does to promote a person past the sphere of their understanding and intellect; all that will end there is chaos. At least Bedingfield understood his own limitations, as so few do, and that understanding, gave me a door to open to my old servants. They were smiling at me, my servants, sitting on their horses and grinning with every muscle in their faces. I could have laughed, I could have cried. Such loyalty and cleverness are things to be most cherished in life. After all the horrors I had experienced in this thin slice of my existence, this was a welcome sight.

"Master Parry knows my business and estates well," I said brusquely. "And perhaps my royal sister had not considered all the responsibilities which would come to rest on your shoulders in this task of imprisoning me?"

Bedingfield cast a dark look at me; he knew he was being laughed at.

"They will accompany us for now, my lady," he agreed reluctantly. "When we arrive at the palace of Woodstock I will send word to Her Majesty to ask her guidance on the matter. If the Queen says they may stay, then they may stay."

I nodded my head as though acquiescing to his judgement, and as my head bowed I stifled a giggle under my chin. Humour often finds a space through the darkness to break free from, and its tickling hand upon the body is a welcome release from the evils of depression. We started out from the banks of the Thames towards Woodstock, and amongst the guards that rode behind me, followed a small band of people, inconsequential to most, but who to me were the very elixir of life.

CHAPTER TWENTY-EIGHT

The Road to Woodstock Palace
May 1554

Our journey from Richmond to the old palace of Woodstock took four days. Four of the strangest and yet most heartwarming days I have ever known.

The detachment of my servants that followed my own main guard was a source of constant agreeability to my heart. Blanche and Elizabeth Sandes were at my side and in them I found some solace for the loss of my beloved Kat. But the striking aspect of that journey, and the thing that really troubled Bedingfield, was the reaction of the people of England to the sight of me.

Everywhere, there were people gathering to see me. Everywhere, those people cried out "*God Save the Lady Elizabeth*!" as we passed.

Everywhere, there was *support* for me.

The scholars at Eton came out to mark my passage; village children were sent to carry baskets of produce and pretty cloth to me; at High Wycombe the women of the town had prepared so many cakes and wafers for us that the litter I was using at the time was completely filled with them. The smell of the pastries and spices were such that the guards started to become distracted by the heavenly scents, their hungry bellies grumbling. Eventually we had to ask the women to stop loading us with their gifts, although by that time tears of gratitude to these people for their offerings were pouring down my face. There were just so many of them, and this sudden outpouring of affection, after all the months of fear and strain in the Tower, quite overtook me.

"I would that you would take them to your own houses, feed your own children and your hard-working men with them," I importuned them. "I have enough here to feed me, but if I could take all the love that made these cakes and pastries, I should be fed for my whole life on your generosity."

Some of the women cried, others grasped at my clothes to whisper their support for me. They told me of how they had been grateful to my estates in years past, for during hard times, especially in the lean winter months, when my tenants had been well looked after. I remembered well the orders I gave to send bread, grain and fuel to those in need on my estates, and it seemed the people I had aided had not forgotten either.

The wages of generosity are love.

If my sister and her Council had thought about my place of imprisonment better, they would have thought that sending me into Buckinghamshire, where I owned vast estates, was perhaps not such a good idea. But to men who cannot conceive of charity unless it be done to advance one's own interests, to purchase a pardon, or to lessen the suffering of one's immortal soul... to such men, the idea of generosity to one's tenants and common folk is somewhat foreign. Because the lords of the Council did not act charitably to their tenants and farmers, they assumed no one else did either. Therefore, they had no true understanding of why the people loved me so. Bedingfield didn't know what to do. To send the crowds away would have caused an insurgence, something he feared most of all, so he had to let them approach, but he limited the time I spent with each huge party of well-wishers.

Poor Bedingfield! He was as much the lamb amongst the wolves there as I was, surrounded by his guards.

Farmers and workmen came out to mark my route, taking time from their labours to doff a cap, or touch their forelock at my progress. In some towns, men rang out church bells as I passed and were quickly chastised or arrested for their support of me. Everywhere along my route there were people eagerly awaiting a glimpse of their Protestant princess; the girl they had loved as a child, the woman who had offered them munificence in their times of need. They returned any such favours to me threefold on that journey; they warmed my heart with their support.

Even when we had passed from my own lands, the towns still turned out to shout "*God Save Your Grace*" to me as we passed. At Wheatley, Stanton St John, Islip and Gosford, whole towns came out to cheer for me, and to try to put on entertainments for us. Dancers and players came to perform for the party, although Bedingfield would not let us tarry long at each one. It was more like a royal progress than a guard escorting a prisoner.

We stayed each night with noble families: servants of my sister's, such as the Dormers, who were supposed to be guarding me and instead seemed to take my visit as an opportunity to attract my friendship, much to Bedingfield's disapproval. Jane Dormer, one of my sister's own ladies in waiting, served me at her parent's house on the road to Woodstock, and although I could tell that she little approved of me, having so high a regard for my sister, she was still warm enough. This meant, I believed, that her parents had much impressed upon her the need to keep the options of the family open, and befriend even a disgraced royal princess when she came to their house. This, and the behaviour of the people of the countryside, gave me hope.

Bedingfield was becoming visibly haggard from the stress of this avalanche of people. As we came into sight of the estate of Woodstock itself, he sagged a little, as though the weight of such a responsibility could not be held up by his broad Norfolk shoulders much longer.

But if Woodstock came as a welcome sight to him, it did not long remain so.

Royal palaces which are infrequently habituated are often in a state that requires repair before the commencement of any lengthy stay, but no such repairs had been made at Woodstock. The estate had been long a royal residence, but one only used infrequently; it came with not only the mundane problems of missing roof slates, smashed windows and broken walls that needed repair, but with another problem, particularly for an erstwhile gaoler.

There were only three doors in the palace which had locks.

CHAPTER TWENTY-NINE

Woodstock Palace
1554

Woodstock had been a royal residence since times of old. My great ancestor Henry I had built it as a hunting lodge, and Henry II had expanded it into a palace to house his mistress, the Fair Rosamund. Some said this was where Henry's Queen Eleanor had tracked down her rival in the maze, and offered her the choice of a dagger or a cup of poison by which to die. By all accounts, the Queen Eleanor was not a woman to meddle with… especially not when it came to her husband.

More recently, my grandfather and father had used Woodstock for hunting, but that now was many years ago. The grounds were fair and pretty, but the house was in a state of much dilapidation. Only some of the chambers were habitable and much of the building was in goodly need of care; broken windows, crumbled walls and a feeling of abject neglect was what I felt when I looked on Woodstock. And all these things put another strain on the back of Sir Bedingfield.

How was a gaoler to lock up a prisoner when there were no locks?

I looked at the dilapidated palace and wondered at my situation. I had never thought to stay in a ruin… How was I to live here, and how was Bedingfield ever to keep those who supported me from infiltrating a house as vast, broken and unwieldy as this royal palace? Even with the profusion of guards he had been given, he would be unable to guard the estate's entirety… Meaning that me and mine would have to be largely trusted to go about our days without effort of escape.

Bedingfield was chewing the inside of his cheek as though he meant to fashion himself a second mouth, so I knew this was as avid a concern to him as it was a pleasurable thought to me. He feared that I was going to escape from this broken-down palace… it might have been easy for me to do so, but I was not going to try to escape from Woodstock; if I did so then the only option left to me would be to meet my sister in all-out war. If I was to defy her wishes and escape, I should have to raise a force to protect my body and self from re-capture. I would be forced to lift a standard of civil war against my sister. I did not want it to come to that.

But that did not mean that I was willing to fade into obscurity in the ramshackle palace in the country that my sister had sent me to. Was I to become as forgotten and neglected as the walls and grounds of this poor palace? No! I was going to continue to be as well–informed as I had been, to rebuild my power and station, and one day, to return to court as an honoured guest. For all those things to occur, I needed my good, careful servants about me once more. No man can make his way in this world without companions to travel with; not unless he wishes for a hard and lonely journey.

The first problems, of where to house me and my servants was overcome quite swiftly as Bedingfield assessed the palace and found it wanting in all ways. He settled for holding us in the old gatehouse. Although he chose for us the largest rooms in the cramped gatehouse, they were barely adequate for the task of housing all of us. We had four rooms; not enough to house all my servants, barely enough to house myself. I complained long and loud on the subject, but since there were few other options if I wanted a roof over my head rather than a bare gap through which to count the stars. I had little choice but to agree to be housed in a place more suited to a few soldiers. My household servants, sent back to me upon my release, had to be housed in Woodstock town, and travel to serve me daily. Only Blanche and Elizabeth Sandes could live with me all the time. I liked not the confined feeling the chambers of the gatehouse gave me, but later, as the winter approached, I had reason to be thankful for that closeness. At least there was not far to move from the fire.

Bedingfield received word that Mary wanted Parry as far from my person as possible, but Bedingfield countered that he was unable to take the role of my Master of Coin or find suitable replacement elsewhere. Parry was therefore allowed to remain in Woodstock, but not at the palace; instead he took a room in the Bull's Inn in the town, and went about his affairs from there.

From Bedingfield's perspective, the situation was horrific. Parry sent dozens of servants each day to me, apparently to conduct our daily affairs, but in actual fact to pass on news and messages that I was never supposed to receive... and Bedingfield could do little about it. The result was that Bedingfield ran from suspicion to suspicion, never knowing which servant was sent to discuss the price of bread and which was sent to give me news of the world outside my prison. Bedingfield spent much time, like a dog enamoured of the disappearing slight of its own tail, turning circles to try and discover what we were up to.

Although this may give you bad impression of me, it was a pleasure to see the man who was sent to be my jailer fighting to retain order in his own house.

There are times in life when one has been so downtrodden, and so badly used, that the slightest hint of amusement causes the spirits to lift to giddy heights. I had come so close to death over the past few months that I will excuse myself of the spiteful pleasures I took in making Sir Henry dance to the tune that Parry and I played. I had had very little to laugh about of late. So I made the man my fool, to amuse me; it was perhaps not commendable to my character, but it still makes me smile even now. I would not have treated him as harshly as I did, if he had not been so incredibly annoying in himself.

Sir Henry Bedingfield was *most* irritating to me, and so I delighted to see that I annoyed him also. It is most pleasing to the spirit to find that when something vexes you, you can give as much trouble back. But for all that, Mary had given me one great mercy by making him my guard. For in Sir Henry there was not that slip of the soul that would allow him to knowingly have me assassinated. He had been asked to guard me, to report on any suspicious occurrences around me, to respect my lineage and position, to keep me away from ill influences and prevent my association with anyone from the outside world. This, he performed to the best of his limited ability, but in that one respect he did me great service. Bedingfield, no matter how annoying he found me, no matter how great a danger he saw in me, would never allow me to come to danger of death under his guard.

I little appreciated it at the time, but my sister's choice of an honest and loyal jailer was just another small favour that may well have saved my life. Mary could not have found another man who should have so doggedly and devotedly attempted to keep his word to her.

Hindsight is of course something that is revealing of many truths. At the time, I simply revelled in seeing Sir Henry twist and turn to our little tune. Perhaps it is the small mercies in life that we come to be most grateful for with time. Bedingfield may have been dull, punctilious, and at the same time, hesitating and annoying, but he did work to keep my person safe from threat of assassination.

So together, my dull gaoler and I, along with every spy that ever there was, sent by Parry, settled into life at Woodstock and I took every chance I could to make Bedingfield dance for my own amusement.

CHAPTER THIRTY

Woodstock Palace
June 1554

Although they could so little about the person of Parry, who from the Bull's Inn was making his own empire of spies wending their way about Woodstock and around the country for my benefit, Mary and her Council could, and did, remove Elizabeth Sandes from my side almost as soon as she had arrived. I knew it would not be long before they did so, but Sandes' appearance at my side as we travelled had given me heart and reminded me of times long past, when our store of troubles was barer than it was now.

Upon hearing the lady was within my house, Mary wrote to Bedingfield that Lady Sandes was "*more Lutheran than Luther.*" Such a phrase, I believe, was at one time levelled against my own mother. Mary wrote that Sandes was "*of evil opinion, and not fit to remain about our sister's person*".

Bedingfield came rushing to us to remove Lady Sandes as soon as he received the missive of my sister; being an ardent and devoted Catholic himself, he came to my cramped chambers in the gatehouse and regarded Sandes with the eyes of one who fears he sees the devil. Previous to this letter from my sister, I would say that Bedingfield had found Elizabeth Sandes to be a most charming woman. But of course, the stain of religious difference is often enough to make a beautiful person ugly, or a good person appear evil, if our own view is pointed in the opposite direction. Our appreciation or disapproval of a person merely depends on which way our perspective is bent.

Bedingfield had to deliver the ill news of Sandes' removal from my household on bended knee. Unfortunately for him, my sister's decrees requiring respect for my position meant that every time he ordered me to do something, every time he denied my wishes, and indeed, every time he reprimanded me like a small child, he had to do so, on bended knee. Even though I was a prisoner, I was still a royal princess, and nothing had been proved against me to stop this little ritual of respect from occurring.

I must confess a type of perverse pleasure in seeing him having to try to order and admonish me, whilst kneeling before me in deference. It almost made up for all the little indignities and annoyances I had to suffer at his hands.

When he told us of Lady Sandes' forthcoming removal from my household that afternoon, we were sad, but we knew that we had been enjoying time borrowed but for a while from the realm of happiness. Sandes grinned at Bedingfield's look of horror at her.

"Don't worry, dear Sir Henry," she said gaily. "I am sure in the few hours we have left together I shall not corrupt the eternal soul of the princess."

Bedingfield did not look at all convinced of that, and he crossed himself, bowed to me and left us to our packing, muttering to himself. As he left the room, we broke out into peals of laughter, and I heard him pause at the door, no doubt somewhat shamed by the sound of two young maids laughing at him.

I said before that my treatment of him does little to commend my character. But I was about to lose another friend and ally to the whims of my sister; I was in no temper to be kind to the man taking Lady Sandes from me.

That afternoon, I walked Sandes out to the inner courtyard. I was not allowed any farther from the palace. It was a balmy afternoon with a soft June wind blowing. Wildflowers were flourishing throughout the ill-kept estate and the grasses which led to the great forests danced prettily in the breeze. Woodstock was beautiful even if it was a wreck; had I not been about to say goodbye to yet another friend, I should have relished the feel of the soft sunlight on my skin, and looked on the flowers with joy. After so long spent inside, the outside air felt good and clean to my body and spirits.

"I shall miss you, Elizabeth," I said as we parted.

"And I you, my lady princess,"

"Where do you go from here?"

"To my father's house in Kent," she then cast her eyes at the slightly removed figure of Bedingfield standing to watch for any trickery as Sandes left me. Lady Sandes smiled widely at him, making him blush and cough, turning his face away as though he but regarded the beauty of the day. I smiled at her, shaking my head. "Although soon," she added, "and if your sister keeps her will for the soul of this country, we mayhap will be moving on, across the waters."

"Would you leave England?" I whispered, feeling mournful at the thought.

"It may well be, my lady that it will not be safe to remain here much longer." Elizabeth looked around again, her voice falling to barely a murmur. "For those of us whom your sister already knows to be Protestant, it seems there is coming a time when we will either have to suffer for our beliefs, or leave, until such time as it may be safe to return."

Sandes looked at me with a gentle smile and pressed her hands into mine. "You are our *hope,* my lady," she said quietly, "our hope that one day we may live in the religion we were born to, the one true faith; to be ruled by one who knows the truth of God's words."

"Hush!" I whispered. "You must speak more quietly even than that whisper if you do not want us to become parted from our heads." I looked around me. No one could have heard us. Bedingfield was still standing nearby, plucking the heads from grasses at the edge of the castle wall, for what purpose, I had little idea. I think he was trying to look as though he were occupied fully with another task other than watching us. The man was as subtle as a dragon wandering amid a herd of cows.

"I would rather that you and others like you were alive and well in the world, Elizabeth," I said softly. "Although martyrs are the blessed of God, I would that if I ever become Queen, that I had many left of my own mind who might come to show the truth of God to others. You cannot do that if you are not in this world. As for myself, I must fulfil my sister's wishes as to my religion, and pretend to be a good Catholic, or I shall surely find myself on the block like poor Jane Grey."

"Aye," she nodded. "And there are enough of us who think the same. We know that you are of the true faith, my princess. Fear not for us. We are strong and true. If your sister brings the fires of the Inquisition to England along with her Spanish husband, then we will have to leave, but we will not travel so far that we might not return as soon as you have need of us, or as soon as we may all have reason to rejoice for the coming of a new age. As long as we have you, we have hope. Keep that in mind, my lady, when things are darkest. You must stay alive. You must survive... for you are the future of our hope and of the light of God."

I kissed her and I watched her leave.

Soon enough there would come a time when Elizabeth Sande's words would echo in my head. At the time, I thought the fires of religious persecution were a far off possibility. Certainly Mary had always had her own zeal for her religion, but she had spoken of tolerance when she first came to the throne and I wanted to believe her in that.

But her tolerance of my Protestantism had barely lasted a few weeks, so when would Mary turn her critical gaze on the rest of her subjects?

A little chill ran down my spine and legs. In the warm afternoon, as we waved off Elizabeth Sandes and her guard from the prison of Woodstock, it was almost as though I could hear the first crackle of wood on a bonfire, and smell the scent of burning flesh on the wind.

CHAPTER THIRTY-ONE

Woodstock Palace
Summer- Autumn 1554

On the 25th of July 1554, my sister did, as they tell us in fairy-tales, what all women must do to secure a happy ending; she married her prince.

Phillip of Spain, son of the great Emperor Charles V, landed in England to meet his bride, and to embark on their adventure of the greatest Catholic union this land had ever seen. Mary was ecstatic; so long had my sister desired the comfort of belonging to a family, something which our own father stole from her when she was but a young maid; and now, she was marrying the man of her dreams.

A Catholic prince, and.... a handsome prince.

Oh yes, there was no denying the good looks of Phillip; all those who witnessed either his arrival, or the marriage in Winchester conducted by the gloating Gardiner, agreed on that point. However much the English did not like the foreign prince come to marry their Queen, they did allow that he was handsome, well-formed and had a good leg.

Two good legs this prince would need for a sure footing on this foreign island.

His hair was blonde. His skin was a little darker than that of the pale nobles of England. He was goodly tall and well-built; he was a warrior, soldier, a noble man, and a prince of a vast empire.

But still, the English were suspicious. Worried that Spain still would try to take control of their country through the bonds of the marriage contract; worried that this Catholic prince from a land of spice and heat would too bring the fires of Spain's infamous Inquisition to ferret out heretics and Protestants and burn them on their *fires of mercy*.

But for now, such worries were for the future. After all, there are few events that people enjoy more in England than a royal wedding, no matter who the people are who are involved.

I heard reports from Parry's spies that Mary was overjoyed with her striking and yet reserved prince. Such luck she had, in not only finding a mate who matched her in lineage and religion, but a handsome one at that! Not all women are so lucky. If Mary was delighted in the attractive looks of her new husband, it was rumoured that Phillip was not so enamoured of his new wife. Mary was about thirty-eight by then, an advanced age for a woman entering her first marriage. Her life had worn her with struggle, hardship and unrest. Beneath the brilliant clothes she wore, I knew well her body was thin to the point of emaciation. Most of her teeth were gone; her eyesight was poor and faded. Her breasts were padded with folds of cloth to give her, in public, a more womanly figure, and her dresses were puffed and slashed to give her figure more life and vitality. Her skin was dressed with cosmetics, plumped up with cochineal and patted with powder to make her look youthful, beautiful.

All this was well enough, in public… but she could little disguise the infirmities of her body to her husband when they came naked to one another in the bedchamber. Then she would be exposed before him; unadorned and un-painted by the skills of the ladies of the court.

In all the truth of the naked body, there is little of the stature of royalty.

With all the harsh imagination of my youth, I curled my lip to think of Phillip's duty in the royal bed; I was much subject to the whim of beauty and therefore could not imagine that he could find much in my sister's body to excite a feeling of passion in him. But royalty does not have the choice that common man may often have; where and when to spill one's seed, and who to mate with, are much more matters of politics than of passion to kings and princes.

Their marriage was consummated on the night of the wedding. And if Mary was most content in this, we heard little murmurs on the wind that Phillip went to his duty that night, and all subsequent nights, with reluctance. In public however, he was the model of a genial and devoted husband. Although there was a strong and powerful side to me which resented what my sister had put me through and her present control over my person, I could not help but feel a little glad for her, that she had someone finally who would at least act as though they loved her in truth.

They spent much of the late summer hunting, riding and celebrating, and the people of England seemed to take a deep breath of relief in this season of celebration that had followed such a time of turmoil. The dreaded Inquisition, who persecuted Protestants and heretics in Spain, did not appear hard on the heels of the new king-consort of England, and so the people began to hope that this new marriage may bring some good to England after all.

As the royal couple frolicked around their estates together, I was stationary and stagnant. The euphoria of trouncing Bedingfield in all the little ways I could muster was wearing thin, and the man was just agonisingly stubborn in his devotion to his duty. To take an example; when first I came to Woodstock Palace, I was not allowed to write to anyone, this was decreed by the Queen, and Bedingfield took this to mean that I was also not allowed to write to the Queen or her Council, a point that I spent hours, meaningless hours, wasted from my life, arguing with the man. Finally, he asked the Council about my request. They passed the request on to Mary, who said she would be "*pleased*" to take my letters.

When finally the dull-witted Bedingfield came to me and, kneeling before me, told me that I *was* allowed to write to my sister, I did not know whether I should slap the man, or embrace him.

Then there was his constant and unrelenting suspicion of me. Now, to be entirely fair to the man, I *was* often up to something I should not have been, especially in my meetings with anyone coming from the direction of the Bull's Inn and Parry's by-now infamous base there. But that fact, I felt, did not give Bedingfield the right to suspect *all* my actions of having a base in wrong-doing. If someone delivered books to me, he sent them to the Council to be gone over by their scribes to find a code or message in cipher; if someone brought presents of cloth or thread to my door, then he searched them; if someone delivered fish, then those fish would no doubt be interrogated thoroughly by his men before they were allowed to my table. The man made everything so intolerably slow and annoying and if I was never very patient with those slower than me, Bedingfield was enough to drive any person out of their wits with rage.

And, there was the journal he kept about me. Such was the importance of his mission to hold me as a prisoner of the Queen, and such were the difficulties he found with that order, that at some stage early in our irritating encounter, he had convinced himself that the only way to be sure that his actions on any matter could not come back to haunt him, cause his arrest or in some way get him into trouble with the Queen and Council, was to keep a record of his interactions with me. Harmless enough, you may think, but it was remarkable how exasperating I found the expression on his face when I could see him making a mental note of what he had to write down when he left. Sometimes during longer meetings, he would scratch out lines with a little quill, which tore at my already fractious soul. When one starts to find a person irritating, it is amazing how fast that escalates until every action, no matter how mundane, become a reason for murder. I believe that in my own head, I had killed Bedingfield half a hundred times during our stay at Woodstock.

Being cooped up together with little other company did nothing to help the situation. As grating as I found him, the feeling was constantly and faithfully mirrored in his own mind. He found me utterly infuriating and although he had to pay due respect to me in person, he started to refer scathingly to me in his little journal as "*This Great Lady*". I knew of this for I had one of Parry's men steal the book, and give it to me, for an afternoon of most interesting reading.

As I said, I *was* usually up to something. But that gave Bedingfield no right to suppose it of me.

The time went on so slowly at Woodstock. The more Bedingfield annoyed me, the more I wanted to annoy him.... Two old cats we were, picking fights with each other in an alleyway over a fish head. As we two felines fought through our days together, there came more news from the court. That winter, Parliament announced the legal return of England to the authority of the See of Rome. Protestant Bishops who had served under my brother, Ridley, Latimer and my own godfather, Thomas Cranmer, were arrested and imprisoned in Oxford and London. The papal legate, Cardinal Pole, once exiled from England for treason during the reign of our father, was cleared of all charges, and invited to our shores. Cecil had been chosen as the man to bring the Cardinal back to English shores, and Cecil wrote to inform me of this, as well as to assure me that from now on, Cecil himself would be known as a 'good Catholic'. Much as I wore the mask of conversion, my good Cecil did so too. It was becoming dangerous to be known as a Protestant, and for Cecil to keep his positions at court and in the House of Commons, he had to profess a change of heart in his religion.

The Catholic faith was returned in truth to England. Although Bedingfield was merry to see these changes, I was not. I knew well enough what such a return meant and if any were in doubt, they only had to look at the arrest of the Bishops to see that Protestantism would no longer be tolerated under my sister's reign. I wondered with fear on Elizabeth Sandes and others I knew from my childhood who would be looking on this ill news as I did. My cousins of the blood of the Boleyns, Catherine and Henry Carey, my servants, my old tutor Roger Asham… would they be now considering whether to fly or to fall? Whether to pretend to be Catholic to stay in their country, or leave their homeland for freedom of religious belief?

But something else happened that had even more significance for me than all of these occurrences. Although Mary was firmly marching her country back into the power of the Catholic faith, into the authority of Rome, there was something of far greater significance that allowed her to do all of this with great confidence.

Barely a few weeks after her marriage night, there came rumours that the Queen was pregnant. After two months, it seemed sure. My sister's old and aged womb had proved itself fertile to Phillip's seed.

In her belly there grew a Catholic heir to her now Catholic throne. All rumours said the same. The Queen was pregnant.

If Mary gave birth to a son, then my position as the heir to the throne would be gone and all my hopes of one day becoming Queen of this realm, would fade… and die.

CHAPTER THIRTY-TWO

Woodstock Palace
Autumn- Winter 1554

I have often had occasion to think, that if we Tudors had not been made for kingship, we may have turned our cap to the world of the stage and made a pretty penny from that living instead. We would have been masters at the trade of play-acting. After all, when my sister was gasping to marry her Catholic prince of Spain, she had handily incorporated the divinity of the Holy Spirit to tell her to do so; a fine tale to tell to all those who might doubt the sanctity of her crown and marriage. Then in this winter, we had another example of her wondrous acting skills.

As my sister returned her divided and uncertain country back to Rome, the newly arrived Cardinal Pole greeted the Queen by comparing her to the Virgin Mary; "Hail; thou art highly favoured, the Lord is with thee, blessed are thou amongst women," the Cardinal said as he blessed Mary upon arrival at the court in London.

That precise moment was when my sister's child, growing inside her thin body, chose to *quicken*, moving in her womb for the first time, supposedly in response to the power of the Cardinal's words. Mary was overjoyed to find that her child was responsive, not only to life, but to her faith. It seemed, everyone said, astounding, that the royal babe should have felt such a response to such an occasion, and everyone was talking of it as though it were a miracle. I personally, have always been a little suspicious of miracles; especially those which involved my sister. Mary seemed to have a lot of miracles occurring in her life; and in general, such wonders all too often turn out to be much more mundane than miraculous… with more in common with duplicity than deity… I did not of course voice this to anyone; such a suspicion is better kept inside the heart. But I could not help but wonder if this miracle of my sister's was much as the last divine intervention had been; at best wishful thinking, at worst deliberate deceit. Bedingfield, on the other hand, was as happy as I had ever seen him. He even whistled to himself as he walked out in the morning on his rounds about the palace. The idea of a continuation of the Catholic line in England made him awfully happy and almost amenable.

I found his joy perhaps more intolerable than his previous sighs and groans.

Parry sent word to me that Phillip was apparently most happy that his nightly duty in the royal chamber was at an end for now, but the Prince had been much surprised to see how swiftly his wife had conceived. Parry also mentioned in cipher to me that Phillip's first wife had taken much longer than a bare few weeks to find herself with child.

It seemed I was not the only one harbouring a few suspicions on Mary's blessed state.

That winter was as chilling to the body as it was to my soul. The gatehouse of Woodstock was most unsuited to weathering a winter;

broken windows and drafts pinched coldness into my very bones. I was not allowed to ride out to warm my blood through motion, so I wrapped myself in wool and fur, trying to find where I had left the warmness of the summer. Poor Blanche seemed to become ever paler and on some days was positively blue. Only Bedingfield, warmed by the news of my sister's condition and the fire of his religion's rejuvenation in the country, seemed unaffected by the horrible conditions we suffered in that old palace. He even allowed my servants to bring greenery into the gatehouse at Christmas, so cheered was he by the news of my sister's growing babe.

I spent much of the winter writing to the Council to protest my innocence still. After haggling with the irksome Bedingfield for weeks on end, I finally had permission to write to both my sister and her Council to petition for my release. If nothing else kept me warm, then the constant scratch of my quill and the unending stream of protestations I made in my own name at least kept me from the chill of death that winter.

In terms of my religion, I had become almost a model of Catholicism for my sister; hearing Catholic Mass as she had asked, even giving up hearing the Litany in English which I had a marked love for. I wished I could hear it still. In some ways it gave me a link to that poor man in prison in Oxford, Cranmer, my godfather, who had translated the Litany during the reign of my father. There was something in it that had hastened to my soul when I first heard it, and giving up this slight thing was a great ache to my spirit. Its words spoke thus;

"Remember not, Lord, our offences, nor the offences of our forefathers,

Neither take Thou vengeance of our sins; spare us Good Lord, spare thy people whom Thou has redeemed with thy most precious blood, and be not angry with us forever."

And then;

"From all sedition, privy conspiracy and rebellion, from all false doctrine. Spare us."

Perhaps you can see why this struck a note in my heart. I thought of my past betrayal of my stepmother Katherine Parr; when her new husband, my stepfather Thomas Seymour had pursued me, a young and inexperienced girl, within the halls of Katherine's own house. Although much time had passed since then, and although, being older, I could look back and see myself as a young girl much taken advantage of by an older man… I could still not erase the feelings of shame from my heart for those months in Chelsea. Nor could I ever truly rest, knowing that poor Katherine had gone to her grave in sorrow knowing that the husband and stepdaughter she had so loved, had betrayed her love and trust in them. Seymour never achieved his ambition to bed me, but yet I still felt a weight of guilt on my shoulders, for past sins, however much they were led and encouraged by another, which had so torn the heart of my good stepmother, Katherine.

I thought too of my own mother and father and the ills they had done, to Mary in particular. I thought of the false doctrine to which I was being forced to bow to by my sister. So, yes, for many reasons, all most personal to me, the Litany was a thing close to my heart for its words and the sentiment of those words. But this happiness too, I gave up to the whim of my sister. Those who would not met their end in fire.

In October of 1554, Protestant Bishops Latimer and Ridley walked out to their deaths. They were to be burned alive. Refusing to turn their souls and convert to the Catholic faith, they would be the first of the Protestant martyrs made by my sister, but they would not be the last. On that chilly day in October, Latimer looked at the pale face of Ridley and perhaps wondered if he saw fear in the heart of the man condemned to die burning beside him. As they stood before the crowds in the pale autumn sunshine, looking on the bonfires which were to become the last witnesses of their lives on earth, Latimer turned to Ridley, smiled, and spoke;

"Fear not, good friend Ridley. For today we light such a candle for faith that shall burn without ever dying out."

There are few people who think to say something truly wondrous at the worst of times. But these people, these few... their words echo through history for ever more.

The two men, flanked by dried wood and straw, suffered their last on this earth in a burning mass of flame and smoke. I hope with all my heart that they had suffocated to death long before they felt their flesh melt from the body, and sensed the fat slipping from their bones to the floor.

Five months later, in March 1555, my godfather Cranmer too left this world in the arms of flame and fire. He recanted his faith at first, to save himself... for fear of the fires of faith he swore to be a Catholic. But then he returned to his true faith and was put to death for it.

Tied to the stake, before the fire had reached his body, Cranmer pushed his right hand into the flames boldly and watched it burn before him. As the flames consumed his right hand, he declared to the crowds about him that the part of him which signed his recantation of the Protestant faith should be the first to die, for that was the part that had betrayed him. But that hand should be the only part of him to suffer; "For all else of my body and soul I know I return to God in the fullness of the true faith."

He died that day in a forest of flame. Cranmer, that man so beloved of my mother, the instigator of the reform of faith under my father... killed by my sister for that same reformed faith.

Poor men... poor learned and devoted men.

They were willing to die for their faith. I was not willing to die. Was I any less brave for wishing to *live* for my faith rather than die for it? I did not want to die, so I pretended to be a Catholic, converted to the faith of the Queen.

The deaths of those Bishops marked the advent of the persecution of Protestants in England.

So began the reign of my sister's terror.

Protestants either burned for their faith, or they ran, or they hid. Many Protestant nobles retired to their country estates to try and live quietly without being seen by the roaming eye of my sister. Elizabeth Sandes and many other Protestants left England and fled abroad, exiles from the Promised Land. Those of us who had not the option to flee, or escape Mary's gaze, put on Catholic masks and covered our faces, praying to God to forgive us, until the day we should be able to show our true visage to the world, without fear of death and persecution.

Run or hide, or burn and die. Those were the choices my sister's reign gave to those who followed any faith but hers.

CHAPTER THIRTY-THREE

Woodstock Palace
Spring 1555

The first feeling of spring is a glorious thing, and never more welcome after a hard winter of little comfort. The first morning I felt the lessening of the chill in the air and the slightest warmth on the breeze, I knew the end of winter had come; I turned my face to the window, felt the still wane sun smile on my skin and felt my heart rise within me as though it were a sunflower following the sun in the heavens with its gaze.

Pale and tired we emerged from that winter at Woodstock; I felt much weakened by the winter. I felt removed from the court, from life, even though my sister had declined to actually take my head the year before, it felt as though she had removed life from me all the same. Woodstock had been a harsh mistress to me and mine that winter; she had taken our spirits even as she chilled us with her drafts. I swore that if I ever again attained my freedom in truth, I should ensure that any palace I resided in would be properly maintained and mended.

I had been at Woodstock for almost a whole year as a prisoner, shut away from the world, kept under the irritating company of my foolish gaoler and still not cleared from suspicion of treason in the Wyatt rebellion. Fears of my own assassination had long-ago lifted and now were replaced with fears that I should simply waste away and die in obscurity. I felt old, after a winter of chilled blood, running noses, painfully cold ears and shooting pains through joints that should be far too young to know anything like the rheumatics of age.

Bedingfield, too, had suffered bodily through this winter; not only with the swollen joints and stiffened hands of an aged ex-soldier, but also with the constant pressure of me as a prisoner. The only thing that warmed me that chill season was the look of impotent exasperation on his face with my every word and deed. What warmed him of course was the news of my sister's pregnancy.

I had begun to think that my sister merely intended to shut me away for good. I would become a myth, a lost princess in a castle sitting around waiting to be rescued by a knight… or in my case, a princess swathed in blankets hacking, sneezing and coughing by her fire as she tried to recall her past courage to keep her warm. There was little to cheer me in soul; Protestants fleeing the country, hiding, or burning for their faith; my sister expecting the imminent arrival of a child who would supplant me as heir to the throne, and I was still a constant captive held under the wishes of the Crown.

In frustration at my continued incarceration, I even turned to verse; one day, taking up a knife used for a delicate cut of meat, I inscribed words which had been turning in my head for some time into the shutter of a window in our chambers.

"O Fortune, thy wresting, wavering state
Hath fraught with care my troubled wit,
Whose witness this present prison late
Could bear, where once was joy flown quite.
Thou causest the guilty to be loosed
From lands where innocents were enclosed,
And caused the guiltless to be reserved,
And freed those that death had well deserved.
But all herein can be naught wrought
So God grant to my foes as they have thought."

Under the verse I wrote:

"*Finis*, Elisabetha, a prisoner 1555
Much suspected of me, but nothing proved can be."

I took then a diamond from my finger and wrote the last line on the glass of the window. Blanche and my servants stared at me as I etched the line into the glass, to be held forever in its visage.

"Much suspected of me, but nothing proved can be."

Bedingfield was not pleased when he saw what I had been carving into the palace shutters in our chambers. They were not undamaged as it was, and he little liked the sentiment of the verse, wondering as ever if he would get into trouble for another of my acts. But I cared not. I was almost resigned to wasting away in this pitiful palace with more drafts than windows, and more leaks than good roof. At least I could leave a few words behind, so that there was some small proof that I had even lived at all.

But then… the spring came.

It is a remarkable thing how the spirits may be lifted by the change of season, and just as one thinks all is lost, salvation comes. It is the sun I think; we grow so used in the winter in England, to losing so much of the day to the night and to darkness… but when the spring comes, we see the power of the light to make the darkness retreat at her coming. We see the flowers start to reappear through the seemingly barren, brown earth… We see life return to the world around us and it gives us hope; for in seeing the world re-born to life, we come to believe that the same might happen for us.

As our chambers warmed in the first soft days of spring, as we started to move back from the fire because it was *too warm*, as Bedingfield allowed us out for short spaces of time into the courtyard to walk; my ladies and I started to breathe freely and to *see* around us once more. In the cold we had become huddled, not only in a corner near the fire, but in a corner of the world, shut away from all else. We had ceased to look about us, and even with the ministrations of Parry at the inn at Woodstock, we were still closed off from the world. With the return of the sun, came the return of hope. Our bent backs and hunched forms unfolded, our tired, cold eyes opened wider. We could step into the air and face the light chill of the spring with humour. We could sleep at night without clinging together to keep warm.

And with the changing of the seasons came the realisation that other things would also change.

In April, Mary and her husband moved to Hampton Court to await the birth of her child. The country was celebrating the coming birth of the new prince or princess even as it cringed from looking at the ongoing burnings of Protestants. I heard of the fires of faith and sighed to be so far from all that was occurring in the country. Although I little wanted to see those of my faith burn at the stake, I wondered if I could not be doing more to help were I there… hiding or concealing members of my faith from the fires of Mary's 'mercy' perhaps. And, then, a letter arrived at Woodstock.

Bedingfield read it to me, kneeling before me as usual with the disgruntled look of an annoyed rodent on his face.

"The Queen, my sister, sends for me?" I asked. The words sounded most foreign and wondrous to me.

"That is so, my lady," he said with his ever-grudging air of respect. "We are to take you to Hampton Court and we are not to call reinforcements. The Queen writes that my men and I will be suitable for the task of bringing you to the court."

I pondered this. Mary was now at ease in her condition, and in that contentment perhaps she was feeling more generous towards me. Whatever the case, and for whatever reason, I was to leave Woodstock, finally! I was to leave my prison, to go into the world once again… I was to go to court! You cannot imagine what effect this had on me. I did not even think much on what might happen to me there; just the idea of a change of station and company was enough to make me quite giddy and girlish with joy.

Much to the annoyance of Bedingfield.

"My sister wishes to share her happy condition with me, Sir Henry," I grinned from ear to ear at him. "Is not it fine that we should travel to see her?"

He looked ruefully at me; he did not relish *any* journey with me, especially not one where he might again have to answer for any joyful reception extended to me by the common man. He feared that if the greeting for my person was too jubilant, then his mistress would be displeased.

I fixed him with a glittering eye. "Come, Sir Henry," I said with barely disguised glee in my voice. "Whether they plan to nurture or murder me once we reach the court, perhaps there will come a time soon when you and I shall part company, and never have to endure each other again. That must be something to rejoice in, must it not?"

He nodded thoughtfully, almost smiled, and then caught himself as though he were about to deny his hatred for me. I waved my finger at him as though he were a naughty boy and felt the wave of vexation that radiated from him.

"*Tusk, tusk* Sir Henry," I cried gaily, waggling my finger at him. "One must not lie. My goodly priest tells me that God sees to the centre of all our souls, so, it does no good to lie. You find me to be difficult as you are unused to the way of princes and *higher* nobility, and I find you difficult as you are totally unsuited in both manner and intellect to perform the task of guarding me. I *understand* this defect in you. It is not your fault, for God made us all, but some with talents... above yours. There is no shame in humility before the Lord, Sir Henry, so we must not lie for the sake of courtesy."

Do you think me cruel? Perhaps, but then you had not endured almost a year of the man.

"My lady," he said with his teeth gritted, fidgeting on his bended, deferential knee to me. "I must go and prepare the household to move and meet Her Majesty's commands."

"Off you *trot* then, Sir Henry!" I said with a little wave as though he was a spaniel I was shooing from before me. As he left the room, muttering to himself, I turned to Blanche and we burst out in a huge gale of laughter.

"To London then!" I said, grasping at her hands. We started to gamble around the room in a little circle of whirling feet and dresses. "And hopefully *forever* to *never* set foot at this ramshackle pile of bricks they called a palace again!" I said as we danced about the room laughing.

We set out for Hampton Court the next morning, and although the exhilaration of freedom from the prison of Woodstock invigorated my blood, the worry of what was yet to come when I met my sister once more increasingly invaded my thoughts as we rode towards the beauty of Hampton Court Palace.

I became thoughtful.... What did my sister want of me now?

CHAPTER THIRTY-FOUR

Richmond Palace
February 1603

The heart plays with us, as though we were puppets that dance to its tune, rather than rational creatures of thought and sense.

That which we wish for, the heart tells us we deserve.

That which we desire, the heart tells us we will have.

The heart is a spoilt, petulant child that knows not the boundaries of its own power, and is continually unfulfilled no matter how many have swooned or cried over it. The heart is an enemy like no other, for we recognize little the traps it places in our path. We think we act on our own virtue, in our own stead, with our own mind, but ever pushing our feet towards its own desires, is the heart.

Traitor! What other being could so betray all that was logical in a person so easily and yet survive to trick us again? What other creation could let us down over and over again and yet remain within us?

Mary may have wanted us all to think that her marriage was ordained by God, that her belly was blessed also in his eyes, but was this truly the work of the Lord? Or was it the hope of a woman, so blinded by her desire to fulfil the path her mother set her on and her father stole from her, that she would do anything, take any step, and see any portent to continue with it?

The heart is our most dangerous enemy. We do not see, until it is far too late, the peril its puts us in, or the damage it is capable of doing.

Mary was following her heart, in all her choices, and it was about to lead her into the greatest pain she would ever know in a life made of suffering, neglect and maltreatment.

CHAPTER THIRTY-FIVE

Hampton Court Palace
April 1555

I arrived at Hampton Court on the 24th of April and was quietly and secretly ushered into the Prince of Wales' Lodgings; apartments which had been built for my brother Edward when he was a child, by our father. Bedingfield released his guardianship over me with a relieved sigh as I was ushered into my quarters. There was no proclamation on our arrival for a princess of the realm, there was no welcome from Mary, there was no delegation from the Council, or even a message from either they or my sister… There was just a little line of guards waiting for us. Quietly and quickly, I was put into another royal prison. This one was just closer to the Queen.

I felt dejected and cursed at myself for my enthusiasm on the journey here. I was fallen lower in spirits now because I allowed myself to become too happy at the message to return to court. What had I expected truly? Wildly, perhaps, I had hoped for my final freedom, to be allowed my former liberty, return to my estates and to my servants… perhaps even for my sister to admit that she had imprisoned me for the past year under false suspicion, although I knew she would never do so in public. But *all* these were false hopes and fool's dreams. I hoped for too much. The euphoria of being freed from Woodstock had been enough to light fallacious expectation in my heart.

I was yet still young enough then, at twenty-one, to dream dreams of justice and honour.

I paced about my rooms, waiting for a summons which seemed never to come. But there was one thing which gave me reason to hope. My rooms had a secret access into the royal apartments; a passageway which ran into the Queen's privy gardens from the one block of buildings and then linked to the royal apartments from there. Something made originally so that our ever-sentimental and privacy-seeking father could visit Edward, his most treasured child, without all the pomp of a courtly visit.

If Mary wanted to bring me to her without the court seeing it, she could.

But my sister did not send for me, not by the secret access, nor by the public halls. I had to merely sit and await her pleasure. The days began to blend into one another like so many brushstrokes in a portrait. I was never very good at waiting for something and with this meeting I was unsure if I dreaded it or longed for it more… the two emotions were bound up together in my heart and my mind, in my fears and in my desires.

All I did know was that I was tired of *waiting* to see Mary once more.

I was told that my sister had decreed that I should play a part in the christening ceremony for her child. Mary did not think to ask me in person of course, but was it perhaps a sign that I was to return to favour? I thought it might be. When I thought of the christening of this child, I could not but help think of the chrysom I had held when I was little more than an infant myself for the baptism of my little brother, the little embodiment of hope for all our father's dreams and troubles.

When I had held that robe for Edward, I had little been aware that his entrance to this world had but taken me one step further from the crown. I but knew that he was more special than I was, more welcomed to the world than I had been. This time, I knew well what the arrival of a child of my sister's would mean to me; a Catholic heir to her now Catholic country would place itself between me and the crown. In this child came the end of all my secret and silent dreams to one day attain the throne of England. In this child came the security of completing the future, and the past, that Mary wanted. Mary could raise this child to know only her version of the past… a past where she was the legitimate daughter of Henry VIII as she had had decreed; a past where her beloved mother was the true and unquestioned wife of the great *Harry*. Mary could create a past where my mother and my own birth were shrugged aside as unimportant; a past where the Catholic faith had continued, unbroken and unchallenged, through the reigns of the Tudors. In this child Mary could install her own version of the events of the past and point her child and her country to a glorious future which only she could see.

But we cannot truly rewrite the past, as Mary was seeking to do so. It is a task impossible.

With these thoughts in my head, I waited. I worried and I waited in those apartments as I had done at Woodstock, and at the Tower. I waited upon the will and pleasure of my sister the Queen. I waited, waited, waited.

And still she did not send for me.

Eventually, fearing that Elizabeth of England would simply be lost to the ravages of old age waiting in her chamber, I sent word to the Council, asking to see them. Duly and perhaps somewhat surprisingly swiftly, a delegation of them arrived at my quarters, headed by Gardiner. A year had passed since we last met at the

Tower and my enemy looked much aged. I tossed my luxurious red hair, pulled my shoulders back, and smiled to see him looking so much more frail and care-worn. All of Mary's Council looked the same; a group of aged men, gathering around their aged Queen. That at least, gave me hope.

I was young; I had much of life left to me. I was the future, and they were the past. The time would come, if I was clever enough, when I would be left to this world and they would be gone. I could be the future… and they would become but a part of my past. For now, though, they were unfortunately my present.

After a short greeting, Gardiner asked me to submit to Mary's suspicions that I had been guilty of treason against her; I refused.

"It would seem, my lady," he said in his oily voice, "that your refusal to submit to the Queen suggests that the Queen's Majesty had *wrongfully* imprisoned you."

I smiled at him. Did this old withered snake think he could trap me now, where he failed to a year previous?

"Her Majesty *is* the Queen," I replied. "It may please her to punish me or reward me as she thinketh good. That is her God-given right as the Queen."

"If you do not think the Queen culpable," said Gardiner slowly, "then you must hold that her lords and her Council are to blame, then, for your long imprisonment?"

I narrowed my eyes and looked again at these men. They were trying to hide it, but they looked worried. I believed I knew why. But a few days after I had arrived at Hampton Court, as I sat waiting for news in my rooms, pacing in frustration, waiting to be called, there was a joyful announcement cried out about the court and through London that Mary had given birth to a son. My heart had stopped full inside me as I heard the shouting from the streets. Bells rang in churches, in the royal chapel, and there was noise everywhere. I had slumped to a chair and sat staring at the tapestry-covered walls, thinking on what this royal child would mean to me. But then, the next day, a proclamation came; the news of Mary's son was false. The Queen was still pregnant, and she had not yet gone into labour. The tidings of the new prince had been a mistake. We all went back to waiting.

For me, this news had been both instantly crushing, and then, when the counter-news reported, confusing. It seemed odd that anyone could mistake whether Mary had given birth; although I had little experience of the act of childbirth, it seemed as though it was quite an obvious affair, with a clear outcome. So how had the news come to be misreported at all? A Queen is not a creature of privacy; her figure, even in her period of lying-in in her darkened birth room of females, was constantly reported on. It seemed strange that a report of the birth of a son could have been so misreported that all of England had started to celebrate, only to be told that it was false...

Here, on the faces of the men who advised her, I saw this puzzlement, and I saw worry too. Perhaps they had rejoiced at my sister's false labour and ideal yet fictitious child's birth. Perhaps they worried that in her advanced age she would die in the labour of childbed. The question put to me, whether I saw *them* to blame for my wrongful imprisonment, demonstrated to me a slight shift in power. If Mary died, or Mary's child died, or if *both* died... I was still the lawful heir to the throne. I was by no means powerless or without friends. Did the Council fear that if I came to the throne, I should exact my revenge on them?

How quickly the balance of power may tip to the other scale. All men should take care where and when they make friends, if they want to avoid falling from the side less favoured.

I inclined my head to them. "They tell me many women have in them a desire to revenge the wrongs of their lives, on whomsoever and whatever they find to be culpable," I said. "But within myself, I have the heart of my father; a male heart; my heart does not dissemble with that which is beneath it. I have found that whilst I may believe wrong to have been done to me and my name, that I do not desire revenge on any. I want to be taken back into the arms and trust of my sister, the Queen, and to show Her Majesty that I am, and have ever been her most loyal servant and sister."

They looked relieved, although Gardiner watched me still with the expression of a serpent eyeing a mouse hole. He was wondering if I was his food or his foe as I sat staring steadily at him. They filed out, leaving me once again to stare at another set of walls and chambers, beds and cushions, fires and windows. I was so very tired of seeing brick and stone, plaster and furnishings close around me. I wanted to feel freedom, I wanted to feel liberty. If it had gone on much longer, I may well have lost all the good senses I had been given by God. Incarceration is not only a state of the body, but of the mind. If one is free and chooses to spend time in a house, or a palace, then all is well, but being locked up and made to stay put is draining on all of the senses, on the imagination and on the spirit.

The gaol of one's mind and the sorrows this causes to the heart and soul can be more dangerous to a prisoner that all the iron bars and locks in the world. They wear on the spirit and they take the fight for life from the soul. It is only by keeping the mind active and resilient that we can survive incarceration at all… and for myself, my spirits were waxing low at that time.

But then, one evening just as I was settling and thinking of undressing for sleep, there came a message from the Queen. The messenger came at ten of the clock to bid me gather myself and come.

Queen Mary ordered the pleasure of my company in her apartments.

"When?" I asked the messenger; I was a little sleepy and hardly ready of wits.

"This very moment, my lady," said the stocky man before me.

I swallowed, surprised. After more than a year of imprisonment for treason, I was about to see my sister once more.

CHAPTER THIRTY-SIX

Hampton Court Palace
April 1555

The darkened hallways were lit only by the glare of the orange torch carried by the thickset man in front of me. The light bounced from one side of the corridor to the other, making the shadow of a giant from the body of a little man. We were quiet as we walked. Our soft feet padded across the dusty floor, little trodden over the years since my brother's death. Through the secret passages I followed the torchlight with suspicion in my heart. Was I truly going to meet my sister, or was a darker purpose at hand?

The passage ended and a cold blast of night air washed over my face as we stepped out into the Queen's privy gardens. In the light of a bright half-moon, I could see the sweet smelling herbs, the glistening pathways and the black ponds, reflecting the sparkling stars above them in the half-light of the night.

The messenger took me quietly to the foot of the stairs that led directly to the Queen's chamber, and I came to think less and less that this was an assassination attempt and more and more that I would indeed finally meet with my sister again. Another torch waited at the foot of the stairs. As we approached I looked up into the face of Susan Clarencieux. A face I had not seen for over a year.

"Lady Clarencieux," I said, with a little relief. Her homely, plain face was not a likely sight to accompany an attempt on my life. "Do I go to see my sister, the Queen?"

Clarencieux curtseyed, but in the smallest way possible and nodded to me curtly. I raised my eyebrows. If the woman had spat in my face it would have been a no less memorable insult to my position.

"The Queen, Her *Gracious Majesty,*" she said, half-glaring at me, "is waiting for you."

Clearly Mary's welcoming party was not going to be overwhelmingly enthusiastic.

Susan inclined her arm at the stone stairs. She waved the messenger away as though she swatted at a fly, and I followed her, walking into the opening of the staircase. The stairs were a spiral, lit by smaller torches burning in sconces up the passage. Our footsteps echoed in the stillness.

When we reached the top, Susan walked me through several antechambers, each hung with Tudor greens and whites, then reds and purples, their walls rich with tapestry and sparkling with gold and silver. Their floors were covered in rushes and sweet-smelling herbs which released fresh scents as we stepped on them. Here and there, sections of expensive carpet lined the floors and great fires roared in every fireplace. Our father had created many such hearths at Hampton Court, so many that every foreign visitor marvelled at the opulent comfort they afforded. No other palaces in Christendom were as well heated as those of our father. I felt the warmth of the fires in each room with relief. Mary's chambers were kept much warmer than mine, and everywhere was warmer than Woodstock. Mary kept herself in comfort here, I thought resentfully as I recalled my frozen winter huddled at the fire in Woodstock wishing and praying for warmth to return to my blood and bones.

Clarencieux stopped outside a heavy wooden door and knocked. The gruff voice of my sister called to her to enter. As the door opened, I took a deep breath, and walked in. It was possible that this was going to be the most important moment thus far of my salvation that I would face. I required courage, and I needed my wits about me.

My sister sat in a great chair near the centre of the room. I walked in, and curtseyed, then went down on my knees before her, my head bowed.

"Your Majesty," I said. "Gracious sister… I am so honoured to have been called to your presence after so long without the comfort of Your Majesty's company."

"Look up at me," Mary demanded. Her voice sounded not only harsh with its usual deep tones, but tired, weary, and slightly irritated. I breathed in again, steeling myself to gather my courage and wits. I looked up at Mary. Still kneeling before my sister, I tried not to gasp or look surprised when I saw how much this past year had altered her.

Mary was much older than I, so I had always been used to her more mature appearance, used to the difference in age between us. But now, she really looked *old*, although she was not more than thirty-eight and I had met older women and men than that. Her thin face was pale, almost grey, and under the light of the candles and her skin was dry and blotched with red and white. Dark, deep shadows lurked under her eyes, giving her face the appearance of a skull. Her hands were thin and looked almost paper-like. Inwardly I shuddered to think of what her dry and papery skin would feel like to touch, flaking off in reams and scabs. Her hair, once a fine thick mane of auburn and red, looked thin and was clearly padded out in places by sections of false hair which did not quite match their surroundings. Her gown, as ever, was rich with purple and red cloth but only served to make her pallor look whiter. Powder and paint sat uncomfortably on her face, not disguising her appearance of illness, and the darkness within her mouth when she spoke told me that she had even fewer teeth left to her than she had done before.

My sister was once a pretty princess, but no man could have told you that upon looking at her here and now. She looked as though Death had already started to take her, even as she supposedly was filled with life.

As for that life... the only part of her that was fat was her stomach; it was enormous, billowing out in front of her, rounded and swollen. And yet, something in that too looked wrong... unnatural. I remembered the flushed and glowing look that Katherine Parr had possessed even in the latter months of her pregnancy and she had looked nothing like Mary did now. It was as though every part of Mary was wasting away and being sucked into this enormous lump on her front; if it was a baby, it was a baby who was consuming the life of its mother in its pursuit of being born. If it was not a baby, as I was beginning to suspect now was indeed the case, then whatever it was... was not benign.

Only Mary's large, dark eyes looked alive as they regarded me from her skeletal face. That way she had of looking at you as though she could see into the depths of your soul had not left her. Boldly, I lifted my chin and looked back into the eyes of my sister; I had done nothing wrong I thought to myself. I had not tarried a year in prison to fail now. I did not flinch from her gaze.

Mary drew in breath from her nose and let it out again as she regarded me. "*You* would say you have been wrongfully punished," she uttered slowly, disregarding a greeting for me, her sister, heir, and only living sibling.

"I must not say so," I reasoned clearly, still on my knees, "if it pleases Your Majesty."

"Then belike your will to others," she said shortly, and looked away from me for a moment. She sighed. I could see her frustration with me. For more than a year she had asked me to say that I had been guilty and that she had been right. It had been the first thing her Council had demanded of me when I arrived. Yet still I refused. If she had to take me back as her sister now, and I still refused to admit any guilt, I would have won.

"You have always been an obstinate and headstrong child," she hissed, "ever since you were young. But then with *such a mother* as you can claim, could we ever have thought you would turn out otherwise?"

I drew breath to try and quench the anger in my heart that sparked as she spoke ill of my mother. I looked up at her and tried to pour waters of sanity on the heart within me which cried out at me to lash her with my tongue for her insults to my dead mother's name.

That is Mary's way, I told myself. S*he will never let an opportunity pass where she might have a chance to abuse the name of your mother.*

"Since Your Majesty, in all your graciousness, was my first and principal carer and friend in this world," I said smoothly, "if I ever had anything of virtue in me, then it came from your goodwill towards me. I do not remember my mother, but I remember, Your Majesty, that we shared a great father. If I disappoint you now, I hope you would put it to the folly of youth, and I would strive to model myself in the future on the example of Your Majesty and of the great father we shared."

Mary looked at me and her lip curled a little. It was not an attractive visage. I knew what she was thinking; that our father was not *our* father, but *hers* alone. She was thinking on how much I might resemble any of the men accused with my mother of adultery and treason. But then, the lip dropped and she viewed me with narrowed eyes... she did not have any love for my mother, but my words had moved her to think of a time when I had been helpless, when I had been her care. In many ways, when I was a child I had been Mary's daughter. All the care and attention that she provided for me when I was an infant, despite hating my mother with a passion, had not entirely left her heart now.

"The model of the King Henry VIII is indeed one that you should follow," she nodded. "For in him were *all* graces possible. You should however also learn from the mistakes of his reign, for even the greatest of kings may be led astray by trickery and evil."

I inclined my head, partly to hide my face from her. It was another sharp dig at the memory of my mother. I wondered spitefully how much of Mary's reign we should attribute to her own actions and wishes, and how much to the machinations of evil around her.

"When my child is born," Mary said stroking her swollen belly with a thin hand. "You will be present to see a new dawn for the Tudor dynasty. It is fitting that a new age should come with the birth of a child, blessed of Heaven, such as my son is. Perhaps *you* may be chosen to repay some of those kindnesses I paid to you when you were a babe, and spend some time with my child as his aunt when he enters the world. But this will only be allowed once I am assured that your faith is bent on the right path. I will have no corruption allowed near to the heir of England, and the salvation of the world."

"I have followed all the directives for the true faith that you have given, Your Majesty," I assured her, choosing to ignore her outlandish reference to her child being the salvation of the world. "There can be no report in all the time I have been your prisoner that would say I have not done all that you asked of me for the salvation of my soul. I have seen the *true* faith, I have embraced it and I understand it in my soul."

I did not say which faith I thought was the true faith, of course, so in effect, I was not telling a lie. She nodded although regarded me with an air of suspicion. Mary knew me well and she knew that I was wily with words.

"That is well then," she said thoughtfully. She seemed suddenly distracted. For a moment, I saw her eyes flit from my face, to a decorated screen covering a part of the room to my side. Upon entering, I had thought little of it. Her eyes came back to mine quickly; the barely perceptible motion she had made however, made me aware that we were not alone.

Someone was behind that screen.

"You will go back to your apartments and await, as I do, the coming of my son. Once he is born and we are past the travail of blessed birth, then we shall talk again, sister. I hope to find that your conversion to the true faith is as you have claimed it to be, as I hope that when my child comes, you will join me in rejoicing for his coming, and be to him a faithful and loving aunt. "

I looked at her, a little amazed. I had been expecting more of a fight to return to her favour than this. Her gaze once again flitted to the screen. I rose at the motion of her hand and curtseyed to her.

"I am most grateful for your attentions, Your Majesty," I stuttered, feeling a little lost. It had been too easy. I was put off my guard and it unnerved me, "and for the honour of being allowed to try to return to your favour. I do maintain my innocence, and would ask that you believe I am Your Majesty's most humble servant. In your present blessing I am overjoyed for you and long to see the heir of England come to life from your body."

My words fell over themselves a little as I strove to get out everything that I had so long thought of and practised to say to her should it come that we met again. I had not been expecting to have a reception where my return was… easy.

Mary's eyes filled with tears at my last, rushed words; there was a puckering about her lips as though she were about to tell me something, something personal and deeply buried in her... but then the darkness of irritation passed over her face again. She never knew whether to believe me or not. She never knew whether she could confide in me or not. But she wanted to. At that moment, she looked so desperately lonely that I felt my heart strain within me for her.

"You can go now," she said gruffly, shaking her head as though she knew not what to make of me. "I will send for you again."

I rose, and curtseyed.

As I walked to the door and towards the hovering figure of Clarencieux once again, I came to a point where the edge of the screen was just visible. Sharply, suddenly, I turned my head and for a moment, I saw a handsome, yet sombre face regarding me with interest. He did not look surprised, or concerned, to see that I had discovered he was behind the screen; he just looked back at me with dark eyes that sparkled in the candle light. As I went to turn my head back to my own path, he smiled, just a little, at me.

I knew who he was.

I felt a shudder of excitement pass through me; the strange sensation of stimulation that a smile from a handsome man may give to any woman. I blushed and turned back to my path leading from the room. As I walked on quiet feet once more down the stairs, across the moon-lit gardens and back to my own apartments, I wondered how much of the reconciliation between my sister and I had been because of Mary, and how much had been because of her husband, Phillip of Spain.

And if the reconciliation had been his idea, as his presence behind the screen and that smile seemed to suggest, then what did the handsome Spaniard want from me?

CHAPTER THIRTY-SEVEN

Hampton Court Palace
Late Spring 1555

There is much in life that we seek to hide from others. Much of embarrassment, shame or humiliation that we feel; those emotions cut deeply into our own sense of ourselves. They wound our dignity. They batter our sense of our worth. For some, shame can be brought to bear on them with something as simple as an insult spoken by another which slashes deep their own wavering self-confidence, for others just a little trip up a stair, or a spill from a cup in public before the braying laughs of others may be enough to make us want to hide our faces. Some of us cannot ever admit our mistakes, for they show us to be less clever than we would have people see us. Some of us cannot bear to be wrong, and so will never accept there is another way to see the world.

For those who live their lives in front of the public, for those who are seen every day by all, there is so little in truth that can be hidden; there is in truth no place to hide.

So it was for my sister, the Queen.

The months of Mary's lying-in stretched on. My sister was supposed to be brought to childbed in April, but then came May, with no sign that the child she awaited was coming. In May, her doctors announced to the court and Council that they had mistaken the date of the Queen's conception; her child was conceived later than they had originally thought, they said. The court and country settled down to wait once more for the arrival of the royal child.

But as May went on and still no babe appeared, whispers could be heard in all the nooks and crannies of the court. They were painful rumours to hear spoken… that the Queen was not pregnant, that the swelling was either a false pregnancy, brought on by the deceit of her mind, or it was a symptom of a disease. But still my sister clung to the idea that she was with child. Not only had she longed all her life for a child, *this* child had been a portent of approval from God, and she could not let it go. I could not help but feel for Mary at this time. How anyone could not feel for a woman in such a situation, I do not know. No matter all the troubles between us, no matter all that was being done in her name to the people of England, I could not help but feel pity for my sister as all in England came to doubt the existence of the babe she was so sure she carried beneath her heart. As she believed she carried a child, so I knew that I carried dual and opposing feelings for my sister, the Queen.

I had felt the same way about my father in many ways. That same dislocation between the father I had loved and adored, and the tyrant he could be to others. I had never reconciled my feelings towards him, and so it was with my sister too. I could fear her, despise her for the burnings done in her name, and yet still pity her for the loss of something she had never had. I could love her for the blood there was between us, and fear her for the hatred she held for my mother, and my faith. Complex, ever, are the feelings we have for our families.

I was not allowed much around court at this time, but I was taken to Mary often. Her wasted body, abnormal belly, and thin, scaly skin repulsed me, but my pity drew me to her with love. I think that Mary herself may have begun to suspect that she carried no child within her belly, but she did not want to face that suspicion, for if she did, then it meant that her most awful moment of humiliation and personal sorrow could be hidden from no one.

After that first meeting in secret under the cover of night, Mary sent for me sporadically at first, and then more and more regularly. At times we just talked, uncomfortably at first, for we had to avoid many subjects which would cause discord between us, and then, as we found moments of our past to relive that held happiness, it became easier. We talked of days when we were all together, Edward, Mary and me; of our little brother, of his love for books, of his desire, always thwarted by our protective father, to run at the rings, or to ride in the joust. We talked of our father, of the times we had had when we were a family together.

We talked of all the moments in our past which did not contain reference to our mothers, all our lost stepmothers, or to religion in any way.

It was a censored picture of our past, but for once I minded little that Mary chose to carve out only the good and leave the rotten behind in the apple of our shared past. After a year of incarceration, a year of fearing I should die in an assassination attempt or from the cold of Woodstock in winter, it felt somewhat relieving to be welcomed into the warmth of my sister's affections and talk to her as a friend. We laughed together. It was as strange for both of us as it was sweet.

For Mary, I think I had become a balm to smear over her present fears. As May went on there was still no sign that the swelling of her body was a child, no movement from the babe supposedly contained within her, no sign of her waters breaking, or of her pains beginning. As the still days of May brought sorrow to her soul, she sought to hide the awful, dawning truth under the constant murmur of our conversation.

Once, I came to her to find her sitting on the floor in her great chamber, utterly alone. Her women stood outside her door, looking at each other anxiously, obviously having been ordered from the room even as I had been sent for. As I arrived, many of them looked at me with disapproval still, but Jane Dormer offered me a little smile of sad relief. When I entered, Mary seemed such a small and huddled form on the floor of her chamber. Her knees were gathered up to her chin, her arms wrapped around herself, and she sat rocking backwards and forwards on the floor like a woman possessed by the devil. I ran to her. Her face was blank and dead as she stared out at me. If tears had rolled down her face I would have been more assured, but there were none.

Her face was as barren as the womb inside her, and in that moment of desperation, she knew it as I did. I gathered her up into my arms, sat on the floor with her and I told her pretty lies: that I had heard often of women being mistaken in their counting of the time before a birth came; that doctors knew little but talked much; that we were all waiting, happily and patiently, for her child to come. Her thin hands, so dry and harsh, grasped at the delicate fabrics of my dress as I lifted her to her chair. She clung on to me. There was more in that grasp than a need for stability in her posture. Mary became desperate for the words I spoke, my pretty little lies that brought her back within the comforting world of fantasy she had created. Soon I had her smiling about her handsome Phillip, and hesitantly telling me which names she liked for her son best.

When it came time for me to leave and go back to my royal prison, for still I was not a free person, she looked at me with grief for my leaving, and greed to have me with her again. In those short weeks where I was at her beck and call, I came to know my sister better than I had ever known another person.

And I pitied her with all I had in my heart.

Was I wrong to tell her lies? For truly, I did not believe she carried a child within her. The swelling of her belly was huge now and yet she looked more wasted than ever. In many ways I wondered if she was dying and I was keeping her company as she did so.

Is it wrong to tell pretty lies to someone you believe may be dying?

That is only a question you can answer if you have ever been in that situation. It can only be judged if you have looked into the eyes of desperation and known what it is to feel your own heart break for another. For myself, I cannot feel bad for my deception. Pity may move the human animal to commit actions of all kinds. If I eased her sorrows only for a moment, then I do not feel badly for my words.

June came, and it was reported around the court that the delivery of the Prince was imminent. But nothing came of it, and still we waited.

Mary was becoming more and more desperate. The swelling in her belly appeared now to be lessening, deflating as though her phantom child was drifting from her on the breeze. She sought to hide it, padding out the dresses she wore as she had padded out the false sections of her hair, as she had lined the chests of her dresses with linen to give her a more womanly figure. But she could not hide the truth, not from us who knew her, who had seen her... Her babe was but a ghost who would vanish in the light of the day. But Mary would not admit it. She clung to my stories and my lies daily. It was a strain on my spirits, I will admit.

One day as I wandered in the privy gardens, seeking a moment of calm to myself outside of the bouts of desperation, sorrow and frantic, fanciful happiness exuding from my poor sister within her darkened chambers, I was startled from my thoughts by a polite cough.

I turned to find Phillip, Prince of Spain, King Consort of England, a little behind me. Unusually, he was alone.

I blushed. This June was warm and wet; a source of great discomfort to my sister. On this day, unusually, there was no rain. Little early roses danced in a balmy breeze and I found myself alone in private gardens on a beautiful day with a handsome man who I will admit, I felt attracted to. There had been little in my life that could be called romantic, but on the face of it, this moment had possibility.

But of course, the man was my sister's husband, the Catholic Prince of Spain. The garden was but an extension of my prison and I was still branded a traitor to the Crown despite my current position as secret friend to my poor sister. Opposite ends of the social scale were the Prince and I then.

The hands that life deals us are never perfect, but we make of them what we will.

"I would not wish to disturb you, my lady," he said in smooth, but heavily accented English. His voice was deep, and his slight mannerisms charming. "I was on my way to see my wife, the Queen, and saw you looking most… ponderous." He smiled at me, his dark eyes danced and I wondered what this serious young man would be like if he had a merry life with less responsibility.

"You always look so solemn, my Lady Elizabeth."

"I was thinking much the same of you, Your Majesty," I started to move to curtsey to him. He held out a hand. "No," he said shaking his head. "I would not have us always stand on ceremony when we have no need to."

I inclined my head. My father often said the same thing to his courtiers, but that was generally for show rather than something he really meant. Princes and kings are fickle things; they long to be valued as real people and yet they cannot bear to be really seen as such.

"You are kind, Your Majesty," I smiled.

"That is much better," he nodded, looking at me with gratification and admiration. "You have the handsome Tudor looks when you smile, my lady, much like my dear wife."

"My gracious sister was always the most beautiful of the daughters of Henry VIII," I uttered smoothly. Another lie; I was becoming most proficient.

"But her younger sister did not miss out on the benefits of the family beauty," he said gallantly.

Philip indicated to a path, as a way of suggesting that we walk together. I could hardly refuse, and I didn't want to. There was something within my character which longed for admiration and attention, and in his eyes I could read quite easily that he found me attractive. It is a heady thing, to be admired by one you admire too. After so long locked away with only the company of women, and Bedingfield, it was nice to bask in the light of his sun shining on me with approval.

"I wanted to thank you, my lady," he said as we walked along the little path. Lavender and rosemary lined our way with just-budding white and purple flowers.

"What for, Your Majesty?" I allowed my hand to trail over the tiny purple flowers of the rosemary. Their spikes stroked my fingers and their delicate scent wandered along my senses.

"Although you would be bound to the devotion of duty naturally," he plucked and twisted a stalk of thyme in his hands, "there is much comfort that you have brought to my wife, your sister, during this difficult time of her… confinement. My first wife, God rest her soul, was also afflicted with the hardships of difficult pregnancy, and thereto, I lost her eventually. I would that the dangers given to women could instead have been faced by men, for we after all are hardened by fighting wars. But as God has chosen my wife to bear my child, I can only thank you for bringing comfort to her at this time. It was a great pleasure to me to see two sisters reunited as it should be, and I know that this event has also brought comfort to your sister."

"And to me," I said. "Your Majesty, I do not need to be thanked for my time spent with my sister. Her Majesty has been evilly advised in previous times to this, and those who would wish me ill have bent my sister's ear against me. I am grateful to be allowed to have a chance to return to her side, and more than happy to have been able to bring her any comfort in such a... difficult time."

His pleasing face nodded. "I think you and I understand each other well, my Lady Elizabeth," he smiled. He looked a little sad beneath the smile, and I knew that he was thinking, as we all were, that Mary was not going to give birth to his child.

He swallowed. "It will be a great consolation to me to become a father once more," his words echoed with hollowness. He did not believe the words he spoke. My heart seemed to plunge from my chest towards him at that moment, like a horse charging into the chase. That awful pity I felt for Mary; I understood he felt it too. There were many men who would have never gone along with such a deception for so long. Even if he was years younger than her, and they were as unmatched in looks as they were in manners, he had enough respect and affection for her to want to protect her from humiliation for as long as possible.

I wondered if Mary knew how fortunate she was as I looked at the handsome face of the Prince of Spain. Although Phillip and I were opposites in religion and perhaps in our paths for the future, I envied Mary at that moment, to have found a man who even if he did not love her or desire her, would still strive to respect, honour and protect her... much as he had vowed to upon their marriage. Such men are a rare commodity in this world, I thought to myself.

"I would," he said, "that the problems between your sister and yourself could be a thing of the past. We go towards a future that will, I hope, be a happier one for you and for Her Majesty. And I hope too..." He turned to me and took my hand. "I hope that as a brother to a sister that you and I may come to be good friends."

I blushed. The handsome Prince of Spain was just a little too good at catching me off-guard. Apart from the extreme and often fearsome attentions of my step-father Thomas Seymour when I was a young girl, I had had little experience with male attention. His glittering eyes and charming ways were making me feel as though I was that child Seymour had pursued once more… as though I was not a rational being who knew well my own strength and power. I spoke sternly to my heart as I felt it beat with traitorous longing to be so loved and admired.

With him still holding my hand, I curtseyed.

"I have ever been in need of good friends, Your Majesty. I do not find they are a commodity one can have too many of."

He smiled. "Then that is settled," he said, kissing my hand as he released it. "Our contract is struck, my lady, and I hope that in all the days of our lives, and whatever outcome for the future, we will both remember this time we walked together and agreed to be always friends."

As we walked back to the centre of the gardens, I looked up at the privy chambers of my sister. Mary was standing at the window; she had been watching us walk together.

As Phillip left my side and walked up the staircase to her chambers, I looked up at Mary's pale face. He was coming secretly to see her; men were not permitted to intrude upon the laying-in of the Queen, even if they were her husband. Mary's expression was unreadable, but her silent stare seemed to emit waves of sadness. I hurried inside, cursing the blushes brought forth by the striking Prince. I hoped I had been far enough away that Mary had not seen them colour my cheeks.

In all incarnations of romance, no matter how fleeting, the men in my life only served to bring me trouble.

CHAPTER THIRTY-EIGHT

Hampton Court Palace
August 1555

At the start of August, my sister Mary, the first sole anointed Queen of England, slipped from her lying-in chambers at Hampton Court unannounced, and travelled to the small palace of Oaklands four miles away. No proclamation was issued, no word from the Queen; just her quiet removal from that female-ruled world of the chamber of awaiting birth.

We all knew what it meant. There was no child waiting to be born in Mary's womb and Mary had finally admitted what we all had known for so long.

Perhaps she could not bear to make her sorrows into words and have them proclaimed to the country. Perhaps she hoped that by saying nothing, that nothing would be said. Her greatest joy had been the possibility of having a child, and now it was gone, and her greatest sorrow was now taken and thrown around like a piece of meat tossed up and torn apart by dogs. People talked of her and *laughed* at her in the court, in the inns and in the streets. Her failure to give any kind of proclamation did not help the wild rumours which grew and grew, growing fatter and fatter on her pain.

Rumours abounded that the Queen was dead, that the Queen had miscarried, that the Queen had given birth to a demon, a monkey, or a hound. They said that she had never been with child at all, but that her mind had made a ghost of a child for her. People whispered that another child, that of a commoner, had been stolen to provide a false prince for the Queen, and that child would soon be announced as her son. Anonymous posters and pamphlets were circulated, and pinned up around the palace, all detailing theory after theory, each more hurtful and abusive than the one before.

Whatever Mary's pregnancy had really been; whether an inflation of the belly due to disease, or the hopes and dreams of a woman made flesh without substance of reality, I could not believe that in my sister there had been that which would seek to deceive knowingly… not on this matter. In her ghostly pregnancy, in her awful desperation, she had deceived only her own self.

Sometimes the thing we wish for, the hopes we have, are so strong that the body seems to listen to the heart, and brings forth sign and symptom of that we hope or dread the most. Mary's heart had longed for a child of her own, so much, I believe, that her body had created every sign that she was indeed pregnant. The one thing her heart could not do by itself, however, was to actually plant the seed that would grow into the babe she wanted so very desperately.

The sight of the papers and pamphlets, containing in them the wildest conspiracies that ever were told on this earth, had horrified me.

Mary's popularity with the people had once again plummeted and whilst, in days previous to this, the people of England had at least always maintained some respect for her person and her crown, now, with this raw sorrow made plain to all, they moved to discredit her utterly. It is an interesting characteristic of the human creature, that when a ruler betrays something of their own weakness to the people, then the people may come either to love their ruler or hate them for it. Mary's weakness here, on top of her marriage to a foreign power, on top of the burnings of Protestants in the fires of her religion, was but a touch paper, to light a fuse of prejudice and hatred against her.

It is a queen's ultimate duty, to produce an heir, to breed well and often, like any bitch or cow, and if this queen could not bring forth life from her womb, the people reasoned that she was not fit in all ways to be the Queen. Men never seem to have this problem; if marriages produce not children, then it is always the wife that is looked to for blame. But here, it seemed that it must indeed be Mary who was at fault. Phillip, we knew, already had offspring; a poor mad son, but an heir nonetheless. In this matter, Mary would be found wanting, Mary would be blamed. Mary's false pregnancy was revealed to the world as a mistake on her part. People asked; if the Queen did not know the workings of her own body, then did she know anything else?

I read some of those papers, thrown into Mary's chambers, nailed to walls about court and all hidden before she could see them. They were horrific. The monarchy under my sister was becoming an institution no longer respected, but one that was game for abuse, for evil words and for disrespect for the God-given and appointed role of ruler.

Then, in late August, it seemed that God had not yet granted Mary all the grief He had stored for her. For it was then that Phillip announced that he had to return to Spain.

It would not be for long, he told the Queen, but his father had decided to abdicate the throne of the Hapsburgs and grant it to his son. The legend that was Charles V was now so old and weary that he longed for peace and seclusion; his son was a man, a proven warrior in battle, a statesman and a smooth courtier. Phillip would go on to make Spain and the Hapsburg Empire even greater than Charles had, and perhaps by handing over the reins now, Charles may have the chance to see his dynasty enter a new phase of greatness under his son.

The royal couple returned to Whitehall Palace at the end of August, and rode through the city on open litters. One of the rumours that had followed Mary's quiet removal from Hampton Court was that she was dead, and now, her health somewhat improved, her piteous belly deflated and flat as an oaken board, she put paid to those rumours of her own demise by appearing to the people. The reception was mixed. I am sure that many standing in those crowds were glad that another situation like the confusing end of our brother's reign had not occurred, and they were not being ruled secretly by some unknown lord or duke who had usurped power following the death of the ruler as Warwick had done. But I am also sure that many were unhappy that this woman, whose rule so far had plunged them from civil war to rebellion, to uneasy marriage to a foreign power and through false hope of an heir to come, was still the bearer of the royal crown.

Phillip sailed away from England's shores. With her ears full of his promises to return in a bare few weeks, Mary went to her chamber and spent hours staring from the window, looking at the river that had taken her husband away from her.

For me, Phillip's leaving was a mixed blessing. Although Mary had said nothing about the manner in which her beloved husband talked to me in the gardens, I knew that she harboured private suspicions that we were attracted to one another. Since our walk in the gardens, I had been careful to not be alone with the handsome Prince of Spain. Although I liked the way his hungry eyes danced over my skin and my hair, although I liked the smooth countenance of his face and the lilt of his accented English, I did not want to lose my head now, after coming so far, for suspicion of adultery with the Queen's husband.

Mary said nothing on the subject; noting that we were good friends was enough for her. Much as she had sought to alter the annals of history by making her mother's marriage to our father legal in law, much as she had turned the country back to the ways of the Catholic faith, much as she had slunk from her lying in chamber without a word, Mary sought to repress all that she did not want to face in life, to revise her world so that all that she thought right was true, and all that she hated was false.

Although I can certainly see the attraction in such an idea, with all the honesty and love for learning that I have within me, it would never be a path I could take. The real truth of the matter is that life is not, and has never been, perfect. But those of us who find happiness in life know this, and do not spend hours of heartbreak wishing it were different; those who spend their time wishing for something perfect will always be disappointed.

I was at Mary's side much during this time. Watching the thin and pale face of my sister strain with the weight of the grief she carried as she watched her husband leave her. It may seem cruel to you that Phillip went from her side a bare month after the sorrow of her lost child was revealed; but princes are not creatures that can always control their own destiny. The common man in the street has more control over his own life than does a prince. We are the staves and the pennants of the land, and we must wave in the wind at the whim of the needs of our countries.

In the autumn, Mary led the court in the Catholic observance of the Pope's Jubilee with me at her side; weeks of fasting and prayer where Mary's bowed head and fast-muttering lips showed me, perhaps only me as I was closest to her, of all the prayers with which she petitioned God during her most desperate times. Lonely, bereft of the comfort of her husband and of the child she had so longed to hold in her arms, Mary prayed long and hard to God for an end to her sorrows. We two sisters, daughters of Henry VIII, knelt on the cold floors of her chamber, her chapel and the royal chapel until our flesh bled and our skin cracked and wept.

I have never been a believer in the idea that God would require the torture of the flesh of his people for his own satisfaction. But I knelt and I prayed, like a good Catholic, with the still-slightly-suspicious eyes of my sister glimpsing at me when she was not ardently asking for God to bring back Phillip, bring them a child and bless her reign. Poor Mary, she had so much, but not the one thing she wanted above all; a family.

As the priest intoned in Latin, and the mist of incense smoke floated around our heads, as the voices muttered prayers and bargains to God, I thought often on the position of a woman in power; the position of a woman sitting and ruling where before only men had been. One day, my head bowed, a thought came to me, so clear and plain that I wondered if God had sent the thought straight into my head, through the fug and the confusion of the Catholic Mass.

Perhaps things should change in the future; perhaps they would not always be as they are presently. But in the here and now, I knew that a woman may reign, may ascend to the throne, but in doing so she must give up her rights to the normal comforts of a woman's life. To reign absolutely, to retain her power, there could be no reliance on a husband; there can be no humiliation of the throne from the rigours of childbirth, or from a lack of ability to produce heirs. A female absolute ruler must stand alone, must leave her personal desires and wants behind as she ascends to that throne. A male ruler may wed a wife, and have her carry any disgrace of childlessness, as our father had done… a female ruler must in all ways be wedded only to her country. The female ruler must be the King and the Queen, the crown and the throne. She must be the embodiment of all hopes and dreams of her people, and never give in to those human frailties which would disgrace her in the eyes of her country.

And no, it was not a fair, nor a comfortable thought. How many times had I said that I did not like the idea of marriage? Yet I had pondered in my past on entering that state… How many times had I thought of the love within the eyes of my mother as she gazed at me and wondered if I should someday look on my own child with such eyes?

We all carry private fantasies and wishes… we all wonder on the outcome of our lives. But at that moment, with swirls of smoke drifting cloyingly around my head, I came to see that if I were ever to ascend to the throne of England, I needed to learn from my sister's mistakes. Her heart had led her only to ruination and humiliation, to the loss of her people's affections… to the debasement of the throne in the eyes of the common people through her personal wants and physical defects.

I could not allow such a thing to happen to me.

With the disappearance of Mary's hoped for heir, I was still the nearest heir to the throne of England. Although I had come to feel both pity and affection for my poor sister in her desperate state, I could not help but see, and desire the glimmer of my own future appearing behind the shadow of her tired and wasted body.

CHAPTER THIRTY-NINE

Hatfield House
Autumn 1555

It was in October of that year that I finally was officially released from the bonds of imprisonment. My sister was returning to the rigours of her government, opening her fourth Parliament, and I was given leave to return to my house at Hatfield.

Mary was entering a challenging time. When last she opened a Parliament she had done so with a new husband at her side and rumours of pregnancy bolstering her popularity. Now her husband had sailed from our shores and returned to his own, amidst wild rumours, I am sorry to say, of philandering on the way. The continued burnings of Protestants caused much fear and dissatisfaction among her people, and Mary had lost, or had never had, the baby she was supposed to have carried. She was in a much weaker position now than she had ever been in before; a much-criticised and ill-loved queen.

Looking older and more tired than I had ever seen her, Mary shook herself off like an old dog caught in the rain, and set to work once more. Plastered in cosmetics and plumped out with false layers in her dresses to make her look well and hale, she walked towards her next duty as queen. She looked like a statue; pale in face, both because of the thick paint she wore to hide her tired skin, and because of the pallor of natural weariness. She wore false hair where her own had deserted her. Her body was so thin and haggard, despite the false padding. From a distance Mary looked like a glorious queen… It was only when you got close to her that you could truly see the cracks appearing. My sister was driven on solely by the force of her own will and mind. For once, perhaps, she was not listening to her heart. For her heart, in its sadness, would surely have told her to lie down and die; but there was one thing which kept Mary's heart burning with life even when she had lost all else… her faith.

Mary was too occupied now with other affairs of the state to want to worry about me. Perhaps she even trusted me a little, loved me a little more after our time spent together. She wanted me close enough to London to call on and keep an eye on, but far enough away so that she did not have to worry about me. It was a relief to be finally free. Although I pitied my older sister horribly and hoped that I had brought her some release from her pain, I could not help but love the idea of my own independence and freedom once more. And I could not love the direction in which she was dragging England; the fires of faith burned bright, and more and more people met their deaths in them each week.

It is a curious thing how we human creatures; that we can hold two view-points which oppose each other so completely, at the same time. I pitied my sister, loved her even for the horrific humiliations she had so recently suffered. Yet at the same time, I hated her for her persecutions of the Protestant people of England. As I had ever thought of my father; that there was a side to him I adored and worshipped, and a side to him that I feared. Perhaps much was also true of my brother, to a lesser degree. Now it seemed that this family trait had passed to another member of my blood. We Tudors... we always seemed to have a talent for dividing opinion, even amongst our own selves.

I rode out from London in mid-October, and the people of London lined my cavalcade with their bodies and their voices; thunderous was the noise that greeted my horse and my personal guard. As they saw my colours and my red head approach, people went wild in the streets, shouting my name and calling blessings on me. The noise of their support for me hollered along the streets of London, echoing against every merchant house, church and street stall, bellowing along the length of the river. It was almighty.

I was their hope, you see. I was their possibility. Not only a figure of optimism for those Protestant exiles from the nobility waiting and watching from the continent where Mary's fires and tortures could not touch them, but I was the figure of hope for all those discontented and disillusioned with my sister's reign. They could see there may be a time, not so far in the future, where an English princess may turn into English queen and they could be rid of Spain, of the fires of persecution, and the nauseating pall of the smoke made from the bodies of those burned for their faith.

The stench in London from Mary's fires of salvation could never really go away. Each breeze or frequent fall of rain seemed to move the smell of burnt hair and flesh into the background... but it never left. You could taste it in every spoonful of broth, and smell it on your pillow as you rested your head to sleep; fat and sinew, flesh and blood, hair and bone... the smell of a roasted human clings to everything, makes everything dirty and soiled.

As the cheers of the people grew louder, I had to ask my men to try and quieten them. Although I was gratified by every shout and well-wisher, I was sipping at my first moments of freedom in a year and a half. I hardly wished Mary's suspicious gaze to fall my way once more, if the people were too over-exuberant in their appreciation of my person.

They did not obey my wishes; I was roared through London.

Arriving at Hatfield, I was overjoyed to find my reception party full of faces I had longed to see; Cecil grinned at me and bowed with all aplomb, Parry's wily tongue spoke greetings and salutations, and Roger Ascham, my dear old tutor, had been sent to continue my education. I had feared greatly for Ascham, knowing well enough the strength of his beliefs; but he, like me, had taken to wearing a Catholic mask under the reign of my sister. He was, in public, a good Catholic man. In private, he was as much a Catholic as I.

It brought such warmth to my heart and soul to see all the faces of the people I loved about me once more. What is better bread for the soul than seeing the faces of those you love, and who love you in return?

Once washed and cleansed of the dust of the journey, I sent for my men immediately; there was so much that I felt I needed to know which I had had little time or opportunity to learn whilst breaking my flesh at the altar of the Catholic God next to my sister. What a thirst for knowledge was upon me then in the liberty of my own house! I felt like a man dying in a sea of thirst, only suddenly to have sailed up an estuary into fresh water and found he is able to both bathe and drink at the same time. I wanted to wallow in the knowledge that my men would have found for me.

They did not disappoint me.

It took many days to catch up on the business of my estates, my rents and my lands, on the harvests and the private squabbles of my people and tenants. Such things may seem mundane to you, but if a prince does not take good care of his own house, how can he seek to rule a country? After that, and seeing that Cecil and

Parry had kept my affairs well in order for me, we turned to the business of the country.

"Phillip is unlikely to return to the side of the Queen as soon as he has said," said Cecil. "I have word that he has rejoined the company of his old mistress in Spain, and is finding her body to be both more fruitful and more enjoyable than the body of our Queen."

"Pray to God then that Mary never finds that out," I replied quietly. "For in Phillip she places all her hopes and love. A heart that is disappointed is often one that turns bitter and does evil."

"More so, my lady, than the burning of her own people?" asked Ascham softly and gravely. "England has never seen such an evil as this. Individuals may have been taken to the stake for witchcraft or heresy, but never have we seen the like of the horrors your sister has visited on us for following the religion laid down by your great father. Countless people have perished in her flames. England was once free of the yoke of all foreign powers, but the Queen has dragged us back under two; Spain and Rome now have more say in the future of this country than any honest Englishman may do. We have become slaves to the might of other nations, and slaves to fear."

"True enough, Ascham," I nodded sadly. "You and I, everyone here gathered, and countless thousands of others have had to hide our true faith under the cover of Catholic masks. Others loyal to our religion have fled these shores, and many others have died for their faith. I wonder how far all this will go, or if my poor sister will ever continue to try and turn back the sands of time to satisfy her God."

"You pity her, my lady?" Cecil asked gently.

"Aye, my lord, I do," I nodded, "for although she has done me much harm, done our people much harm, she too has done equal harm to herself. Look and tell me how many of our countrymen would follow her now to battle as they did when first she came to the throne? Tell me now if you can, what portion of the country love her as well as they once did? She is alone, friendless and making no new allies. She is used by Spain and ridiculed by her own people. I do pity her, for power is a lonely place for a woman to reside."

"Not all women are suited to the position," grinned Ascham. "But I believe I know one who is equal to the task." He smiled at me, and I reflected his smile with mine.

"There are many waiting only for the Queen to trip up once more," said Parry, "who would gladly place another on the throne"

It was suggestively put, although not incriminating. A typical Parry-ism.

I sighed and shook my head. "Gentlemen, although I value every faith you have in me, or with me, I have only these past few days become freed from suspicion of treason. I do not wish now to become embroiled in any reckless plan made by rash young men, as all these plots seem to be. I believe in the sanctity of the Crown as you well know, and I would wish no harm on the head of the Queen. If God wishes me to one day rule this land then such will become so. But I will not become involved, nor have my servants involved, in anything that would endanger my sister, my own good name, or the common people of these lands, who are always the first to suffer from the plots of the nobility. If any man comes plotting to these walls, gentlemen, be sure to tell him to plod and plot away from my house."

I smiled at them. "It has not been a time of ease or merriment for me these past many months, I think that perhaps some small entertainments may be devised for my diversion in the evenings. The days, gentlemen, I give to you for all the planning and the watching we must needs devise, but the evenings, I shall take as my own for if I do not hear my own laugh once again soon, I shall forget I ever had it at all!"

They laughed with me; good men, good servants and good friends. I had much in life to thank God for.

"But there is one thing that I must do, now that I am once again at my liberty," I said and they all looked to me in readiness. "I doubt I will need your assistance on this task, good masters, for it is only a letter, and a favour I hope my sister will grant after all this time I have spent at her side. Our party is as yet incomplete."

Parry looked at Cecil, who looked at Ascham, then they all looked at me. I very nearly laughed at them, for it is a strange thing to see men of such intelligence as the three before me stumped on such a little riddle.

But that is often the way of men; they forget there are others just as important as they are, in the world.

"We are missing a *Kat*," I smiled at them again. "My household is never complete without a house-Kat, my lords. Kat Astley must return to my side once more! This is my first, but most likely not my final, demand in my new freedom."

They smiled at me with affection and passed a wry look between them. Inwardly I smiled. They might think that Kat Astley was little important in the grand scheme of things, but they were wrong. For in all times of my life where I have been without that lady, I have been ever incomplete and unfinished as a person. There are some people who give life to the soul, who are the very substance of all you are. Kat was the very fibre and flesh of my being, and if I could bring her back to my side, I should indeed be free and complete in truth.

As I plotted for the return of my old governess to my side, Mary's own Parliament plotted to remove from her the power to reign as she wanted in England.

CHAPTER FORTY

Hatfield House
Autumn 1555

My sister was feeling generous towards me.

When she received the petition for the return of my old governess to my household, she allowed it, and soon, my greatest friend in this world was restored to my side.

Looking once again into the eyes of my dear Kat, I felt as though I were coming home.

A feeling, almost indescribable, as though of constant, nagging, hunger, had pervaded my soul since her removal from my side, and now that she stood once more before me, I felt it escape from my body like a sigh.

"Kat," I smiled warmly as she was brought into my presence chamber. "Too long have you left my side this time."

I rose and walked towards her, and pushing aside the formalities that should have come from a servant entering the presence of their master, I opened my arms wide and embraced her. There are some people in this world who embody that feeling of security and faithfulness that one arrives at when coming within the boundaries of one's own home. Kat was such; the last and full most link between the Elizabeth of now, and the little girl I had once been. Kat clung to my body, weeping tears of relief and of joy.

"My lady," she sobbed. "I have longed only to return to you."

"Let us hope this time will be the last you are parted from me," I said, my eyes also wet with emotion. "I feel I am never a whole person without you."

The return of my greatest friend to my side was of comfort to me. Indeed, with Kat's homecoming, my household was complete. It could almost be that we had stepped back into time and I was but a girl, a princess learning her lessons in the palace of childhood. But it was not so in truth; some things had changed beyond anything that the girl I had once been would have recognized, or thought possible.

As one Kat came home to my life, another Catherine had to leave.

My cousin, Lady Catherine Knollys, daughter of my mother's sister Mary Boleyn, and sometime companion of my childhood, was leaving the shores of England with her husband Francis; more of my friends who would rather flee the lands of their birth than renounce their true religion were leaving my side. Although I understood the reasons for Catherine and her husband leaving with absolute clarity, and in some ways celebrated their pragmatism, I could not help but feel a sore pull in my heart for all those figures, shrouded in distance and mist, all those people I had loved in my short life, who were having to leave the shores of England, to but worship God in the way they felt was right.

In my heart I also wondered… Was my faith as sure as theirs? They would give up home, hearth and country to be free to follow the faith they truly believed in, and yet I remained, playing at being a Catholic for the chance to survive in my own land. I prayed to God often, to hope that He did understand me. Should I leave these shores, it was likely I should never return. If I fled these lands now, and if Mary died, then it was more than likely that some other claimant might take the throne for which I was destined. If I followed the heart of my faith, I could never bring that faith back to heal a country as divided as this one in its heart, soul and mind. Did God understand me? I hoped so. That is all we mortals may have sometimes… Hope.

My cousin, Catherine, wrote to me before she left, explaining that the suspicion upon their shoulders was growing too great; her husband knew that soon he would be taken to the Tower to answer questions for his faith, and risked being burned for heresy in the greedy fires of Mary's unrelenting faith. When it was safe to return, Catherine wrote, they would not hesitate to come to my side.

"For in you, is our hope," she wrote in her bold hand.

When I read those words, it was as though a multitude of voices all called out to me at the same time. Not just the gentle voice of my cousin, but the voices of all those exiles watching their homeland disappear as they stood on the bows of mighty ships and merchant vessels, all those who walked to their deaths by the flames of my sister, all those who had waited in their dark prisons in the Tower of London or in the city gaols.

They all spoke to me at once of the same thing… hope.

I could not let them down.

Such a weight was to be carried on my slim shoulders, I thought. I could only hope that I would be worthy to the task set to me by the destiny of dynasty.

I burned Catherine's letter to me; it contained too many affectations that could become incriminating should my house be searched. But I did dare to write back to her, signing myself "Cor Rotto": the "Broken Heart". I wrote to, "think on this *pilgrimage* rather a proof of your friends, than a leaving of your country." I wove the letter into a dense background of alliteration and riddle, so that if my letter to my dear cousin was found, there would be many possible interpretations of each and every phrase held therein. That way, I could not be accused of open treachery, for if my words could hold many meanings, then they could be held to interpretation in many ways.

Yes, under my sister's reign and tutelage I had become the wily vixen slinking in the undergrowth; I was determined never to be caught by her indelicate Council oafs again. For every sentence that slipped from my tongue or quill, there would be a hundred meanings and readings to come from those words. I would be shut away in allegory and allusion.

It is a good lesson to learn, that words and books, verse and stories may have as many interpretations within them as there are readers to read them. I, who loved so well the written word and the contents of chronicles, came to use the power and the magic of ink on paper to conceal my true self, and yet reveal it to those with the imagination to understand my mind.

We can take up a book, and in reading it, find that we agree with so much the author has said that we can believe ourselves to know truly their heart, and feel ourselves close to authors who might have died a thousand years hence, or be living yet within the same land. Such is the magic of words and of books; to bring us together, or to hide us in plain sight.

I wrote letters to those of my faith in those hard years, where it seemed as though we might be wiped from the face of the land we loved so well in the scorching fires of Mary's Catholic rejuvenation. For those who knew my heart, those letter were easy to read; to find the hope I knew they needed, to see the pain I felt in every death which came to fall on those of the Protestant faith. But for those who would seek to steal those letters and use them against me, there was but a myriad of metaphor and a confusion of concept within. Those who were the enemies of me and my people knew not the truth of my heart, and therefore, they could not read my words in clarity or in truth.

I had learned to conceal myself. I had learned to be careful. Perhaps this, most basic of methods of survival was the greatest lesson my sister ever impressed upon me, however unknowingly the lesson was taught. I had become disguised in words, hidden in allegory.

I was no mere woman any longer, but a veritable book of fable and fictions.

CHAPTER FORTY-ONE

Hatfield House
Autumn 1555

There was growing unrest with Mary's governance of the realm.

Dissatisfaction with the path Mary was leading the country on was increasing, and it was starting to show even within the traditionally most-loyal of institutions in England.

Mary had started her reign on an ocean of approval but now, rebellion, an unpopular marriage, her failed pregnancy and the still-burning fires of faith were all stacking against her in the hearts of her people. Many Catholics of the land, not as violent in their views on religion as my sister, were opposed to the killings done in the name of faith, as of course were any Protestants still hiding their beliefs.

Many of the common people were tired of fearing for themselves, and their neighbours, and many of the nobles of the land felt much the same. Many Catholics may have been behind Mary in her determination to restore the Catholic faith to England, but they still baulked at watching their countrymen burn to death. They liked not the imposition of such "*Spanish*" ways thrown about England's unwilling shoulders.

People in the streets talked of the days of *Bluff Hal*, our father, with the tones of rosy hindsight. They talked of his days as the Head of the English Church as though it had been then an institution of inclusiveness and compassion. They did not remember truly that our father had executed as many Protestants for being heretics as he had Catholics for failing to adhere to his position as the commander of their faith. The people now talked of King Henry VIII as though he were a paragon of virtue and religious tolerance. Whilst this was not true, it was telling of the tide of popular feeling against Mary and her Council in their ruling of England.

If my sister was a wise woman, she would have listened.

She did not.

The Parliament of England was but an occasionally used institution; called and dissolved by the monarch when required to pass acts on matters such as increased taxation of the people of England, particularly in times of war, or on matters of law and legislation. In the thirty-seven years of our father's reign, he called only nine Parliaments. Our brother had called two Parliaments, and Mary was now opening her fourth. It was due to the rapid religious and cultural changes that she had called so many in such a short space of time.

The Crown and its Parliament were not supposed to be at odds with each other; their natural position was one of cooperation, for Parliament to bring about the wishes of the monarch, without reducing the country and her people to servitude, as they had once been under tyrannical rulers such as Bad King John.

Upon opening her fourth Parliament, Mary therefore found to her surprise that many members of her elected House of

Commons were minor gentry much under suspicion in matters of religion. Many of them were suspected of being secret Protestants, or sympathisers. Many were known to have talked against the marriage with Spain. Since Members of the Commons were elected by men of England who owned the relevant amount of property, the sudden influx of dissenters to the will of the Crown to the House of Commons was telling. This should have told Mary of the bent of the people's minds in her country. When the higher institutions of the land come to be filled with those who question the rights of the Crown, the Crown should know troubles are not far behind.

Mary was not as well-supported as she had been at the start of her reign, but she still had her loyal guard-dog Gardiner at her side. He opened the Parliament in his position as Lord Chancellor of England. His first act was to propose an increase in taxation on the English people for the needs of the Crown, a common ask of Parliament, which passed with fair ease.

Soon enough though, Mary would come to see that her narrow view of the world was not shared by all in her land. Although, generally, I would not wish to bore you with the fine details of all the arguments that occurred during the fourth sitting of Parliament of Mary's reign, there are some elements of it which are most important to my tale.

For the most part, Parliament to me has seemed like a clumsy way to ensure that the people of the country are allowed a say in their governance; red-faced men quipping and shouting at each other from one side of a room to another, trying to impress each other with their cleverness. Should anyone enter an inn during a cock-fight in London, one will see much the same scene and, most likely, the same outcome. If the vast majority of those who stand for Parliament would leave their overwhelming sense of their own importance at the door to the House, we should get a lot more done in this world.

Having said this, however, I cannot find in my wit another way to ensure any kind of fairness; our system of government does not necessarily protect its people, but it is the best system we have managed to erect, flawed though it may be. Although I have ever believed that God Himself chooses the monarch of any country, I also have to admit that some chosen to rule as monarchs are as little concerned with the welfare of the people they govern, as those bellowing out in Parliament.

They say that God works in mysterious ways, and with that I am in agreement.

My sister, the Queen, wished to pass two pieces of legislation in this Parliament, both close to her heart and beliefs. The first was a Bill which would return to the Catholic Church lands and estates that had been confiscated by the Crown during the reign of my father and that of my brother. These were rich properties, not just abbeys and monasteries, but farmland, river routes, roads and estates. Rents, tolls and dividends from these holdings currently went into the pocket of the Crown, but now Mary wanted those tithes and all the rights that went with them to return to the Catholic Church, and so ultimately, to Rome. The second Bill was to allow the Crown to confiscate the lands and properties of those Protestants who had fled England for fear of prosecution and execution for their faith. If those exiles wanted to retain their property, then they would have to return to England, placing them firmly within the hands of Mary's Catholic investigators. It was a plan intended to serve up more sacrifices on the altar of Mary's Catholic reformation.

The Pope must have been licking his lips in anticipation of an early New Year's present from England… on both counts.

The first Bill was brought to The House of Commons, and it was not popular.

The Crown was already in debt; indeed, the first act of the Parliament had been to agree an increase in taxation on the people of England for the needs of the Crown. Yet here was my sister, with her belief that holding Church lands was heresy, offering up another portion of England's dwindling riches to the Pope, a man in another country who already lived in opulence. But it was not only Crown fortunes that Mary wanted to grant to the Pope in Rome; she also wanted her lords to give back the lands that had been granted to them from the spoils taken from the Catholic Church when our father and brother reigned.

Mary held out her hand for more money from their left pocket, even as she sought to make them open their right pockets to the greedy hands of the Pope. She was taking their riches, and they liked it not.

It was madness. A ruler may command many things, but the impoverishment of a nation's landowners for the sake of her own personal morals showed that Mary understood her people not at all. Our father's reforms and reallocation of the wealth of the Church may have once upset his people, but now those lands, that wealth, was seen as *English* wealth. It was not a right of the Catholic Church to have such wealth… it was a right of English men. To ask that her landowners and nobles give up their rights to lands and estates granted to them, to ask that they impoverish themselves for her beliefs was unacceptable to them. If this act went ahead, then the common people would suffer greatly; they would have to give a portion of their incomes and harvests to the Church in addition to what they already paid to the nobles whose land they toiled… and what the nobles asked of the people of England would now also be increased to pay the nobles' share to the Pope in Rome.

Mary herself would feel little change as a result of her proposals; as the Queen, she would continue to be maintained in a manner expected of her situation and station. If that money came from her lands, or those of her subjects, it mattered little really to her. It was all the people down the chain that would suffer for my sister's ideals. All those landowners who would lose income and have to draw increased, unpopular, tithes from their tenants, all those living on small farms who would have so little left spare to feed themselves, after raising most of their crops and animals to pay their dues to their masters.

The people of England were already being subjected to increased taxation; this act would only increase poverty and discontent amongst her people.

Mary thought what she was doing was moral and good, but really she was plunging her country and her people deeply, into danger and hardship. Mary could not see this. She never took time to try and understand any view that was not her own. She saw the holding of these lands as a heretical act; perhaps she thought that if she returned them, then God would act to help her country, and her own personal dreams. Perhaps she thought that if she sacrificed this wealth to Rome, to the Pope, then God would take the time to look her way, and to grant her all that she desired so much; a family, a husband at her side, and children at her breast.

I believe that God gave us the ability to think for ourselves, gave us Free Will in order that we might weigh up the balance of our actions for ourselves. There is an old saying I remember much from the fables of Aesop, that if a man would have help from God, he must first try to aid himself, and that fable was never more in my mind than when I thought of this political obtuseness of Mary's. She believed in offering this sacrifice to God, and that in doing so, He would protect her people. I believe that she should have tried to see what was best for her people and in doing so, work God's will for compassion in her reign.

Just as this first Bill was going to its vote in Parliament, Stephen Gardiner, Mary's Lord Chancellor and Bishop of Winchester suddenly died. Although he was much aged by then, and had been long a sufferer of dropsy and illnesses of the liver, his death by a sudden ceasing of the heart was unexpected. The first attack weakened him, and brought him quickly to a bed he never again left. On his deathbed he was read the story of the Passion of the Christ and was said to have spoken the words "erravi cum Petro, sed non flevi cum Petro": "Like Peter I have erred, unlike Peter I have not wept." For a man who spent much of his career at court in bending to the will of his ruler, perhaps those were apt words of both regret and resolution.

I heard the news by a missive sent to Hatfield. My first feelings were those of disbelief, that a man who had so plainly made himself my enemy since the coming of my sister to the throne, had been so quickly and quietly removed from my path. Then, I will admit to you, I felt relief. I could not express sadness for the death of the man who had been my mortal enemy, who had sought at every turn to ensure my demise in these short years. It had never been proved that Gardiner was the man who had sent the forged order for my immediate execution to the Tower of London when I was imprisoned, but *I* was sure it had been his hand which moved to try and have me removed from life. Gardiner had been Mary's most important weapon in her struggle against the Protestant faith, and whilst the will and order to execute those of my faith had come from her, they had been carried out by Gardiner.

No, I could not mourn for such a man, but I could pray for him. He would need those prayers when he came to face his maker and answer for his earthly deeds.

Mary replaced her Bishop Gardiner with a cleric called Bonner. If the people had hoped for a reprieve in the stench and horror from the fires of faith upon the death of Stephen Gardiner, they were to be sorely disappointed. We came to see over the next months that Gardiner had been the lesser of two evils. Bishop Bonner soon became know as 'Bloody Bonner' for the pleasure he took in the pain and suffering of others. One of my enemies fell by the wayside; another rose to replace him, like the many-headed hydra, for Bonner had even less love for me than his predecessor. The arrests and the persecution of Protestants grew apace under Bonner with the sanction of Mary's Cardinal Pole; and the whole of England shivered in fear for any who fell under their gaze.

As the fear of religious persecution intensified in England under the appointment of Bishop Bonner, so Mary's fourth Parliament continued to struggle with the will of its monarch.

Until the reign of my sister, contention between the wishes of the King and the votes of the Commons in Parliament had been rare; usually, but not every time, a king of England would have what he wanted from his Parliament.

In order to have her Bill on the return of lands to the See of Rome passed, Mary took drastic action. Feeling there was much opposition to her will the Queen had the members of the Commons kept as virtual prisoners, locked inside the House without food or water until her men felt certain that they had enough votes to achieve her wishes. The Bill passed, but it was by a slim margin.

Usually there would be little opposition to the Crown. Mary had attained victory, but only through imprisoning her Parliament. Having passed a Bill that would effectively impoverish both her country and her people, Mary went on triumphantly to make her next move, so much supported and encouraged by Cardinal Pole that I began to think the second Bill had been his idea. The lands of those who had fled England's religious tyranny would be confiscated; those exiles wishing to retain their lands and properties would have to return to England, forcing them to face investigation into their religious beliefs… and we all knew what that meant.

If Mary could not bring the Protestants of England to face her Catholic investigators by fair means, she would use foul.

Mary, however, had not fully appreciated how angry the House was due to the treatment of its Members regarding the last Bill. She had also not appreciated that the many Englishmen now living in other lands had family and friends here still in England. Most of all… she had not appreciated that something done once, may be done again.

It came down to one man in the end; one good Englishman who had a fine bawling voice and enough charisma to thwart Mary and her minion Cardinal Pole. When the Bill was read, Sir Anthony Kingston of Gloucestershire, with the help of the sergeant-at-arms and guards of the House, locked the doors on his fellow Members of the House, roaring out in a clear voice that whilst they had been forced to pass the last Bill, this one at least should not be passed *"by any honest Englishman for the impoverishment of his neighbour"*. I doubt the Members of the House were overly keen on once more being locked into the House, this time by the opposition to the Crown, but they took their votes I hope with their consciences, rather than for fear of their monarch.

Mary's second Bill was defeated. It was most unusual for such a thing to happen. Three days later, Mary dissolved her Parliament in great anger, and Kingston was arrested and sent to the Tower. Members of the House were supposed to be free from threat of arrest for their votes within the House. Mary was once more thinking with her heart, rather than her head. It was leading her to disobey English law, and even if one is the Queen, disobeying the doctrine of law is a dangerous thing to do; if the sovereign can ignore law, then so can the common man.

I wonder how my sister felt when she realized that her own people were against the measures she proposed to bring the religious exiles to her heel. Although she could rejoice at the return of property to Rome's already overflowing coffers, she had not managed to enforce the return of the religious exiles to her land. They had escaped her clutches, with the help of their fellow Englishmen.

But more than that; it was now clear that Mary reigned over a country that was fast becoming dangerously divided.

Such lands are always ripe for rebellion. Dissatisfaction is the mother of all unrest. We all want to have enough, to be appreciated within our own spheres, to be seen and heard and to be treated with fairness. Mary was blind, deaf and dumb to her people; a living embodiment of all that should be feared in a monarch. She put the wishes and wants of her heart above those of her people, and covered it all in a mask of religion.

The heart is the most dangerous enemy.

In all ways and in all things, religion should be a force of goodness. If ever something is done in the name of religion that brings naught but disorder and destruction, then you can take a fine bet that it is not the heart of God that is involved, but that of man. When we follow but our own hearts and our own vanity, we are blind.

I looked on my sister's reign now with the eyes of one learning a lesson in how *not* to reign. I promised myself that if I should ever attain the throne of England, I should take every lesson, however harsh, that was granted to my sister, and I should learn from it… where she learnt nothing.

That Christmas as we prepared our feasts and succour for our servants, there came to Hatfield a visitor who had not thoughts of Christmas cheer in his mind.

Once again, rebellion was lifting its angry head in England.

CHAPTER FORTY-TWO

Hatfield House
1555- 1556

That Christmas, as was the custom of England, my servants had gone forth into the forests and the parks about Hatfield to bring in greenery to decorate my house with, but on Christmas night at Hatfield, as the sounds of merry making rang out from the halls below us, a different kind of offering was brought into the house, a most secret one.

Whilst snows fell on the frozen lands outside our windows, and the common man gathered fuel to warm his fire in the depths of winter, we came to know that the hearts of some in England were being warmed by a different flame than that found in the hearth.

Rebellion against the Crown was once more on the march.

I sat waiting in a private chamber, alone but for Kat, when Sir Christopher Ashton was brought to me by Parry. Ashton came alone, and with only one man as his travelling companion on the snow-covered roads of England. If I was to meet with any of these men who presently plotted against my sister, then I wanted the number to be as small as possible to minimise the risk of discovery. As Ashton walked through the chamber door and bowed to me, little flakes of melting snow fell from his travelling cloak, collecting in tiny puddles on the fresh-smelling rushes of the floor. I nodded to Parry to close the door, so that I could listen to what my secret visitor had to say.

None knew of the meeting but my closest of servants and friends. Whilst I feared not for the loyalty of my household, I wanted not to endanger them with the knowledge that I had chosen to meet with one of those seeking to bring disorder to the rule of my sister. The fledgling rebels wanted my support. As heir to the throne, I was valuable to their plans. But I was yet unsure in myself which way I thought on their plans. Although I had told my servants in no uncertain terms when we first arrived that I wanted nothing of plotters in my house, the last few months, as Mary had taken our country ever deeper into trouble and despair had weighed heavy on my conscience. I believed in the God-given position of the monarch in any land, but with my sister's advances into lunacy and economic tyranny, I was coming to wonder if it was not a sign that I *should* be willing to depose her, to take the throne myself and to put right the wrongs she was visiting on these lands.

But I was, as I often have been, of two minds about this. Too often does vanity control the taking of decisions. Was I any more worthy than my sister to take the throne? Should I become embroiled in any plot that might endanger the rightful passage of the crown from one king to another? Weighty questions for any, but especially for a twenty-two-year-old maid, bowed down with the responsibility of living in the shadow of the crown. But when knowledge of this plot had come to us, by Parry's spies and Cecil's contacts of course, I had come to think that I must at least find out more, and to use that knowledge to decide my mind. The acquisition of knowledge is never a bad thing; it is only the choices one makes upon that knowledge that may be good or evil.

Parry knew well the bent and turn of my mind; he could read me better than any. I believe that is why Parry convinced me to allow Ashton to come into my house to reveal this plot, when he should have, at my orders, sent him away.

I looked the man up and down, and could not help but smile when he looked up at me. Christopher Ashton was my kind of man; he was a risk taker, a gambler, but he was also as loyal as a lion and as brave as a bear, when given the right master. I knew him from court of course. Ashton was rich; he had married a wealthy widow, Lady Catherine Gordon, who had been kin of King James IV of Scotland. The lady had led a troubled life; her first husband had been the notorious Perkin Warbeck, that pretender to the English throne who had arrived during the reign of my grandfather claiming to be Richard of York, the younger of the two child-Princes who were murdered in the Tower under the reign of the usurper Richard III. Perkin's uprising failed, although along the way, he apparently managed to convince many people, including the King of Scotland, that he really was the fabled Duke of York. Personally, I have ever wondered if James of Scotland had really believed that Perkin *was* Prince Richard. I would not have put it past James of Scotland to have supported Perkin's uprising simply to annoy my grandfather, for James had no love for the throne of England, despite later marrying my aunt Margaret Tudor.

After Perkin's execution, Catherine had been kept much as a respected prisoner of my grandfather, and was a lady in waiting to my grandmother Elizabeth of York. She married another two times, burying each husband, and had also once served in my sister's household. Despite being essentially a prisoner, Catherine was protected by the good-will of my grandfather and father, who, thankfully for her, found her as personally captivating as she was politically dangerous, for she was spoken of as one of the most beautiful women any man had ever seen. Catherine died in 1537, passing her wealth to Ashton, her last husband. Ashton was therefore rich enough, and influential enough, to prove a serious threat to Mary. His name had been mentioned in the Wyatt rebellion, and he was a known opponent of my sister's match with Spain.

There are some families, it seems, which are ever-bound to the service of rebellion and revolt.

Ashton stood from his bow, and I nodded to him to start to relay the ideas he and his fellow plotters had put together. Ashton looked sideways at Parry, and received another nod from him. It seemed Ashton was seeking assurance that he would have a measure of protection he had perhaps requested before entering my house.

"I will not repeat anything which is said within this chamber, Sir Ashton," I said, looking at him, "as long as you offer the same assurance; as far as I am concerned, this meeting has never happened. That is assuredly what I will tell any who ask."

Ashton grinned at me and bowed again, "my lady."

Then he started to talk, and I started to listen.

Ashton, it seemed, was far from alone in his thoughts of rebellion against the Crown. Another plot-prone noble, also from a family bred for rebellion, Sir Henry Dudley, had also promised support. Related by blood to the infamous Warwick, who tried to steal the throne from my sister and place our little cousin Jane upon it, Sir Henry Dudley was well-versed in revolt and eager to rise against the Crown. Sir Anthony Kingston, that self-same man who used my own sister's tactics against her in the House of Commons, was also involved. Luckily for that rebel knight, the law of the land had swung in his favour, and my sister had had to set him free from the Tower, despite her dislike of him. The charges against him had not been sufficient, to my sister's irritation, to condemn him, nor keep him imprisoned. He had, after all, not actually *forced* the votes of the House of Commons; he had but held a door shut.

Ashton tried to impress on me that there were others involved in the plot, and many more that would rise to join their forces, once the standard of rebellion was raised. He, of course, called it loyalty to England, rather than rebellion against her queen. I smiled a little as I thought to myself that whether history should come to call it that depended entirely on the outcome of the rebel plots.

The plot unfolded into my little ear and as it did, I had to refrain from letting out a sigh. Perhaps expecting originality was a step too far.

The plot was really much the same as Wyatt's had been. Forces would be raised from all corners of England under the command of Ashton, Kingston, Dudley and others, to march on strategic points. Protestant exiles in France and the Low Countries would engage foreign mercenaries and send them to England to take the ports and coastal towns. London would be taken as all the forces converged. Mary would be deposed, I would be married to Edward Courtenay and we would be made king and queen, refuting the power of Rome, and ruling England for the English alone. Courtenay had, some months ago, been sent into exile and was now in Venice, but the rebels were keen to see him return, to take my hand in marriage.

My eyebrows must have lifted at this notion, although I believe I managed to ensure admirable control over my face considering my disgust at the idea; once more I found myself matched to that dullard Courtenay. How many more times would men seek to saddle me with such a fool? This was not the fate I wished for.

I looked at Parry as Ashton continued with his speech, and behind Ashton's head I saw Parry smile briefly and shake his head a little at me. I almost grinned at the man; he and I thought alike so well.

I heard Ashton out. Although I found him to be both engaging and charismatic, a fine speaker, I could not help but feel irritation move through me as I heard his plans. Why could these men never see that their ideas were all the same? Why did I *always* have to be married off to some remnant of a lost dynasty? Why could they not think of me as anything but a tool to lever in a king? Why could they not pause to think, that perhaps I did not want to be married off to some dullard more suited to becoming a court fool than a king? Why could they not think that Elizabeth of England might have something of worth in her, other than a finger on which to place a ring?

There was never anything more dangerous, or more tiresome, than the absence of originality.

I had seen my cousin, Jane, used as a tool of men. I was never going to allow that fate to become my own. If I was ever to rule, then *I* should rule. I was not some mere figurehead for the wants and wills of another. I had my own will.

My thoughts raced angrily through my mind as Ashton continued, not noting the slight frown on my face which would have alerted any of my servants that they were wading into danger. At my side, Kat was trying to smother a grin; like Parry, she knew my mind well and could feel my temper rising. But Ashton was gleefully unaware of the danger he was paddling into.

The main difference between this plot and Wyatt's was that the temper of the country was swiftly turning against Mary. Where Wyatt's rebellion had failed, many people then still being loyal to Mary, Ashton thought this present plot should truly have the support of the common people.

This at least, I had to give to him. But I was unconvinced by the plot and more than slightly irritated by his eagerness to sell me off to marry Courtenay. Listening to the plot, I found I little wanted to become embroiled in another plot that might see me, should it all come to nothing, once again facing the prospect of losing my head on the same green that took my mother's life. And, should it succeed, I might well find myself saddled with a most unwanted husband.

I listened to Ashton; I admired him in some ways. He was bold and reckless in many regards, but he was also quite captivating and interesting. I had to talk sternly to my heart a few times during our secret interview when I found myself impressed with his manner of speaking… Just because a man can inspire you to fight a war, does not mean he can win it.

I could see Parry thinking the same thing…. Almost hear his keen mind whirring and clicking behind Ashton's engaging figure in the room. There was too much to risk here by coming out boldly in support of the plotters. So I gave Ashton my usual assurances, and my usual evasions. I confirmed nothing, and I denied nothing. I let the mask of the vixen steal over my features once more. I was not willing to walk as yet from the deep shadow of the undergrowth, to the light of the open field.

This plot was not for me, not now, but I was glad that I knew of it, so that I might be prepared whether they succeeded or not. Much the same as when Warwick and my sister had waged war for the throne, I would settle within my house in the countryside to see what would come of this new struggle for power. I would not raise my hand against my sister, but I would not stop others from doing so either. Mary had not won my loyalty, but she had not yet earned my outright treachery. I would wait and watch, as ever was my way.

Ashton rode out from Hatfield as he had come, under cover of darkness. I am sure in his mind he thought I was as eager for his revolt as he was. But I would wait and watch; if they succeeded then we should see if I was merely to be married off to whomsoever *they* decided.

I would have my *own* say in the matter. They would not find me to be a silent, malleable tool in their hands.

The rebellion began to take its first steps into action. In secret, the plotters raised forces and gathered supporters. Parry reported to me that they even succeeded in robbing the Exchequer, taking bullion and treasure with them as they sailed to France to raise troops there. During the first months of 1556 I was restless and anxious, wondering if at any moment, they may in fact succeed where so many others had failed, and invade at the head of an army of English Protestants and foreign hire-swords. These thoughts made me uncomfortable, for my soul told me that the country should not rise against its queen, and yet… how could I blame them for trying, when Mary had inflicted such misery on her people?

I was torn, in mind, in heart, in loyalty… I knew not which I wanted to succeed, nor which outcome I should truly want.

But then, as so many of these plots do, it all fell apart; the rebels were betrayed by one of their own men who confessed all to Cardinal Pole. I never found out the name of the man who betrayed Ashton and the others, nor why he revealed the plot to my sister's men. Perhaps the man had been a dual-agent all along, operating two faces on behalf of my sister. Perhaps he was weak-willed and bent under the pressure of so many secrets, perhaps he was tortured. But for whatever reason, the plot was unfolded to the ghastly Cardinal Pole. Ashton and Dudley fled to France, and all the plotters left in England were arrested.

The investigation was handed to Mary's Catholic Councillors, and they were brutal in their methods of excavating the truth. My old gaoler, Bedingfield, now Lieutenant of the Tower, found himself vomiting upon seeing the vile state of the cells the prisoners were thrown into. Piss and rats and bile, mud and blood and faeces; those were the things which kept those men company within their cells in the Tower of London. They were questioned, they were tortured… they started to talk.

When I heard news of their capture and torture, I felt fear quake within me once more. With the rebel leaders Ashton and Dudley in France, out of reach to the Councillors and to Mary, would her sights once again fall upon me as the instigator of rebellion against her throne? As the plot was unravelled I came to fear that my life was once again in mortal danger.

If my sister had suspected me of treason when I had but received a message from a rebel in the last plot, what would she do to me if she found out that this time, I had in fact been meeting with those who wanted to see her deposed?

CHAPTER FORTY-THREE

Hatfield House
June 1556

It was with the worst feeling of deja vu that we watched the arrival of hundreds of royal troops at Hatfield.

"When troubles come, they come in force," Kat mused, looking out from the window at the approach of the Queen's Guard.

"And every man is for himself," I grimaced.

"Lucky that we're women, then," Kat said with a touch of her old humour still showing, under the quaking of her voice in fear.

I reached out and took her shoulder. "We have faced this, and worse, before, and yet here we still stand. We must remember all that has saved us before and use those lessons well. Confirm nothing that they wish confirmed, deny all that cannot be proved. Stand strong and survive. This is a test of endurance, not that of speed."

I wished that I believed those words as easily as I said them, but in truth, my heart was beating fast enough to kill me even as I spoke words to comfort my friend.

Parry came in. "They are here," he said, rather unnecessarily, but I nodded to him.

"Who leads?" I asked.

Parry made a rueful face "Sir Henry Jerningham and Sir John Norris."

I am sure my face looked as ill as Parry's upon those words. Jerningham was one of Mary's inner-circle of Catholic Counsellors, if there was ever a man in England closer to being a part of Spain's brutal Inquisition, you would have been hard pressed to find him. Norris too was a passionate Catholic. Unfortunately, neither were unintelligent. It seemed my sister was serious in her attentions for my arrest this time.

"Come then," I said. "Let us go and let them have what they want of us. Let us just remember, my friends, there are things I want of you, too; your loyalty, and your good quiet tongues."

Parry and Kat nodded. We were becoming seasoned soldiers now in this type of battle. But that did not mean we were less afraid; only that we knew now what we had to face. Kat was quickly arrested and taken from me; it was clear to most people that the continual return of my governess to my side was important to me, and therefore my enemies thought it would always weaken me to have her taken away.

"How many times must we do this?" she whispered to me. Her face was full of anguish. "So little time with you, my dearest one."

"But yet, how many times have you returned to me?" I replied as I slipped the ring I gave her when we were parted before once more into her hands. She clutched it in her fist with a dark look of anger and pain on her face and in truth, I almost smiled. Kat Astley was as much of a lioness as I; I should very much like to see any man try to remove that ring from her clutches. They took her to the Tower of London; once more my poor Kat was a prisoner within those walls. I feared for her, for the horrible memories the Tower would bring back to her spirit, and I hoped that her courage would hold out during her time there.

My servants and my ladies, including my poor Blanche, were all arrested and taken away, also to the Tower. Parry was sent off under guard to his uncle's house, and I was put under house arrest at Hatfield.

Mary's guards searched Hatfield and my other houses. They found a cache of books and pamphlets in Kat's apartments at my residence of Somerset House that not only attacked Catholicism, but also satirized the Queen and her beloved Phillip. The papers were planted, of course. Kat was many things, but she was not stupid, nor foolish enough to leave incriminating books in a place we were not staying in. We had enough secret hiding places for the books and volumes we valued to hide them well enough from Mary and her inquisitors, and we never left anything behind to leave a trail.

I believe Mary was looking for a reason to take Kat from me for good, and so created one. All that Mary ever believed of Kat was that she was a bad influence on me. But then Mary often saw things upside down; for it had been many, many years in fact since I had become the main influence on Kat, not the other way around. If anything, *I* was the 'bad' influence on Kat these days.

My enemies had much more evidence than the last time I had been under arrest, and more reason perhaps to strike me down. I was growing very afraid of what else they would "find" to incriminate me. There was however, one saving grace for me in all this sudden torrent of horror… Phillip of Spain.

Mary, being the devoted wife that she was, sent word of all that had happened to her beloved husband and asked, as was her wifely duty to do so, his opinion on the matter and what was to be done. It is the only time I have ever come to bless the servitude that marriage often places on the shoulders of a woman… or the involvement of a foreign power in the matters of England.

You see, in asking Phillip's opinion, Mary opened up what should have been a merely a matter of the here and now in England, into one of future possibility and empirical scope. Phillip was not a disinterested third party, and he had a longer gaze than that of his wife; as the ruler of the Hapsburg Empire, Phillip was as much a slave to the best interests of his country as any other ruler.

If I was removed, without an heir from the body of Mary, then the next Catholic heir to the throne would be our royal cousin, Mary Stuart, Queen of Scots and Dauphine of France. Despite being excluded from the will of our father, our cousin of Scots was more attractive as an heir, I believe, to Mary than our Protestant Grey cousins, or our odious cousin Margaret Douglas, Countess of Lennox. For Phillip however, there were other considerations. On the one hand, Mary Queen of Scots was Catholic, bred and raised and therefore much more attractive than I in terms of religion. On the other hand, and especially poignant from Phillip's point of view, Mary Stuart was married to Francois, the Dauphin of France. If Mary Stuart became Queen of England, then the position of France, one of the great enemies of Spain and her territories, would be greatly, and perhaps for Spain, fatally, strengthened. France would have a foothold in Scotland, England and Ireland as well as controlling all territories belonging to France at present, thus forming a great barrier between Spain and her territories in the Low Countries. France would rule the seas betwixt its lower southern end and the shores of the upper islands of Scotland. It was not something the Spanish would ever want to see happen.

The prospect for Phillip of dealing with a Protestant heir was much more attractive than handing the power of England over to the French once my sister Mary was dead. And perhaps, just perhaps, there was in his protection of my life an inkling of his own, personal, fondness for me. He did not delay in sending his answer to Mary. I found all this out from the secret messages that Cecil still managed to sneak to me even under house arrest. There were few cracks in the wall through which my clever men could not find a passage to me.

After a bare two weeks of house arrest, I was sent an extraordinary message.

The guards were sent away and I was informed that although some of my servants had been complicit in action of rebellion against my sister, that I was innocent. My sister sent word that she could "*never believe*" that I would have acted against her, as I was "*too wise and too prudent*" to have done so, and she even sent me a diamond, a symbol of purity, to show her affection for me.

I was informed that my servants who were suspected of being complicit in acting for the rebels would not be returned to me, but that I was no longer under any suspicion.

Well versed was I in the production of protestation to cover any suspicion of treason. Less well prepared was I, then, when thinking I should be surely arrested and executed, to suddenly found myself exonerated.

Fleeting is the shadow of the axe that falls before the sun.

I was saved this time not through my own wit, nor through my own steadfastness, not by the loyalty of my servants, the quickness of my mind or the love of the people of England... but through the actions of a powerful friend. It was a sign that the tide was turning in my favour; the most powerful Emperor in Europe thought that my life was worth preserving.

The seasons change, the tides turn, and day frequently becomes night. Nothing and no one stays the same as they were. It seemed that the wheels of Time and of Fortune were turning, and I, for the first time in my life, was starting to ride the crest of a wave that carried my favour.

CHAPTER FORTY-FOUR

Hatfield House
Summer 1556

The events of the Ashton-Dudley rebellion slowly but surely trickled away like water down a drain. I was not given back my servants, but they had not been accused of treason or executed, for to do so would be to implicate me. Many of them were under house arrest in the homes of their families, although this was not made entirely public.

Instead of my own household, I was given Sir Thomas Pope and Sir Robert Gage to take on the duties of my house. I was under custody and watch, but I was also allowed freedom of movement and freedom to write, and at least Hatfield was a house in good order with warm rooms, unlike my last prison. It seemed that Phillip had told Mary that all charges of suspicion were absolutely to be dropped against me; that I was to be freed of all touch of treason and the matter forgotten.

Extraordinary, you might well think… as I did.

That is the measure of politics however. What is treason one day may be excused in the name of practicality the next; strange bedfellows are made in the halls of power.

My life at Hatfield was quiet and mellowed. Mary requested me at court, and I declined for a while, thinking that whilst Phillip had arranged my pardon, Mary must surely still be angry with me. Her anger with my person would be better reduced by allowing her time to calm herself; for although I had not countered the rebel's plans, I had met with them. I could understand that my sister must see me as a threat to her reign. So, I wrote to her instead; letters full of the praise that is required when one writes to princes, but also including small inferences to our time together when she had lately despaired and I had helped her. Perhaps the only time I had ever been good enough to her to return the affection and attention she bestowed on me when I was but a babe; perhaps the only time when we two pawns of power, had been as sisters.

In October of that year, Kat and other members of my house were finally freed from the hideous confines of the Tower, but none of them were allowed to return to my household or to write to me, officially at least; Parry however still found ways to reach me with messages, even if the others could not. Mary still thought Kat an evil influence and was determined that I should never see my old governess again. However sad I was about that matter, I had other reasons to rejoice. In the same month as my servants were freed, so was I. Although the custody I had been placed in was not onerous, it still felt as though an iron door had clanked open when Robert Gage and Thomas Pope were removed as my wardens and I was given back control of my household.

What energy may be found in the freedom of one's independence! There have been a few times in my life when I have truly had reason to exult at the feeling of liberty, never more so than under the reign of my sister. If you have never felt bars close around you, you do not understand the full beauty and majesty of the freedom you have. It is only when one has faced such a time of incarceration that one truly appreciates the feeling of sovereignty. To step free, ungoverned, unwatched and unknown... to ride across hilltop and know that you command those very hills… to hold in your hands the power of controlling your own life! Ah! These are the things that drive the heart to beat and the blood to pound. The essence of our lives comes in our own recognition of freedom. None can teach it, none can tell it. But all those who have lost it and found it once again would never devalue it.

I spent a long time out riding that autumn; wet grass and muddy lands, flooded fords and ripping winds; there was never a sensation more glorious than that of England as her rough weather battered my face and my skin. I would rather ride through an English storm than bask in a foreign sun; for a foreign sun would burn me, where an English storm would feed my soul.

It was as though the weather mirrored my feelings of savage enjoyment in the freedom of my person. Rain fell, wind blew and tempests raged… but still I rode out to face them. Each night when I returned, wet through and exhausted, I slept like a babe without a care in the world.

We received word soon enough that the Earl of Devon, my erstwhile suitor Edward Courtenay, had died suddenly in Padua. Although I had scarce ever known the man in truth, I felt a little sad at his passing. Perhaps it is silly to mourn for a man who really only brought me trouble, so often was he *affianced* to me in the plans of rebels, but when I heard of his death I could not stop thinking about the man who spent most of his life imprisoned in the Tower, only to emerge and be exiled from his home; such a small and a sad life of little and spare freedom for one born to royal blood.

Eventually Mary asked that I attend the Christmas celebrations at court that winter, and I was eager to attend. Although I had relished the return of my freedom, long months of little company had left me hungry for London. At the end of November, I rode into London towards my residence at Somerset House amidst two hundred of my men dressed in the most expensive black silks and velvets... and the roars of the crowds of London cheered their princess home once more.

CHAPTER FORTY-FIVE

The Court of Mary I, London
Winter 1556

Before I came to meet with my sister that winter, there was the pressing matter of replacing the members of my personal household that had been removed from me. Those servants suspected of treason were still under house arrest with their own kin and were not allowed back into my service. But it does not do for any prince to be without the servants of the body which prove the respect and honour of rank. Two ladies came to me to beg for a place in my household and I came to take both into my house.

Anne Calthorp, Duchess of Sussex, was as unconventional a woman as she was unconventional a noble; once part of the inner *salon* of Queen Katherine Parr, Anne, to the horror of her husband, a pious Catholic, had turned to the Protestant religion during the reign of my father and that of my brother. There were rumours that she also dabbled in the arts of magic and sorcery, although, upon meeting her, I found this hard to swallow. So often, when women are but outspoken and self-assured, rumours spread about them having demonic powers. It is more often than not a way to discredit them in the eyes of the world. It is something we should all beware of, to take gossip and slander as fact.

I found Anne most interesting from the very start. Ordinarily a married woman would have no place in my household; highborn maids were usually served by noble maids rather than matrons; there were exceptions of course, such as my dearest Kat, but Anne's husband had lately managed, with great difficulty, to divorce her on the grounds that she was "*unnatural*". This piqued my interest first of all; how often had it been impressed on me that *I* was beyond the realms of natural behaviour for a woman, after all? But my first meeting with Anne suggested to me that she was a woman of intelligence and bravery; the kind of person I admired and turned to. I could see nothing unnatural in her, and I relished her company.

The second lady was Elizabeth Brooke, and I believe she may have been sent into my service by my sister. Elizabeth Brooke had married the Marquis of Northampton, William Parr, who was the brother of my own dear stepmother Katherine Parr, after he had divorced his first wife for adultery. My sister, however, had refused to recognise Parr's second marriage and this left Elizabeth Brooke in somewhat of a difficult position. In her own eyes she was married and was the Marchioness of Northampton. In the Queen's eyes however, she was nothing of the sort. Left as a wife who was no wife, a Lady who was no Lady, she could not come to court as the Marchioness of Northampton, nor live honestly with her husband. My sister also stripped Elizabeth's husband of his titles, and so they each forced to seek service in the houses of others more highly born than they were.

I believe my sister, although disapproving of the match between Elizabeth Brooke and the Marquis, had, all the same, sympathised with Elizabeth's plight at knowing not what to do with herself now. So, I believe that Mary had sent her to me to become a part of my household. I warmed to Elizabeth Brooke immediately; she was pretty, and I was always attracted to beauty in my women, but also had a spirit to her and a loyalty that came from the very best in her heart. In the following years, she became one of my closest confidants.

So, with my new and interesting ladies in position with me, I was ready once again to meet with my sister.

Three days passed residing at Somerset House before my sister sent word to meet with her. The whole court would be there to see *"my own sister return to the heart of the family"* Mary wrote. The letters Mary sent to me were warm and friendly, marking nothing of the latest troubles that had beset us.

And therein, in all that warmness, I began to suspect that something was afoot.

We rode through the streets to Greenwich Palace, towards the court, crowds cheering and the coats of my hundred attendants flashing in the morning light. I waved and smiled to those people who had stood in the streets for hours waiting to see me. London and its people were ever such a balm to my spirits. When we arrived at the great palace of my forebears, we were taken in great state, and very publicly, to the presence chamber of my sister, and there, amidst the sound of cheers and music, I was brought before the figure of my sister Mary again.

Richly dressed in cloth of gold and bright red velvets, she sat on the dais looking regal and richly dressed. Around her throat shone diamonds and emeralds, twinkling at me in the light reflected from the windows. On her head, covering her thin hair was a hood of black and white decorated with pearls and sapphires. On her skeletal hands there was no decoration save the simple gold band that signified her marriage to the absent Phillip, and her ring of betrothal to him. But her face was grey with tiredness, and her eyes encased in dark shadows. Cosmetics had been used to cover her face in pale majesty, but cracks in the paste which opened and moved as she talked showed clearly that the skin beneath was as parched and tired as she was at heart. I dropped to a curtsey on the floor before her, and spread my arms as though I were a penitent coming to the altar of the Lord in Heaven.

"Rise," she said, and I did so, standing before my Queen.

"I am so pleased to see you looking so well, Your Majesty," I lied as the court waited to see what should happen between us. "It has been so long since last I had the privilege of looking upon Your Majesty's grace."

"Indeed, sister," she smiled. "It is gratifying to see you return to our court; we should not be without our *most loyal* of subjects and friends for so long."

I curtseyed again at this compliment. I could almost feel the court wondering *what on earth was going on?* But, however confused they were as to my arrival as a most honoured guest when they had likely suspected recently that I should be arrested and executed, the court did not ask questions in public. They applauded, in the most sycophantic manner possible, at the surface image of we two Tudors, we two sisters, reunited apparently as the best of friends.

"Later sister, we must meet and discuss matters that I know will be of *much* interest to you," Mary said. "My husband, although he is still absent from our shores on matters which cannot be put aside, also writes to me of many things that will interest and entertain you." She paused and smiled warmly. Her thoughts were with Phillip then, and they were pleasant to her. "His Majesty writes often to me," she continued. "Although the matters of his empire are most arduous, there is never a part of my dear Phillip which is not thinking of England and our matters here."

"His Majesty is the most devoted of husbands and consorts," I replied, "and I pray the matters that hold him away from England will not do so for much longer, Your Majesty. He must long so to return to you."

"He does," Mary said shortly. A little cloud passed over her eyes and then she shrugged it away.

"You will come to my inner chambers later this very day, sister, for there is much we must tell each other of this time we have been apart."

"I will count the hours until you send for me, Your Majesty."

Later that afternoon, the message came to my apartments that I was to meet with my sister in private. I was nervous, but interested. I could not help but wonder what sort of meeting Mary and I should have this time. Should I be portrayed as publicly innocent before the court and yet barraged in private with accusations of treason? Would Mary resent that her husband had stepped in to protect me from this latest accusation of betrayal? Was I once again to be subject to a storm over her suspicions that I was still a secret Protestant?

I never knew, with Mary, what might happen. Such a mask she managed to wear over her true face before the court that I knew not where she really began and ended. Perhaps she felt the same for me; we two sisters were ever destined to dance around each other in different costumes and guises, like two seeking to know each other at a masque, our knowledge of the other was ever incomplete.

My ladies, Anne and Elizabeth, could see that I was worried. I sought little to hide things from my personal servants; if I wanted their loyalty then I needed honesty with them also.

Anne pressed my hand. "Your reception with Her Majesty was goodly and gracious," she counselled. "You must not see ghosts of troubles where there are none as yet."

"As yet," I said ruefully.

"The future is never written in ink, my lady," Anne smiled at me. "It is writ in chalk, for it is something ever-changeable and never sure. What matters is that we face it and choose as best we are able to do with all that God has given us."

"That is true," I nodded.

"And your spirit is such that words never fail to come to you when you have need of them," said Elizabeth Brooke, coming to my side. "Within your own self, my lady, you have a formidable weapon."

"It is not what is within that I fear, Bess," I replied. "But what is without. My life has ever been controlled and thrown around by those about me. One day perhaps, I should like a chance to rule my own life myself."

"So should we," said Anne.

"Come then," I smiled at them. "Take me to the Queen, for whatever it is that causes her to smile at me like a spider to a fly, it cannot be as bad as I would imagine here."

I was wrong.

CHAPTER FORTY-SIX

The Court of Queen Mary I, London
Winter 1556

Anne and Bess escorted me through the court to the privy chambers of my sister. From there, I was met by the handsome and lively, Lady Jane Dormer, and taken to the Queen. Jane, it often seemed to me, was an odd choice for one of my sister's ladies; Mary habitually preferred the company of rather drab, serious and pious ladies, much matching the reflection of her own soul. Jane seemed to me rather like one of my own ladies; more of the feisty spirit and indomitable loyalty that I tended to favour in a servant.

My sister's chambers seemed to be kept unnaturally warm, even for the time of year. By the time we reached Mary's inner chambers, I could feel sweat beading on my forehead and a thin line of perspiration running slowly down the curve of my spine. When I commented on the heat of the chambers, Jane almost pulled a little face of disgust, but then, to my amusement, seemed to remember herself and said formally, "The Queen, unfortunately, feels the chill of this winter most keenly."

The obvious point was there, but left unsaid; my sister was not a well woman. For no one who was hearty and hale should need to fend off the winter airs with such a stifling heat as that which shimmered around me.

"Her Majesty, my great sister, has the royal line of Spain within her blood as well as that of England," I said mildly. "I understand Spain to be much warmer in all seasons than England. It is only natural that the Queen's blood may need a little more warming than those of us just who carry only the blood of the English."

Jane looked at me sharply, and then tucked her lip slightly in a smile that was both grateful, and a little pained with sorrow. I was touched; Mary had an unfortunate habit of remaining distant from people, even as she desired above all things to be loved. Because she held others away from her with a practised hand, precious few ever came to love her truly. Whatever problems I had with my sister, I was never unhappy to see that someone near her really did care for her.

Love, especially for members of your family, can be a complicated thing.

Jane took me into the chambers of my sister; Mary was standing at the window looking out onto the river as we entered. I dropped to a curtsey but Mary came and touched my shoulder, indicating I was to rise. Then, to my great surprise, she opened her thin arms and embraced me.

"It does me good to see you, Elizabeth," she said warmly.

I reached my little arms around her, and as I did so, I smelt the most unpleasant odour emanating from her body. Not quite sweat, not quite dirt or mud or waste, but something cloying, sweet, and… rotten. Like the fug which rises from a waste heap invaded by rats. It was ghastly. Without letting her know, I had to hold my breath to endure the embrace. As she released me,

I looked at her keenly. Close up, she looked even more wasted and jaundiced than she had done at a distance. Her skin was indeed grey under al her paint, tinged with a yellow hue, and blotched here and there with patches of red and pink. There was a scaly rash, not quite hidden by a little lace ruff on her neck, and her hands looked as dry and bare as a skeleton; bones only just covered with a thin veneer of nearly transparent skin. Her hair was almost entirely made of fake pieces, and her breath was pungent with desiccation.

My sister was ill, perhaps sick unto death. None standing near her, nor smelling the funk that came from her body, could doubt it.

"You have been… well, Your Majesty?" I asked.

"There has been much that has kept me occupied in matters of the kingdom, sister," she indicated that I was to walk with her to the window. "I feel both the absence of my beloved husband and also the chill of the airs of winter this year, most keenly. But then," she paused and touched my face gently, her papery skin scraping and catching on my soft flesh, "I am not as young as you are now… Youth is wasted on the young, for they do not appreciate what they have until it is gone."

She laughed a little. It sounded gay, but there was an undercurrent of bitterness that made me uneasy. All this show of friendliness was unnerving. What was going on?

"You said, Your Majesty, that you had much to discuss with me?"

The warmth of the room and the strange behaviour of my sister were both starting to close in on me. I felt as though I were slowly suffocating in the heat.

"I do," she said, "and matters of the highest importance… to you, at least, I am sure."

She paused and looked from the window.

"When our father was alive, Elizabeth… when I was much the same age as you are now… there was one thing I wanted that our father was afraid to grant to me; the office and comfort of marriage. I desired a family, and a babe of my own to hold in my arms, but he would not endure the idea of me marrying, nor seek out a husband for me, as most kings would, to further the dynastic strength of England. I resented that our father would not allow me to marry; it was wrong of me to think so, but we are only ever fragmented beings when it comes to goodness. Only now do I see that our father's decision to withhold on my marriage allowed me to contract with the greatest man that ever lived, and so only now am I grateful for the long gap in my life without a husband at my side. It was indeed *God's* will that I be married to Phillip, and it must have been the hand of God ensuring that I remained a maid to wait for the most perfect of men. But such a long wait to have the comfort of a husband is not befitting to all women. The natural state of a woman is to marry with one who will *complete* her, and bring further glory to her name and her lineage. My husband and I have decided that such a fate as mine should not await you; you will have the comfort of marriage soon, Elizabeth. We have discussed the matter at length and come to a conclusion; you will be married to Emmanuel Philibert, the Prince of Piedmont and Duke of Savoy. He is a fine man, a good Catholic prince, a strong general, and, a close ally of my beloved Phillip and his empire."

The heat in the room was stifling, and I suddenly felt as though I could not breathe. I stared at my sister. The oppressive warmth of the chamber and the words which came from Mary's mouth seemed to have stolen my wit from my mouth or my mind.

"You say nothing, Elizabeth," said Mary, her bright eyes shining at me as though flamed with fever. I believe she was enjoying the look of horror that must have stretched across my face.

"Are you not grateful for such a match, to such a man? The gratification and peace that comes from marriage *completes* a woman in truth, there is nothing like the harmony that is brought to a woman through finding her lord and master… even for royalty such as we, there is always a man to make us whole."

I swallowed; my throat had gone very dry.

"You would intend on sending me from England, Your Majesty?" I almost whispered my voice harsh in my suddenly tight throat. I had not been expecting this.

"Not all of the time," Mary smiled benignly making her look like a cat. "I believe your marriage would be much the same in practise as that between my beloved and me; although of course, Duke Philibert has far less extensive territories than those of my treasured Phillip. You would spend some time in his territories, and some in yours. The Duke is also the Lieutenant of the Netherlands, a position granted to him through alliance with the Hapsburgs, and so will have duties in those lands as well."

I swiftly understood this plan of my sister and her husband. Duke Philibert was a pawn in the pocket of Spain; a Catholic noble, a lord loyal to the machinations of the Hapsburgs and their interests. Duke Philibert owed the Hapsburgs his position and standing; he was their man. My sister and her husband were seeking to control me, and dilute the threat I bore… through marriage. In any marriage, the husband is the legal lord and master of his wife. She becomes his property, as does her wealth. Only spare few women ever came to wield their own power within marriage, and even then they were usually censured as unnatural creatures.

With a Catholic husband controlling me, I could be kept a Catholic. With a husband mastering me, I could be melded to the will of Spain. My destiny would come to be controlled by Spain, through their ally. If they could marry me off to this Duke of Savoy, then I would be in the palm of Spain for the rest of my days, guarded and mastered, subject and never truly the Queen even if I came to that title in time. They would *own* me, mind, body and soul, both now and in my future. I would no longer be my own person, have my own power… I would be mastered, through marriage.

Mary was staring at me; I realised I had not said anything for quite some time. I was sure that all the blood must have fled from my face, but yet it still felt hot and flushed.

"Your Majesty," I stuttered, feeling at a loss for words. "I am very grateful for the honour and attention that you and His Majesty have shown to me, but I feel I am too young to consider such a proposal."

Mary's eyes narrowed and a dangerous glint came into them. She had been hoping, I am sure, that my narrow brush with danger this time might have made me more pliable to her plans here. Finding me not so, finding me as her rebellious younger sister once again, was not pleasing to her.

"You are not so young," she said bluntly. "Twenty-two is a good age to become a wife, and you must consider that you will need all the good years you have left to produce children. Many women marry much earlier. You will need all the goodly years you have to breed, and give children to your husband."

Children! My heart stopped in horror again. Little Catholic babies that I should have no freedom to raise in the faith I believed in. Images raced through my head of myself becoming older and sadder, watching my phantom children worship in the confused manner of the Catholics and never once knowing the true touch of God's grace. Images of a husband who would use me, my body and my position only for his own ends, forcing me to lay with him, taking the country I loved, ruling where *I* should rule and all sanctioned in law by the subservient position of a woman who was married. The terms of Mary's marriage had been ordered and beaten out to exclude Phillip from real power over England, but I doubted the same concessions would be done for my marriage… that would not be what Mary and Phillip would want… they wanted me caught under the boot heel of Spain. They would ensure the power of marriage rested with this Philibert, and therefore in the Empire of the Hapsburgs… Look at the wives of our father, controlled and subject to his will and whim on pain of death… should my fate become as theirs?

I could not become so enslaved. I could not be so ruled. I could not let my spirit and freedom be taken by Spain, by a husband, or by my sister… I could not let this happen.

I had already considered for a long time that I might never choose to marry at all, for all I had ever seen of that estate was fear, danger, disgrace and loss of power for a woman…. But to be told that I would be forced to marry a Catholic lapdog in the seat of Spain? No! This could not be my fate.

"Your Majesty," I said, swallowing again. "I have no inclination to marry at this point in my life. I am grateful for the honour done to me, and the attention given to my situation, but I must refuse this proposal of marriage as it goes against all my natural inclinations."

"*Natural*?" Mary's voice grew high with anger. "What is there that is natural in a woman refusing the hand of a fine prince in marriage? *What was there ever in you that was natural and not… perverted?*"

She spun around and walked up the room. I stared after her in dread and shock; the mask that she had worn to welcome me so warmly to her presence was gone. She must have suspected already that I would refuse, and my refusal to bend to her will had once more filled her with fury.

Mary was anger. Mary was *wrath.*

"All our lives you have tripped and pranced your way along, always managing to slip out of trouble like an eel!" Mary shouted, her hands flailing about in the air and spittle flying from her dark, toothless mouth as she spoke. She was furious, red in the face, her eyes like burning sea coal in the hearth. "Much like your *mother*, oh, she knew well how to *charm*... to *slither* out of blame for whatever evil she did, and look where she ended! Our father ne'er did a finer nor greater thing than to order that swordsman of France to slice off the head of that heretic witch! And now here you are... looking at me with *her* eyes... pretending and charming and slithering your way through life just as she did! You protest often of our joined lineage through my father, but you are more in truth like your mother than any other! See to it that I do not decide to send you once again to the Tower where I truly believe you belong!"

I fell to my knees and held my hands out to her. Her rage was escalating and it was quite terrifying, but I could not leave these rooms with my hand and my independence given away to some lackey of the Hapsburgs.

"Mary," I begged, holding my hands out to her and shaking slightly. "*Sister*... Your Majesty... Please believe me when I say that I am grateful for all you have done for me, and for the belief that you have had in my innocence in matters treasonous and rebellious... But I cannot make my heart marry where it screams to me that I should not! Surely, you would understand that? Surely as *you* refused to marry, unless it was to Phillip of Spain... you would understand, too, my wishes to marry only where my natural inclination led me?"

Mary pulled up and turned on me. Her eyes glinted and flashed like agate and her hands whipped out around her like she was possessed by demons.

"*My* marriage," she hissed, spitting the words at me, "was *sanctioned* by the Holy Spirit! It was intended by *God* that I should marry Phillip, for there was none other in this world that *the Lord* wanted for me. *You*! You seek to compare yourself to me? You are still suspected of holding religious beliefs most abhorrent to God! You are secretly a heretic in your heart, I know this well enough. Perhaps that is why you refuse this honourable match! You think you may still be able to marry a heretic *heathen* like yourself, do you? And to take my throne as yours? Well, any such plans shall come to nothing if you end your days in the sanctifying fires of salvation! What do you say to that, *My Lady*?"

I pressed my hands closer together and tried to remain calm. If I was not careful I should find myself either locked in the Tower, beheaded or burnt at the stake due to my sister's rage.

"Mary," I implored. "I am your sister… I don't believe you would ever sanction my murder. *Please, sister*! Your Majesty…." I burst into tears that were not feigned nor faked in any manner. I don't believe in any of the situations I had ever faced, that I had been as afraid as I was on that day facing the full and unpredictable wrath of my sister.

Mary drew herself up. She breathed in, attempting to calm herself. "If you do not accept this proposal of marriage that has been most carefully chosen for you," she spat, her jaws clenched as though she was a wild beast waiting to bite me, "then I shall have no choice but to publicly declare, through Parliament, that the issue of your bastardry makes you unfit to be the heir to my throne. I will have you stripped of all lands, titles and possessions and the position of heir to the throne shall instead be granted to our cousin of Scots, Mary Stuart."

I stared at her, aghast.

"Surely… that would not be in the interests of the Hapsburgs," I pleaded, stuttering. "Surely Phillip would not want…"

"*Think not that you understand the mind of my own husband!*" Mary screamed in my face, her previous controlled coldness vanishing under a fresh torrent of rage. "Think *not* that you are the only one who understands anything about everything! *Vain, conceited and self-centred* you have always been and this blinds you to everything else in this world, and beyond it! Even if I did not leave the throne to Mary of Scots, there are more possible claimants to the throne than just yourself and our Catholic cousin, *sister.* You are easily replaced in line to the throne of *my* gracious father."

Mary turned away again, fighting back tears of frustration and bunching her hands into fists and then out again. Her back shook with tremors of anger and I could hear her trying to catch her breath. I trembled before the might of her wrath. "You will leave now!" she shouted with her back to me. "Go back to Hatfield and think on all I have said. I will not have you at my court this Christmas; *vainglorious, foolish, treacherous* girl that you are. If you will not submit to me as you should through all duty and for all the graces I have shown to you, then I will remove you from your position in the royal house... *One way, or another.*"

I was still on my knees, staring at her, when she turned back to me and screamed, "*get out!*"

I stumbled to rise. My legs were weak and I felt sick. I staggered to the door and wrenched it open, lurching past Jane Dormer who was standing just outside. Jane ran past me and into the arms of Mary who clung to her like a limpet. I ran from the room, faltering and tripping into the arms of my own ladies, who almost carried me back to my rooms.

When we reached my apartments, I vomited long and hard into my chamber pot. I could not stop shaking. I was under threat of death or the loss of my position if I did not marry the man they had chosen. And if I did marry him, I should lose all the singular power and independence that I had, or might have had, as queen in the future.

I was trapped; not by the walls of a prison this time, but by the fast-approaching bonds of marriage.

On the third of December my party made its way back to Hatfield. The people of London cheered and yet I could barely wave back to them, my body felt so ill and my head so scared and confused. My breaths came in short, panicked bursts that made me light-headed and faint. When we arrived at Hatfield

I collapsed and was taken to bed. Although I had often feigned illness to escape a dangerous situation, this was no feint. For days I hovered in fevered dreams between life and death, subject to a raging temperature and a mind that knew no quiet and no peace.

When I awoke from my sickness I was plunged into a realm of misery and darkness; for in all the times of my life, I had never felt at such a loss to know what I should do. Imprisonment and suspicion of treason I could escape from with words, but as the law stood, Mary was my sovereign and master… and if she insisted that I marry then I was bound by the laws of God and man to obey her.

CHAPTER FORTY-SEVEN

Hatfield House
January 1557

In times of need one finds out who one's friends truly are. There was never more truth in this than during the peril of marriage that beset me in the early months of 1557.

My sister threatened imprisonment, debasement and perhaps even death if I did not come to heel and marry the lapdog of Phillip of Spain; only if I married Philibert would she officially name me her heir. Only by doing as she commanded would I escape her threats of loss of position and titles. But to do so would not only rob me of my own independence and power, but would, in reality, amount to accepting my God-given position as heir to the throne of England from the hands of Phillip, King of Spain, and place me firmly in the palm of Spain for the rest of my life.

The idea outraged me. Perhaps Mary had always resented the idea of me as her heir, so disgraced was she by the treatment that she and her mother had received as a result of the fortunes of my own mother. But whether Mary liked it or not, I too was a daughter of Henry VIII; I was named heir to the throne after Mary in the will of our father. If my sister passed from this world without heirs of her own body, then the throne was mine.

There was no possible path I could walk on which I would bargain to be granted my God-given position by the hands of Phillip of Spain.

No one likes being forced to do something. In my case, as I am sure is common with many others, it made me all the more determined to resist such a position. But what could I do? Once again I faced the prospect of prison, debasement or death, this time for stating I wished not to marry the man chosen for me by the Hapsburgs.

It was then that my instincts upon choosing my own ladies of my house really proved their worth.

It is a truth rarely acknowledged in this world that women can be as great in mind as their male counterparts. Perhaps this is because men generally hold the reins of power; perhaps it is because women work in less obvious ways than men. But for whatever reason, the influence of women on world affairs is generally overlooked, and that, to my mind, suggests that females are much better suited to the practise and persuasions of *covert* operations.

My ladies Anne and Bess had watched over me at Hatfield in some horror during the tenure of my illness resulting from the verbal abuse and threats thrown at me by my sister. They had waited over my bedside, fed me chicken pottage and boiled rice like a child, and as I lay, prostrate with fear and worry, they conceived a plan between them that might enable me to stretch out my arms to new friends who might help me in this time of trouble.

As I recovered in private, they kept up in public the rumour that I was ill. As I gained my strength, they spoke gravely of my weakness to other servants. Much as I had so often hidden myself under a cloak of illness when it seemed politically expedient to do so, they hid me under a blanket weaved of their words. As I recovered, they un-hatched their plans to me; that if I had gained the support of Phillip, whose powerful friendship had saved me in the last plot, they reasoned, then it was possible now, perhaps, to make powerful friends in *other* quarters of the world to save me from this marriage.

Anne and Bess sat on my bed and whispered their ideas to me. If the Spanish could not be trusted as friends, then why not turn our sights to their natural enemies, the French?

"As one door closes, so another opens," Anne counselled, with all the wisdom of Moses, it seemed to me then. "There may be powerful friends that can be cultivated here and now, who may serve you well, my lady."

I nodded. I could see well the virtues in gaining support from our near neighbours, however unlikely it would be that they would remain so for long, an ally is an ally for only as long as the need is mutual.

"I will remain abed," I said. "You must get word to Parry, and to Cecil on this matter, and do so secretly. I will remain within my chambers and you will keep up the rumours of my illness. I need time if you are to speak to the French Ambassador Noailles on my behalf."

"Me?" Anne exclaimed in a slightly girlish fashion.

"Who else?" I asked smiling. "Although I would gladly send either of you, it seems to me that you, Anne, should take up this task. I want no man-servant riding into London in my livery to be noticed by all, putting this plot into risk. No, it shall be you, but you will not go to the French Ambassador as *yourself.* You will take a disguise and find entry to his house, therein you will pass messages to him of this proposed marriage and we shall see if there is anything the French can do to help us oppose it. It is not within their interests to see this marriage go ahead, for it favours the future fortunes of Spain, after all. The French would be more likely to want to work for my deposition as heir and the recognition of their Dauphine, Mary Stuart, in my place. Let them know I am opposed to the match; if they think there is a chance to better their own interests they will help us."

"And what if you are deposed as heir as consequence of this?" Bess asked quietly.

I paused. "Mary of Scots is in France and I am here," I mused. "If I can avoid being stripped of my properties, arrested or executed by my sister, if I can avoid being married off to some underling of Spain, and can outlast the life of my sister, then it may well be that no matter who is named as successor in Mary's will, that the English people would prefer a princess they love and know to a stranger from a foreign land to be their queen. Warwick tried to set another queen in place of my sister, and the people rejected her in favour of the laws of my father's will. I believe they may yet do the same for me, if it came to it."

"Amen," said Bess resolutely. "That is a goodly share of avoiding to be done, though, my lady."

"Then we had better become well-versed in the art of footwork," I uttered ruefully.

They both laughed, but we had serious matters in our heads. I had a husband to avoid, a position to protect, and a throne emerging in my sights over the horizon. Separation from my sister's threats and her stinging words, time to think over my position, and the help of my dearest new ladies of the bedchamber started to bring the colour back to my cheeks, and the spirit back to my body.

I could not give in now; I was a survivor, and the reward for my many sufferings was near at hand.

So it came to pass that later that week, my first female scout left Hatfield House under cover of darkness and, with a small party, rode into London under an assumed name. Being of little interest as just another minor noble woman, she was largely overlooked, and Anne smoothly succeeded in gaining entrance and audience with the Ambassador of France, disguised, I believe, as the type of lady who frequented the French Ambassador's house with regularity. Upon realizing that she was not there to merely pleasure him, Noailles said something that amused me greatly when his answers were repeated to me...

"The Lady Elizabeth sends scouts draped in silk rather than iron; for well she understands that the might of *ardour* is more powerful than that of *armour*."

Spies in silk dresses, like spiders who weave their intricate webs afresh each night; they are hard to see, and ruthless in their efficiency.

Within one moonlight meeting, we had a new ally.

CHAPTER FORTY-EIGHT

Hatfield House
Winter 1557

"And what does he say of the possibility of my flight to France?" I asked.

The chamber was shadowed in darkness; the flickering lights of the candles and the fire only dimly lit the faces of my ladies gathered around me in the cover of the night. Anne had returned from her mission to the French Ambassador, flushed with success at having visited Noailles' house twice undiscovered. My scout was quite excited at the triumph of her first mission.

The French Ambassador, Antoine de Noailles, was more than willing to be drawn into a conversation with our party; here and now, the French and the Spanish were once again at war. Henri II of France had broken the terms of the treaty between France and Spain and had resumed their age-old war for possession of Italy. The English were, as yet, still apart from such conflict; the terms of my sister's marriage to Phillip had come with the *proviso* that England should not be drawn into war on Spain's behalf.

The French wanted friends on this side of the sea; they feared the involvement of another nation supporting Spain in their war, and they knew that if Phillip put pressure on Mary, then it was likely that England would become a war-ally of the Hapsburgs against them. But they looked also to the future; Mary was not hale, she was growing old, she was childless. If their war with Spain continued on past the boarders of her life, then they should like very much to have the heir to the throne as an ally for the future.

The messages that came back contained both assurances of friendship, and a disappointing lack of commitment. But the messages too advised caution and patience… qualities that I had ever held dear.

"He would not advise that you leave England," said Anne. "He begs you to remember the situation that your sister herself faced under the reign of your brother, when she was similarly threatened over her refusal to abandon the Catholic faith and she considered escape to Spain. If she had taken such a path then she would have not been here when your brother suddenly died, and therefore would most likely have lost the throne to the plotting of Warwick and the Grey family."

I nodded. The same idea had occurred to me also, but it always helps to hear your own thoughts confirmed by another. Thought of fleeing the country was only a last resort, but I liked to have all roads covered.

"He offers the friendship of France," Anne continued. "And hopes that you will always remember such when…" She paused, her lips knotted together as though she wanted to say more, but feared to do so.

"When what?" I demanded.

Her face clouded a little. "He believes that your sister may not be long for this world," she said. "He has women who report to him placed in the Queen's household, they tell him of much she tries to hide from her court. Noailles believes the Queen's health is precarious and on the wane. He thinks that if you are able to hold out, to parry around the idea of marriage, then there will be a time, not too distant, where you will be able to choose a husband for yourself." Anne paused and smiled widely at me. "He suggests that within the household of the King Henri of France, and his wife, Catherine de Medici, there are many sons who would most cherish such a comely and clever wife."

Anne grinned a little at the face I pulled upon her words; there were rumours circulating that the princes of France were unhinged.

"The Ambassador says that French men are not as foolish as those of England or Spain," said Anne. "He says French men prefer a wife who is more than just an ornament to hang off their doublets. They would like a wife like you, *as gentle as a dove, as wise as a serpent.*"

"When you see him next, you must relay thanks to him for his attentions, and let him know that when we have liberty to make our own choices, that the sons of France shall certainly be considered as a worthy match for a daughter of England."

"Would you really consider so, my lady?" Anne asked and smiled. "I have heard reports, not from the Ambassador certainly, that would suggest the sons of France are a lot less savoury than those of other noble houses in Christendom."

"Less savoury than which house, Anne?" I asked, raising my eyebrows. "Than that of Spain, perhaps? Wherein is housed the mad Don Carlos, son of Phillip of Spain who they say has a hole in his head and enjoys flaying the skin from dogs and horses for his own entertainment? Than that of Scotland, where every male heir seems to run headlong into battle and perish quickly therein? Of England, where every noble lord with a scrap of royal blood seems to believe he is destined for the throne? In France the sons show strangeness and fits of shaking sickness, I have heard. There are but few princes in this world; their blood may be royal, but their behaviour is less so. Should I ever have the choice, Anne, I should need to examine any suitor rigorously, for to be saddled all my life with some craven, or fool, with some idiot or infant, would certainly not be in my interests, nor those of England."

"Would we all not like to examine our future husbands… rigorously, my lady?" asked Anne with a naughty look on her face. I slapped her arm lightly. Although I found her amusing, it did not do for her to become too scandalous in her speech.

"I am sorry, my lady," she said, rubbing her arm a little. "I spoke out of turn."

I nodded, but I was not really thinking on her bawdy joke. I was wondering what should come next, but I did not have long to wait to find out.

In early March, Phillip of Spain sailed back to England. Mary was overjoyed at his return, although in truth everyone knew she was not the primary reason for his visit. Phillip had two ideas in mind when he came back to our shores, and both were politically motivated: the first was to have the English join his war against France: the second was to have the problem of the English succession settled… by marrying me to Prince Emmanuel Philibert.

I was summoned back to court for his arrival. My sister did not formally receive me when I arrived, and obviously did not want to see me. My attendance came at the specific request of Phillip himself, and only after his arrival at court was I sent for to meet with Mary and her husband.

When I arrived at the privy chambers at Greenwich they were both awaiting me. I walked in and curtseyed deeply to them, feeling my heart shake slightly, both at the prospect of having to fight for my right to remain an unmarried maid, and because it had been a long while since I had looked on the handsome face of the King of Spain and King-consort of England.

When I was given leave to rise, I looked at both Phillip and my sister. The contrast between two people could not have been much greater. There was the withered figure of my sister, her grey face and her reeking body, next to the lithe and spirited form of Phillip. His face was a little darker from time spent in the sun on campaign but flushed with vigour; his hair had grown blond streaks in it, also from the sun… His beard had been trimmed a little shorter than I remembered, but his dark eyes still held in them that hungry little spark which ignited as I looked into his face, and his features were still as solemn and as desirable as they had been to me before.

I willed myself not to blush as I looked into his face.

"Sister," he smiled welcomingly at me. "I trust that God keeps you well?"

I curtseyed again. "Well enough, Your Majesty… although I have been much troubled with thoughts of other matters these past weeks." I looked at my sister, whose grim face darkened as I gazed over at her.

"It is those matters that I have come to talk to you of, Lady Elizabeth," he said warmly.

"For which you might feel grateful," came Mary's harsh voice, "that His Majesty takes such an interest in your matters."

The warning was there in her voice and it was clear. Phillip's arrival back in England had postponed any plans that my sister may have had to deal with me in another manner. Perhaps she had planned to finally remove me from the succession. I wondered how long and darkly she had talked of me in private.

Phillip cast a look, somewhat of veiled warning, to his wife, and I was surprised to see her blush lightly and cast her eyes away from him. She could not bear any mark of his disapproval with her, I thought, a little wonderingly. There had been few times I had seen any real sign of this in public, but there it was. Mary was as much in the thrall of Phillip as ever she had been; he was the master of her heart.

My mind turned quickly upon itself; if Phillip controls Mary, then I must have some means to control Phillip, or else my cause would be lost.

Phillip walked over to me. "I have spoken long and often with my wife, Her Gracious Majesty, on the proposal of marriage put forward between you and the Prince Philbert of Piedmont, Duke of Savoy," he said. "I believe it would be an excellent match on all sides; allowing you formal recognition of your titles and place in the succession, granting you a husband who is not only a noble man and fine soldier, but one who will bring wealth and honour to your house and country. Prince Emmanuel Philibert is also not born of a country that has ever had ill relations with England," he continued. "And I believe that the English people would be more... accepting of a man who comes not from a greater house than their present King."

I stared at him. It was a balanced speech, taking into consideration the suspicious nature of the people of England. They would always suppose dark things of the men who came to be the husbands of their princesses if they came from other countries. If only I could believe that that were all the interests that he had in a marriage between Philibert and me. Phillip did not mention, of course, that such a match should see my personal powers overshadowed by a husband, nor that placing his ally, a man who was dependent on Spain for all he had, would give Phillip and Spain a foothold in the affairs of England for the foreseeable future. Philibert, I had discovered, held but an empty title, for his father had been deposed of his throne by the French in the same year my mother was executed. All that the Prince had, or may have in the future, was subject to the whims of Spain, and if he was to gain those lands back to add to his titles, then he had to stay on their good side. He was, therefore, their tool. And they were happy to use him to their advantage.

No, no, I thought. You are clever, Phillip, but I am not to be bought with such assurances and quips. I must play for time.

"I had not had the proposal put to me in such a way before, Your Majesty," I said calmly. "I would beg some time to think on such matters a little. I would not wish to feel that I had not considered all options and advantages to the match before giving an answer."

He gazed into my eyes shrewdly. He was as clever as I, and perhaps he realized I was delaying. But he was willing to give me time. There was gentleness there in those dark, flashing eyes…. Eyes which warmed a part of me that had not felt life in a long time. I noted the curls near his neck, the rich cloth that covered a body well-made for riding and fighting. Oh yes, Phillip of Spain was a most attractive man.

He looked at Mary. "You see, my love? There was just a matter of finding the right words to fit the situation." He smiled and she reflected his smile with her own instantly, her tired face suddenly lit with the exhilaration of her love for him, and her desire to always win his approval.

"Perhaps I was too… brief… in my explanation of the advantages of this match." Mary uttered shortly. "I sometimes forget that my seemingly *clever* sister is still very young, and may yet be *ignorant* to some of the advantages that are not immediately apparent to one who is so… *inexperienced* with life, and politics."

I curtseyed; partly to keep my tongue from snapping back at her loosely-veiled insults. "Your Majesty is most benevolent to me. I little deserve such grace at your hands."

She nodded condescendingly, quite agreeing with me. I had to grit my teeth slightly to imprison my tongue which longed to lash at her.

They sent me forth from them again. I was to have time to consider the match anew. Mary seemed quite at ease with the notion, seeming to believe that her Phillip could charm any woman into agreement with him, as he did with her. But although I found the presence of the handsome Phillip distracting, I was not about to sign over my freedom and my power without a fight.

I wanted with all my heart to become an eel, just as Mary had said I was; too slippery to grasp, too clever to rise to bait… a smooth fish that could not be easily caught. I needed all the slipperiness and all the caution and wit I had, to avoid the traps that were being laid out for me in the great waterways of the court of England.

CHAPTER FORTY-NINE

Somerset House, London
March 1557

On that visit to England, Phillip brought with him two female cousins, the Duchesses of Parma and Lorraine, and although it was not necessarily unusual for an entourage to come with a king or prince when travelling, their presence was much commented on, and wondered at. Royal men usually travelled with noble men; aside from wives or mistresses, women had little place in the upper ranks of male royal households. Phillip's mixed party was unusual.

The arrival in England of the Duchess of Lorraine was commented on much behind the velvet sleeves of court, for she had once been Christina, Princess of Denmark and then, by marriage, Duchess of Milan, widowed at the age of only thirteen. When my father was seeking a wife after the death of Edward's mother, Jane Seymour, he had seen a portrait of the fair Christina, and had been much enamoured of her pale beauty. He had sent

Ambassadors to woo the princess for her hand in marriage, but Christina, then a young widow of sixteen years made clear that she was much opposed to the match; in the courts of Christendom it was already widely whispered that the English King Henry VIII had a habit of mistreating his wives.

Christina was obviously then not given to much subtlety in her youth as she refused my father, saying that if she had two heads, then *one* would surely be at the disposal of His Majesty of England. This rude refusal of his hand had greatly embarrassed my father, but this did not stop him continuing to pursue the match for over a year. Despite himself, my father often had an attraction to spirited women, it was a trait which bred true in all his wives but Jane Seymour, and even with her, I often had reason to suspect that the lady who unseated my own mother could not have been as placid and docile in spirit as she appeared about court. Christina's remark was much bandied about in secret at court, and I of course heard of it from Kat. Despite the insult to my much-beloved father; the not-so-veiled reference to my mother, and her death by beheading, led me to understand that others on the continent viewed the demise of Queen Anne Boleyn with eyes which did not agree with my father's official version of events. It seemed to me there was more sympathy for the fall of my mother from grace in the halls of other courts, than that of England, and perhaps others were aware that she had been removed for political reasons, rather than for being truly guilty of what she was accused.

Phillip tried often to bring the Duchesses into my company, as though wanting us to be seen together. They were genteel ladies enough, and well bred, but although they were warm on the surface, both ladies seemed closed in some manner I could not express. I also found Phillip's insistence on travelling with them constantly to be strange and unnerving. Never before had he seemed so to insist on the idea of female company.

One day he came to Somerset House, my seat in London, and requested time to talk with me. My ladies entertained the Duchesses as he and I played at cards together in the far corner of the room. Every now and then I raised an eye to see if Anne and Bess were doing the tasks I had set them; I wanted to know what these ladies were about and why they were here. If I could not glean that information from Phillip, perhaps my ladies could learn something from them.

Phillip talked of trivial matters for a while, and then came to his main subject. Had I had a chance to think more on the matters of my marriage? I sighed a little and looked up at him over my hand. I had a good chance of winning the game, but I wondered whether I should win this contest in my own life…

"I have thought on it, Your Majesty."

"Have you reached a conclusion?" he asked.

I looked into his dark eyes, and they softened slightly as he saw the look of disquiet fall over my face. However deeply he was politically motivated, there was an element of Phillip that desired and perhaps even cared for me.

"I still feel, Your Majesty," I ventured, "as though I am too young to marry."

"Therefore," he said quickly, "you should be advised by those who want the best for you. The Queen and I have more worldly experience than you; perhaps you should allow yourself to be guided by us."

"I have not even seen a portrait of this prince you propose for me," I faltered. "I know not what he may be like in person or in character. Although others give good report, how am I to know what manner of man I pledge my life to?"

"Royal marriages are often made so, my lady," Phillip shrugged. "But I can arrange for a portrait to be brought to you so you might look on his face. I am surprised Her Majesty did not offer to show you one herself. Philibert is a most handsome prince and a fine general; you would be married to a strong and worthy man."

"There are other men, who could also be worthy… *more* worthy…." I said quickly, then, dropped my eyes suddenly to my cards. He looked sharply at me, but I was re-arranging the cards in my hand as though fascinated by the game.

"There are?" he asked, his voice a little harsh with a tinge of jealousy which I almost smiled to hear. "Know you of any such, my lady?"

I looked up. My dark eyes met his and I saw him take in a little breath. My eyes were vastly pretty, I knew well. Much like those dark glittering eyes of my mother's, they had a magic in them which seemed to work well on the sensibilities of men. "Although I have been kept much from the company of men, much in seclusion, I feel as though there may well be a man that is worthy of my hand." I cast my eyes downwards. "But I fear…"

"What do you fear?" his voice had become gruff, he leaned forwards, his eyes intent on my face. He was starting to understand what I was suggesting and he was interested by it. The thought had come to me a few days before this, that if Phillip desired me, then perhaps just the seed of an idea might stop this marriage… If Phillip believed I wanted to marry *him*, then perhaps he might prevent the marriage with Philibert, to wait until the death of my sister… to marry me himself.

It would give Phillip influence over England once more, and he would have a younger, much more desirable bride than the one he had now; one young enough to bear children. A lineage for England that was also born to the line of Spain... I was offering him a continued place at the head of England, an expansion of his Empire, and the fulfilment of his desire for me. Passion, power and politics combined were a heady mixture for any man.

Terrible though it was, perhaps, to play with a man's emotions, to bargain with the idea of my sister's death, I could not blame myself for using any and all advantages that I might have. Think badly of me if you will, for in that game of cards I called on Phillip to imagine future pleasures he might have with me, once the pitiable figure of my own sister laid dead. Not such a thing should a Christian woman do, and yet I did so. There are many causes in my life to look back and regret for. I do not regret my actions in that chamber, but I do regret that I was forced to take such action.

The weapons that women have in this world are often more dangerous and more subtle than those of men.

"I fear," I said falteringly, "...I fear that I may have already seen the man I should wish to marry, and yet he does not see me."

"How could anyone not see you, my Lady Elizabeth?" he asked, leaning forwards intently and for once, past the courtier's appearance, there shone the heart of a man who was truly infatuated with me.

"Your answer brings me hope," I smiled warily. "But if that hope is yet to remain, then any talk of marriage, such as this proposal to Prince Philibert, would have to be abandoned. I would hope.... I would wait... given only very little faith to survive on, if there was a chance for something... *greater...* for me, in the future."

He looked at me carefully; I could hear his mind clicking like a clock. If I was kept unmarried, then doors would be open to him back into England upon the death of my sister... But could he trust that I meant what I said? It was a gamble, but Phillip was a man who enjoyed a fine bet, and he believed he could see the desire he felt for me, mirrored in my eyes. And perhaps it was... I admit I found him attractive, but I was not a slave to the flickering notions of desire I felt for this man. Phillip believed he could charm any woman as he did so successfully with my own sister, and he believed he had my heart in his hands. How could a young maiden such as I resist *such* a prince as he after all? Taking a chance on keeping me an un-married maid now, may pay dividends in the future for Spain, and for Phillip. He was not to know that it was all a lie; I had no intention of marrying him, even if I did find him attractive, only in keeping my hand free of the bonds of marriage so that I might maintain my own power and freedom.

I took a ring, a little diamond set in gold, from my finger and slipped it into his hand. "For friendship," I whispered, "and to remind you... of the promise that the future might bring... for both of us."

He took the little ring. It fitted on none of his fingers, so he slipped it into a link on one of the golden chains that hung from his neck, and kissed it. Then he unhooked a brooch from his chest, a crest of his house made in gold over the carved and polished sphere of a sapphire. Quietly he handed it to me.

"For friendship," he replied warmly, "and for the *fulfilment* of promises."

I kissed the brooch and pinned it to my breast, and then I looked on him with admiring eyes that did not need to feign the desire I had for him.

When he left my house, Phillip of Spain thought himself betrothed, even though his wife was still living. For my own part, however much I desired him, and it was a powerful draw that he invoked in me, I would not countenance receiving the position and power *I* was destined for at the hands of anyone, and never from the King of another country. I was not going to marry him, and I was not going to marry anyone else he might deliver to my door.

To be great, to be powerful, both England and I had to be independent of the wants and the wills of other nations... and of men who would seek only to control us.

CHAPTER FIFTY

Whitehall Palace
June 1557

The true purpose of those elegant ladies who accompanied the short visit made by Phillip to England that year became clear through the network of informers of the French Ambassador Noailles. Although the Ambassador could little come out in open support for me, he was happy to keep me informed; the secret messages passed from his house in London to my ladies were of much interest to me.

It was my lady Bess Brooke who brought his warnings to me; one day as she walked in the gardens at Whitehall as we resided at court that summer, the Ambassador came upon her and my other ladies as though by accident. The years of my sister's reign were unusually wet and grey; rain fell through the summer and the coming of a rare warm day was a welcome and scarce commodity, well worth a turn in the sun to admire. People whispered that God caused rain to fall so often on England to put out the fires that still burned the flesh of Protestants caught and executed by Mary, her Bishop Bonner, her Cardinal Pole and her Council. God wept, the people said, spoiling the harvests and keeping the ground sodden, to show His displeasure at the fires of faith. It was becoming a veritable fable of the English, and one that was heard whispered in many places.

Who can say what is in the mind of God? For my part, there were so many dismal summers and cold, biting winters as my sister's reign passed, that I could not help but think that God had indeed turned His face from this country in sadness. God did not want to look on the ravages of my sister's reign and so England was made cold and miserable as He turned the light and warmth of His face from us.

As my Bess wandered in the gardens, the Ambassador crossed her path… by accident of course, you understand… Noailles suggested she show him the rose gardens for which Whitehall was famed. Stopping to admire the beauty of the early budding flowers and their subtle fragrance, the Ambassador proved himself a friend to me by passing on a grave warning about the actual purpose that those two Hapsburg cousins of Phillip's had been brought to undertake.

"They are here to offer a disguise," Bess whispered to me breathlessly within the confines of my chambers. She had come running to me through the halls of court when she heard what Noailles had to tell her. "A front of respectability for a plot that Phillip hatched before he came"

"And the plot itself?" I asked slowly.

"If you were not amenable to the marriage with Prince Philibert…" she said carefully, "…Phillip would take you prisoner, abduct you, ship you abroad secretly to some stronghold of the Hapsburgs, and therein have you married to the lapdog by force."

My face must have paled. Phillip had come to these lands determined to take me as a vassal for Spain in one way or another.

For all the courtly manners and sometime desire or affection for me he showed, he was truly a ruthless man at heart.

"I would rather die!" I cried loudly. Bess and Anne looked about themselves, fearing my words should be heard.

"And *that* you can return word for word to the Ambassador," I spat. My heart was pounding and my flesh felt cold. I felt as though I had already been duped. I had not thought Phillip capable of such barbaric behaviour. What manner of man was this prince that should a maid refuse a husband he would have her abducted and forced into marriage? Would he too ensure my new husband raped me to secure the match? I would not put anything past Phillip upon hearing his plots to abduct me. Suddenly the attraction I felt for him dimmed much within my mind and body. I had liked not the idea of being required to do his will through legal means. I liked it even less when the thought came that I should be truly subjected to the will of the King of Spain by force.

"The English people would never stand for such, my lady," said Bess. "There would be open war against the Queen, if not with Spain, too."

I nodded. Long ever had I held that the most important aspect of nobility or royalty was the love of one's people; this was never more true than now. Should I be so abducted, the people of England would not stand for it. They would rise to fight for me, and for my honour. But would Phillip have completed his plans by that time and forced me to wed and bed his underling?

My ladies were obviously thinking in tune with my own thoughts; Anne shook her head, looking concerned. "I doubt that the truth of any abduction would be discovered, before they had forced Your Highness to marry their man," whispered Anne carefully. "We should take this warning with all due consideration and seriousness; you must never be put in a position where it could come to fruition, my lady."

I thought a while on their words. Both sets of information were true enough. But even if Phillip had come to England with the idea of forcing me to marry his servant, would he now continue with such an idea, if he thought I was to perhaps become his own wife in the future instead? It was good, I thought, that I had not known this plot when I had convinced Phillip that I would marry him after the death of my sister… had I known he was bent on such brutal tactics to bring me to heel then I doubt I could have flirted and flattered him as I had done over that game of cards. But now, Phillip did believe that I wanted him as my husband, and so would he still resort to abducting me to force my hand?

I thought not, but I also thought, it does not hurt to be careful. The man was obviously capable of a great deal more ruthlessness than I had imagined.

"I believe the risk to be small," I said. "But we will also keep in mind your warnings, Anne. Send secret word to Cecil and to Parry of this plot that they may keep watch on it, and too that if I am suddenly gone or they hear naught from me, then this is what may have happened. Get them to keep a close eye on Spanish vessels or merchant ships at the ports. Should it come that I am abducted, I will be expecting a rescue before I have left the sands of the English shore." I nodded to the both of them. "Thank God for all your work for me, ladies," I smiled. "I am well served in my house."

"We want nothing more than to serve you, my lady," said Anne fervently. "You are our greatest care in this world. When we were most in need you took us into your house and gave us the protection of your grace; these are not things one easily forgets."

"Indeed not," said my loyal Bess. "You opened your home and family to us, my lady… We are ever in your debt."

I reached out and took a hand from each of them. Tears stood in my eyes. The devotion of people to your safety can never be undervalued. It was true that they owed me much, but they returned all my payments of riches, or of position, with their loyalty and their love. Such qualities, in this world, are of constant and unrelenting worth.

We returned to our usual game; to watch and to wait, to never trust any who was not within our confidence, and all the time we did this, we danced and talked, laughed and conversed with every noble and royal at the court of my sister. Oh, my women were well versed in the art of appearing to care for nothing, whilst taking care of everything. Flitting through the life of court like little butterflies who care only for the warmth of the sun and the touch of the flower, and yet with every dance and every giggle, they gathered information on wings of silken grace.

But there were others also working for me, and seeking to enter my household. Now that the threat of my arrest or execution seemed to have disappeared through the intervention of Phillip, there came a steady yet increasing flow of peoples to my house, seeking a place or position in my household. Their numbers were not vast to start with, but the increase in demand for places in my house showed that there were others, not just I, who were watching the turn of Fortune's Wheel, and placing a bet with their lives that as Mary's sun faded, mine was rising on the distant horizon.

It put me in some trouble, to balance my books well. Positions and appointments have to be paid. I said before that if a prince cannot take care of his own house then how can he be expected to rule over others? There are, however, times when certain expenses must be met in order to lay a foundation for the future. If I turned away all who came looking to me for favour, in those early days when much was still uncertain in my position, then I should be turning away those who might instead give their persons and loyalty to another candidate for the throne, or to the continuation of my sister's wants. No, there are times when balancing the books also means weighing up the stakes, and sometimes, risks have to be taken.

My household was increasing in size, but my sister was unwilling to add to the already generous income left to me by our father. I was not surprised that Mary did not want to offer me more money; she could see well enough to count and she knew that my household was growing. She could also guess at the reason, although I doubted that she would have wanted to. None would say it to her, but all in England could see that her tired body, old before its time or turn, was of the past, and I, with my fresh face and nubile form, was poised to enter the future with England at my side.

So I spent time making concessions in one place to facilitate the gain of allies in another; I took far less for my own gowns and books, I ordered no jewels; instead of worldly goods I started to quietly amass a fortune of fellows at my side, a plethora of peoples, a wealth of wits. A woman may have all the jewels in the world to sparkle on her breast, but her greatest fortune lies in the friends and allies with whom she can surround herself with in times of trouble. The men and women who came to me then were taking risks just as I was. Choosing their alliances now, with my sister still living, meant they were willing to weigh the future, to take a risk, to make a bet. I enjoyed gambling, but I never took a bet that was ill-informed. It was my earnest hope, that my new servants would not either.

Hopefully, I should turn out to have been a sure bet, on which to gamble a future.

In June, we were still caught in a between time, a between world; Mary still waiting for me to give an answer on Philibert's hand, myself and my servants waiting and watching to see if the plan to have me abducted should go ahead; Phillip paying court to me, talking in ciphers when he visited about a time when we would be man and wife… whilst all the while in court, talking to me warmly of marriage with Philibert. I had to use all the talents I had for make-believe to ensure that the Prince of Spain saw none of the disgust I felt for him in attempting to take my will by force… each time he left my company, I felt as though I was befouled by the presence of a man I had once desired, and now detested for his willingness to do anything to master me. It was a hard task, but it had to be done. Should Phillip suspect that I did not desire him, or want to marry him then he may well have gone through with his original plan to abduct me. I was playing for my own freedom.

And amidst all that, as we all danced around each other trying to see the truth past the webs we spun, the French brought England into a war that Mary's Council had previously declared their country would never fight.

The war between France and Spain had begun, as most wars do, over lands and territories. In 1551, France had declared war upon Spain for control and possession of Italy, for whoever controlled that territory would also dominate the affairs of Europe. Both France and Spain had hereditary claims to control Italy, and both had fought for her in the past. Until this time, the terms of Mary's marriage had kept England a neutral party in the wars on the continent, but then, in 1557, the French struck at England, and drew her into war.

Perhaps thinking they should unsettle England before she entered the war as Spain's ally, the French sent Sir Thomas Stafford, an English traitor to the Crown, with a volley of men to ruffle the feathers of the English Queen. Stafford's mother had been Lady Ursula Pole, and he was therefore a cousin of the odious Cardinal Pole, Mary's beloved papal legate. Stafford had been involved with the rebellion of Wyatt in 1554, and had been much opposed to Mary's match with Spain. When the Wyatt rebellion failed, Stafford had been captured and imprisoned in the Fleet prison, before bribing his guards to grant him freedom, and escaping to France. A known intriguer with other English exiles of Mary's reign, Stafford was a prime candidate for bringing unrest to England once more.

Stafford and his men reached English shores under cover of darkness and they took Scarborough castle with but a small force. Stafford marched into the largely unprotected castle and declared himself 'Protector of the Realm', calling on honest Englishmen to join him in rebellion against Mary to return the power of the Crown "to the true English blood of our own natural country."

Stafford and his men were quickly overcome. It took the Earl of Westmorland and his men only three days to take back the castle and place Stafford and his men under arrest for treason. The men of England had not risen to the call of Stafford to arms and to rebellion; they had seen what happened to the last rebels against Mary's reign. The English were becoming still with fear for what their queen would do to those who opposed her. The burnings of Protestants and hideous torment and executions of rebels to the Crown were, it seemed, a constant sight during my sister's reign. Although the people of England had ever seen a trip to public executions as a fine day out in the last reign, they were becoming sickened by the constant and unrelenting stream of deaths which seemed to emanate from my sister's skeletal hands.

Stafford and thirty-two of his followers were executed for treason that May; Stafford went to the block and lost his head for his failed invasion of England, his men were not so lucky. Base-born and lacking noble blood, they hung from the neck until their eyes bulged from their heads, their legs kicking against the coming of their deaths in desperation, then they were freed from the rope only to endure the extraction of their entrails before them, and finally the sweep of the axe which finally brought blessed Death to them as a welcome friend.

The Queen had had enough of mercy to those who opposed her.

Even though this 'invasion' of England was quashed quickly, the threat was such that Mary and her Council quickly spat defiance in the face of the King of France, and declared war on France, joining their forces to those of Spain. It was foolish of France to have acted so rashly, and I could not help but wonder if somewhere, somehow, Phillip had been at the back of some plot to encourage this reckless act of Stafford's. It was of much advantage for Phillip to have another ally in the war, and France must have known that sending such a small invading force was at best a gamble.... Was it too much to think that perhaps Phillip's own men, working covertly in France, might have engineered this platform from which England was launched into war?

As war was declared, my ally, the French Ambassador Noailles, was forced to make a hasty retreat back to France.

Although the marriage contract between Phillip and Mary had stipulated that England would not be encumbered to take part in any Spanish war... England went to war. Having achieved at least one of the objectives he set himself to do when he came to England, Phillip announced he was once again leaving for Spain, and then for his armies, to lead them in battle against the French.

Less than a month after his ship sailed for his homeland, Mary announced once more that she was pregnant.

CHAPTER FIFTY-ONE

Richmond Palace
February 1603

Life is made of so many partings; there are some that cripple us, those that bear down on our souls so that we cannot see the light of day without shielding our eyes from its glare. The death of those we love, we carry with us, as great weights that only slowly, and with time, we learn to shoulder.

We do not learn to love those people we have lost less, nor feel the rent of their absence any less keenly. We learn only to carry our sorrows with us; we learn to bear the grief of their departure from our lives as we continue on, without them.

And then there are those who die, distant from our lives, people who were once so close to us. Those people who may well pass quietly from our lives as we are distracted by other events and moments.

But there is no death that does not deserve reflection. There is no passing that does not deserve a moment to think on the life that has gone.

In the years and events I relate to you of my life, I was entirely captured in the present of my existence; a young woman, who still felt like a child, struggling to keep her head above the murky waters of the court and of international politics. And as I waded through those waters, trying to keep my head above the surface, an old friend, an aunt… a *once*-mother, slipped quietly from this world.

In the dark night of July 16th, 1557, the last remnant of my father's never-ending search for love died quietly in her bed. At forty-two, she was not old, and since my sister's ascension to the throne, she had kept her Protestant person most discreetly in the background of court life, appearing only for the most vaulted of occasions. Her position, not only in England, but in her homeland, spared her from arrest for her religion, but she was also a woman who knew well how to avoid trouble and danger with long-honed skill and ability. If I gave her not as much thought then, as she deserved, I can give it to her now.

The Princess of Cleves and of England, Anne, was the soul who took the hand of Death at this time and left our lives. My father's fourth wife was the one who lived the longest of all those he loved. And it was she he had loved the least.

They say that my mother, and her cousin Catherine Howard, were the wives he loved the most, in life at least… and they were destroyed the fastest. The force of love can be as such. At its best it is a joyous power that binds loyalty to life… At worst, it is a force of destruction which whirls in the darkness, crushing and vanquishing all in its path.

Anne had been a pragmatist, and she had survived marriage with my father... only one other woman could claim that. Anne of Cleves had granted my father all that he had asked of her, and agreed to annul their marriage without even a whiff of a fight. No other wife had done such. My father had rewarded her richly for acquiescing to his will, making her his royal 'sister' and a princess of England.

Anne had left the idea of love, or marrying again, and had lived her life as a rich, free, noble woman, much loved by her servants and close friends. Living as she did, much removed from the Catholic court of my sister, was Anne's choice. Never was there a woman I have known before or since, who knew more acutely when to make curtsey and slip away. Perhaps you could say the same of her death; a quiet passing in her estates in the country, Anne left her life behind just as the land she loved so well was thrown into war and conflict.

As England went to war with France; as my sister gloated over a belly that we all knew was swollen not with child but with disease; as I grew eyes all over the country to try and keep all in sight… then passed from this life the greatest and least celebrated survivor of my father's reign.

Anne left me jewels; some sit now on my breast and on my hands, even with the thousands I own, they are still precious to me. For they remind me of that woman who instinctively understood naturally all the lessons in carefulness, pragmatism and expediency that I should only learn to hone with time and practise.

Never honoured for her true worth in her lifetime; I hope yet Anne of Cleves will take this praise from an old woman, sure to see her soon in the Kingdom of Heaven.

"Blessed are the meek, for they shall inherit the Earth"

CHAPTER FIFTY-TWO

Whitehall Palace
July 1557

As the forces of England followed the armies of Spain out to France, I received an unexpected visitor.

It was a normal enough July-day for England during the time of my sister's reign; heavy rain pelted the outside world, the world was wet and heavy, grey and brown and drab. The gentle summers of England had deserted us in Mary's sovereignty, it seemed, and all there was about us was the constant pounding of rain on the roof above our head, and the lather of seas of mud on the roads. Riding had become more and more difficult recently, the roads through and about London more and more impassable, even for the fine horses of my sister's royal stables. My ladies and I were forced inside once again, to play at cards together, to read and to embroider.

I was feeling like a wolf kept in a cage; so relentless was the bad weather that year that I felt penned up and hemmed in. It did not help that my mind was constantly barraged by this plot or that to either see me killed, deposed, abducted or married off. How I longed to be free, back at Hatfield, where I could ride out even in the storms on roads not marred by the passage of so many carts and horses and people… where my every action would not be commented on and passed around as court gossip. There are many kinds of imprisonment… I felt as though I had given up the walls of my former prisons only to be kept captive by the will of my sister and the confines of the court.

My book sat in my lap as I looked not at the words of the master I was reading, but instead stared despondently from the window at the watery world before me. London was grey; through the glass the city looked as though it were sick, pale and insipid where at all times it should be alive with laughter and conversation. Those unfortunate enough to be outside, huddled under their coats and jackets; those fortunate enough to have the choice, stayed absent from the wet and the cold. But all were as miserable as the weather. The world looked empty and forlorn. I was weary of seeing England so. I sighed as I looked at it.

And then Anne came to me, smiling in a light and cheeky manner that told me something of pleasure was afoot.

"What is it, Anne?" I asked "Why do you look like the child who found the cakes hid for Christmas night?"

Her smirk broke into a smile and she curtseyed. "How well you read me, Your Highness!" she beamed. "You have a visitor."

"Who calls?"

"A gentleman who says I am to convey all greetings of grace to you, my lady," she said, grinning. "And who asks also if you had ever had cause to wonder if the life of a pirate would have ever been preferable to that of a princess?"

For a moment I stared at her, not knowing of what on earth she spoke, and then a memory came to me; one from so long ago that it felt barely real, from a darker time, when hope had seemed a distant reality. My face must have lit with a little understanding, as she giggled.

"What does he look like now?" I asked, my voice low; a little smile played on my lips as I thought of the handsome young man I had once known.

"A *fine* man," she replied warmly. There was admiration in her voice.

"A fine man, indeed?" I smiled. "Well it is for certain that he has made an impression on my ladies. Let not your head be turned by a handsome face, Anne," I continued with a little edge to my voice. "I need you looking in the right direction at all times, not distracted by a pretty visage."

"No, of course, my lady," she bobbed eagerly on her heels. "Will you receive him?"

I thought on it a little. I was curious I had to admit, about the man waiting upon me in the other room; once a young boy who had been so close to my beloved brother, this man had become embroiled in a plot with the rest of his family to give the throne to our dead cousin Jane. I remembered the message he sent to me through those children at the Tower of London in my darkest days. I still remembered his words, which he had sent to me at great personal risk.

And now, here he was.

"He was released from the Tower, then?" I asked, "I had not heard such."

"Many have been released on whom the suspicion of treason was growing old, my lady," said Anne. "They have been given the chance to fight for England, against France in the coming wars and redeem their honour in that manner."

Sadness pervaded my heart; sent from prison into the jaws of war. Just another type of jail devised for those who would threaten the realm. The idea had been used often enough in my father's reign, to send those once suspected of treason to exonerate themselves on the field of battle. But I felt a little sad that this man should be sent from England to perhaps die in France. The thought of him touched parts of my heart's memory which I had thought long since buried and cold.

"I will receive him," I instructed. "I am interested to know what the years have done to him. Bring him in."

I stood up and straightened my gown, pinched some blood into my cheeks. I had, even then, a tinkling sort of excitement in my skin, a pleasurable racing in my blood.

After a few minutes, in walked Robert Dudley.

He bowed to me, a deep and long bow that spoke volumes of his respect for my position. When he straightened, I nodded to him, and took a long look at the man before me. For this was no boy any longer. Gone were the dangling limbs and clumsiness of the youth I had once known. Gone even was the still-boyish plumpness I had seen on his cheeks when I had attended his marriage at court so long ago. I barely remembered the name of his wife... Amy was it? But well I remembered those dark and sparkling eyes... Gone was the boy who once neared me in height, and instead was a powerful figure that stood a fair shoulder and head above me. The dark hair on his head was thick and curled a little near his neck, his beard was short and fashionable, trimmed to merely accentuate a strong jaw. His form was lithe, kept slim I suspected from his years in prison, and yet he looked strong and healthy, just a little pale from time spent long from the rays of the sun.

And his face... was just simply the most handsome I had ever seen.

There are moments in life when our paths are decided for the future; times when we are cast like dice into the path of a game. The outcome may well still be within our power to affect, but the way we will fall, the course of our paths, are set as our fortunes leave the hands of the players and we are thrown to the whim of Chance.

Do you believe that a person can love at first sight? If you do, I would call you a fool. For love is born, it is cultivated and grown only through time, and only in time can one know if one's love is true. True love takes up the challenges set to it and does not falter in the face of adversity or fear. It manages hurt and pain, it weathers the storms of life and it survives even death. Love can be measured in the longevity it has, in the trials it has overcome, in the battles it has fought, and in the continuance of its passion, still standing strong after every test.

There are few people in this world who, truly, have known love and had it returned in kind to them.

But the *seeds* of love may well be cast in a moment. This is what people speak of when they talk of love at first sight. As the farmer throws his grain to the field, so can one heart fly out to another and find an echo of its own beat within the body of another person. Perhaps those who have never encountered more than this first jolt of love may ascribe more depth to it than one like I, who was fortunate enough, and unfortunate enough, in equal measures, to have loved in truth.

I looked into the face of Robert Dudley and a thousand memories of the past, of my brother's reign, my father's and all those times that had gone before fell into the stream of my thoughts as I did.

"My Lady Elizabeth," he said, bowing again.

"My Lord Dudley," I said eventually. "Seeing you has brought all manner of memories to my mind. I find myself quite lost in the past."

He smiled. It was charming and easy, a warm smile, and a faintly mischievous one. I could not help but smile back at him. "I hope they were pleasant memories, Your Highness?" he asked.

My smile clouded a little. "Some were, my lord," I said. "Some… were less so."

"I believe I may guess which were less so," he tucked his lips together. "You have faced much hardship since we talked together in the gardens of your brother as children, my lady."

"And do you still hate Cicero as once you did?" I inquired, smiling at him.

"You remember." His voice was warm and he seemed so pleased that he quite forgot his formal addresses to me, but I did not mind. "So much time has passed since then that I wondered if you would remember such a slight conversation from so long ago."

I laughed. "It was a memorable conversation, my lord. Did you not swear that you would make me a pirate queen some day?"

Robert laughed. It was a good laugh, deep and rich; it bounced from the walls. Suddenly I remembered my father's laugh, the way he had of commanding a room just by being in it. Robert Dudley had the same type of bearing, the same type of charm.

"I hope you will forgive that boyish comment now, Your Highness," he pleaded. "One feels that such a path is not necessarily the one either of us would take now."

"No?" I asked and smiled at him mischievously.

He raised his eyebrows a little. "Perhaps we can always keep it as an option, my lady," he said, "for the future."

He spoke to me as though we had long and ever been good friends; I felt the same ease with him. But I had to remind myself to hold this conversation in check; Robert Dudley was obviously used to getting his own way with women.

"For the future," I repeated, nodding, "but what now of the present? My ladies tell me that you are shortly to depart for France to fight in the war."

"Her Majesty's Grace has allowed me to prove my worth, and my loyalty, by joining the war," he said earnestly. "I long for the honour to fight for her, and for my country."

"You are not worried that you may not return?" I queried, feeling a troublesome pang in my heart to think of this handsome man wounded or dead. "Many do not return from wars, however loyal they may be to their queen and country."

He smiled again. I could see in his eyes there was a thirst for battle, for action. After all, he was a young man, and most young men dream of such things. "After so long spent in a prison, my lady," he said, "I relish the feel of the free air on my face, whatever Fate may hold in store for me."

"I understand that well enough, my lord," I muttered quietly, thinking suddenly of the day I was released from the Tower of London.

He bowed, his face suddenly concerned. "I would not have wished to bring such memories to you that would cause sadness, my lady. All England must praise the day that the Lady Elizabeth, by the grace of God, walked free from suspicion of treason and returned to the favour of Her Majesty."

Most carefully said; he was a clever speaker that I could happily grant him.

"I remember such a time, however," I said, "when I was much without friends, and yet, another prisoner, shut away from the world as I was, importuned me to remember that *many in this country love her.*"

I paused and looked up at his face. He looked like a boy, awed that I remembered his message to me in the Tower.

"It is still true, my lady," he murmured softly.

I nodded. "I remember well my friends, Robin Dudley. And a friend of but fair weather is not one I value. Luckily, God has gifted me much foul weather in this life, so that I might see who are my friends in truth. I do not forget my friends, if they do not forget me."

Robin smiled and bowed a little again, "I too have known much of the storm. But I had a flame on which to fix my eyes, and her light was what saw me through."

He stopped and locked his dark eyes to mine. I almost blushed, so intense was the rush of blood to my head upon the meeting of our eyes. "My eyes are still locked on this light," he said. "So you see, I cannot fail, nor fall, for soon she will become a light for all, to lead us from the darkness."

For a moment we did little but stare at each other.

"I wish you good fortune in the battles which are to come, my lord," I murmured eventually. "And with the grace of God, will pray for your safe return."

He bowed. "There is no man in France, Spain or England who could prevent my eventual return to these shores, my lady," he said boldly. "And when I do, I would like to petition for a place in the household of Your Highness. Whilst now, treason still clouds the name of Dudley, I hope to prove my loyalty to Her Majesty, the Queen, and come home to take a position in the house of her loyal royal sister."

I smiled. So that was the purpose of this meeting, was it? Another man asking to join me and mine, full of promises for the future... and yet, there was something different in Robert Dudley; something exciting, bold and adventurous. I liked well these qualities in men.

I laughed suddenly and he looked up at me. "Done!" I exclaimed gaily. "Done, my Lord Dudley! Go and array yourself with honours on the battlefields of France, and when you are returned, should my sister allow such, I will have a place waiting for you in my household."

I smiled at him, and he dropped to one knee before me. I held out my elegant, long-fingered hand for him to kiss. As his beard brushed my skin, I felt a thrill of excitement pass through my body, making my blood... and other parts of me... tingle with strange and enticing warmth.

"Your position will see us evened, my lord... A position in my household as payment for the comfort of a message, sent to a princess in the Tower, long ago." I said as he rose.

"Nay, my lady," he shook his head. "That message was my payment to *you*... for the comfort you brought to me as a prisoner, given when I looked from my window each day in the very depths of despair and misery, watching a beautiful woman light up the darkness of hell." He kissed my hand again. "You gave me hope then, where there had been none."

"It would seem then, that you are further in my debt, Robin Dudley," I teased. "You will have to work hard to see these lines of credit balance."

He smiled. "One day I will repay all that Your Highness has bestowed on me, that I swear."

When he left my company that afternoon, I felt exhilarated. The appearance of this interesting and engaging man had blown all frustration and annoyance from my countenance and filled me with life. Gone was the pensive Elizabeth sat staring at the grey rain, and in her place was a woman with cheeks coloured pink with enjoyment, ready for any battle she had yet to face.

Such was the effect that Robin could have on a woman. Such was the effect he always had on me; to lift my spirits, to raise my soul. There was never another man in all the world like Robert Dudley.

Later that week, he went out to France to join the armies of England. The fight had begun.

England lifted her head, and roared into war.

CHAPTER FIFTY-THREE

The Court of Mary I, London
Winter 1557

War is something that no ruler should ever enter into lightly, or without realization of the risk involved, not only to their country or people, but to their own reputation as well. When the French King Henri heard of England's involvement in the war between France and Spain, he laughed, and said that the English Queen would do anything to *pleasure* her husband, which riled the temper of Englishmen as they heard their queen's honour insulted. Even if they were not fond of Mary themselves at this time, no man wants to hear of his monarch being insulted by another.

Early victories at Saint Quintin gave the French reason to fear, and the English reason to hope, but as we gloated on the easy success of our troops, the French took a terrible revenge; one that stabbed deep into the heart of the English monarchy.

We princes of England have long since styled ourselves also as the natural rulers of France. We have held many claims to that throne through years of marriage and spilt blood. Edward III claimed the throne of France in 1340 as the male descendant of the last Capetian monarch, Charles IV of France, and thus the long years of the wars with France commenced. When our ancestor Henry V invaded France and won at Agincourt, felling the flower of the French nobility, we had seen France come within our grasp as truly part of our territories. France was then taken as a property of England; the French King, Charles VI surrendered to England and assented to make Henry V his heir. Henry would take the kingdom of France as his own upon the death of the defeated Charles. Henry was wedded to the beautiful daughter of Charles VI, Catherine, and came home to await such a time when he would inherit his lawful property.

But then, disaster struck. Henry V died; a sudden fever from his army camps took his life and left the throne of England to an infant, his son Henry VI who had only just started to open his eyes to the world as his great father entered the Kingdom of Heaven. The French saw their chance; as England was rendered weak, they went back on their promises to grant the throne of France to England.

In the long struggles of the civil war that followed in England under the weak rule of Henry VI, Lancastrian fought Yorkist for claim to the throne; the territories in France that English blood had fought so hard to claim, were lost piece by piece and taken back into the arms of France.

When our grandfather Henry VII finally took the throne, winning it from the usurper Richard III on the field of Bosworth, there was only one part of English soil left in France… Calais. All through our grandfather's reign and our father's, Calais was an important territory of the English Crown, equally for making peace with the French and for invasion into French territories.

Our father was most fond of telling us the tales of his own invasion of France, and the Battle of the Spurs; so-called as French were greatly surprised by the vast English numbers brought to the battle field, and ran away so fast that all any could see of them was the light glinting from their spurs on the horizon. I am sure the French have a different version of this tale, but I cannot help but enjoy the English version more. It was one of my father's favourite stories of his youth.

Calais was the last stronghold of English power on the continent; the last bastion of a time when English kings had won an Empire. Calais was the last great reminder of a conquest which had vanquished a people; a time when all the people of the world had looked at England and trembled.

On New Year's Eve, 1557, the French army, under command of the Duke of Guise, attacked Calais. Despite warnings sent from scouts watching the French, neither the English nor the Spanish had made an attempt to fortify the city. Poorly garrisoned, poorly equipped and defended mainly by the great, if crumbling fortifications made by our forebears, English Calais was outnumbered. The forces of the Duke of Guise lashed against the fortress like the waves of a great storm.

It did not take long…

Calais fell to the French.

It was an attack of brilliance. No one had thought the bold Guise captain would dare to mount such an attack in the dead of winter, so large were the risks of a long and drawn out siege, leaving his army susceptible to disease and starvation. There were rumours that the English forces inside the castles and battlements of Calais were too drunk on New Year's cheer to notice the threat. The outer-lying castles of Calais surrendered one by one, and by the time the English forces had marched out to make battle, the day had already been won by the French.

As news was brought back to us of the terrible defeat we had suffered, it was as though a grave and heavy groan of sorrow and humiliation came from deep within the throat of England herself. Calais was not just a piece of land; it was the last territory of our Empire, a symbol of English pride. The horror at having lost such a strategically important part of our lands was awful; the humiliation of our dignity, far worse.

Phillip offered to march a counter-attack to re-take Calais, but the English Council said they could not afford to take part. They sent what meagre fees they could raise from the English people, already so taxed and despondent that even this small fee caused unrest and riot within the towns and cities, but it was not enough. My sister's ill-managed reign, the bad harvests, the poor weather, heavy taxes, the return of English wealth to Rome, and now the war we had plunged into, had drained the money from the pockets of the English, and many of the common people were struggling to survive the winter. I had instructed that my tenants and those living in my lands should be given succour from my houses whenever possible and wherever the need was the greatest. But my purse and means too were becoming stretched with those coming to my household, and by the demands Mary's rule put on all her people.

It was the hardest of times, a brutal time, when I came to realize that the pride that people take in their country is so dependent on the right choices of its monarch. I cursed the French, but I also saw that our troops had been defeated by their own lack of imagination. I cursed at my sister in my mind. She seemed little aware of the horrors into which her choices had plunged our great country.

The Council could not seem to decide what to do to address the situation; Phillip's new envoy to the English court, the Duke of Feria, despaired daily of the infectiveness that fogged the Council and its efforts in the war. They seemed unable to make a choice between them. I knew how he felt; I looked over the battle plans, at the territories held and lost, and despaired of the English involvement in conflict that brought the threat of war so close to our own shores.

War was bleeding the country of resources, and it was sapping both the souls of the people and our own sense of pride.

England entered the year of 1558 as a nation humiliated and dishonoured. But our queen sat on her gilded throne, ignoring the stain on our national honour, and the growing desperation of her people, gloating once more over the phantom of the child that she believed lived in her swollen womb.

No one truly believed this time that she was with child... no one but Mary.

It seemed that Mary cared nothing for her country or her people anymore. She cared but for the lives of her beloved Phillip, and his child that she believed she carried under her heart... which throbbed with everlasting love for her prince, deafening her to all other cries within her realm.

CHAPTER FIFTY-FOUR

The Court of Mary I, Whitehall Palace
London
Late Winter 1558

In early 1558 I removed from the court to my country estates once more, but was soon called back to London. Mary summoned me to see her before she retreated to her lying-in chambers to await the birth of her child.

Fantasy moved within Mary during this time as freely as the blood roams the body: fantasy that a child would come to her by the grace of God; fantasy that our lost territories in France would be restored by her hero Phillip; fantasy that her husband would come home to her at last. It was as desperate as it was sorrowful. As her subject and her sister, I was obliged as all lords in her realm to humour the Queen during this, her latest awful daydream of pregnancy.

She called me to see her a few days after my arrival in London; and what a poor sight met my eyes! Mary's chambers were darkened, and they were still kept so warm that sweat trickled down my back under winter layers of English wool and costly velvets.

Jane Dormer told me that the light was hurtful to my sister's eyes, but in the heated gloom that awaited me, I felt as though I had entered a world of shadow, where truth was hidden under layers of shade, and smothered by the oppressive heat.

I bowed before Mary as she sat up in her bed, supported by masses of cushions and pillows. She was too unwell, too "weighted down" by "the child within" her, she explained, to receive me sitting in her usual chair. That smell which I had noticed when she embraced me previously, had now ventured forth from her body and hung, like a sickly blanket, over the fug of heat that shimmered in the dark rooms. It was a cloying smell, a heavy and sultry smell, too strange, too repulsive and too persistent to ignore. When I left Mary's chambers later I had to order a change of gown and strong perfumed oils for my hair, for the scent of death seemed to cling to every fibre of my clothing and every hair on my head.

"We are pleased to see you, sister," rasped Mary as I rose before her, "and joyous that you have come to see us before we enter the time of our most blessed state."

She paused and her dark eyes glinted in the dim candlelight as she looked on me in triumph. "Finally," she said, her voice growing stronger and louder. "Finally, God has listened to our prayers and has advanced a child unto us for the preservation of our realm and our faith."

Her eyes shone with a glassy, febrile look; her words sounded so much more confident than they had done over a year previous when she had first thought she was with child. There was no doubt in her mind now, as there perhaps had been then; the force of her conviction told me all that I needed to know.

Mary was unhinged, her fantasies made real to her through the force of her own want and desire. I liked not the way in which she regarded me with her too-bright, febrile eyes. She was more dangerous now in this altered state than she had ever been before, for all doubt had been removed as her sickened body plunged her into a state that teetered on the cliff tops of madness.

How fragile is the mind of the human; affected by the ever-tenuous and susceptible body, or bent by the desires of the traitorous heart.

Mary's eyes glowed in the shadows. It was like facing a predator skulking in the undergrowth; some great cat that was all the more dangerous because it was wounded.

"I am grateful that Your Majesty chose to call for me to witness the miraculous event of your pregnancy," I said carefully. "Truly, you are blessed by God, and He will ensure your safe delivery, and that of your child."

Mary's skeletal face loomed into my vision as she shifted herself forwards. Her face was a deathly pale grey, her skin as pallid as the moon, but her eyes… her eyes burnt like fire. A fierce hold on my courage only just stopped me taking a step back from the vision of horror that my sister had become.

"I would that I could hope as you do, sister," she stared at me with her heated gaze, fixing me with her stare. I felt I understood then why a mouse freezes before a cat; for fear that moving even a whisker may bring the power of the beast down on their throats. Mary continued "but I believe I may not live to see the child that God has blessed me with. Such is the trial of the task He has granted me." She dropped back on her bed; her breathing was laboured and wheezed from her painfully. "But if I should not live to see the face of my beloved child, I will know that he is left in the best of care."

"Please, Your Majesty," I begged and bowed again, my skirts rustling against the rushes on the floor. "Please speak not of leaving us. Your child, my own nephew the Prince, will need his mother as well as his father as he grows."

I heard a little snort of laughter from the shadows. It held no mirth.

"I am *sure* that is what you want, sister," she muttered. "But the wants of men are not always aligned with the will of God... That much I have learnt in my long life; that much *you* still have to learn. It is our duty to submit to the Lord's will and if He has decided to take me into His Kingdom, then I should never stand against those wishes. I have such dreams, sister..." She trailed off and then sat up again, her eyes locked on my face as she struggled to hold herself up with hands like claws on the sheets that covered her.

"The Holy Spirit comes to me again, at night, in my sleep," she said. "As he did when I was brought low with the choice of whom to marry. The Holy Spirit whispers to me of the child I will have; a fine boy he is, sister, a strong boy, who looks much like my own father but I see in his eyes the wisdom of my beloved mother. This child will be the one to carry this realm into the light, after so long hidden in the darkness of revolt and heresy. I am but the *vessel* to bring forth such a child; although I could never think myself as worthy a vessel as the beloved Virgin, I know I have been *chosen* to give life to the child who will be the Saviour of England. My son will lead first the English, and then all the peoples of the world to a true understanding of God. All heretics will fall to the wayside as he approaches, and God's angels will fight at his side to reclaim the world for the true faith of Christ."

She smiled at me; her grey face was so dry and hard that it looked as though the smile would crack through her skin. As though her face would shatter like a broken mirror.

"My child *is* the Saviour," she proclaimed. "And although I may never live to see him perform the task that God has given him, I know I will have given my own life to ensure his and thusly, to save the world from all evils." She fell back on her bed again and panted slightly. The effort of talking had exhausted her.

"In that end," she whispered. "I can take comfort and die a woman who has achieved all she could for her country and for God."

I hardly knew what to say. Mary was convinced, in her illness and her growing madness, that she was not only carrying a child, but that her child was to be the Saviour of the Catholic faith, the Saviour of England! Saviour of the world! Such lunacy, such *arrogance* to believe that she was the vessel for the redeemer of the world!

But I could hardly say that to her. Such a confession would surely have seen me sent to the stake to burn at the hands of a queen who had clearly lost her mind.

"All England will praise the day that Your Majesty gives us your son." I said and curtseyed.

"Go now," Mary rasped from her bed. "The time of my lying-in approaches and I have women, ample and able to the task of caring for me. You will return to your country estates and pray for me. Perhaps sister, this will be the last time you and I see each other in this world."

I went to contradict her, but she stopped me.

"Should that be the case," her voice was becoming faint and weak, "I would urge you, not only as your sister and your sovereign, but as one *soul* to another, to put aside these heretic beliefs that I know well enough you still harbour in private. I have protected you in this world well enough, but when you come to face the Lord God in truth, there will be none who can protect you from the force of His vision. God will see the truth of your heart. When you come to face the Lord of Heaven, Elizabeth, do so as a disciple of His True Faith, or face the burning fires of hell and the removal of true grace from your eternal soul forever."

She paused and coughed a little. "You and I may not always have honoured the same ideals in life," she said, "but I would be sorrowful if you were not taken to the arms of God when you face death as I do."

"Go now, please." She croaked and rolled over, spluttering out a dry and hacking cough which turned to dry retching over the side of her luxurious bed. Her ladies ran forward to aid her in her struggle to breathe. They waved me away as I took an involuntary step towards my sister.

By God, Mary was a pitiable creature, even as she was a dangerous one.

I curtseyed again, and was led from the rooms by the candle of Jane Dormer.

As we reached the outside chambers, I started to breathe once more, and I gulped in the clean air, relishing its fresh taste, not polluted by the hideous scent of death or the encroaching heat of Mary's inner chambers. Jane, too, breathed in deeply, filling her nose and her chest with the heavenly scent; I could not imagine what it must be like to be in those awful chambers every day, all day.

Jane's lively face was pale and drawn with sadness. She knew as well as I that my sister was deluded in her conception. She knew, as I did, that my sister was dying.

"I hear you have lately become promised in marriage," I said. "I congratulate you; although I am sad to hear your marriage will take you from England. The Duke of Feria is a good man, so I understand, a clever man, and his titles and lands are vast. You will become a woman of great standing."

"Thank you, my lady," she nodded and looked back at the door towards Mary's rooms. "Although I have promised Her Majesty that I shall not leave her until... after the birth of her child." Her face puckered and her eyes filled with tears.

I reached out a hand and squeezed her shoulder. Jane looked at me with grateful eyes, although neither of us acknowledged the truth staring us both in the face.

"It is a hard time," I counselled. "But I take comfort from knowing that my sister is surrounded by those who truly love her." I paused. "That is indeed all that she has ever wanted in life."

Jane nodded. "*Many* love Her Majesty," she said defensively. "She is a great queen, and a good woman."

"I hope that she will continue to reign over us for a long time yet," I nodded, but my words sounded hollow. As long as Mary lived, I should be in constant danger and turmoil. My sister had spoken to me of how she had protected me from my enemies. How strange that she could not see that she herself, had been my enemy; that she had placed me often and readily in the path of Death.

Jane excused herself and walked back to the dim, oppressive chambers of my sister, her candlelight disappearing through the darkened, muggy gloom until she was out of my sight. I walked back to my own rooms, left in a pensive and pondering state. When I reached my ladies I bade them strip me of my clothes; so cloying was the clinging smell of Mary's body that I washed and bathed in winter.

Later that week, we departed once again for my estates in the country. I was removing to Hatfield to make preparation for the coming of a storm.

CHAPTER FIFTY-FIVE

Hatfield House
Late Winter 1558

As the war continued into 1558, we seemed to receive nothing that was not bad news. My sister had become enveloped in a world of pure fantasy that protected her from all that was not right and good and her Council dithered and dallied incompetently. Perhaps the reason Mary's Council was so ineffective in the making of decisions to further our efforts in the war, was the almost complete state of denial in which Mary appeared to be residing.

Convinced that our territories would be won back by Phillip, that the victories of the Spanish were as much ours as theirs, Mary appeared to ride on a crest of happiness and contentment, believing that as long as Phillip was in charge, everything would be well.

I did not wonder that people despaired of her belief; a total incapacity to see the facts is not a good trait in a ruler. She seemed almost to have taken Phillip as a deity; it was not in fact armies of men that fought and died on the battlefields of France, but just Phillip, apparently taking whole cities and territories single-handedly. He had become Hercules, he had become Mars… He was her saviour and that of her people. Mary had lost her hold on reality.

Many ascribed the bent of her mind to being affected by illness. Mary believed, and she believed completely, that she was once again with child. In her mind, Phillip had left her pregnant, and had gone to win an empire for their child. She was convinced of this, and she had the authority of the highest state to confirm it; that of God. It appeared however, that my sister was not convinced she was going to survive the trial of the coming 'birth' of her child.

In March, Mary made her will. A copy of the will made its way into my hands through the offices of men working for Cecil who thought I would be interested to see it, which of course I was. Although I could not help but stare in horror at its contents, as Mary wrote me out of history and created her own fantasy world, I also could not help but feel pity again for my sister.

Cecil, along with Parry and Blanche, had made their ways quietly back to my household at this time, much in secret, for my sister would not have approved their return. Cecil held positions at court, and was therefore but a sometime visitor to my household, but now that I was once more in my country estates and removed from court, I felt safe to have Parry and Blanche return to me, hoping that my sister and her Council would be too occupied with war and the piteous state of England to much notice the return of my servants. The only person missing to complete my household and my heart was my dearest Kat. But we should have to wait a little while longer before dear Kat could return to me once more. Mary still viewed my old governess as being an evil influence on me, and Kat's position, kept within the halls of her family home in Devonshire, was still watched over to ensure she did not escape to join me once more.

As many of my old servants slipped secretly back into my house and rejoined my service, I felt once more powerful; the having of friends and allies close to me was a tonic to my blood and bone.

Which was as well, for the hastily copied will I held in my hands brought little comfort to this heir to the throne.

Mary's will bequeathed the throne of England to the child she believed she carried within her. Mary believed that she would die in the forthcoming birth; I was not mentioned, not even as a possible guardian for the spectral baby. Phillip was named as the legal guardian of both her unborn child, and of the country of England. Mary named Phillip, the King of Spain, as the Regent of England. Phillip would control the country, protect the prince or princess, and ensure the continuation of the Catholic faith in her realm in the event of Mary's death.

Given her age and physical state, Mary's death in childbed was not an unfounded concern.... provided of course, that she *was* pregnant. I was not the only one to see her swollen belly, the gait of her walk and the pallor of her face and to know that it was not life that she carried within her, but death.

Cardinal Pole was asked in the will to ensure that revenues from the Crown continued to feed the Catholic Church, and to re-bury Mary's mother, Katherine of Aragon, in her proper place, as an honoured Queen, in Westminster Abbey.

Mary extolled her subjects to honour and obey Phillip as their King, as though they themselves had also married him. She wrote that his *"endeavour, care and study hath been and chiefly is, to reduce this realm unto the unity of Christ's Church and true religion, and to the ancient and honourable fame and honour that it hath been."*

"She must be without her true mind!" I wondered aloud to Cecil who sat quietly watching me as I read the hastily written parchment containing the contents of the will. "What else but that could affect her so that she could think the people of England would accept Phillip as their King?"

Cecil smiled sadly. He was a good man, and although he despised my sister and her reign, he was not without human sympathy. "I think it more troubling, my lady, that once again the Queen is convinced that her body is with child, when all about her can see she is dying. Even if there *were* a child of her body to take the throne, the English would never accept the rule of a foreign power over them as Regent. It would make us beholden to Spain, it would make us weak."

"Weaker than we are already, Cecil?" I asked ruefully. He shook his head sadly.

"There is much to be fixed here," he mused, as though England were a table with a broken leg. "But I believe we are still a great country… or could be, if lead by a great ruler, my lady." He looked at me pointedly.

"Thank you, my lord," I smiled briefly, and then pulled a little face of disquiet as I looked on the copy of the will once more. "My sister is unpredictable and strange at this time, my lord," I continued. "She seems to have left behind sense and reason and instead languishes in whimsy. I fear her now perhaps more than before; she has the eyes of one who can see that the end is in sight, and may act to remove that which she has always distrusted."

"You must take care now, my lady," cautioned Cecil. "It is too true that when the end of a race comes within sight, so often those who are not set sure to their purpose may trip and fall. We have so long worked in the shadows here, but the time is not yet right for us to come to the light."

"But when that time does come, we must be ready, Cecil." I said. I looked down at the paper in my hands and a sudden anger came bubbling to my blood. For all that had ever passed between us, for all the affection and the hatred, I had never thought Mary was really capable of writing me out of the line of succession, and yet here was indeed the proof. She had not intended for me to see this document until the demands within it had already come to pass. If she died, and this will was upheld by her Council, then I would have a fight on my hands for the throne. Mary had wanted me to be taken off-guard, for me to not know or expect the contents of this will, but thanks to clever Cecil and his men, she had failed.

"My sister will not succeed in erasing my name from history!" I cried, my temper flaring. "However much she may dislike it, I *am* the daughter of Henry VIII and I *am* the heir to the throne."

I looked up and saw Cecil smiling at me.

"It does not do, my lord," I spat waspishly, "to badly judge the bent of a prince's temper by *smirking* at them as they rage... Such things may advance one rapidly into trouble."

Cecil wiped the smile from his lips. "I am sorry, my lady, I smiled not at the temper brought forth in you, it was just..."

"What?"

"I was thinking... how like your father you seem when risen to anger. It is almost as though I could see him here before me inside the flash of your eyes, the set of your mouth and the toss of your red hair. I meant no insult, my lady."

My temper dropped. I smiled at Cecil. There were few compliments I liked more than being compared favourably to my father.

"You are forgiven, then, my lord," I paused. "My sister thinks like my brother did; that she can control the destiny of the throne from beyond the grave. But just as my brother sought to give the throne unlawfully to our cousin Jane, I shall not allow the crown to be granted by our sister to the King of Spain. I believe the people of England think as I do. If England is to continue as a country, then it will continue *as* England, under the reign of the Tudor kings, not under the yoke of a foreign empire."

I leaned forward to take Cecil's arm. My former anger had passed, and now there was on my mind a sense of urgency to complete this meeting and come from it with a sense of purpose renewed.

"My sister's reign is waning," I said softly. "When the time comes we must be ready to move before anyone else has thought to. There are other claimants to my throne; the living Grey girls, sisters to my poor cousin Lady Jane, are at my sister's side at court, and they have a slim claim; the Catholic Queen of Scots in France too has a claim; my odious cousin of Lennox and her family, and now my sister has given us another, the King of Spain himself! I know well enough how you and Parry have worked to keep me safe, and I know what resources are at your hands. When the time draws near we must have as many in the government and the nobility as possible ready to take our side."

I paused and fixed Cecil with grave eyes. "My household grows in number each and every day with those coming to support my claim to the throne, but we *must* have more. Make sure that this year we are cultivating all those who we have as yet been unsure of. Make friends with both the Catholics and the hidden Protestants… with any on the Council who have an ounce of wit. We will have them all on our side even if they are not on each others'. When the time draws near, we must be ready to act with all speed and lawful endeavour, to take the throne in my name. I will converse with Parry soon enough, but I want to be prepared on both fronts; should it come to it, I will have Parry mobilize men to take the throne by force. But…"

I smiled at him, breaking the gravity of our converse slightly. "Perhaps being so often brought to trials of trouble, good Cecil, I have ever preferred the route of peace to that of war, so I want *you,* my lord, to be prepared to take the throne in my name wielding ink and pen as your weapons. Get me my throne through proclamation and through law, my lord, without a drop of English blood spilt."

Cecil rose and bowed to me; he remained on one knee and kissed my hand. "It will be done, Your Highness," he said.

"See to it, Cecil," I nodded, "and you shall not find me ungrateful. Should we succeed, then I will make you one of my chief advisors on the Council, and my Secretary of State."

"My lady!" he exclaimed.

"You are well suited to the task and position, Cecil," I smiled, shaking my head. "As well you are aware."

Cecil grinned at me.

Our pact and our plans were set, and a partnership was made. Parry would be advised to secretly raise forces so that if we had to fight for my throne, we could. Cecil would cover every legal recourse and action, so that if we could avoid fighting, we would.

Once more, I sat down to wait and to watch and see what the future would bring to me.

CHAPTER FIFTY-SIX

Brocket Hall
Spring 1558

There come times in life when one must disappear from centre stage, if only to ensure that one's return to the story is done both with ease and with glory. But as all actors of the stage will know, as the audience keeps its eyes fixed on those carousing around on stage, much of the real work is put in place far, far behind the curtains.

When we officially removed to Hatfield, we did not tarry long. We soon made another move which was not, at first, well known to those at the Queen's court. My household, under Parry's guidance, proceeded to the estate of Brocket Hall, some two miles or so north of Hatfield. Brocket Hall was a less vulnerable estate than the rambling lands of Hatfield and it was from there that we sent forth the tendrils of messages and missions that came to ensure my succession. With the River Lea just to the side of the mansion itself, we also had a goodly means of communication at our disposal.

I have ever been an advocate of planning, and in those months of 1558, my household and my staff became embroiled not only in the day-to-day tasks that beset any house, but in the operations of the task most dear to my heart, and ambitions.

The throne of England was coming within my sights and as it came closer, I thirsted for it more and more.

Cecil and Parry were both carrying out the orders I had given to them; to bring about my claim and ascension to the throne of England. The *right to claim* a throne depends on the blood that flows within the veins, the *power to take* a throne, to *hold* a throne, depends on the strength of the one who wears the crown. And to all that, we must add that watching and waiting, preparing and planning can never be undervalued. I would not be caught unawares by the machinations of those who did not want to see me take the throne that was mine in law, and by right.

My supporters had grown; now numbering men on Mary's Council, despondent with the fragmented present rule, as well as those who saw me as the hope for the return of the Protestant faith in England. In houses and in villages, in the town and the cities of England, I started to amass a following of those who turned to me as the last lights of Mary's reign glimmered in the darkness.

Parry had found support for my cause in men like Sir John Thynne, once a servant of the ill-fated Duke of Somerset, Edward Seymour, who had waited long years to return to a seat of power in the government. Thynne was powerful and promised us his whole standing army should the acquisition of my throne require force. Another ten thousand troops came promised from the garrison of Berwick-on-Tweed, the largest battalion on English soil. Thomas Markham, a captain in the garrison, came with papers cleverly written to assure me that these troops would be provided, if needed, "*for the maintenance of her royal state, title and dignity.*"

I have ever been impressed with those, like myself, who can succeed in writing so plainly and yet cover their meaning so convincingly, for really, the "maintenance of my royal state" could have any one of a hundred meanings.

More men came to us; Lord Clinton, the Lord Admiral and commander of Her Majesty's forces in the Fleet came to my banner through his wife's admiration for me. Elizabeth Fitzgerald, Lady Clinton, had been a friend and companion of mine in childhood. When Mary and I lived together at Hunsdon she had come to live with us, and eventually became one of Mary's own ladies. Lady Clinton was another of those women that I admired as much for her spirit as for her beauty. When she was a young woman, the Earl of Surrey, that reckless son of my uncle Norfolk, had written poetry for her, immortalizing her as the, "*Fair Geraldine*", and it was as such that I came to call her. I have ever liked having my own names for those I have affection for. My Geraldine had started out her career at court as one of Mary's ladies, but as time went on she had become less and less able to hide her true religion from her mistress. She had left the court, as had so many others, to take refuge in her country estates, awaiting a time when her religion should not place her in mortal danger.

Her husband, the Admiral, was bold, witty, wise, and was about the only man on the Council that I found I could stomach with ease. He clearly adored his Geraldine, and seeing a man so wise in that respect, I liked him even more. It was Geraldine who brought her husband to me, and she who ensured such an important player in the game of politics, with such a force behind him, became my supporter in earnest.

My lady Bessie Brooke brought to me her beloved husband, William Parr. He was her husband who was not her husband, their union not being officially recognised by my sister who had refused to acknowledge his divorce from his first wife on grounds of her adultery. I think Mary was likely to have disapproved of the pair anyway, as Bess and William's relationship, as it was whispered, had started long before the end of his last marriage, and the pair had been a leading power in the reign of our brother Edward, under Warwick.

But in my eyes, William was wise for having fallen in love with such a fine woman as my Bess. And he had another claim on my affection, being the brother of my stepmother, Katherine Parr. When he arrived at my house, I held out my hands to him, and noted with pleasure that in his face shone those same warm grey eyes which reflected light and colour around them. Such the same had my beloved stepmother had, and seeing the ghost of her eyes in his, made me feel immediate affection for him.

"Uncle," I said happily, and he looked at me both surprised and pleased that I should acknowledge such a tenuous link, by marriage, in our families.

"My lady… niece," he stuttered, slightly uncomfortably, and his wife Bess stifled a giggle at his face. He looked at her and she nodded to him before he turned to ask me for his own favours. William came not really looking for position or titles, although I am sure he would not refuse such if offered; he offered support to me, in exchange for the recognition of his marriage to Bess.

How soft can a man make a woman's heart become when we recognize the trials of true love in him! Perhaps it is all the more touching to us when a man thinks of his love first and foremost, because it happens all too rarely in world of ambition and greed.

My bargain with William Parr was one I was most happy to strike; he, being another who had hidden his religion for fear of burning at the stake, would make one more fine ally for me in the future. My dear Elizabeth Brooke dropped at my feet and kissed the hem of my dress in a manner that made me want to cry.

"Come, dear Bess," I said gruffly, feeling tears well up in my eyes at the sight of her happiness. "You have served me well and you know that I will always work to do the best for my friends. It does not do for a man and wife to be parted for so long. There is precious little of love in this world, without denying that which any fool can see is real and should be venerated; not censured."

Many more men came to call at the house, ostensibly to ask after my health, or for favour in one matter or another, but in reality, to offer their support to the next daughter of England chosen to take the crown. Amongst them, and to my great happiness, was Robert Dudley, returned from the wars in France as talks of peace had started between France and Spain. He was brought to me along with others, but I found that in my excitement at seeing his handsome face once more, I could hardly concentrate on the messages the others brought.

When Robert's turn came and he stepped forward, I took a little time to worry on how thin I saw he had become. The war had done none of us good, I thought, and now it had thinned not only the pride of England, but the health of our men as well.

"It is good to see you, Lord Robin," I said using the version of his name I liked more. "It seems I was wrong to fear that you would not keep your promise to return."

"My lady," he bowed. "The idea of seeing you once more was all I needed to keep me from death in France. What could compare to the want in my heart to see you again?"

I laughed. "A pike or dagger might, should they have had a chance."

"Many struck close, my lady, but none could dent the *armour* of your promise to me."

I smiled at him. Others in the room were looking a little amused at his over-embellished phrases, but I did not mind. Under all that praise, there was a spark of truth in all he said. I could feel it.

"Well now you are returned, Robin," I said. "And have you come to claim my promise of a place in my household?"

His dark eyes sparkled at me with mischief in them. "No, my lady… At least, not at this moment."

I was astonished. What did he mean by turning down a place in my household when it was offered? Others in the company looked equally shocked, and there was a muttering of disgruntled voices. It was a slight on my name and titles to be so refused by a man of lesser standing. Anger began to rise in me.

"If I may, my lady..." he entreated.

I nodded curtly. Let the man explain himself!

"I come on this day, my lady, to make an offer of my own wealth, such as it is. I place it at your disposal, for your own needs, which must be many. I do not seek a place in your house at this time, but I seek to offer my wealth and my own men to you, knowing that you will make good use of them." He smiled; a knowing and a most charming smile. "And I hope that you will remember your friends in the future; remember those who served you to the best of their ability when *you* had need of *them*."

The anger in my chest stopped pulled up on a short rein by the proposal he gave me. I looked sideways at the figure of Parry who stood, as always, quietly at my side. Parry's face was unreadable to most; years of practise in subterfuge had given him a good mask to hold out to the world, but I, who knew him so well, could read him well too. Our resources were indeed under strain, although this was not a fact that we made clear to any who came wanting a place in our household or those to whom we promised money and title to in return for service now. But the growth in our supporters had led to a bleed on our resources. There was so much now to be planned and bought, paid for and promised in return for the support of our smooth ascension that we were fighting to keep good our accounts. My sister would forward us no more money, for the simple reason that she wanted me no more powerful than I was presently, but here was a lord with a good understanding of our situation, who offered the help we needed, when we needed it.

Clever Robin, I thought, to so easily see into the heart of a problem I had sought to hide, and to offer help without stain or insult to my name. He had refused a place in my household now, and instead offered me his own wealth and men, because he knew the rewards would be greater if he but waited a little longer. I liked clever men. They were so much more refreshing than those who looked beautiful and yet were of limited understanding. Such men are like flowers. Flowers are very pretty, but one can only regard them for so long before longing for the wisdom of a beautiful book.

His proposition was also clever; his present offer of money and men would spur the other Lords to realise that doing the same might in turn see a great reward for them when I became Queen. He may well have increased our revenues threefold on this day just through one speech. And I had not had to ask for a single coin.

Clever Robin; he saw right to the centre of a problem, and saw, too, what should be done to best advance his own interests and my own. A bright set of eyes this one had, taking into account the present and the future, I thought to myself. My loyal lord, my clever Robin… my good eyes.

"I once said, my lord," I said, looking at the dark eyes of Robin that twinkled back at me, "that I was glad God had sent much of foul weather my way, for a friend in times that are foul is of much more weight to me than friends who come only in times of clement skies. It is pleasing to me that you would offer me both men and money for the preservation of my honour and titles. I will accept, but I make to you this promise. Such service as you do me now shall not be forgotten and shall be returned to you *threefold* when the time comes."

Robin bowed to me, a swift a graceful movement. I wondered suddenly if he still danced as well as he had when we were children. There had been little chance for dancing in these sparse years of danger; I hoped there would be chance of it in the future. I should very much like to dance with Robin Dudley.

As the day's visitors filed out, I turned to Parry.

"What think you, Parry?" I asked. "It turned out to be an interesting, and profitable day did it not?"

"Indeed my lady," he replied. "The acquisition of income is all the more enjoyable when it comes as a surprise."

"Does he have much, then? My Lord Robert?"

Parry nodded cautiously. "Many of his own estates were returned when he was released, although many of his father's and brother's lands have not been returned to him. They are still property of the Crown I believe. But his wife came from a family of some means and lands in Norfolk." He paused.

"I do not believe that Lord Robert has as much as he would like others to believe. There is much of the clever courtier about him, to cover the dignity and honour lost as a consequence of those charges of treason and his family's fall from grace. But what he has will certainly help us." Parry looked rueful. "The demands on the coffers have been great of late," he said.

"I had almost forgot that he was married." I pondered, quite ignoring Parry's slight criticism of the state of my coffers. For a moment I felt a little sad, but soon I brightened.

"So much the better," I laughed a little, "for I prefer a man to keep a wife at home. It leads much less to those proposals of marriage that so mar a friendship, do you not think, Parry?"

Parry smiled at me. "As you say so, Your Highness."

I looked around us. I trusted my household, but we must never be too bold on that count.

"I thought perhaps, Master of Horse?" I said quietly to Parry, "for the Lord Robert."

Parry nodded. "He is an interesting man, my lady," his great brow furrowed as he thought. "For he understood well enough, and better than others, what our cause needed and how to offer it, and that shows a greater understanding than most of these lords who come now to offer their support. But he also comes from a long line of traitors, my lady; his grandfather, his father and most of his brothers were executed for treason to the Crown. Every branch of your tree has had to deal with a Dudley working treason; do you wish to have one of such a family so close to your person? Could you ever trust one who has so lately been kept in the Tower for scheming against the Crown?"

I smiled. "Do you forget, Parry? Who else was lately kept in the Tower?" I laughed a little. "It was not so long ago that Robert sent messages to me as *I* was held for treason, not so long since *you yourself* were held there too. There are many past traitors amongst those who serve me, but I do not care for what they were accused of once, only what they may do for me in the future. I do not deny that the ancestors of the Lord Robert have been tried and found traitors to the Crown, but whilst they lived and worked with the Crown, they were valuable servants. A traitor in one reign can become the chief advisor in the next."

I paused and reached out to take his hand. "Parry," I said. "I am in truth surrounded by liars and schemers. The only thing that I want to have assured is that they are *my* liars and schemers and no one else's. I want Robin as my Master of Horse. If he is equal to the task then he shall keep it, if he betrays me then he shall lose both his position, and that handsome head."

Parry nodded to me and I laughed at his serious face. "Come, Parry," I sang. "There is still much of this business of housework yet to be done before our day is done."

CHAPTER FIFTY-SEVEN

Brocket Hall
Summer 1558

As the year continued it was both a time of much activity and of much watchful waiting. In August an outbreak of a sweating sickness came to England, borne on the sea mists that came from France and Spain. Men and women fell ill and died, some within a day, they said, so virulent was the disease for some. The sweat had long been a curse on these isles, first come to England with the armies of my own grandfather Henry VII when he brought mercenaries to fight with him at Bosworth, but combined with long seasons of poor harvest and the damp weather that had plagued my sister's reign, it became a force to be reckoned with.

Blanche, Anne and Elizabeth all suffered mildly with it, and I too was taken low, but our sufferings were luckily of short duration, and did not prove serious. My sister, too, was taken with the sweat, and her already weakened body was undermined further still by this disease. In August, we thought we might at any time hear that she had died. By September she had rallied enough that the Council sent forth joyous exclamation and proclamation for her return to health. But by October, it was clear that for Mary, this had but been a momentary reprieve. She was sick unto death, and we all knew it.

Her doctors sent regular messages to Phillip; not only on her health, but on her wishes to see him once more before she left this world. He sent his Ambassador, Feria, back once again to England to care for her, but since Phillip's father, Charles, was also dying in Spain, Phillip himself could not come to his wife's side.

Bereft of the company of the one she loved more than any other in this world, and pressured by her Council who could see no babe growing in the woman dying before them, Mary made an addition to her will.

"God hath hitherto sent me no fruit nor heir of my body, and it is only in his most divine providence whether I shall have any or no."

The admission that she might not have been pregnant must have been a painful one as she lay on that bed, in those sweltering darkened rooms.

"In the absence of mine own issue and heir, I shall become succeeded by my nearest heir and successor by the laws of this realm. I ask them by the bowels of the mercy of God to respect my bequests to the Church of Christ and to protect the land of England."

I looked at the dispatches in my hand; another clever copy made by those in Cecil's pay and sent to us at Brocket Hall. My feet tapped on the rushes on the floor, sending up sweet smells of rosemary and thyme that I crushed beneath my heel and toe as I thought.

"Even now…!" I cried, my voice lifted in anger even as my spirits felt weary. "Even now, she will not acknowledge me as her heir. Look here; I am '*them*'! Or perhaps," I frowned, "I am no such… and she seeks to replace me still with another…"

Parry stood near the window; he had already read the dispatches, of course, and so was well aware of what they contained.

"Does she seek to send England to civil war or to rebellion again?" I muttered angrily. "If she names no successor, then others will come to challenge me upon her death!"

"They may do so in any case, my lady," Parry reminded, turning and walking to me.

"Mary Queen of Scots and her husband the Dauphin already state a claim to the throne of England... and even if they are far away in France, they still have an army at their back. Those Grey girls... Katherine, and the crookbacked Mary Grey; even though their sister Jane died at the block you still see them prancing around court as though they were the foremost heirs to the throne. The Lennox family headed by your cousin the Countess Margaret Douglas... They have another slim link to the throne, and that woman is relentless in her ambitions for her son! Even once we have achieved our aim here, my lady, however easy or hard this first step may be, it will still only be a first step. We will have years of new challenges to contend with, and there will always be those about you who hold a claim, no matter how tenuous, to your throne. They will always be a risk to you."

He looked at me and bowed. "Your royal father and grandfather understood, my lady, that the only heirs that a king can risk trusting are the heirs of his own body. All other claimants should be... removed."

"Stop, Parry," I moaned ruefully. "You will make me faint away with all this good cheer you bring to me! A prince can only take so much of festival and ease you know..."

He smiled at me and bowed again. He often did this more when he knew he was making me uncomfortable. It spoke volumes of Parry's wariness of my temper. "But it is the truth, my lady," he said. "Long has been your preparation for the throne, but once we have you seated on it, we shall have to become masters of the art, and put aside those tools we used as novices."

"We will have all resources to hand then, Parry. I know well of the challenges we ride out to meet, but what I do not want is to start my reign fighting for my crown against the Greys, the Lennoxes, the Valois or the Stuarts. It seems to me that even if such a war is won, the people of England will still be the ones to lose, for once again their country will be rent apart, their villages and towns burned and looted, their crops destroyed. No, if we can do this without a war, my good Parry, then I shall be a content woman. I will fight for my throne if I have to, but if I can gain it in peace then I will. All other steps, whatever they may be, can be taken after the first as long as it is placed well on the road ahead."

"Of course, my lady," Parry bowed his head.

"There is other news, my lady," he said as I stared despondently at the paper before me. Why it should have brought such sorrow to my heart that Mary would still not acknowledge me as her heir by name, I know not. But it did. In these, however many days or weeks we spent on this earth together, Mary still denied me the titles and rights which were mine. She still denied me my place. In all we had seen together, from childhood to youth and beyond, she still sought, perhaps for her still lingering hatred of my mother, to remove me from the position to which I had been born. She still, in some ways, denied that I was her sister. Although it did not surprise me a great deal, it wounded my heart still.

"What news?" I asked.

"The Duke of Feria has arrived back in England as special envoy to the English court," said Parry. "Cecil sends word that Phillip wants you named as successor, and has sent Feria to ensure that Her Majesty is aware of this."

"Of course," I snorted. "The slippery King of Spain hopes to replace one daughter of England with another in his bed as soon as it draws cold on him. We will take the support of Feria and Phillip now, but when the time comes the King of Spain will find that not all women in England fall so easily to his wants and desires as my sister did."

"I should expect nothing less, my lady," Parry struggled to hide a smile. "Feria has already requested that you would grant him an audience, once he has seen the Queen and Council."

"I would be most pleased to receive the envoy of Spain," I smiled. "But if he wants to see me, then he must needs come to Brocket Hall; I'll not travel to the heel of any servant of Spain again."

"I will relay the message, my lady," said Parry as he bowed and left.

CHAPTER FIFTY-EIGHT

Brocket Hall
Autumn 1558

"The Lady Jane Dormer asks for an audience, my lady," Bessie Brooke's soft voice startled me from the pleasure of the walk I was taking in the gardens at Brocket. The autumn was passing fast, and this November was chilly and cool; sparkling frost stood on the remaining golden-red leaves of the gardens gilding everything with a glitter of silver sparkle.

I had taken to walking in the mornings and evenings; just a short stroll out in the fresh air to relieve the tensions of my days of bargaining and planning. In these past few months, sleep had become a stranger to me, evading me at night, leaving me to stare from the covers of my bed into the darkness of the future and what it might hold for me. Parry had suggested that exercise might help me to find the restful sleep that I knew I needed so, and although neither these strolls, nor my regular rides in the parks had helped me into the arms of sleep, they did indeed help to quieten the rigours of a restless soul. Even a moment or two of peace, a bare few minutes without talk or thought, helped my mind to calm itself, and to prepare for the next barrage that beset me.

I turned; Bess was standing wrapped in her cloak and fur-trimmed hood, a vision of an English rose in a garden of winter. My ladies did not like coming out into the cold with me, but they did so because it was their duty. Anne and Blanche were at my side, and I saw in their faces the same interest in Bessie's words that had sparked inside me.

"What does the Lady Dormer want?" I asked.

"She comes with a message from Her Majesty, the Queen," Bess replied. "But any more than that, she would not reveal to me; she said the message was for your ears, my lady, and no others."

I raised my eyebrows. Mary was sick unto death, but still struggled on living. Messages from the court suggested that she still hoped God would send her a miracle and present her with a child. That horrible hope, a delusion created from desperation, continued to keep Mary from naming a successor to her throne.

"I will come," I said. "Bring the Lady Dormer to my privy chambers."

We went back inside the house, Blanche and Anne clearly relieved to find the walk cut short for this morning. They went into the great hall to warm themselves at the vast fire which burned there. In the privy chambers, I was removed of my own cape and hood, and sat down to await the coming of my sister's favourite lady in waiting.

In came Jane Dormer. Her lively eyes were rimmed with red and grey for long hours of toil at the sick-bed of my sister, and for the grief she suffered on seeing her mistress brought so low. Her pretty face was pale from much time spent indoors, but her expression was set with the task she had been sent to perform.

She curtseyed to me, low and deep in a respectful manner. And when she rose I spoke.

"What news of my sister, Her Majesty?" I asked.

Jane's face puckered a little, and ready tears leapt to her eyes. "My lady, Her Majesty sends her love to you, her royal sister. The Queen is troubled in mind, and most ill in body."

"I am sad to hear so," I said honestly. "Does Her Majesty know much pain?"

"The pain the Queen knows in her natural body is of little significance to her, my lady," Jane replied stoically. "Her Majesty faces all hardship with the grace of an angel and the strength of a lion. But those things which trouble her in her mind plague her most, for in all things, the Queen has ever desired to do only the best for her people, to ensure their future and protect their souls."

"What is it that troubles my sister so?" I asked. "And what might I do to relieve that suffering? Since you are here, there must be something that Her Majesty wishes of me."

Jane nodded. "There is indeed, my lady," she pulled herself up and pushed back her shoulders. "Her Most Gracious Majesty has sent me to your house as her emissary, my lady, to relay to you that she has named you as heir to her throne to her Council. In return for this honour, Her Majesty asks two things of you when your time comes to take on her mantle. The first: that you will pay the debts owing in the name of the Crown so that in matters worldly the Queen can rest at ease."

I nodded... a feeling as though someone had opened a window in my heart on the first day of summer flooded through me. "You may tell Her Majesty, my sister that I am grateful for the honour she does to me in naming me as her successor. I can only hope that I prove as worthy as she believes me to be. Tell Her Majesty also that she may set aside her fears for her earthly cares, assured that any remaining debts from her reign will be settled by me. But what is the other condition she names?"

"My lady, that you keep the Catholic faith in England, as it has been restored to the people of England," Jane said. "So that in matters spiritual, Her Majesty may rest in peace, knowing that the souls of her people, of her *children*, are safe from heresy and corruption."

It was not unexpected. With her last request, Mary wanted me to keep the people of England shrouded in superstition and myth, always subordinate to the power of Rome. She must have known that even if I acquiesced to this demand, I was unlikely to keep my word, so against all that I held dear in matters religious and worldly was this request. But I could hardly say that to Jane. She sought this last reassurance, to give peace to a dying, misguided woman.

"I have, through the reign of my sister, been a true Catholic," I prayed to God in my head that He would understand and forgive me for the lies I was about to infer. "Tell my sister that when the time comes, I will maintain the Catholic faith of England, as she requests."

I did not mention however, for how *long* I would maintain the Catholic faith of England once I was Queen… Although that likely does me little credit in your eyes, it was not *precisely* a lie.

Jane fell to her knees and let out a little sob. These past months had been hard on this good woman who truly cared for my poor sister with all her heart. Perhaps she was the only one in the world who loved Mary so well. I could not claim that position, for my feelings for my sister were ever in turmoil. I rose and went to her. My touch at her shoulder caused her to lift up her head and look at me.

"You have suffered much, I think, for your devotion and love for Her Majesty, my sister," I said gently. "This I well know and I would thank you for it. I am sure that the fidelity and affection you have shown has come of great consolation to Her Majesty in times of need. Whatever else has passed between Her Majesty and me, she is my sister and I will always be grateful to you for the care and warmth you have given her."

"Whatever love I have shown Her Majesty," Jane looked up at me with eyes that shone with tears, "has been inspired by the love and honour she has shown to me. She is a great lady and a great sovereign."

I nodded. I could hardly argue on that point, however much I wanted to, given the circumstances. "Your Duke Feria comes to court, so I am told," I said. "Has Her Majesty given you assurance on when your marriage may take place?"

"It will... not be long now, my lady. The Duke is most keen to be wed, and I have missed him a great deal."

"Perhaps soon enough Jane," I smiled, "you will have a different type of comfort in your life. There are dark days yet to face, but your prospects for the future with Duke Feria seem bright. Let those prospects light your way now, and as you give comfort to my sister, let Her Majesty know that I love her, that I pray for her, that I remember most keenly all that she did for me when I was a motherless child, and all that she has done for me since. Give her such words of comfort from me, and let her know that I harbour only love for her in my heart."

"That will bring her peace, my lady," Jane sniffed a little on her tears. "Although she has spoken but little of the times that passed between you, I believe she has always loved you and wanted well for you."

"As I have done for her," I said, feeling the lies told at a time of death stick in the back of my throat. But then, were they all lies? Complex are the emotions when dealing with a sister, especially one who has posed a constant risk to your well-being. That was true enough for both Mary and for me. Had we never been born to be queens, would we have felt differently about each other? Would our love, which I was sure *did* exist in each of our hearts for the other, never have become tainted with the stains of distrust and jealousy?

Who can say, and who may know, but God?

Perhaps one day, if we are reunited in the Kingdom of Heaven, in a place where these rivalries and dangerous suspicions are not present, perhaps we should come to know what value there may be in the simple love of sisters.

It was just as I was thinking on these things with sad affection that they were once more ruined for me by Mary. Before she left, Jane gave me a gift from Mary; jewels that were from the Queen's private collection. Amongst many plain gems and brooches was a ring with the initials H and K entwined in gold over a little diamond. It must have belonged to her mother; so small and delicate a ring could never have sat on our father's giant fingers. And such a treasure Mary would never have parted from without reason.

I sighed as I turned the ring over in my fingertips; even at the last, as she demanded that I work to maintain her wants and desires, Mary could not help but remind me that in her eyes, I was, and always would be, a bastard.

CHAPTER FIFTY-NINE

Brocket Hall
Autumn 1558

A day after Jane Dormer's visit, emissaries of the Council, always just that slight step behind everyone else, came to tell me that I had been named heir to Mary's throne. I don't believe they had known about Jane's visit to Brocket Hall, for I saw them view the jewels I wore to their audience with me with surprise. They recognized those jewels on my breast as ones from Mary's private collection, and they wondered how, when and why I had been granted them. It amused me to see them wonder. Let them so! It had not been so long ago that I had stood before many of these men fighting for my life under accusations of treason. I had not forgotten that I had been treated in a manner that was disrespectful to my title and position. I welcomed any discomfort, small or large, that I could impose upon them.

They informed me, with a little pomposity, that I had been named as Mary's successor, and rattled off the same conditions that Mary had given me the day before. But to that, they added another condition which I knew was their wish, not Mary's; that the Council as it was now, was to remain unchanged if I ascended to the throne.

I could have laughed. What arrogance these men had, and how plain they had made their fears to me! What fools they were to come and lay bare the alarm they felt in being removed from their posts in the Royal Council! I smiled at them. Although I had given Mary all assurance that I would maintain the religion of superstition in England, I wanted also to assure my Protestant supporters, of which there were many, that I would remove it and the stain of its fires from England.

"I will promise this much," I told them on the matter of religion, "I will not change it, provided only that it can be proved by the word of God, which shall be the only foundation and rule of my religion."

They looked perplexed, as well they might. It was not a sentence intended for the removal of doubt, but one intended to keep my own options open. Let men read into it what they would.

"And in the matter of my Council, my lords," I spoke briskly, narrowing my eyes at them. "Every prince that has come to this throne has had the right and freedom to choose his own advisors, and I will exercise that right, as is my privilege and my duty. There is no man amongst you that can hold me to retain any of the Council that now exists, for should that rule have been passed, then, long since now, the King of England should have been advised and counselled only by corpses and ghosts. I assure you that I will take the utmost care in deciding who is fit to counsel me. I will retain those who are worthy, but I will not ensure the continuation of any on the Council whom I find to be wanting. This much, I will promise to you."

They left looking rather shocked and bruised. It was a risk to speak as I had done, but I was daily assured by the numbers swelling in our cause, by the garrisons promised to us, and by Mary's eventual, reluctant confirmation of me as her heir, that the throne was close enough that I could start to rule as I meant to when I came to sit on it.

If my sister's rule had taught me anything, it was that if I was to sit on the throne of my forebears, then I had to do so in perfect understanding of my own power, and in bold confidence for my own will. There would be no hesitations, there would be no woman ruled by her husband or foreign power. I would not part with any aspect of my power. If I was to rule, then *I* was to rule, and I wanted that truth well established in everyone's minds even before I came to sit on that throne.

I would *be* the Throne. I would *be* the Crown.

I would be the Queen, and I would be the King.

I was a prince of England, born from a line of great kings.

I was a princess of England, raised from the blood of its land.

I would rule and none would rule me.

CHAPTER SIXTY

Brocket Hall
Autumn 1558

There comes a time in any long preparation when you start to feel as though your target is within your sights. I could almost feel the crown on my head, the throne under my skin, the sceptre in my hand… but I was not queen yet.

Secretly, and with great care, for I still did not want any interference with our other plans from Mary's Council, I ordered that Kat was to be brought from Devonshire to Brocket Hall and hidden amongst the many servants I now had there. Officially, Kat was not meant to be within my household, or anywhere near me. But now, Mary and her Council were much distracted by other matters, and I thought the time had come to once again bring my old governess home. Her family were pleased to release her to me from house arrest within their estates; they knew as well as all of England, that the time of Mary's reign was drawing to a close and mine was about to begin. They wanted Kat back in a position which could do them the most good, and they knew, too, how much she had longed to return to my side.

One night, as the dark blue dusk started to paint the land with a hazy hue, and the frost sparkled like diamonds on the grass, there came a knock to my door. I nodded to my ladies and smiled, for we knew who was coming to us this night. Bessie Brooke rose and opened the door, a deep look of interest and hunger in her face, for she wanted to see the woman I had trusted all my life, and had missed with all my heart.

Kat was heavily cloaked. A deep cowl of black had covered her head and face as my trusted men had snuck her through the frosted lands of England to the halls of my house, and brought her to my rooms. As she stepped through the door, and the other ladies around me stepped back, Kat pulled back her hood and revealed to me that face that was most dear to me in the world.

I rushed towards her, but she dropped suddenly to a curtsey before me. Raising her face, I noticed with a great tug to my heart that she looked so much older than she had done when last we saw each other, and her skin was pale, as though she had not seen the sun this last summer at all.

"My lady," she murmured with the greatest warmth and love in her voice. "Thank you for bringing me back once again to be with you."

I reached down to her. This level of formality was not part of our former relationship, but I was struck with the new awe she seemed to hold for me; recognition that I was closer than ever to becoming not only her mistress, but her queen.

I touched her shoulder. My eyes clouded with tears of joy to see her once again, and I raised her up. "Kat…" I said. "This will have been the last time you ever have cause to leave me, I *promise* you that."

Kat smiled; her eyes too foggy with tears. "I would be grateful," she smiled, "to never have to miss you again, my lady." Tears rolled over her lower lids. "The most pain that anyone ever gave to me was not the cells of the Tower, nor was it the shouts of interrogators; it was the torture of not being beside you, my lady," she paused. "My Lady Elizabeth… my little girl."

I hugged her. My long fingers reached deep into her brown hair, my tears soaked into her shoulder just as they had done when I was just a small child, and she had held me, protecting me from bad dreams. Finally, I felt complete once more, as my old governess, and my oldest friend, came home to me.

I pulled back and laughed through the tears. "Come and warm yourself, Kat," I said. "You must become acquainted with my other ladies. Well they have served me well since you were taken from me, and I know that you will love them as I do, for in your absence they have become my own guard of lionesses, watching and protecting my every step."

Blanche and Kat embraced; they were grateful to see each other once again. The other ladies, Elizabeth and Anne and my Fair Geraldine who was also visiting Brocket Hall, looked Kat over with some interest, for often and well had I spoken of her. They helped her out of her wet and heavy travelling clothes.

By the time an hour was spent, we were having a rather riotous time in my private chambers. Wine and sweetmeats were brought in; we laughed and chatted to each other in a merry throng and Anne played on the lute as the others sang. As the evening wore on, we cupped goblets of warm, spiced wine in our hands and sat before the fire on great cushions, talking of a time when our happiness, would become the happiness of England, too.

The next day I slept late. The evening had worn on into the small hours with my ladies, and afterwards, Kat and I had lain side by side in my bed still talking as the others slept. Sleep mattered not as we talked, so much was there was to tell each other.

"It would seem my mistress has grown into a king..." Kat softly wondered as I told her of all our plans and all of the plotting that had taken place since she had been gone.

"Needs must," I said. "The throne comes closer to me now than I could have ever imagined when I was a child." I sat up and turned on an elbow to her. "Did you ever think it was possible Kat?" I asked, my whisper low in the darkness. "When I was a girl, there was but little chance that I should ever come to the throne. I thought my brother should have lived to have his own children; he was so young after all... And then when Mary came to the throne, although there was more hope, I thought that she still stood a chance to bear her own line. But now, Edward is gone, Mary lies sick unto death, and I am named heir to the throne."

Kat shifted in the great bed; the warm covers of wool that clothed our bodies were snug around us. "You will be a great Queen, my lady," she said. "And if it once seemed unlikely that you should take the throne, it offers more proof that it was God's will that the throne would be yours. When I look at you now, I still see my little Elizabeth, with that proud, knowing look you had when you were a child... How I remember your scowls and the determined set of your mouth when you were crossed! But I see now also the shadow of your father in the woman before me, and I hear the wit of your mother in your tongue." She paused. "They would be proud of you, Elizabeth. I know that with all the certainty in my soul. "

Tears leapt to my eyes once more. If I had once heard that sentence from either of my parents, I should have been overjoyed, but neither spoke such to me when they were alive.

"I think of my father often now," I whispered. "When I was in danger, in the Tower, I thought of my mother more, but as I come to the throne, to the court, I find that I think often on what my father would have done, or said. Do you think that strange?"

Kat shook her head. "No. For in her lifetime your mother was bravest in her most troubled times, the times she fought for her position, the times she struggled to protect you. Your father was at his greatest in the times when he was most gracious, when he ruled the country through love. It is fitting that each of your parents should have taught you something to help you survive in each challenge you have been given, and fitting that you should learn from *both* of them. No matter what any person says, your mother was a fine lady, a woman of learning and grace, and your father was a great king, a strong king and one whom the people loved… Even when they feared him, they still loved him."

"It does make sense," I nodded.

Kat rolled over so that she, too, was on one elbow; our eyes sparkled at each other in the fleeting moonlight shimmering through the curtains.

"And now, you will be Queen," she murmured. "And you must needs decide what type of rule you wish to have over people. Should you be just as your father, or should there still be in you a part that is your mother?"

"I can never truly acknowledge my love for my mother in public. The stain on her name is such that it is still used against me; my enemies call me *bastard* and *little whore*, but I know well enough she was a good woman, and died innocent of the crimes she was accused of. That is enough for me."

I paused and thought. "I want the people to love me as they have done since I was a child, Kat. But I understand the value, as my father did, of fear. There must be no man who can call my reign into question without reprisal; there must be no one near me who can endanger my life. I have good men that I will take to my Council; I have good women with whom I will surround my private body. All those nearest to me will be those I trust and they will protect me. But I mean to rule with a stubborn will; I will not let my state and realm be overtaken by the petty factions that so ruled my brother and sister, and I will not step backwards from the truth as my sister has done. My reign will be based on all I have learnt. I hope to be a fair ruler, but I will not retreat from punishing those who stand against me."

"A king must be ruthless at times, my love," agreed Kat. "Rulers do not have the luxury that simple folk have, to walk away from a fight. But I know you well enough, my lady, Elizabeth." She smiled. I could see the edge of her grin in the darkness. "You will be a good Queen, a fair Queen. You will make our England fine and good once more."

"Kat," I whispered. "When the time comes, I am going to appoint you my Chief Gentlewoman of the Privy Chamber."

There was a little gasp from the shape beside me, and a warm hand fumbled against mine in the shadow of the bed.

"My lady," she said in a voice most humbled. "There are others far more titled and worthy than I take that role. I am happy just to serve you and be by your side again. I do not need such titles."

"Hush, Kat," I said, slipping my fingers inside hers. The warm cup of her hand was smooth; it brought back a thousand memories of my childhood.

"I need those around me, closest to me, whom I can trust without question. And there is no one more suited to this role than you. How long have you served in my house, comforted me? Who fed me and looked after me when I was a child? How many times have you proved your loyalty to me under arrest and capture by mine enemies? How many times have you advised and helped me in times of most desperate need? In all ways and in all things you have proved yourself to be my most trusted companion and friend, protector of my person and confidant of my soul. I would have you honoured in my reign just as you were slandered in the last. You will become the Head of my Chambers Kat, the most important post I can grant to you. I will brook no refusal on that point."

"My lady," Kat said, acceptance in her voice, "you need not wonder on how you will rule. For the Elizabeth I have always known becomes like a king already crowned, when she sets her mind on something."

"You accept the position?" I asked, laughing.

"I would obey from fear of offending you, my lady…" Kat laughed too, "if I was not already moved to accept by my love of you."

"Then I have already achieved my desired style of rule," I said impishly, waving my hand in the air. "Fear and love in almost equal measure, with love outweighing the fear."

"Only by a *short distance,* my lady," Kat said cheekily; I slapped her lightly on the arm and she laughed again. "My mistress still has quick hands I see!"

"As quick as the thoughts that drive the hands," I smiled.

"Fear and love, my lady," said Kat. "But you will find, I hope, that more come to love you as I do, with all their hearts."

We grasped each other tightly, tangled together in the darkness so that for a while none could have told where Elizabeth started and Kat ended. Long we talked into the darkness, and as the early lights started to appear, Kat fell asleep beside me, a little smile on her face. As the dawn rose, I looked into the face of my old governess and saw, to my pleasure, that she looked younger than she had when first she came through the door to my chambers. The strain and pressure of being somewhere other than where you long to be can cause the body to look older than it really is, I thought. Happiness may make us young again, as sorrow makes us old.

As the grey dawn soaked over the skies outside, I lay my head on the pillows and watched it. A new day was dawning.

CHAPTER SIXTY-ONE

Brocket Hall
Autumn 1558

The next evening, we were a merry party at Brocket Hall; Bess had brought her William to the house, and Geraldine's husband, the Lord Admiral Clinton, had also arrived. I called for a feast, for we had also heard that the Duke of Feria, Phillip's envoy from Spain, was wending his way to Brocket after talking with Cecil in London. I wanted him to see that this prince of the realm was no longer hiding in the shadows behind the throne.

Feria arrived just before the evening's entertainments were to begin. He seemed surprised that such a merry throng should be around me, perhaps thinking that I should still be removed from all friends and allies, as the Spanish no doubt had hoped. During the meal, there was much talk and laughter. Although Kat was not present, because I wanted none to know she had been secretly brought back to my house, the very idea of her presence so nearby had raised my spirits.

As the banquet of sweets drew to a close, I turned to the Duke. He was a fairly handsome man; dark eyes and hair, his beard fashionable and short and his body clothed in the dark robes that the Spanish seemed well to favour. Diamonds sparkled on his doublet, and pearls on his sleeves; although he looked simply attired compared to some of our English gallants, he was dressed in jewels and cloth that must have cost a goodly fortune.

William Parr and the Lord Admiral removed themselves at my signal, and the Duke and I were left with just the company of my ladies and the musicians who took up a mournful tune as we turned to talk.

"I would that you would speak in your own language, Your Grace," I said in Spanish. "For my women know only the English tongue, and I would want you to speak freely. It will save time in your visit here, if we speak with honesty to each other."

Feria smiled. "I would not mind if the whole world knew of what we said to each other. My master and I have no fear, my lady."

"All the same, Your Grace," I smiled. "Your master strove to protect me in times when I needed such; it would be of comfort to me, to return such friendship to his emissary now."

Feria nodded and acquiesced. It was not in the nature of any Ambassador to deny an offer of secrecy when it was presented to them. How was he to be aware that each of my ladies had good knowledge of the Spanish language? He was not conscious that my women and I often conversed in Latin, English, French, Italian or Spanish when we were in our private lodgings; keeping our knowledge of each alive through daily practise with each other. Blanche was even teaching the rest of my ladies some Welsh, although their tongues tripped often over the complexities of that new language.

If this emissary wanted to bargain with me for Spanish advantage once I became queen, I wanted witnesses to his demands now.

My ladies gave no signal that Feria could have seen, but they understood me well enough. Between themselves, they talked quietly, but I could almost see their ears growing, elongating, as they worked to hear our conversation as they minded to their own. It is a skill that many women have, which men do not seem to have ever learned; to be able to clearly hear another conversation as they make one of their own. Whenever I have asked men of it, they have looked at me with confusion, perhaps thinking it a feminine ruse of some kind. But I counsel you now to remember, good gentlemen, that those of the fairer sex have many such covert skills at their disposal, unbeknown to their male counterparts. So, be careful what you say in the company of women, my good lords, for not only do they remember all, but they hear all as well.

"It is fitting that you should begin, Your Highness," Feria said in his heavy Spanish, "by talking of a debt owed between yourself and my master, Phillip of Spain; for although it will not have been made clear to you, it is through his actions alone that you have been named as heir to the throne. The Council and the Queen were moved by his arguments in your favour, and so in addition to the protection he offered you when you were most in need of it, my master now offers you the throne of England, through his own graciousness and good-will."

I stared at the Duke for a moment, my anger rising in my chest. What did this man think of me, that I should believe that I owed my right to the throne to the whims and favour of his master? I tried to cool my rage; the Spanish *want* you to believe this, I thought, so that they have you in their pocket… as they wanted to do so before, by marrying you off to their lackey Philibert.

I clenched my teeth together. It would not do to slap the emissary of Spain, however much I wanted to.

"It is the people… The people of *England* who have given me my present position, Your Grace," I replied smoothly. "In recognition of my own heritage, my own royal blood and titles, and in recognition of their love for me. I was made heir to this throne of England by law in the will of my father, the great King Henry VIII, but it was the will of those I mean to rule that has vouchsafed me this throne in truth. *Nothing*, do I owe to your master in that regard, and nothing to the nobles or royal seat of any house, other than those of *England*."

Feria tried to cover his look of surprise. He was skilled at masking his horror but I spoke more plainly to him than he had ever expected. Ambassadors are used to dancing their way through lies and gaining truth through subterfuge, but I wanted his master in Spain to be in no doubt, about who was going to rule this country… and who was not.

The time for interference by foreign powers in the matters of England, was done.

"It is the people of England who place me on the throne to rule over them, Your Grace," I repeated, just to make sure he had understood me completely. "And no one else."

I smiled at his serious face. He had been hoping to easily dupe a young maid into obedience to his master; I almost felt sorry for him. He had no idea who he was dealing with; his master should have seen him better prepared than this to face me. I reached out to his hand and touched it lightly.

"Your master once tried to have me married," I said gently, "to a lord from foreign shores. But I refused to do so, for I know well enough that the Queen, my royal sister, lost the love of her people because she married a foreign power. There will be no such mistakes now. The people of England place an English princess on the throne and they make her the Queen, and their love will decide my actions in the future. I will be ruled by none," I affirmed, my eyes glinting at him as the musicians took up another tune. "Other than by God, my conscience, and the love of my people."

Feria swallowed. Things were not going according to his plans. "Will you be governed not by the Council?" he asked.

"Not by the *sheep* and *goats* that surround my poor sister now," I laughed. His face for the first time registered a look of shock. "Yes, my lord," I nodded. "You heard my words correctly. I call them such for such they are. The *sheep* are those my poor sister inherited of my father and brother, beasts long since past their best meat, now just fit for mutton; and the *goats* are those she chose herself. There are some in that Council who still have wit and reason, and they will survive the cull I intend to make when I come into possession of the herd, but *I* will choose my own flock." My face darkened. "And my men will be chosen from those who have not wronged me, as so many on the Council of my sister have done."

"It would not do credit to your name or titles," Feria frowned, "to show a desire for vengeance or revenge; it is not *womanly* to show such characteristics, and would much upset the image that most of the world has, of you as a good and kind Catholic princess."

I smiled ruefully. "And we would not want such an image to be disrupted, Your Grace… I will not seek *vengeance* on those who have done me wrong, on those who once slandered my name and stood by as I was abused and defamed. I will ask that those members of the Council who did such to me acknowledge their faults in that matter. I will pardon them as I let them go. I will have no use for them, but I will not seek to ruin them, as they once did to me. So you see, Your Grace, I do not carry vengeance in my heart."

"What men will you then trust, Your Highness?" he asked. "Your Council will be made of new men, none accustomed to the governance of the realm as those who are trained and experienced in their roles… as the men that sit therein now."

"Experience does not necessarily bestow success or wisdom," I smiled. "Especially if all one is experienced in is failure and folly. I believe you know already whom I will favour when the time comes, Your Grace. But I will make it easy for you. Look to my audience chamber when you come to take your leave on the morrow. Therein you will see many faces of the new age that approaches." I smiled at him and pressed my hand over him on the table. "I know well enough that you have made many friends in the present Council, and that you seek to defend them for that friendship. But you, and your master, my dear *brother*, should sense well enough, that the tide is turning on these shores of England, and a new order comes. Do not find yourself stuck on the sands for having missed the opportunity to assess the power of the waves, Your Grace."

He went to talk again, but I held up my hand and silenced him. Although he looked outraged, he was silenced at my signal.

"I have had enough talk this night of politics, Your Grace," I said merrily. "Tell me of your plans to marry my sister's lady in waiting, Jane Dormer. I have met her and found her to be a woman of much courage and grace. I hope you are aware that you take an English bride with English spirit; I wonder if you are ready for such a challenge?"

I eyed him mischievously. Oh, he was a fun one to poke at, this Spaniard! So painfully aware of the proper way of behaving. I hoped, for her own sake, that Jane would find some way of loosening the drawstrings on his humour.

"I thank you, Your Highness," he said stiffly. "My Lady Jane is a good woman. I hope that our union will not be long in the waiting."

"I wish you all possible happiness in marriage, Your Grace." I lifted my goblet to him. The wine inside mine was far weaker than in his, for I did not like a head clouded and muddled from the excesses of drink.

My ladies picked up their goblets, as did Feria, and all looked at me to make the toast.

"To love," I cried in English, "between a man and a woman, or a duke and a lady and to the love between two countries," I fixed Feria with my sparkling eyes. "May greater *understanding*, lead only to harmony and love between our nations."

"To love!" my ladies and Feria cried loudly, toasted and then drank.

As my ladies and I rose to go to bed, Feria bowed and took my hand to kiss it. "I understand you, perfectly, Your Highness," he said.

"Then I am glad, Your Grace, for I mean to be well understood in my own house." I smiled.

As Feria went to leave the next morning, he came, as instructed to my audience chamber. Therein were the faces of the new age; Robin Dudley, Parry and Lord Clinton, and new supporters of my position; Nicholas Throckmorton, Peter Carew and John Harrington. Men we had amassed, those that had come to me, those that had come through my present servants. Only Cecil was absent, being still in London making our arrangements.

I saw Feria pale slightly as he came to take my leave in the chamber, and I smiled once again to see him so discomforted… as well he might be. He and his master might have hoped that I would reign under Phillip's influence, or become a puppet of Spain, but they were wrong. They might have hoped that I would retain Mary's Catholic Council, but they were wrong. They might have hoped they would have a foolish, untutored child to deal with, *but they were wrong.*

My new Councillors were young, vigorous, bold… And almost every one of them was a secret Protestant, as well Feria knew.

I let him leave early; after all, bad news is so much harder to write than good news… and he had a letter full of bad news to compose to his master in Spain.

I took some satisfaction in thinking on what Phillip's face might look like when he opened the letter… my enjoyment, I felt, was justified seeing as the Prince of Spain had once plotted to abduct me and force me into marriage with his underling. I only wished I could have been there to see the light drop from his eyes, when he found the heretic heir to the throne of England had spat defiance in his face.

CHAPTER SIXTY-TWO

Brocket Hall
Autumn 1558

The day after Feria left our little court, Cecil came riding home.

Although Parry, ever the cautious military man, advised against it, Cecil believed that we should remove from Brocket Hall and take our growing court back to Hatfield House.

"The time has come to establish our base for your ascension," Cecil reasoned as Parry and I listened. "We have all in place, and each day I expect news of the Queen's death; we should repair to a palace more in keeping with your new status, my lady."

"When you say *all is in place,* good Cecil," I questioned, "by what means do you refer?"

Cecil looked briefly at the ceiling in my privy chambers. He often wont to do this when he was thinking and placing those thoughts in order to be spoken.

"I have the documents of proclamation for your ascension prepared," he said. "Fast riders are positioned up and down the route to London, so that we might send message or proclamation to the Council by them, and I have the majority of the Council on our side, expecting that if they proclaim you as Queen on the death of Her Majesty, they may yet have hope to retain their present positions." He paused. "Moreover, I have a new Councillor's oath drawn up, so that when the time comes, we can have every man of them swear to protect and assert your titles. We are as prepared as can be, my lady, for your reign to begin in smooth adherence to the will of Henry VIII. "

"There is still a risk that we will need to call on those men and garrisons promised to us to take the throne by force," argued Parry. "I have them ready to mobilize with spare little warning... And if we need to muster troops to take London, Brocket is a more defensible base than Hatfield in which to defend Her Highness."

"Let all those instructions stay in place," nodded Cecil. "It never hurts to remain cautious. However, I believe that the country and the people are behind our cause. We have enough proof of it from our men who send news to us of the murmurings in the countryside and towns. Enough of the Council is willing to support us, and all those men who have gathered to the side of our lady are enough that no one, unless a true fool, should look at our forces gathered and think that they stand a better chance to take the throne."

I looked at both my men; Parry and Cecil were like two sides of a coin, and both were as cautious and as devoted to my cause and to me as I could ask. In each one of them there was sense spoken, but I felt that Cecil was right; we must place ourselves where we could be easily found when we were called to the throne. To remain in such seclusion at Brocket Hall might look like cowardice, or reluctance.

"We will remove to Hatfield," I said and held up a hand as Parry started to protest. "All military preparations will remain in place, Parry," I continued. "We will be but four miles from Brocket should we need to come back to establish a defensive stance. The house will remain as it is. There are more than enough guards that we might take some to Hatfield and leave as many here. In that way, we are prepared for both eventualities. And as Cecil says, we must arrange ourselves at a palace more befitting our station than this house," I paused. "Do we also have fast riders positioned to send word to those garrisons promised to us, should we have the need?"

They nodded almost in unison, and I frowned. "But yet you only tell me of those ready to ride out in the event of a peaceful succession?" I shook my head at them. "Gentlemen, although I may still look like the girl you knew, I am to be your queen most imminently. As such, although I value your desire to protect me, I must advise you to keep nothing from me. The time of our childhood is gone." I looked at them. "In all things and in all preparations, I must have the truth from those around me. Nothing else will do, or my reign will certainly fail as has that of my sister."

"Forgive me, my lady," Parry apologised. "It was not a thing done on purpose; I did mean to tell you, but in truth there has been so much preparation and action in your cause of late, that there are most likely many things I have not outlined to you. But please believe me, all preparations, for each possible outcome, have been thought on, and plans set in motion to allow for each."

I nodded. "I understand, Parry. There has indeed been a great deal occurring of late. But you will need to share a little more in your dealings," I smiled. "I know well enough I can trust you both. Long have we all been together, and if we shared in the horror, the abuse we suffered before, so shall we share in the glory. But remember, gentlemen, I am of a mind most inquisitive, and therefore you do me more service in revealing too much to me than you do in hiding anything from me."

They bowed.

"Now," I said. "We should prepare to move to Hatfield at once. Cecil, you are to stay with us here from now on, then? You are not needed at our affairs in London?"

"When the time comes," Cecil agreed, "I should be at your side, my lady. I have the best riders and messengers in the country at our disposal and I can have a message to London within an hour or two with ease. All other plans are ready, and you have many loyal servants in London working to carry out our orders, from men placed in the Council, to those who will watch the body of your sister. I have men observing the ports in England, France and Spain. If there should be any inclination of attack or invasion, the Lord Admiral will be ready to take your side. I have women placed to mark the movements of the Grey sisters and others watching your cousin of Lennox. There are those placed in towns and the city who will monitor for any sign of rebellion, and those placed to herald and proclaim your coming as a new age of tolerance and plenty up and down the country."

He paused, trying to think if he had forgotten anything. "From your side," he continued, "I will be able to issue forth the proclamations that will make you the Queen in law, and from your side I will be at the best vantage point to ensure any last minute problems can be smoothed."

I smiled at him. Dear Cecil! His careful and exacting nature was so like my own. We shared a common spirit, I believe. Had I been born a man, I might well have been Cecil's twin. And my dear Parry! His quietness often allowed him to slip into the background unseen, and yet he was indeed a force to be reckoned with, a military man, a man of action, with all the careful plotting and planning of a general most experienced behind him.

They had done me good service.

"You both have taken all possibilities and wrapt them up in silken cloth for me," I said to them. "We are prepared indeed."

A little flutter, like the wings of a bird, flew through my chest. I took a deep breath as the gravity of the situation started to dawn on my soul. Such a responsibility for one so young to shoulder! I was twenty-five. I still felt young to be handed the reins of government, and yet at times, amidst all the troubles we had seen, I felt as though I had lived a thousand lives.

My soul was quivering against my chest as the motions of moving house were begun. Servants ran here and there, gathering those belongings that were wanted or required in Hatfield; the kitchens, the furnishings and the wardrobes of my house were loaded onto cart and horse, and everywhere there was a sense of anticipation and activity.

As the house rushed into a hive of organised commotion I stood at my window, trying without success to ease the panic that was rising in my chest, and to sort through the myriad of thoughts that raced through my mind.

CHAPTER SIXTY-THREE

Hatfield House
Autumn 1558

Later that day most of the household was moved to Hatfield. My darling Kat was once again hooded and hidden with the other servants for the short journey, and my ladies went ahead to prepare my rooms for me. My great bed was moved from Brocket to Hatfield and as the last preparations were made, I turned to Parry

"I will ride out a little, my lord," I said. "I need some fresh air." I held up a hand for he had already started to protest. "Send as many of your men as you like to follow my horse… I do not care if there is a garrison behind me as long as I might feel some air on my skin!"

He looked relieved. I knew what was in his mind. At this late stage in the game we played, he feared that I might be removed from my place in the line to the throne by some assassin. A lucky strike from a musket, a swift move with a dagger, or a shot from a bow might well see me removed from the succession and instead send me to herald the way for my sister's arrival in Heaven.

But the nearness, the suspense of waiting was too much for my young soul. If I could get out, get out and ride, even if for a bare few hours, I knew I should become more calmed in my spirit than I was presently.

In the afternoon, Parry sent scouts out ahead of my passage, and with some of his fastest and best men mounted on horses behind me, I rode out into the countryside. I rode fast, without a care as to where I headed, only relishing the feeling of the wind as it bit at my cheeks, and the rain as it fell from the skies against my hot skin. My horse seemed to sense my feelings, and snorted white mists from his nose as he plunged through forest and over field. His great feet flew as I moulded my body to his, and leaning forwards, seemed to become the horse himself as our forms ripped through the countryside like an arrow.

The men behind me rode fast and wild as they fought to keep me in sight, but I was not thinking of them, nor of any possible assassin in the woods or trees, hidden on hill or knoll. The faster I rode, the more all thought other than the thrill of the ride was expelled from my mind, and the more that feeling gave me peace, the more I wanted.

As my mind cleared of all its worries, all its panics, all those thoughts that betrayed my weak and scared heart, I started to feel a sense of peace fall on me; in body and in spirit I welcomed it with open arms. Finally, my mind started to un-twist itself and my thoughts began to fall once more to the order and calm of a mind that was cool and composed.

I pulled my horse to a stop on top of a little hill, and looked out into a world made of grey and blue in the falling light of the winter day.

From the edge of a great wood, near to the river that fed the farms below, I could see the smoke rising from earthen chimneys, warming simple homes in the little hamlet before me. Some miles away, there was the clipped echo of an axe chopping at wood, and the bleating calls of sheep as they were driven home by their masters. Dogs barked high and loud in excitement far down the hill, and there were the far-away shouts as a watchman called goodnight to farmers headed for their hearth and home.

The little lights, of firelights and torchlight shone out dimly in the fading day. Before me now was a tiny seat of English families finishing their toil for the day. My horse panted; sweating beneath me he tossed his head, nodding, as though signalling his enjoyment of our race together. I patted his wet neck, feeling the tight, strong muscles beneath my long hands. The men behind me, tracking my every move, had almost caught up, but they still rode furiously to reach me. I smiled, thinking of how Parry should scold them for not being able to keep up with a little slip of a girl.

I had not ridden so as to lose them, but to lose myself, even for a bare moment; to feel… as though I were not *this* Elizabeth, about to step into a role that I felt both ready for, and for which I was yet unprepared. Just to feel as though I was still my *own* Elizabeth, even if just for a moment.

So much in my life was about to change.

For so long I had been the princess on the outside, the *bastard* daughter of a king, the sole offspring of a woman who some held to be a Protestant saint, and some held to be a traitorous heretical whore. For so long in my young life, I had lived under the shadow of suspicion and treason. I had been a prisoner and a princess; a captive and a master. I had fought and struggled to where I was now, narrowly avoiding death, execution, betrayal…. and all had been for the moment that I might call myself the Queen of England; placed in a position of safety, protected by my trusted servants and loved by my people.

But the closer I came to this place where I had thought I would see the end of my struggles, the more I came to know that this was not the end of my fight.

Tenuous is the state of a queen, fragile and delicate. I had seen enough of in my sister's reign to know this was the truth. I had enemies who would hate my religion, rivals who thought they had a claim to the throne I sat on, foes who simply would like my lands to add to their own. As I stepped from one danger, I would only be placing my foot near another.

I looked down on the villages and hamlets that speckled the countryside along the banks of that river. The lives of those who lived there were a continuous struggle to ensure that their basic needs were met; they worked merely to survive, and to continue their own lines, their own families. The humble people of England had survived through the ravages of rebellion, of war, of taxation and poverty, of poor harvest and ill weather, and yet they still were standing, still living and still looking to a time when things might get easier.

Much like me.

We were survivors, England and her people. We fought to survive, and to live. And that struggle was not one war or one battle, but a constant stream of challenges that we must ride out to meet, or else see all we held dear crumble and fade. I looked down on those little houses, those pens of animals and small gardens which still showed flecks of green from the winter vegetables these people struggled to grow.

If they could do it, then so could I.

In my palaces I did not hunger, I was clothed in silk and jewels… but I faced more danger to my life and to my person, than those below me would ever know. I would give them a true sovereign once more; I would not show the fear I felt for the dangers that beset me, for the people of England deserved a monarch they could respect. They deserved an image of their country as strong as they were.

But more than that; I owed it to them to make their country great once more, to bring them out of the times of starkness and hunger, to hold back the threat of rebellion that had broken their lives over and over, to give our country time and peace enough to heal itself. This land was fertile, and it could give us riches, and that richness, I was determined, should see all the fortunes of all the people of England rise.

Stuck in my thoughts, I was startled when the captain of the guard moved behind me on his horse asking if we were to leave, for we would return after dusk as it was. I smiled at him. "Fear not, good captain," I said. "I shall tell Parry that it was my choice to ride so far. You have done naught wrong but obey your mistress."

He nodded, but I could still see worry in his eyes. Parry was a master to be feared, then, I thought. How interesting to see my servant from the view-point of another.

"Come then," I went to turn my horse. But before we left, I took one glance backwards to the villages in the fading light. The white smoke that puffed from their chimneys mingled with the mists of the darkening skies, so that no one could tell where the earthly world began, and that of the measureless skies ended. I would give them something to believe in once more. I would give them an England they could be proud of, and a queen they could believe in.

England would have its Elizabeth, and I would have my England.

CHAPTER SIXTY-FOUR

Hatfield House
Autumn 1558

The man that stood before me watched me nervously as I read the letter he had provided. As well he might… for the letter was from a man, who, during Mary's rule, I had come to look on with much disgust and revulsion.

Cardinal Pole.

Although Mary had been the instigator of those hideous burnings that had brought persecution to all those of the Protestant faith, her Cardinal had approved of those burnings, and encouraged them with the blessing of his master in Rome. The letter before me was written in a hand I loved not, for the man who sent them was, to me, the essence of the control the See of Rome held over our country and our people.

"I read here that the Cardinal has no hope for the Queen's life," I said to Seth Holland, his messenger. "He asks me to remember my promise to see the true faith live in England."

"He asks that you would remember that it is the greatest wish of Her Majesty, your sister," affirmed Holland. "But also to inform you that my master himself is a sick man, sick unto death. He wishes to leave this world ensuring that all worldly matters are taken care of, and one most particularly with you, my lady."

"What matters are those between the Cardinal and I that he might not rest for?" I asked.

"He merely wants to assure himself that there is no ill will between you and him," said Holland. "Matters of this nature wear on him in his weakened state."

I tapped the paper on my leg as I thought. "You say he is sick, unto death?" I asked again.

"Indeed my lady," nodded Holland. "The Cardinal will not be long for this world."

"Then you should tell him to rest easy," I affirmed, "for even if there were cause to concern the Cardinal, in matters to do with me, those cares shall not touch him in death."

Holland looked a little perplexed, so I elaborated; "Tell the Cardinal there is nothing to concern him," I said, "and he may take his path to the Gates of Heaven assured that I bear him no ill will."

Holland looked relieved. I wondered suddenly if Cardinal Pole was, in actuality, dying, or if this was some subterfuge to enable him to wriggle his way out of my clutches when I came to the throne. I was willing enough to put aside my grievances with him in this world if he was dying; if he lived, however, my generosity would most likely become less magnanimous.

The burnings the Cardinal and Mary had sanctioned had seen over three hundred people of England bound to the stake and burned to death in the flames of persecution. Perhaps near to a thousand of our people had left these shores and sought refuge in foreign lands. Many friends and companions had left my side to flee for their lives. And how many countless had died through torture or abuse in those dark cells of the Tower and the prisons of London?

How many had suffered for my sister's vision? For her desire to make England Catholic, and turn back the sands of time, to make the past as she wished it could have been?

Cardinal Pole was Mary's papal legate, and Chief Councillor; if the stain of those deaths, those exiles and those disappeared touched her, then it also spread over the soul of Pole. Each was as guilty as the other for the savagery rent on the people of England. Was it true then, that two such souls, two people so linked in life, should be as linked in death? Did God call to both of them at the same time, to account for the actions they had taken in life, side by side?

The news that Pole lay dying on one side of the Thames in Lambeth, as his mistress lay dying in St James' palace, seemed to me to have an almost unbelievable symmetry. When God called to them to explain their actions, I wondered if their souls should still be as linked as they were now. Would death keep them friends and allies, or would the guilt of their earthly actions be too much for them to preserve that loyalty still, in death… before Almighty God?

Holland left to take my message back to his master. I turned to Cecil, who, when not busy scribbling at his desk, was to be found by my side.

"Send Throckmorton to London," I ordered. "I want no false report of my sister's passing to interfere with our plans. Tell him that when Mary is dead he is to bring to me the engagement ring that Phillip gave to Her Majesty. When I see that parted from my sister's body, I will know in truth she is gone, for she would never allow it from her person unless she were dead."

Cecil nodded.

"Any other news?" I asked, my mind still on the thought of Pole escaping me through death.

"Perhaps something that may divert you, my lady..." Cecil smiled. "There was word from Lord Paget that upon his return to London, the Duke of Feria came to him to say that he thought you, my lady, should be wedded to a suitable Catholic husband as fast as possible."

I burst out laughing. "You see Cecil!" I exclaimed. "They use marriage to try to subdue me once more! Come... tell me, what did Paget say to Feria's demands?"

Cecil allowed himself a chuckle. "Paget said that he was weary of such talk, my lady; that he had arranged the marriage between Her Majesty and King Phillip and the people had learned to hate him for it. He said he wanted nothing more to do with royal matchmaking and would have no part in it. Then, he sent this word to me, and thusly to you." Cecil grinned. "I believe Feria was much disappointed to find that there was little support for his idea."

"He took one last chance to try and have me shackled," I laughed. "He and his master are disappointing in their lack of imagination. A husband! That is all they can think of to bring me to heel! A husband!"

"One day my lady..." Cecil said, "and for the sake of the realm, as soon as possible, you *will* need to find a husband."

I waved my hand. "There will be enough time for that later Cecil," I said dismissively. "Look at me! I am not my sister who came to the throne already a woman old and past her prime!" I narrowed my eyes at him. "And if the time comes when I choose a husband, that will be *my own choice* Cecil, and I will listen to no other opinion than that of the people of England. I will not marry where I would lose their love, and no handsome face nor well-formed leg shall sway my mind where it did my sister's. And most of all, I will have no husband saddled to my back who seeks to subdue me and flatten my faith or power with his will."

"Certainly not, my lady!" agreed Cecil, a little aghast. "Your husband will be most carefully chosen, and his power limited according to his station."

I sighed. "Let us not talk of things so far in the future now, Cecil," I said. "I believe that we have enough to worry on presently, without adding concerns so far removed from the present."

"Of course, my lady," Cecil acquiesced, but as we turned to talk on other matters, I saw a little worried frown crease his forehead.

I think that Cecil, who understood me so well, started to worry then that I did not wish to marry at all. Although I had voiced an opinion akin to this before, no one really took me seriously. It was the place of a woman, no matter whom that woman was, to marry and produce children, and if that woman was a queen, so much more important became that office.

But my duty was different to that of every other woman, and even every other queen. My position altered from the natural state of every wife and mother. If I wanted to retain the power and independence to rule as I saw fit, then I could never become saddled or shackled to a husband, for he would always seek to rule over me, and over the country I loved.

In this house, there would be but one mistress... and no master.

CHAPTER SIXTY-FIVE

Hatfield House
17th November 1558

In the late afternoon of 16th November 1558, my sister Mary lay half in this world, and half in the next, flitting between dreams and consciousness in her bed at St James's Palace. When she had awoken, she told her ladies that she had been surrounded by children singing and playing. She believed that they were angels, welcoming her into Heaven.

Later, during the early morning Mass, Mary responded to the priest. But soon afterwards, sometime before the chill winter dawn made its appearance over the horizon, when her women believed her to be once more sleeping, Mary I of England, eldest daughter of Henry VIII, the first sole anointed and crowned Queen of this realm, passed quietly into the arms of God. Over the water, in Lambeth palace, one of Cardinal Pole's chaplains told him of the death of the Queen. In the late afternoon of that same day, Pole heard Mass, and then he, too, took his leave of this world. The news spread through the country, and from each church the voices sang *Te Deum laudamus* for the souls of the Queen and of the Cardinal.

The news of Mary's death reached us in Hatfield long before the rest of the country was aware of it by way of Cecil's men.

For my own feelings, I can tell you but little. Complex were the sensations that sprung to my heart when I heard my sister was dead. Grief, shock, relief... all had equal measure within me. My enemy was gone, but with her went a sister who once cared for me like her own child.

Throckmorton had ridden out to Hatfield, bearing the ring of Mary's engagement to Phillip, cut from about her finger upon her passing. When he placed it in my hand I knew already that my sister was dead, as Cecil's men had sent word to us on the moment her passing was known to her women, but I thanked him for his pains in any case. Then, I asked that my people leave me for a moment alone, so that I might pray for the soul of my dead sister.

I held the ring in my palm, looking on a worldly possession which had once meant everything to my dead sister. I took it to my chambers and I placed it in a locked chest next to two books which had once been my mother's; next to letters written by my father; by my stepmother Katherine Parr; by the Admiral Thomas Seymour and my beloved brother Edward.

All those who had contributed to this little chest, were now lost to me.

I looked on that ring, sparkling in the dim light within the box, sat on a platform made of my family's words. And then I shut the wooden chest and locked it, tucking the key into the pocket of my dress. There would be much of my life now that would never be private again, but these few treasures of my past, tokens of the strange and complicated workings and ties of family, I was determined to keep as solely my own.

Every woman keeps her secrets.

As I struggled with both the sorrow and the relief of my sister's passing, Cecil's well-oiled clock sprang into motion as the death of the Queen signalled the commencement of all his careful plans.

On the morning of my sister's passing, Members of Parliament and the Council were summoned to the House of Lords, where they were told of Mary's death and of my accession to the throne of England. Nicolas Heath, the Lord Chancellor spoke to the lords gathered about him, telling them that it was both right and proper that they mourn for the death of Mary, but that they must also rejoice in my ascension…

"*we have no less cause another way to rejoice with praise to Almighty God for that he hath left unto us a true lawful and right inheritrix to the crown of this realm, which is the lady Elizabeth, second daughter to our late sovereign lord of noble memory, Henry VIII, and sister to the said late Queen.*" There was a meaningful pause before Lord Chancellor Heath added… "*Of whose most lawful right and title to the crown, thanks be to God, we need not doubt.*"

The Commons and the Lords cried out, "*God Save Queen Elizabeth*!"

Dear Cecil had placed my supporters well. Although it was not a legislative act, all were placed to show their support for my ascension to the throne, and none came out to contest it. They went to Whitehall Palace to await my proclamation, which, of course, Cecil had already sent by messenger.

Cecil had been at his desk since the news had reached us early in the morning, and when the news of the support of the Lords came, he was ready. My accession proclamation had been already sent to London almost as soon as the news that Mary had died reached us. Cecil's network of fast horses, many riders covering the ground between Hatfield and London in stages, worked well. It arrived therefore in remarkable time, ready for the Lords and the Commons to receive at noon on that very day. The proclamation informed my new subjects that;

"*they be discharged of all bonds and duties of subjugation towards our said dear sister and be from the same time in nature and law, bound only to us as their only sovereign and lady.*"

The speed at which Cecil had moved to proclaim my titles and the support of the Lords and of the Commons meant that no other claimant had a chance to even raise a standard before the wheels of my reign came crashing into motion.

The Queen is dead… Long live the Queen.

CHAPTER SIXTY-SIX

Richmond Palace
February 1603

There are times in my life when I have had just cause to remember an image in perfect precision. There is so much in life that merely slips away from the mind, becoming lost to time and shadow.

But there are some images I shall never forget….

The flickering golden light of a fish tail as it swims in a glimmering pond.

The dark glittering eyes of a woman gazing with love at her child.

The red coat of a wary vixen skulking in the shadows of the undergrowth, travelling through the darkness of the night.

The cobalt blue of a morning's sky, touching dark, black, waters lapping gently against the side of a boat.

The shining light of mischief in the dark eyes of a handsome man stood before me.

The febrile eyes of a mind maddened by desperation burning like coals in the sultry gloom of a palace chamber.

Many thoughts, many colours, many images to light the fire of my memory.

On that day, on the day I became the Queen, I added one more picture to the annals of my memory….

Red-gold leaves of the oak, dancing in a light breeze, lit by the sun of a dying day.

CHAPTER SIXTY-SEVEN

Hatfield House
17th November 1558

Beneath an old oak, in the grounds at Hatfield, I stood waiting. The day of my ascension was growing old. In London and in my own house, all our preparations and plans had come to order under the watchful eyes of Parry and Cecil, and thanks to them, all had gone smoothly. My name was proclaimed as queen and none had moved to stop it. The Council were on their way to inform me of this, as though I did not already know, and to pledge themselves to me. We had not needed the guards raised by Parry to take the throne by force should another claimant to the throne risen… but I had not ordered them disbanded as yet. It never hurts to be prepared.

I waited for the Council. I wanted them to find me in the gardens, as though I was not fully and completely prepared for all that about to occur, as though I *was* just the young maid I appeared to be. It does no harm for a queen to hide some of her arsenal from those she means to rule. Just as it does no harm for a lady to add a sense of the dramatic to occasions that should be remembered well.

This was one of those occasions.

I looked up into the almost bare branches of the tree. It was fitting that I should take up my title under the branches of the English oak. No better or stronger wood was there in all the world, and no more true symbol of our country. As I looked up into the branches, I saw there a few leaves, still clinging on to the tree through the spell of late autumn. Green no more, but golden, brown and red they shone against the pale sun above. The flickering light, through the branches and against the leaves, did not hurt my eyes.

I looked with a sense of calm, and of watchful purpose, on the red-gold leaves of the oak tree. I was a little removed from the house, my ladies behind me, standing some way apart from me as I had requested.

There are moments when one needs to stand alone.

The red-gold leaves danced in a gentle breeze above me. The sun twinkled between them. There were no jewels in the entire world more perfect and beautiful than that image. Across the path, I saw the delegation of the Council arrive and I stepped out into the sun, letting the light touch on my own red-gold hair and crossing my hands before me.

They jumped from their horses and walked to bow before me. Nicolas Heath, the Archbishop of York and Lord Chancellor, spoke of my sister's death, and of my proclamation as Queen.

I took a deep breath, for I had thought long on what I was to say to them.

"We are much sorrowed to hear of the death of our royal sister," I said in a strong voice that reached not only the Councillors before me, but also my ladies, and all those servants now gathered to watch this little scene.

Behind me, I knew, were Cecil and Parry, Kat, Bess, Blanche, Anne, Geraldine, William Parr, and John Astley. And beside them were all the servants of my house, coming out in little streams at first, then becoming like the great flow of a river. All standing behind me and listening to the words of their mistress, and their queen. The Councillors looked at the gathering crowd behind me, and I saw nervousness in their eyes. But those people were not gathered to harm them; they gathered thus only to honour me.

"I am amazed at the burden that hath fallen to me," I continued. "But I am God's creature. He has granted to me the grace of this crown. This office is His design; I will do all in my power to uphold His will, and protect His people."

I paused. The Council delegates were still on their knees and I made no sign to allow them to rise. I wanted their full attention.

"In this great task ahead of us, I ask for the great care and assistance of all our subjects, so that I with my ruling, and you with your service, may make a good account to Almighty God. I mean to direct all my actions by good advice and counsel, for the preservation and protection of my people."

I paused, and glanced back up at the leaves of the oak behind me. The fading light of the day lit my gold-red hair so it shone like flames against my pale skin. My dark eyes sparkled as I looked onto the faces of those who had once sought to imprison and trap me, those who had once sought to take my life... now, my servants. I was their master.

I unfolded my hands and spread them before my body as though praying.

I spoke, loudly and clearly. "*A Domino factum est; Et mirabile in oculis nostris.*"

"This is the Lord's doing; it is marvellous in our eyes."

As Mary's former Councillors dropped their heads in prayer, I noted something on the horizon. In the distance, a rider on a snow-white horse came plunging towards Hatfield. I smiled as I recognized the rider. No one else would ride as boldly as the Queen's new Master of Horse. Robin Dudley was riding to my side, his sense of occasion as dramatic as my own; riding on a great white horse to his princess, to his queen. A knight of old, a hero of the new age… at least, so I hoped.

In the light of the fading sun, under the strong branches of the oak of England, I stood… their queen. Standing with my arms outstretched, Councillors bowed before me, and my household bowed behind; I was surrounded by both those who had made me queen, and those who had sought to destroy me, all bathed in the last light of the day.

With a gentle gesture I bade them to rise.

We had much to do.

I am Elizabeth… Queen of England.

ABOUT THE AUTHOR

I find people talking about themselves in the third person to be entirely unsettling, so, since this section is written by me, I will use my own voice rather than try to make you believe that another person is writing about me to make me sound terribly important.

I am an independent author, publishing my books by myself, with the help of my lovely editor. I write in all the spare time I have. I briefly tried entering into the realm of 'traditional' publishing but, to be honest, found the process so time consuming and convoluted that I quickly decided to go it alone and self-publish.

My passion for history, in particular perhaps the era of the Tudors, began early in life. As a child I lived in Croydon, near London, and my schools were lucky enough to be close to such glorious places as Hampton Court and the Tower of London to mean that field trips often took us to those castles. I think it's hard not to find the Tudors infectious when you hear their stories, especially when surrounded by the bricks and mortar they built their reigns within. There is heroism and scandal, betrayal and belief, politics and passion and a seemingly never-ending cast list of truly fascinating people. So when I sat down to start writing, I could think of no better place to start than somewhere and sometime I loved and was slightly obsessed with.

Expect *many* books from me, but do not necessarily expect them all to be of the Tudor era. I write as many of you read, I suspect; in many genres. My own bookshelves are weighted down with historical volumes and biographies, but they also contain dystopias, sci-fi, horror, humour, children's books, fairy tales, romance and adventure. I can't promise I'll manage to write in *all* the areas I've mentioned there, but I'd love to give it a go. If anything I've published isn't your thing, that's fine, I just hope you like the ones I write which *are* your thing!

The majority of my books *are* historical fiction however, so I hope that if you liked this volume you will give the others in this series (and perhaps not in this series), a look. I want to divert you as readers, to please you with my writing and to have you join me on these adventures.

A book is nothing without a reader.

As to the rest of me; I am in my thirties and live in Cornwall with a rescued dog, a rescued cat and my partner (who wasn't rescued, but may well have rescued me). I studied Literature at University after I fell in love with books as a small child. When I was little I could often be found nestled half-way up the stairs with a pile of books and my head lost in another world between the pages. There is nothing more satisfying to me than finding a new book I adore, to place next to the multitudes I own and love… and nothing more disappointing to me to find a book I am willing to never open again. I do hope that this book was not a disappointment to you; I loved writing it and I hope that showed through the pages.

This is only the first in a large selection of titles coming to you on Amazon. I hope you will try the others.

If you would like to contact me, please do so.

On twitter, I am @TudorTweep and am more than happy to follow back and reply to any and all messages. I may avoid you if you decide to say anything worrying or anything abusive, but I figure that's acceptable.

Via email, I am tudortweep@gmail.com a dedicated email account for my readers to reach me on. I'll try and reply within a few days.

I publish some first drafts and short stories on Wattpad where I can be found at www.wattpad.com/user/GemmaLawrence31. Wattpad was the first place I ever showed my stories, *to anyone*, and in many ways its readers and their response to my works were the influence which pushed me into self-publishing. If you have never been on the site I recommend you try it out. Its free, its fun and its chock-full of real emerging talent. I love Wattpad because its members and their encouragement gave me the boost I needed as a fearful waif to get some confidence in myself and make a go of a life as a real, published writer.

Thank you for taking a risk with an unknown author and reading my book. I do hope now that you've read one you'll want to read more. If you'd like to leave me a review, that would be very much appreciated also!

Gemma Lawrence

Cornwall

2015

THANK YOU

…to so many people for helping me make this book possible… to my editor Brooke who entered into this with me and gave me her time, her wonderful guidance and also her encouragement. To my partner Matthew, who will be the first to admit that history is not his thing, and yet is willing to listen to me extol the virtues and vices of the Tudors and every other time period, repeatedly, to him and pushed me to publish even when I feared to. To my family for their ongoing love and support; this includes not only my own blood in my mother and father, sister and brother, but also their families, their partners and all my nieces who I am sure are set to take the world by storm as they grow. To Matthew's family, for their support, and for the extended family I have found myself welcomed to within them. To my friend Petra who took a tour of Tudor palaces and places with me back in 2010 which helped me to prepare for this book and others; her enthusiasm for that strange but amazing holiday brought an early ally to the idea I could actually write a book… And lastly, to the people who wrote all the books I read in order to write this book… all the historical biographers and masters of their craft who brought Elizabeth, and her times, to life in my head.

Thank you to all of you; you'll never know how much you've helped me, but I know what I owe to you.

Gemma
Cornwall
2015

Made in the USA
San Bernardino, CA
16 December 2016